SAVING
THE
GUILTY

SAVING
THE
GUILTY

A Laurel Highlands Mystery

LIZ MILLIRON

To the readers who have followed Jim and Sally this far.

Praise for Saving the Guilty

"This is one of the best books in this long-running series and I can't wait for more exciting adventures with Jim and Sally."—DruAnn Love, Dru's Book Musings, 2017 MWA Raven Award winner

Chapter One

Defense attorney Sally Castle hoisted the bags of groceries from the back of her new Toyota bZ4X and closed the liftgate. The SUV was new enough that the metallic red paint gleamed through the speckles of slush from the early December snow. It had been a wrench giving up her trusty Camry, but she'd been forced to give in to the reality of her circumstances. She was a big dog owner. Pixel, her retired-racer greyhound, could curl into an impossibly small space, but the back seat of a sedan was just not enough room for long trips.

If she had to carry Rizzo, Jim's rowdy Golden Retriever, at the same time, forget it.

In addition to the dogs, she'd moved from the city streets of Uniontown to Confluence, Pennsylvania, where leaving town meant four-wheel drive came in awfully handy. But she refused to buy a gas-guzzling behemoth. Thus, the new electric SUV.

She tapped snow off her boots at the back door and deposited the bags on the kitchen table. At the same time, her phone trilled from inside her purse.

Her boyfriend, State Trooper Jim Duncan, came inside, trailed by both dogs. "Need any help?"

She scrabbled for her phone. It was a FaceTime call from David Sturgess, an old friend from her days in Allegheny County. "Can you get this?" She waved at the bags.

Jim held up a hand to indicate his understanding and began putting groceries away.

Sally tapped the green icon and focused on her call. "Dave, how the hell—

1

what on earth happened to you?"

"A heart attack and triple-bypass surgery." A smile stretched across Dave's broad face, which held none of the healthy color Sally remembered. He reclined in a hospital bed, an IV in his arm and a heart monitor beeping next to him. "I'm at Presby."

"I hope they're taking good care of you."

"I have no doubt that without these fine folks, I'd be in much worse shape." He shifted on the bed.

Sally shrugged out of her jacket one arm at a time. "I'm not complaining, but if you're in the hospital, why are you calling me? Don't you have more important things to do than catch up with old friends? Or should I be worried?"

Dave's laughter was as infectious as ever. "No, no. This isn't me making my final goodbyes or anything. I need a favor."

"Anything."

"Can you talk privately?"

Sally glanced over at Jim, who shooed her away. "Give me a moment," she said. She went to the back room and closed the door. Two weeks ago, when Sally decided to move in, Jim declared she needed her own space. They chose to convert the fourth bedroom into her office. She snapped on the lights and sat in her executive-style desk chair. "Okay, now you've got my curiosity at eleven. This is obviously not a social call. What gives?"

Dave tugged a pillow up behind his head. "What do you know about the Wilson murder?"

She thought. "Only what was in the paper. Husband accused of the brutal murder of his wife in Monongahela County. Marsdale, wasn't it? I read you were the defense counsel and got a change of venue to Fayette County." Like her, Dave had left prosecution in Allegheny County for defense. They'd lost touch years ago, but she'd heard through the legal grapevine that Dave had gone to the rural county south of Pittsburgh.

"Correct on all points."

"The jury returned a guilty verdict right before Thanksgiving, didn't they?"

"Also correct." He squirmed again. "Damn pillows are thin as cardboard.

Anyway, it's bullshit. Alec Wilson shouldn't have been convicted. The cops led him to believe they were just talking."

Sally could hear the air quotes. "No Miranda warning?"

"Nope. They said he wasn't in custody. My ass. What else does a reasonable person call being in the back of a patrol car and then in an interrogation room?" His expression left no doubt as to what he thought. "The judge agreed with the DA and denied my motion to suppress Alec's statement."

Sally couldn't remember all the details. She'd been involved in her own case with Noah Freeman at the time. "I'm sorry to hear that. Are you going to appeal?"

"I was. It's clearly evidence admitted in error." Dave made a circular motion with his finger at all the medical equipment. "Then this happened. The court appearance to present the appeal is set for a week from tomorrow, and I'm benched."

Suspicion took root in Sally's mind. "Oh no. Don't even say it. It's impossible."

"You're a damn fine litigator, Sally. I've heard nothing but good things about you, first when you went to the Public Defender down there and now that you're on your own. Alec couldn't ask for a better defense attorney." He grinned. "You know, if he can't have me."

"Dave, I think lack of oxygen scrambled your brain. It's Sunday afternoon. I'm flattered you think so highly of me, but I can't build an appeal for a case I know nothing about in five days. Not one that has a snowball's chance in hell of succeeding." Sally's partner, Tanelsa Parson, would have kittens if she took this on.

Any trace of mirth left Dave's face. "Sally, I wouldn't ask if it wasn't serious. Alec's in a jam. He's facing a life sentence without the possibility of parole. Technically, this is a death penalty case. Besides, I've done most of the heavy lifting. Your job is to stand up in court and present it."

She huffed. "Pennsylvania hasn't executed anyone since 1999. The moratorium from 2015 is still in effect."

"But death warrants are still issued."

She tried another argument. "I can't just read your work. I have to get familiar with the case and be ready to answer any questions."

"I'll give you all my notes and research. Sally, we need you." The seriousness in Dave's expression matched his voice. "Alec spent every last dime he had on his defense. I can't walk away from him."

"You want me to do this *pro bono*?" Never mind kittens. Tanelsa would have a full-blown meltdown.

Dave held up the hand with the IV. "I wouldn't do that to you. You'll get paid out of my fee. I'll take care of it."

He'd be generous, too. He was that type of guy. "Your client is okay with the switch?"

"Completely. Alec trusts my judgment." Dave rubbed his forehead. "Please. Just read the case file. After you do that, if you still don't think you have a chance of pulling this off, I swear I'll leave you alone and find someone else who can give it a shot."

"Who?"

"No idea, but I will."

She drummed her fingers on her desk. She'd been looking forward to a quiet few weeks before Christmas, the first she and Jim would spend in the same house. Making sure she could present a credible appeal in five days would definitely cut into that time. Yeah, Dave could try to find another substitute, but that person would have just as hard a time. Jim would understand, but that didn't mean he'd like it. "I have to clear it with my partner."

Dave sagged back, as though the tension that had held him up had left his body. "Of course."

Sally spun her chair to face the wall. "Send the file by overnight delivery, and I'll see what I can do."

"Already done. You'll have it first thing tomorrow."

She wanted to groan. "How'd you know I'd say yes?"

Dave's answering chuckle sounded both mischievous and amused. "You always were a soft touch for a hard-luck case."

Chapter Two

Duncan put the last items away and closed the cabinet as Sally emerged from her office. He took one look at her expression and knew her phone call had been both unexpected and unsettling. "What's wrong?"

She tapped her phone against her chin, two little creases between her eyes. Their deep green color meant she was lost in thought.

He waited a moment. "Sally, what was the call about? There isn't a problem with your sublet, is there?" He hoped that wasn't it. He doubted it would mean a change to her plans to finish moving to Confluence before Christmas, but not having to pay rent for the last three months of her lease would be helpful.

She started a little, as though she'd forgotten he was there. "Sorry. Lost in thought. No, it wasn't about the apartment. Everything is still a go for all I know."

"Good." He poured a cup of coffee for her and handed it over. "You've got that look on your face."

"What look?" She accepted the mug and blew on the contents.

"The one that says, 'Oh crap, how am I going to pull this off.'" He poured a second cup for himself.

"You know, it's like reading people is a part of your job or something." She took a seat at the table. "The call was from Dave Sturgess, a friend of mine. He asked me for a favor."

Duncan leaned against the counter. "What kind of favor?"

Sally picked up the creamer from the table and added a splash to her mug.

"Before I answer, let me ask you something. Did you hear anything about the Wilson murder?"

"You would've had to be living under a rock to have missed it. Even in Pittsburgh, an incident like that would cause a major stir. Husband kills wife using a carving knife from their knife block, six major stab wounds, dozens of nonlethal cuts, and leaves her body in the kitchen." He shivered thinking about it. He'd never seen photos, thank God. Even fourteen years on the job couldn't prepare him for something like that. "But for it to happen in a rural county like Monongahela? It was the biggest thing to hit Marsdale since, well, ever."

Sally focused on him. "Was it a State Police investigation?"

"No. They have a county police department over there. But PSP assisted."

"Did you hear about any details?"

He shifted. Why was she asking about that case? "It happened in September of last year, before I made the jump to Criminal Investigation. Like I said, Monongahela has its own county police. They ran the show. We just helped out as needed."

Her gaze sharpened. "Yes, but you just said it was a big deal. I can't believe you didn't hear anything through the grapevine. Especially after the change of venue motion put the trial in Uniontown, smack dab in the middle of Fayette County."

He tried to laugh it off. "They weren't giving daily briefings about it in the Uniontown barracks, Sally."

"Jim." She set down her coffee. "These non-answer answers are not helping. Is this something you can't talk about? Or you don't want to?"

He should have known she wouldn't be put off easily. He ran a hand through his hair. "Let me ask you this. Why do you care? It's not your case, and the crime didn't happen in this county."

She held up her hands. "Fair enough. It has to do with Dave's call. Humor me, please? You tell me what you know, and then I'll explain why I'm interested. I don't want my involvement coloring your—"

"Testimony?"

She crumpled a napkin and tossed it at him.

He dodged. "I don't know anything specific, all right? I didn't talk to any of the troopers involved or see any of the evidence. What I'm telling you is what I heard around the water cooler, so to speak."

She waited.

He stalled a bit more by taking a drink. "I also don't want to play armchair quarterback. Situation like this, you have to make snap decisions and live with the consequences."

"Jim, stop tiptoeing around. If you ethically can't say anything, just tell me."

"There was a lot of scuttlebutt about the procedure, or lack of it, during the arrest." He went to the table and sat. "Things were pretty cut-and-dried to start. A 9-1-1 call came in to the Emergency Operations Center. Late at night, I think it was. The husband claimed he'd come home and found his wife in the kitchen. Emergency personnel were dispatched to respond. Upon finding the deceased woman, they called the county cops, who sent their own detectives to handle the investigation."

Sally leaned on the table. "Sounds pretty routine."

"That night, it was. The husband was taken to the Monongahela County HQ for questioning. The way I heard it, he talked during the ride in. Depending on who you listened to, the cops either subtly encouraged him or said nothing. The *conversation* continued at HQ. As a result of what he said, and the fact his story was weak, Monongahela PD made the arrest. Husband pled not guilty. Insisted on going to trial, even though the Mon County District Attorney offered a deal that would at least give a chance at parole. At trial, he'd be looking at life, if not worse."

Sally's fingers twitched, as though she wanted to be taking notes. "I'm not seeing a problem here."

He eyed her. "I know you followed this at least as closely as I did. The defense attorney made a motion to suppress the husband's statement before he asked for an attorney. It was the guy who called earlier, right? Said his client hadn't been properly Mirandized. Police and the prosecution argued Miranda didn't apply because Mr. Wilson was not in custody and was not being interrogated." He set aside the cup of now lukewarm coffee.

"The judge denied the motion to suppress." Sally tapped her nails against the cup. "He ruled Mr. Wilson had made a voluntary statement and upheld the DA's rebuttal. They quit when Wilson asked for a lawyer and issued the Miranda warning once the interaction turned from a conversation to an interrogation."

Duncan shifted. "You know all about it, then. Why are you asking me?"

"To get your take. Call it the opinion of a disinterested third party." She rested her chin on her fist. "You've used that tactic. I seem to remember you *talking* to a guy in a men's room, trying to get information."

He pointed at her. "That was different. You know as well as I do that custody isn't only about being arrested. It's the denial of freedom to the extent associated with an arrest. Mark Framingham was definitely not in custody. We were at that legal dinner. It was the bathroom, for God's sake. He could easily have left. But yes." He spread his hands. "I played on the fact that most people are so eager to appear innocent they talk when they really ought to shut up. Also, I wasn't trying to get him to incriminate himself. I was after information about someone else."

Sally leaned back. "What's the difference with Wilson?"

Duncan stood and gathered the mugs. "He was in the back of a car, for crying out loud. How do you leave? At HQ, he was questioned in an interrogation room, and you've seen those. It's an intimidating environment, designed to get suspects defensive. That's why there was a split. Some of us felt the Miranda warning should have been issued as soon as they arrived at HQ, if not earlier. Hell, what normal person feels he can waltz out of a police station? Or refuse to get in the back of a squad car when asked?"

"I would have zero problem with doing that."

"Not the same." He put the mugs in the sink. "You are an experienced defense attorney, not the common citizen. I'm sure they asked Wilson very politely. Made it seem like he was doing them a favor. I'm also willing to bet it wasn't guys sitting around going over what happened. From what I heard, the questions asked were specifically intended to elicit an incriminating response, and that's the textbook definition of an interrogation."

"To be clear, what side of the fence did you land on?"

How could she even ask? His posture stiffened. "What the hell do you think?"

His tone must have said it all because she smiled. "You'd have issued the warning on the spot, made damn sure you had proof he acknowledged it, and not said another word until Dave Sturgess showed up."

He relaxed a smidge. At least she knew him that well.

She pushed away from the table. "Dave is appealing the conviction. Evidence admitted in error and all that. I'll find out the exact details tomorrow."

"Come again?"

"Dave can't continue with the case." She told him about Sturgess's health problems. "He asked me to take over the appeal. It has to be complete in time for a court appearance a week from tomorrow, which means I have to get it done this week." She went to the fridge and opened it.

"Aren't you forgetting something?"

She didn't turn around. "What?"

"You promised you'd be fully out of your place by end of day on Friday so the new tenant can move in."

"Shit." She closed the fridge and leaned her forehead against it. Then she faced him. "Well, I only said I'd *look* at the file. I have to talk to Tanelsa, of course. It's not a done deal."

He shook his head. "Sally, don't kid yourself. You're gonna take this case and convince Tanelsa to go along. Admit it."

She huffed. "I'm not a pushover, Jim Duncan. I have commitments and priorities of my own."

"But you *are* a softie, and this is exactly the kind of thing that gets you fired up." He went over and wrapped his arms around her. Then he kissed her forehead. "Don't worry. Duncan Moving at your service. It's not like I have anything on my plate this week. Cavendish and I wrapped our last investigation a couple of days ago."

She draped her arms around his neck. "My hero. This is why I love you."

"Yeah, my muscles and the fact I know a guy with a truck."

She kissed him long and hard. "There are other reasons, too," she said, voice husky.

Chapter Three

The promised file showed up early Monday morning. Sally signed for it and returned to her desk as she pulled the strip to open the thick envelope.

Her partner, Tanelsa Parson, didn't look up. "Why on earth are we getting a delivery before nine in the morning on a Monday? You expecting anything?"

"I was. This might be our next client." Sally hurried back to the warmth of the main office. The door had only been open for a minute, but it had been a minute too long in light of the December cold.

At that, Tanelsa did lift her head. She hitched her cashmere pashmina closer, set down her pen, steepled her fingers, and fixed Sally with a hard-eyed glare that shouldn't be able to come from deep brown eyes enhanced by impeccable makeup. "Care to explain that statement?"

"It's like this." Sally gave Tanelsa an overview of her conversation the day before with Dave Sturgess and the follow-up with Jim.

Tanelsa rested her head in her hands. "What on earth were you thinking, Sally? Five days to come up with a respectable appeal? Did it ever occur to you that if we lose, this guy will blame us?"

"Hey, it's the same amount of time Dave had. According to him, it's practically done." Sally dumped the contents of the package on her desk. "If it craters, Wilson can't possibly blame us."

"Famous last words. As far as the client, he can and he will." Tanelsa aimed a finger at her partner. "If Jim is right in how the cops played it, and he probably is, this thing is a shitstorm waiting to happen."

Sally ignored Tanelsa's response. "Besides, I didn't accept. I said I'd look

11

over the file and let Dave know our decision. I made it very clear you had to be on board."

"Gee, thanks." Sarcasm dripped from Tanelsa's voice. "Another freebie. We can't keep doing this."

"You didn't let me finish. Dave is going to pay us out of his fee." She snuck a glance at the other woman. "Dave's rates are no joke. We could make more on this appeal than everything else we've done this year."

Tanelsa tapped her deep-red nails on her desk. "Not like we couldn't use the cash. Wilson." She bit her lip. "Marsdale? Wife murder?"

"With a change of venue to Fayette County. Uniontown. We don't even have to travel."

"That was an ugly one." More tapping. "Did your friend give any details as to the grounds for his appeal?"

"Only at a high level." Sally wheeled her chair over to Tanelsa's desk and handed her half the stack of paperwork. "Let's start reading and see what else we find out."

* * *

On the same Monday morning, Duncan and his partner, Trooper Jenny Cavendish, pulled up outside an aging Victorian farmhouse in Farmington, a small community about twelve miles southeast of Uniontown, down Route 40. A marked state car was parked in the driveway, lights off. Behind it was one van with the logo of the Fayette County coroner and a second van from the crime scene investigation division. "Another day, another dead body," Duncan quipped as he got out of the car. He tugged his gloves into place, then zipped his jacket up to the very top. The sky was bright blue, but the frigid air cut right through the legs of his pants. A good two feet of snow covered the yard, the edges by the road dirty from passing traffic.

Cavendish answered in a deadpan voice. "It pays the bills." She gazed around the neighborhood. "You're not exactly living on top of your neighbors out here, are you?" The wind caught her hair, and she held it to keep it off her face. "First round's on me if we can find a witness who can give us anything."

He doubted she'd be paying up. The house stood a good fifty feet back from the road. There was a ranch-style home off to the left, but far enough that it would be hard to notice anything at the Victorian. Farmington was small, part of the town of Wharton. All of the businesses were on Route 40 proper. This little loop of houses was too far away for anything to be seen by a motorist on the National Pike. Witnesses would be hard to come by.

Cavendish pulled her stylish leather jacket tighter. "I hate winter. I hate the cold. Did I ever tell you that?" She picked her way up the driveway, which was at least mostly clear.

Duncan followed, bemused at his partner's barely adequate outerwear and footgear. "How long have you lived around here? Don't you know how to dress appropriately?" He'd swapped out his own dress shoes for sturdier ones. Still professional, but better suited for snow.

Cavendish didn't turn around. "Bite me."

Just outside the scene, they were greeted by a familiar face. Trooper Aislyn McAllister was definitely dressed for the weather in heavy boots and a cold-weather jacket issued by the PSP. Thick gloves hung out of the jacket pocket. "Morning, Boss. Cavendish."

Cavendish grunted a greeting.

Duncan's spirits lifted. McAllister was no stranger to a death scene as a responding officer. She'd have her procedure in place and the information he needed ready. "Morning. What's the story?"

"Call came in at eight-forty-five from a Mr. Edward Rosen." McAllister read from her notes. "He arrived here at eight-forty, looking for his friend, Ellis Martingdon. Martingdon is the resident. Mr. Rosen's suspicions were aroused when the front door was unlocked and slightly ajar. Not only was it in the teens overnight, he swore Martingdon would never have left the door open."

Duncan removed his own pad from his pocket. "So he's missing?"

"Oh, no." McAllister brushed blond curls off her forehead. "Mr. Rosen entered the house. If you are thinking this was a risky move, he was carrying a Dan Wesson DWX."

Cavendish whistled.

McAllister continued. "I confirmed he is licensed to carry. Anyway, as soon as he came in, he found his buddy in the living room. Face down, shot through the back of the head." She closed the notebook. "The closest neighbor, who lives in that ranch over there, said he didn't hear anything he'd think was a gunshot last night. And he took one of those ZzzQuil sleep tablets." She waved at the few other houses. "None of these folks are home right now, so someone'll have to come back."

"World War III could've happened, and that guy wouldn't have heard shit." Duncan looked over the property.

"Indeed." McAllister raised a finger. "However, he did see a quote, big-ass black pickup, end quote, in the driveway here around ten. Mr. Martingdon owns an aging gray Dodge Ram, and it's in the garage."

Cavendish shielded her eyes against the glare of the sun off the snow. "Except there aren't any lights. How'd he know it was black?"

"That's what he said. Black."

"Don't suppose he saw a license plate."

"Negative." McAllister jerked her thumb toward the house. "Rosen *claims* he doesn't know anyone who drives a black pickup."

Duncan's ears perked at the stress she put on the word. "You don't believe him?"

"Not entirely. Come on, who walks around carrying a Dan Wesson DWX?" She raised her eyebrows. "It's not a compact, concealed-carry gun. That's firepower. If you're toting one of those, you're expecting trouble."

"And why is he bringing it to breakfast?" Cavendish asked. "Where is Mr. Rosen?"

"In the kitchen." McAllister ran a hand through her curls. "Tommy-boy is in the living room with the deceased."

Duncan took out a coin and faced his partner. "Heads, I get the suspect."

Cavendish waved him off. "Forget it. I don't think you're playing with a legit coin, Duncan; I lose every time. Besides, if by Tommy-boy she means that deputy coroner friend of yours, you can have him. He's weird." She strode off into the house.

Duncan turned to his former trainee. "Impressions of the scene?" He took a few steps toward the house.

"Clean. Very clean." McAllister put her hands in her jacket pockets as she followed. "No sign of a struggle. No sign of forced entry. Victim has a lot of cash on the property. I found packs of used twenties in a box in the basement. I haven't counted it yet, but I wouldn't be surprised if it turns out to be five thousand or more."

Duncan tapped his shoes against the porch to get rid of loose snow before donning a pair of paper booties. "Drugs?"

"Nothing. I did find some handguns. A Taurus and a couple of Berettas. Boxes of ammo for each of them. But no loose or packaged drugs, no drug paraphernalia. I haven't had a chance to see if the guns are registered."

Inside the house, he accepted a pair of paper booties from a tech and put them on. "What else?"

"Nothing suspicious. That makes me more antsy than anything." She gave him a lopsided grin. "You did your job too well, Boss. On the outside, this is the well-maintained, but older home of a single guy who might dislike banks."

He unzipped his coat. "Which, of course, makes you think he had something to hide."

Her blue eyes widened in mock innocence. "Don't you?"

Chapter Four

Armed with coffee, Sally and Tanelsa went to the conference room and began reading. Both women took copious notes, working in silence. Through several cases, they'd developed a pattern. They became familiar with the facts independently, made their own observations, and afterward, they pooled their thoughts. Working this way allowed one to see things the other didn't and offer fresh ideas.

Sally finished slightly ahead of her partner. She warmed up her coffee while she waited.

Tanelsa set the last pages aside. "What a mess." She glanced at her pad. "Looks like the entire case hinged on the husband's statements the night of the murder."

Sally returned to the table. "What happened that night starts off uncomplicated. According to Alec Wilson's statement, he left the house around four that afternoon. He admitted to learning earlier that day that his wife, Vivien, was having an affair and was supposedly leaving him. He said he was angry and argued with Vivien. She laughed at him, and he left."

"But there's no one to corroborate that story."

Sally continued. "According to Alec, he went to a local bar to get drunk. The night bartender, who arrived around six, confirmed Alec was already there and stayed until approximately nine that night. They cut him off around eight-thirty, confiscated his keys, and called an Uber. The Uber driver gave a statement that he dropped Alec off at his house sometime around half past nine. According to Alec, he went for a walk to sober up and didn't go inside the house until almost eleven. That's when he found

16

Vivien in the kitchen, called 9-1-1, and tried to give CPR. The uniformed police and ambulance arrived at eleven twenty-two. The paramedic saw that Vivien was obviously gone and pronounced her dead at the scene at eleven fifty-three. The medical examiner's report said the victim had been dead less than six hours before she was found. At the trial, he said livor mortis had barely begun. That means whether Wilson went inside at nine-thirty or eleven, he could have killed her."

Tanelsa got up and wrote the timeline on the whiteboard. "Here's where it gets hinky. The police report says while at the station under questioning, Alec changed his story. He said he'd gone in the house upon arriving home, *then* went for a walk. Where's that transcript?"

Sally rummaged through the paper. "Here." She read.

Question: What time did you get home?

Answer: The car dropped me off at nine- thirty.

Q: Did you go inside?

A: No. I tried, but I didn't have my keys.

Q: What did you do then?

A: Went for a walk to sober up. I hoped Vivien would come home so we could talk.

Q: You didn't speak to Vivien?

A: No, I told you. I didn't have my keys.

Q: In the car on the way here, you said you went inside to talk to her.

A: No, I {pause} I didn't have my keys.

Q: Do you have a spare key at the house?

A: Yes, in a fake rock in the garden. I know; stupid. Vivien's idea.

Q: So you used that key to get inside.

A: Yes, no, I mean no. I was drunk. I didn't even think about it.

Q: But that's not what you said on the way here.

A: Why are you bullying me?

Q: We're not bullying. We're having a friendly conversation. Just trying to get the facts straight.

A: Don't I have the right to an attorney? I want a lawyer.

{Interview ended}

Sally set aside the paper. "From what I just read, Dave is hanging everything on the fact that the exchange was an interrogation while Wilson was in custody. At least, he believed he couldn't leave, which is the same thing under the law. He should have been Mirandized. It's a violation of his Fifth Amendment rights against self-incrimination. They only stopped when he asked for an attorney."

"I can't believe the judge denied the motion." Tanelsa set the marker on the table. "It's textbook Law 101. The prosecution should be ashamed." Tanelsa sat on the table. "What do you think of this?" She handed Sally a sheet from the file.

"The witness?" She reread the statement. "He was on Dave's original list but disappeared before the trial. Dave asked for a continuance so he could look for the man, but the judge denied that, too."

Tanelsa went back to the board. "Is the witness's name in there?"

Sally shuffled through the files. "Kyle Palmer. He lived across the street from the Wilsons." Sally scanned Dave's notes. "I have a statement here that is signed by Mr. Palmer. In it, he says he saw another man enter the Wilson house at seven and leave in a hurry thirty minutes later." She picked up the phone and dialed the number in Palmer's contact information. She hung up. "Out of service."

"He lives in Marsdale?" Tanelsa groaned. "That's not exactly a trip around the block."

"No." Sally gathered up the dirty coffee mugs. "But we might have to run out there anyway."

* * *

Duncan snapped on a pair of nitrile gloves and went to check in with deputy coroner Tom Burns while Cavendish searched the rest of the house.

The younger man was bent over the victim, briskly going about the business of death investigation, humming an off-key tune while he worked.

Duncan, although not musically inclined himself, shuddered at the noise. "You need a tune-up."

Burns didn't flinch. "If all you're here to do is offer auditory criticism, there's the door. But I've heard you sing, my friend. People in glass houses and all that."

"I'm not." Duncan stepped around the deceased. "Walk me through your findings."

Burns sat back on his heels. "The victim had some serious enemies."

"How can you tell?"

The younger man pointed. "Single gunshot wound to the back of the head. No exit wound, small entry. He was on his knees, facing away from the shooter. You can see the hole here and the stippling from the burn."

"Execution style." Duncan made a note. That might narrow the field of suspects a bit. Random murderers didn't do executions. In Duncan's experience, that meant drugs or some other criminal activity.

"Yep." Burns continued his examination. "No signs of defensive wounds. Livor mortis is fixed. Rigor is well set, and he doesn't show signs of coming out of it. I know you love it when I speculate. I'll humor you. My guess is he has been dead anywhere from twelve to twenty-four hours. We'll have a better estimate after a full autopsy, of course."

"Let's say between nine yesterday morning to nine last night for a working theory." Duncan scrawled a note. "Anything else?"

"He's a little on the overweight side. I don't think the ambient temperature slowed or sped things significantly." Burns waved at the thermostat on the wall. "That thing is set at seventy-five degrees. He wasn't beaten before he was shot. I've been half-listening to the techs. They haven't found any brass. I think your actor was pretty professional."

"Great. That means we won't get a ton of prints." Duncan surveyed the deceased. He wore a faded sweatshirt and matching sweatpants. His feet were bare, but a ratty pair of blue slippers weren't far away. The TV remote was on the floor, a couple feet away from the victim. A bowl of potato chips and a can of beer graced a nearby table. Judging from the ring of water around the can, it had been cold but was now room temperature. He picked up a chip in his gloved hand. It still had a crunch, which led him to estimate the time of the shooting on the low end. Much longer, and the chips would have lost a bit of their crispness. "Any clues as to an ID?"

Burns slipped paper bags over the victim's hands. "You don't usually have your wallet in your pocket when you're sacked out watching the tube."

"Touché." Duncan looked over at the flat-screen in the corner. He estimated it to be at least sixty-five, maybe seventy inches in size. "Do you know if it was on?"

Burns paused. "It was dark when I got here. You'd have to ask the techs."

"I'll do that. Thanks." He stepped around the body and went over to a tech who was dusting for fingerprints. "Hey there."

"The TV was off." The tech focused on his work but allowed a faint grin. "I heard you talking to Burns. Honestly, Trooper, this place is clean. Much cleaner than I'd expect."

"You haven't found anything?" Another argument for a professional hit.

"I didn't say that." The tech sighed and gave up his work. He put away his brush. "Clean, not immaculate. We got prints from where you'd expect them. The TV remote, the light switch, the beer can. I'm not the best at the whole betting thing, but my guess is that they'll all match the victim. You can check with Anita in the kitchen, but I don't think she's found much out of order, either." He straightened. "It looks like the guy fell out of his chair onto his knees and croaked. I mean, I know that's not the case. You don't shoot yourself in the back of the head. But whoever did this took a lot of pains to follow an old Boy Scout rule."

"I was a Boy Scout, and I have no idea what you're talking about. Murder 101 wasn't a badge back in my day."

"Be prepared. He, or she, either wore gloves or did a decent job of cleaning." The tech tilted his head. "Probably the former. If everything had been wiped down, we'd come up empty."

When was the last time we had a professional hitman in these parts? Not within recent memory. "Find a wallet?"

"Nope, but like I said, check with Anita." The tech went back to work.

"I'll do that." Duncan headed for the kitchen, but he didn't get far.

Cavendish appeared, holding a plastic card. She stretched out her hand to Duncan. "Everything in the house seems to say the resident's name is Ellis

Martingdon. I found a license, a copy of the rental agreement, and a couple of utility bills."

Duncan looked at the license picture. It showed a man who looked a lot like the victim. Same hair color, same doughy complexion. "Burns, what color are the deceased's eyes?"

Burns peeled up an eyelid. "Brown."

That also matched. "You said *seems* to say. What's the issue?"

She nodded toward the license. "Take a closer look."

Duncan inspected the plastic. At first glance, it appeared legitimate. He stepped over to a lamp and held it under the light. The holograph was blurry. Instinctively, he flexed the card. It gave a bit, then snapped. "Fake."

"That was my take." She looked over at the victim. "We'll check with the landlord, but I doubt our John Doe needed more than the driver's license to get the rental. The utilities would be cake after that."

"Of course, that begs the question." Duncan dropped the pieces of the license in an evidence bag.

"What's his real name?"

He looked up. "Well, yes. But I was thinking more along the lines of why did he need a fake ID in the first place?"

Chapter Five

Sally headed over to the county jail around ten-thirty. Tanelsa had stayed at the office to work on tracking down Kyle Palmer. Between public sources and the major databases they subscribed to, the same ones used by private investigators and skip tracers. Sally hoped that Tanelsa would be able to find the elusive witness. Meanwhile, she would talk to their client and get his side of the story.

She lucked out and scored a parking spot not far from the courthouse, which connected to the jail via its own version of the Bridge of Sighs. *Good thing, because I think I'd freeze if I had to walk there today.* Typical of early December, the temperature had plummeted to below freezing. A stiff breeze nipped at her face as she hurried toward the building under leaden gray skies. The folks at the local ski resorts had to be loving the cold snap. Her, not so much.

Despite the cold, she slowed her approach. The Fayette County courthouse looked as impressive as ever. The heavy gray stone and single spire with slate gray roofs and simple clock face loomed over the street. Sally had spent the better part of five years working here when she was with the public defender's office. She'd made the right call to go into private practice, but part of her missed coming to the imposing building.

Inside the front doors, she put her bags on the conveyor belt to be scanned and stepped through the metal detector. She retrieved her things and thanked the county sheriff's deputy on duty. She'd have to stop and see Doris, the secretary at the PD's office, before she left. The older woman would never forgive her if she learned Sally had been in the building and didn't stop to say hello.

At the jail, she presented her identification and asked to see Alec Wilson. After she surrendered her phone, a security guard escorted her to an interview room. While she waited, she arranged her materials, including a small digital recorder.

It didn't take long for the guard to return with the prisoner. On the tall side, Wilson had dishwater-blond hair that flopped over his forehead. He didn't look like a man who worked out a lot, but neither was he overweight. His prison jumpsuit didn't strain at the seams, nor did it hang on his frame. He fidgeted with the metal rings on his wrists and shuffled into the room.

Sally waved at the wrist and ankle shackles. "I don't suppose you'd take those off, would you, Officer?"

The guard fastened the chain on the prisoner's wrists to a ring in the table. "No, ma'am. You know the drill." He went to the door. "I'll be outside if you need anything." He left, giving them the required privacy.

Sally took a moment to size up her client. His brown eyes held the haunted look of a man who'd spent time behind bars but still couldn't quite believe what had happened. "Mr. Wilson. My name is Sally Castle. Your attorney, David Sturgess, is a friend of mine. Due to his health problems, he's asked me to take over your appeal."

"He told me." Wilson leaned forward. "I didn't do it. I swear."

She held up a hand. "We'll get to that. Before I commit to the case, I want to hear your version of the events on the night your wife died. If you don't mind, I'd like to record this session. That way, I can share what you say with my partner, and I'll be free to focus on you instead of taking notes."

He glanced at the machine. "Sure. Where should I start?"

"At the beginning of your night." Sally pressed record and situated herself. "I want to know everything that happened up until the point you were charged."

"Hasn't Mr. Sturgess told you all this?"

"Yes, but as I said, I want to hear it in your words." She folded her hands. "Go ahead."

"I guess it started when Vivien and I got into a fight that afternoon."

"What was the fight about?"

Wilson picked at his cuticles. "Vivien told me she was gonna leave. We'd been having problems for a while, at least a year. I kinda suspected she might be, you know, seeing someone. I was right."

"She was having an affair." Sally knew her words sounded brutal, but there was no sense sugar-coating anything. Not when the man's freedom was on the line. "Did you know with whom?"

"No. I didn't want to. Anyway, I got mad. We yelled some. I told her she needed to think things through before she threw our marriage down the drain. She wouldn't want to make a decision she'd regret." He swallowed. "I didn't mean I would hurt her or anything. You see, we'd had a good thing at the beginning. I wanted to work on it. I didn't want her to walk away and realize she'd made a mistake. Not that Viv ever admitted her mistakes, at least not to me."

"Why didn't you want to know the name of the man?"

"Would it have made any difference?"

Sally would have wanted to know, but that was her. "I understand. What did she say?"

"That she'd thought about it plenty." He slumped in his chair. "She laughed and said the only thing she regretted was marrying me in the first place. We'd been together since high school. She'd always been...demanding, I guess you'd call it. High maintenance. I knew I wasn't the catch of the century, and she made sure she told me that every day. But her choices were limited in Marsdale."

"I'm surprised she didn't move to Pittsburgh. Plenty of men up there."

His shoulders twitched. "All I know is that Vivien liked being in charge, pulling the strings. She had a way of getting me to do what she wanted. Eventually, she decided to go after someone else, someone more, I don't know, exciting I guess." He looked up. "I'm an insurance actuary. Not exactly a thrill-a-minute profession."

Sally waited a moment. "What did you say to that?"

"Nothing. I never do. I used to, not that it ever got me anything. I know my place. Anyway." He blew out a breath. "I was mad, so I went to the bar. I wanted a sympathetic ear and to drown my sorrows. Bartenders are always good listeners, at least on TV."

"What time was this?"

He scrunched up his face. "Around dinner? Late in the afternoon. Whenever it was, by nine, I was blotto. I sorta remember the bartender taking my keys away and calling me a ride. At home, the house was locked. I couldn't get in because I didn't have my keys."

"What about the spare key?"

Wilson shook his head. "I didn't even think about it. I was that drunk. Somewhere in my mind, I thought it would be better to wait for Vivien to get home, even though I knew she'd find a way to make the whole situation my fault, like it always is. All the lights were off in the house, so I figured she'd gone out, maybe with Mr. Right." His voice dripped with self-pity. "I decided I didn't want her to see me hammered. I didn't think I could take her abuse. I went to the park and walked the running track until I felt a little more sober."

Sally thought about the statement he'd given the police. "Did anyone see you?"

"No. It was a Friday night, late enough to be dark. I guess people had gone to bed or were out somewhere." He picked at his nails again. "I went home; don't ask me when. This time, the house was open. I thought Vivien had maybe left the door open for me. I went inside to the kitchen to get a glass of water before sacking out in the spare room." He shot Sally a guilty look. "We haven't been sleeping in the same bed for a while."

She ignored the statement. "That's when you found her?"

He paled and nodded. "She was a real mess. Blood everywhere. I know people say that all the time, but it looked awful, worse than anything I'd ever seen on a TV show. Her clothes were soaked with blood. It was in her hair, under her head, on her throat." He gulped. "I tried CPR, tried to find a pulse. I wasn't thinking."

If he was telling the truth, shock might have caused his behavior. "Try to remember. Was her body warm or cold?"

He blinked. "Um, I wasn't paying attention. Kinda warm, I guess. It was warm outside, so if she'd been cold, I think I would have noticed that. The blood was sticky, but not dry. Does that mean something?"

"Only that she might have been killed recently." The coroner's report said death had been within a couple of hours. *Right about when he admits to getting home from the bar, left, and no one can corroborate his story.* "Then you called the police."

"I dialed 9-1-1, yeah. The EMTs said Vivien was dead. That's when the cops took me to the station. At first, they were sympathetic, but I could tell they'd started to look at me as a suspect before long." He rubbed his face with his hands. "The questioning seemed to go on forever. Finally, I wised up and asked for a lawyer."

"Did they stop at that point?"

"Yeah. But I'd already put my foot in it."

Sally thought. "You said abuse earlier. Was Vivien abusive?"

"She never hit me, no."

"I mean verbally or emotionally." She'd seen both in her career, and they were often worse than any physical action.

He squirmed. "Vivien was high maintenance, like I told you. She always had been. I learned a long time ago it was better to go along with her and keep her happy."

It was Sally's first conversation with her client, but Vivien seemed like a textbook case of an emotional abuser. At the very least, she had been difficult to live with. Unfortunately, that only fed Alec's motive. The abused spouse who finally snapped. But Sally's job wasn't to cast doubt on his guilt. Not yet. First, she had to get past the appeal. She leaned forward. "Mr. Wilson, this is important. Did they ever advise you of your rights?"

He gave her a blank look. "Like they do on TV? No. At least not until I asked for my lawyer. I didn't even think about it."

"Did they tell you that you could leave at any time?"

"Well..." Wilson stared at the wall, lost in thought. "Not in so many words, no. They kept saying we were only talking, but I definitely got the impression that if I'd tried to leave, they would have objected. The way they asked their questions, though, it was uncomfortable. Like they were waiting for me

26

to trip up." He licked his lips. "I wanted to go home. But I needed them to understand I was innocent. I didn't kill Vivien. I thought that leaving, or refusing to talk, would give the wrong impression."

Sally pulled the folder with Sturgess's notes toward her and looked for the statement. "The police say that you initially told them you went in the house when you arrived home from the bar."

"No, I went *to* the house. I never said *in*." He licked his lips again. "Not that I remember. I was so drunk, but I think I would know if I went in my own house."

She scanned the trial records. "The key from the garden was on the table."

"I don't know who put it there, but it wasn't me. It must've been the killer." He clutched the table. "Or maybe Vivien forgot her keys and used it."

"Your wife's keys were in her purse." Perhaps the house had been unlocked when she got home. "Did you see anyone nearby after the Uber dropped you off?"

"No."

"Do you or your wife have any enemies? Someone who'd wish to hurt either of you?"

Wilson ran his tongue over his lips. He swallowed hard and dropped his gaze to the table. "No. No one like that."

She fixed him with a stare. "I advise you to tell me the truth, Mr. Wilson. No matter how you think it sounds."

He raised his head, but he didn't quite meet Sally's gaze. "I don't know of anyone who'd want to do that to Vivien."

She studied him for a long moment. He was scared, that was certain. Of going back to prison or something else? She wasn't sure. "Do you know Kyle Palmer?"

Wilson's eyes widened, and it took him a moment to answer, as though the change in topic had thrown him. "Kyle? He lived across the street from us. Weird guy. Never spoke to him much. Just a quick hello if I saw him getting his mail or whatever. As my grandmother would say, he was an odd duck. He didn't go out of his way to be friendly, but he didn't brush me off, either. But I never made it past the sidewalk in front of his house."

"Then why would he be on the witness list for your trial?"

"No clue." Alec's confusion showed on his face. "I know Mr. Sturgess was going to call on him, but honestly, I don't know how it would have helped. I didn't see him that night. But he didn't show up when he was supposed to testify. Mr. Sturgess asked for a...what do you call it when you need more time?"

"A continuance."

"Yeah, that. But the judge said no. We had to go forward without him." Alec rubbed his face. "That didn't piss Mr. Sturgess off as much as when he argued everything I'd said shouldn't be used against me. You know, on TV, the cops read people their rights at the drop of a hat. That didn't happen to me."

"It should have. Are you sure you don't have anything else to tell me?" Sally tried to keep her voice from sounding accusatory. She'd been doing criminal defense long enough that her gut told her Wilson was holding something back. Either because he was ashamed or he didn't think it could be helpful. Either way, she didn't care. She'd had clients who withheld information before, and it wouldn't necessarily stop her from taking the case. But she didn't like being kept in the dark. "The best thing you can do for yourself, Mr. Wilson, is to be completely honest."

He let the silence build, but finally, he met her gaze. This time, there was no hesitation in his voice. "No, Ms. Castle. There's nothing."

Chapter Six

Duncan and Cavendish did a detailed search of Martingdon's house. He knew forensics was doing the same job, but he couldn't help himself. "I haven't found a single thing that indicates the victim had another name, have you?"

Cavendish pulled herself out from underneath the bed. "Not even a hint. Every bill, every piece of junk mail; hell, even the registration for that truck is in the name of Ellis Martingdon."

Duncan thumbed through a pile of envelopes. "Doesn't look like he had a checkbook."

"It seems to be a trend these days. Don't get me started on all the mobile payment apps. Talk about an invitation to get hacked." Cavendish went to the closet and tossed articles of clothing out in a pile after shaking them out and searching the pockets first.

"Times change." Duncan opened each drawer in a dresser and ran his hands under and between the clothing. "Maybe we're looking at this wrong."

She paused. "How so?"

"Maybe it isn't the name that's fake. Could be the age."

She snorted. "According to the ID we found, he's forty. Who fakes that?" She returned to her task. "What did your coroner buddy say?"

"That he looks like a man in his late thirties or early forties." Duncan abandoned the dresser. "But that's a guess. What if he's older and, for some reason, needed to lower his age. Or even the opposite. Humor me. Have we run that name?"

"Not yet." Cavendish pulled out her phone. "I'll get someone at the office to start on it." She held the device to her ear. "Kincaid, I need a favor. Start a search for a man named Ellis Martingdon." She spelled the name. "Anyone from mid-thirties to early fifties. Check all the usual sources. Thanks." She hung up. "What about prints?"

"Burns gave me a card. I'll run it through AFIS when we get back." Duncan left and went to the bathroom.

"CSI say anything about the prints they lifted?" Cavendish called.

"They appear to match the victim's. Nothing unknown." He picked up a prescription bottle of cholesterol meds. The name on the bottle was Ellis Martingdon. Either the guy went to a pro and got a whole new identity, or they were missing something on the ID. He put the bottle back.

His partner appeared in the doorway. "Nothing? I find that hard to believe."

He checked in the toilet tank, a clichéd but still used hiding place. "Our actor was pretty thorough. Either he, or she, obliterated everything else, or Mr. Martingdon doesn't get visitors." The interior of the tank was rusty and water-stained, but free of items that didn't belong there. He replaced the lid and turned his attention to the linen closet. It held a selection of threadbare and scratchy towels, but nothing else of note. "This is pissing me off."

"Tell me about it." She leaned on the doorframe. "We've looked everywhere. So have forensics. Face it. Either Mr. Martingdon is who he said he is, and for some reason known only to him and God, he has a fake Pennsylvania driver's license, or we've fumbled the ball completely and missed something."

Duncan didn't want to admit it, but facts seemed to indicate Cavendish was right. "This place is a bust. Let's check the truck and get out of here."

"To where?"

He tossed the towels back into the cupboard, not bothering to fold them neatly. "I want to canvass the neighbors again."

* * *

Sally swung by the deli on the way back to the office and picked up sandwiches for her and Tanelsa. She arrived and presented lunch to her partner. "I come bearing gifts."

Tanelsa didn't look over from her monitor. "You better after what I've been doing for the past couple of hours."

Sally sat at her desk and unwrapped her turkey-and-swiss on rye. "Find anything on Kyle Palmer?"

"Yes and no." Her partner made a few mouse clicks. She ripped open the bag of chips, popped one in her mouth, crunched it up, and swallowed. "I just sent you the report. I've looked in all of our usual databases. Palmer has a pretty solid history. He rented the house across the street from the Wilsons for a couple of years. He worked as a general contractor for several firms over that time. It looks like standard jack-of-all-trades, master of none stuff to me."

Sally wiped mustard from her hands. "Did you call any of his past employers?"

"Yes. Not all of them, mind you, but the ones I did connect with said pretty much the same. He did grunt work, nothing that required special skills." Tanelsa turned her attention to her sandwich.

"He leave or get fired?"

"He had a pattern. After anywhere from six months to a year, he'd get bored and look for another job." Tanelsa smeared aioli on the bread. "I asked if there were any issues with his work or if he ever missed a day without explanation, but nothing. He showed up on time, did what he was told, did it competently, and went home. He wasn't one to offer to stay late or work weekends, but that's hardly a crime." She took a bite.

Sally held her sandwich in one hand and scrolled through the report with the other. "Doesn't look like he was in serious debt."

"Rent was on time, one credit card that usually had a small balance but was paid regularly, all utilities taken care of promptly. He drove a Ford F-150 that was about fifteen years old. At least he did until he sold it."

"What does he drive now?"

Tanelsa unscrewed the cap on her water bottle. "Nothing. I can't find his name on any current registration in the DMV records." She took a gulp.

"Sold for the cash, and he couldn't buy a replacement?" She glanced at Tanelsa, who had a mouthful of sandwich but made a noncommittal gesture. "Looks like he had a few brushes with the law."

The other woman swallowed. "But not for anything that resulted in a conviction. A warning for possession of weed back before the medical marijuana days. He received a couple of warnings for bar brawls, but nothing ever came of them. Looks like he inched up to the line, but he's never crossed it."

"You're right. This is pretty boring." Sally opened her own bag of chips. "Why did you say 'yes and no'?"

"Because this past October, he disappeared." Tanelsa looked at her monitor. "Left the house he was renting, sold his truck, and emptied his account at the Marsdale bank. He canceled his credit card. The number your buddy Sturgess had was Palmer's cell, and it's out of service. No forwarding address with the post office. He didn't even renew his driver's license."

Sally skimmed down the report, but Tanelsa had covered it. For all intents and purposes, Kyle Palmer had ceased to exist.

"One more thing." Tanelsa brushed off her hands, got up, and pulled out a folder from the material Dave had sent. "Your buddy hired a private investigator."

"To do what?"

"See for yourself."

Sally took the folder. The contents were slim: a contract to find Kyle Palmer, a paid invoice, and one meager status report. "Do you think the PI found Palmer?"

Tanelsa crossed her arms. "There's nothing in the file. Then again, Palmer's name is definitely on the witness list for last month's trial. Maybe Sturgess was hoping he could be located in time?"

Sally reached for her phone. "There's only one way to find out."

* * *

Duncan watched Burns zip up the body bag. "When will you get to the autopsy?"

"We're booked today. Tomorrow morning. It'll be up to the boss, but that's my feeling. Give me a hand, will you?" He grabbed the head of the bag.

Duncan lifted the feet, and together, they got the body onto the gurney. "Text me with the details?"

Burns strapped down the bag. "You got it. If you get any info on John Doe here, remember to tell me so we can update our files." He trundled the gurney out of the house.

Duncan reviewed the pile of evidence bags that forensics had gathered thus far. "How fast do you think we'll get the DNA processed?"

Cavendish shook out her blond hair and gathered it up. "The state lab is backed up, as usual. They say six months. Maybe we can coax them to move faster, but don't hold your breath. This isn't high enough priority for a rush."

"Of course. Maybe we'll get lucky when we run the victim's prints." It happened, but he didn't have a good feeling about this one.

His partner slapped him on the back. "Why don't I take this stuff back to the office and start the search in AFIS? You can do the door-to-door."

"Why do I have to be the one to trudge through the snow?" He raised an eyebrow. "Is this supposed to be some sort of chivalry? I let you be all warm and toasty while I freeze my ass off?"

"Nope." She gathered up the bags. "You have better people skills."

Part of that was bullshit. Cavendish was a fine interviewer. But he did have to admit her brusqueness, a trait honed by being a woman in a male-dominated field, sometimes put witnesses off. "Fine. But you owe me."

"I'll meet you and Sally at Whiskey & Rye tonight. First round's on me." She left.

Duncan reviewed the list of statements from McAllister. He'd have to come back to the houses where there'd been no answer. Of the remaining three, one claimed not to have seen or heard anything, one might have heard a car backfiring late last night, and one flat-out refused to talk. Duncan decided to tackle the "hear no evil, see no evil" neighbor, a man named

Newsome, who lived across the street, first. At least the house was on the other side of the road. All the houses seemed to be separated by anywhere from twenty-five to fifty yards.

The man who answered the door gave a grunt of obvious annoyance when he saw Duncan's ID. "I told the woman who was here earlier. I didn't hear or see nothing."

"I need to follow up. Matter of procedure." Duncan stamped his feet. "Mind if I come in? It's pretty cold out here."

The man huffed but opened the door. "What is there to follow up on?" He barely waited for his visitor to get inside before shutting the door.

"Mr. Newsome. Are you sure you didn't hear anything? This is a pretty quiet area."

Newsome crossed pudgy arms. "Nothing."

"I live in Confluence. Same size community. If someone had shot my neighbor in the head, I think I'd hear it."

Newsome startled. "In the head?"

Duncan gave a solemn nod. "Execution style. Bad enough, a man got killed in your hometown. Only certain kinds of people do execution killings. They aren't the type of folks you want coming to the neighborhood picnic in the summer."

Newsome waited, perhaps mulling over the idea of a contract killer, or the type of people who attracted such visitors, living in Farmington. "I really didn't see or hear anything. Nothing I'd consider out of the ordinary."

"What about things you'd consider run of the mill?"

Newsome shifted on his feet. "I did hear an engine last night. Like after eleven. At least, the late news had started."

"Did it sound like a truck?" Duncan took out his notepad.

The other man thought. "Nah. Well, maybe. Whatever it was, it was big. Either one of them big-ass trucks or a muscle car. Like a Hemi, that kind of thing. I can't tell you exactly what kind, but it was not a Honda Civic."

Duncan wrote this down. "Did Mr. Martingdon often get late visitors?"

"I didn't pay much attention. Martingdon didn't encourage small talk."

Duncan looked up. "He was unfriendly?"

"Not that." Newsome went to the table and grabbed an open can of beer. "Standoffish-like. Everybody else had candy for the kids on Halloween. His place was dark as a hole. Oh, he'd talk if I saw him out, but never about anything more than the weather or stupid shit. No complaints about the potholes, or the mayor, or comments about when the Beverlys down the street had a knockdown fight a few weeks ago. I never saw him sitting on his front porch or mowing his grass, although someone took care of it."

Duncan wrote all this down. "Anything else?"

"No. I really wish I could help, but honestly? Sometimes I forgot the guy was there."

Duncan thanked him for his time, gave him his card, and left.

The next neighbor, Margie Allington, was a little more talkative. "It was a loud bang, like an engine backfiring. I heard it clear as day when I put Sammy out. If I don't let him pee in the middle of the night, he has an accident. Poor dear is getting old." She waved at a Labrador with a gray muzzle but whose tail thumped enthusiastically, as though he knew the humans were talking about him.

"Could it have been a gunshot?" Duncan asked.

She shook her head. "No, definitely an engine." She pursed her lips. "Then again, it might have been a gunshot. My husband, God rest his soul, used to hunt. Not that he was in the habit of firing a rifle in the house, mind you. But we had a little cabin, and we'd go for the first week of deer season. I'm familiar with firearms." She tapped her chin. "Never mind. It was definitely a car backfiring."

"Did you see the car?"

"No." She scratched Sammy behind the ears. "I was in the backyard. If I don't keep an eye on him, he wanders. Old age. It happens to us all, even dogs."

"Of course." Duncan handed her a business card and urged her to call if she remembered anything.

The third neighbor, Jeff Somers, was downright rude. "I told the first cop. I can't help you. I'm watching *Judge Judy*. Sorry, I can't talk." He shut the door.

So much for my people skills. Duncan knocked again. "Mr. Somers. I promise I won't take much time." No answer. "I already have two people who heard a car last night. If you could add anything, I'd appreciate it." Still nothing. "A vehicle with a large engine. Mr. Newsome thinks it was a truck or muscle car. Mrs. Allington said it backfired. Any details you can add would be helpful."

The door flew open. "Figures Newsome wouldn't know his ass from his armpit on cars. And that Allington woman is looney. Weren't no engine. It was a gunshot. The truck was earlier."

Duncan hunched his shoulders inside his jacket. The wind had picked up and was icy against his bare neck. "You did hear something."

Somers said nothing. He turned around and walked off, leaving the door open.

Duncan took it as an invitation and followed. He found Somers in the front room, settling into a BarcaLounger with frayed seams, shiny patches on the fabric, and a bit of stuffing poking out of the arm.

The older man put up his feet and muted the medium-sized flat-screen TV. "All right. You got me. Let's get this over so I can go back to my show."

The room was bereft of any other furniture, so Duncan settled into a more comfortable stance. "Let's start with the truck. When did you hear it?"

"It showed up earlier, around eight. Football game hadn't started yet. It left late. I mean, real late." Somers popped the tab on a can of Iron City. "One of them classic movie stations was running *The African Queen*. I like Bogie, so I watched. Movie started, what, eleven? I heard it a little after that." He held out the beer. "Want one?"

Duncan held up a hand. "No thanks. I'm on duty. Could you tell what kind of car? Or did you look out your window?"

"Didn't look." Somers slurped some beer. "I used to be a mechanic. It was a big one, eight-cylinder. Nice throaty roar. They don't make many of 'em like that anymore."

It wasn't much, but it would have to do. "When did you hear the gunshot?"

"After I heard the engine the second time. The movie was still on. Don't bother to ask me what kind of gun."

The times worked with what Burns had given him earlier. Given the style of the killing, there wouldn't have been much conversation. The rest of the time would have been spent cleaning up the scene before the shooter left. Police the brass, wipe down prints, attempt to get rid of anything that might yield DNA. "Anything else?"

Somers threw his arms wide, slopping a little beer onto the carpet as he did. "What more do you want? The name of the guy driving the truck? Bet I told you more than those other two nitwits."

Duncan suppressed a sigh. "Yes, sir. Thank you." He held out a business card. "If you think of anything else, please call." When his witness didn't take the card, he set it on the rickety table next to the lounger.

Somers set his beer can on top of the card. The liquid from the side of the can ran into the paper. "Yeah, I'll do that."

Chapter Seven

Sally checked the time. Twelve thirty. "Gut check. We've spent half a day on this. Are we taking the Wilson appeal or not?"

Tanelsa's expression betrayed a hint of surprise. "You're asking me this time?"

"Yes. I should have been doing it from the start. Are you in or out?"

Her partner scanned all the paper before her on the desk. "We get to right a wrong *and* get paid for it? Hell yeah, I'm in. Besides, I see more holes in the prosecution's case than there are in a slice of Swiss cheese."

Sally schooled her expression, but a wave of relief went through her. "All right then." She got up and went to the conference room. Once there, she started writing. "I think our best bet on the appeal is the whole evidence admitted in error angle. Dave's already done most of the work. It should be easy to show the judge erred in overruling the motion to suppress."

Tanelsa followed her. "I agree, although the writing can use some finesse. Keep the missing witness in our back pocket. If we find him for the appeal, great. If not, maybe we can still call him if the case gets sent back to trial or for additional proceedings."

Sally made two columns. "I concur. You're the better writer. You start reworking our argument for why that motion should have been granted. I think there's plenty in Dave's notes for you to start with."

"I've also been looking into precedents we can use." Tanelsa picked up a marker and wrote the relevant case names in the Suppression Motion column. "I appreciate your compliment on my writing skills. I take it you're gonna continue looking for the missing Kyle Palmer?"

"You got it. And researching those holes. I saw them, too. The police had a serious case of tunnel vision on this one."

Tanelsa laid down her marker. "I think you've taken the hard part. I sifted all through those databases and couldn't find a damn thing. What's your strategy?"

"Simple." Sally wrote a name in the Witness column. "I'm going to call that private investigator."

* * *

Duncan got back to the office in Eighty Four right before one. He'd stopped on the way and bought lunch for him and his partner. "I hope you didn't eat already." He dropped a bag on her desk and shrugged out of his overcoat. "Any luck?"

"You, sir, are a prince among men." Cavendish ripped open the bag. "I'm famished. A Cuban? And it's still warm? How'd you manage that?"

"I turned on the seat warmers. I may also have broken the speed limit a bit." He dropped into his chair and attacked his own sandwich, roast beef with cheese, onions, and peppers. "Lay it on me."

"You first." Cavendish took a huge bite of the first half, and sauce oozed out over her fingers. "Any luck with the neighbors?"

"Some." He gave her the high points. "Personally, I put more stock in what Somers said than the other two. He was surly, but once I got him talking, I think he was more sure of himself."

"Then we're looking for a vehicle with a large, powerful engine that was in the area the night of the murder."

"But it drove away before Somers said he heard the gunshot."

"Driver leaves the shooter. Shooter walks away. Or the driver came back much later, and no one heard him. Any CCTV?" She grabbed a napkin.

"In a residential neighborhood in Farmington? Get real. Although." He paused. "None of the neighbors I visited had one of those video doorbells. That doesn't mean no one on the street has one. We should send a uniform over to check. They have to go back to the neighbors who weren't home anyway. I'll get McAllister to do it."

She wiped her fingers and made a note. "You definitely had better luck than I did."

"How so?"

"I ran Ellis Martingdon's prints through AFIS. Nothing."

"What about NLETS or the National Crime Information Center?"

She shook her head. "He hasn't been arrested, doesn't have any wants or warrants, and even the feds don't have anything in their fingerprint records."

Duncan stuffed a stray slice of pepper back between the bread. "I find that hard to believe. The way he died strongly suggests he wasn't your typical street thug."

"I feel the same way. However, while that may be a dead end, there is this." She pawed through some paper and tossed one on his desk.

He was careful to wipe grease from his fingers before picking it up. It was an inventory sheet from the search of the scene. "Traces of white powder identified as cocaine. Also traces of a light brown powder, identified as heroin." He looked up. "Did they find any packaged product?"

Cavendish's mouth was full, so she shook her head and held up a finger. "Nope," she said after she swallowed. "They found the residue in the basement on a table. My guess is Martingdon used the table for dividing the drugs into baggies, maybe cutting it along the way."

Lunch abandoned, Duncan turned to his computer. "But Martingdon doesn't have any drug convictions."

"Based on what we found today, I'd say it was only a matter of time. It's possible he gave what he had to his distributors. Or sold it, if he handled everything himself."

"Maybe he was cutting in on someone's turf." Duncan searched. "Who've we arrested recently for cocaine or heroin distribution in that area?"

"I haven't had a chance to look it up." She popped a bit of bread in her mouth. "In addition, there were records in a metal filing cabinet near the cutting table." She found the evidence bag and pushed it across.

Duncan opened it and took out a plain three-subject spiral notebook, exactly like one a student would use. The last third was blank, but the first had "Sales" written on the divider. The second was labeled "inventory." He skimmed the columns. "Looks like he was starting out. There are dates and amounts here. Money and weight. And initials. People he sold to?"

Cavendish picked up the second half of her Cuban. "That would be my theory."

He flipped to the second section. Again, there were columns of dates, initials, and dollar amounts. "He kept immaculate records. I'll give him that."

"If he was horning in on someone's territory, that person, or persons, would be seriously pissed."

Duncan studied the figures. Martingdon had unexpectedly neat writing for a man trying his hand in such dangerous business. "I know where we may be able to find out. Or at least get the hint of where to look."

Cavendish lowered her Cuban. "Really? Where?"

"I have a source." He picked up his phone and dialed.

* * *

Sally arranged to meet Gerald Harper, David's private investigator, at a Panera in Uniontown. When she arrived, she spotted him almost immediately. He had taken a table in the corner, his back against the wall. She took a minute to size him up. Even though he was seated, she could tell he'd be tall from the length of his legs, almost matching Jim's six-foot-three. He was dressed in a dark winter jacket, dark-wash jeans, a navy pullover, and a white turtleneck. His gray hair was cut close. From the way he surveyed the other tables and where he'd chosen to sit, she pegged him as former law enforcement or military, most likely the former. She made her way over, unbuttoning her coat as she walked. "Mr. Harper? Sally Castle." She held out her hand.

He shook it once, his grip firm. "Ms. Castle. Hope you don't mind. I got here early and grabbed a seat."

The restaurant was not crowded. Even the tables near the gas fireplace were empty. "Not at all. But you make it sound like you had to fight for a space, and there are only three or four people here." She shrugged out of her coat and hung it over one of the extra chairs. "Military or police?"

His face didn't move. "Uniontown cop, twenty-five years. How could you tell?"

"My boyfriend is a state trooper. Between your haircut, the way you keep checking out the others in the restaurant, and the fact you picked a table in the corner, not one by the nice, warm fire, I knew it had to be one or the other."

His laugh sounded sharp, but amused. "I think I like you, Ms. Castle."

"Please, call me Sally." She pulled out her wallet and nodded at the cup in front of him. "You need a refill or a snack?"

He held up his hands. "I'm good. Get yourself something hot, and I'll be right here."

She returned minutes later with a steaming cup of coffee and a chocolate croissant. "Thanks for meeting me. I really wish you would have decided I was okay without bothering Dave, though."

"In my business, you can't be too careful." He reached down for a folder and placed it on the table. It wasn't more than half an inch thick, an indication his investigation hadn't been lengthy. "Here's what I have. Shame about Dave. I hope he recovers."

"I'm sure he will. From what he's said, his doctors are optimistic." She pulled the folder to her and opened it. It held a collection of photographs and a handful of paper. "Can you talk me through your investigation?"

"Dave approached Palmer to be a witness in the original trial. Palmer agreed, or seemed to. According to Dave, he failed to appear. Couldn't be found at his house—or anywhere else for that matter." Gerald took a drink. "How much do you know about Palmer?"

"A little. We know he disappeared." Sally told him what Tanelsa had managed to find. "Our trail goes cold about two months ago."

"Mine as well. I know where he was between last spring and October, but it looks like he liquidated everything about that time. His lease ended at the end of September and he hasn't been seen since." He pointed. "I didn't take those, but the photographs are what I could find online. He had a Facebook account, but the newest post was six months old. He was never very active."

Sally flipped through the photos. Her first thought was that Palmer could blend in almost anywhere. The man in the pictures had no remarkable features and no visible marks, such as scars, tattoos, or birthmarks. One of the pictures showed him in a t-shirt and jeans. He looked like he might have a bit of a paunch. From the picture of him standing by a truck, she judged him to be of average height. "What about friends or co-workers? Does he have family in the area?"

"His parents are both dead. He has a sister, but she lives in Pittsburgh. I talked to her. She said they aren't close. She hasn't seen him in years." Gerald took another gulp from his cup. "Neighbors say they rarely saw visitors. Co-workers say he was a close-mouthed SOB. Never wanted to go out drinking after the job, never showed any kind of social graces. He came to work and went home. Ate a boxed lunch by himself."

"Hmm." Sally set aside the photos and turned her attention to the papers. One of them looked like phone records. "What are these highlighted numbers?"

"Burners." Gerald set aside his cup. "He made four or five calls to each one over a period of a week, maybe ten days. Then that number isn't seen again. Right up until his own was disconnected."

"That's not suspicious at all." There were few legal reasons for people to use burners.

The comment earned another laugh. "I take it you've encountered the folks who tend to use those kind of things."

"I started in prosecution in Allegheny County. Then, I spent a few years with the public defender here in Uniontown. I'm quite familiar with the game."

"Your boyfriend either loves talking shop with you, or he hates it."

"Mostly the former, when the rules allow, of course." She thought a minute. "Was the telephone account closed by him or by the provider for nonpayment?"

"He closed it. He never missed a payment, not on anything from what I could find."

43

It was consistent with Tanelsa's findings. Sally finished with the records and turned to what looked like bank statements. "Interesting. He'd built up some cash, hadn't he?"

Gerald leaned on the table. "He certainly had. For years, his bank balance was pretty stable, or at least the pattern was. He'd get paid, gradually spend it over two weeks, get paid again, rinse, repeat. But in the three months before he disappeared, he had cash coming in from somewhere. By the time he closed the account, he'd saved almost ten grand. That's on top of his paycheck." He pointed.

"You haven't found a trace of him. Do you think he left Marsdale?"

He shook his head. "I can't find his name on a legal document of any kind. Could be he's living with someone and borrowing a car. He hasn't gotten a new job or a new bank account. Marsdale is too small for him to have disappeared so thoroughly, so yeah, I think he's in the wind. However."

Sally looked up, waiting.

"It doesn't seem like he just *left* Marsdale. He pulled out in a hurry. One day, he was there, and the next, he wasn't. He didn't even quit his last job. He was absent without explanation for three days, and they fired him. The day before the last time he was seen, the neighbor across the street said a man in an oversized black pickup came looking for him. A rather large Black man with a lot of tattoos and wearing clothes that, quote, made him look like a city street thug." Gerald's fingers made air quotes, and his expression conveyed his thoughts about the phrase.

Sally didn't have to struggle to get his meaning. "He ran from something. Or somebody."

"Bingo."

Unexplained money. Sudden disappearance. Sally didn't think either of those things had to do with Palmer's willingness to be a witness for Alec Wilson.

Chapter Eight

Duncan pulled into the gravel lot outside a squat gray cinderblock building on the outskirts of Confluence. Icicles hung from the gutters and someone had cleared a path through the snow to a heavy gray metal door that looked newly cleaned or recently painted. A small slot at eye level was the only opening. The building did not have windows. The other car in the lot, a gleaming black Lincoln Navigator, told Duncan his source was inside.

He and Cavendish exited the unmarked state car and headed for the door. Ten paces away, he turned and held out his hand. "A couple things before we go in."

She folded her arms. "I've dealt with informants before."

"I know, but Eddie is, well, you'll see. This looks like a pissant operation, but somehow he has his fingers on the pulse of the Fayette County crime scene. Kind of surprising for a fat man who doesn't get out much."

"Got it." She took a step.

"One more thing. Do not, under any circumstances, blow a gasket if he calls you Pretty."

"Excuse me? I certainly will." She tried to step around him.

Duncan blocked her. "No, you won't. For two reasons. One, if he does, it means he likes you. He's said it to McAllister and Sally. It's just how he is."

"What's the second reason?"

"If you go after Eddie, Stanley will eat you alive."

She scoffed. "I've handled bodyguards before."

"Stanley is at least three inches taller and fifty pounds heavier than me."

He held out his arms in a rough approximation of the hulking doorman's size. "Those things matter in a fight. Trust me."

Cavendish glanced at the building. "This is your informant. I'll let you take the lead. But don't expect me to stand around and say nothing if they start making me the butt of their jokes."

"Just be polite, and that won't happen." He led her to the door and banged on it.

A couple minutes later, the door slot opened to reveal a pair of dark-colored eyes. "Duncan. What the hell are you doing here?" The gravelly voice sounded more surprised than angry.

"Hello to you too, Stanley. I need to talk to Eddie."

The eyes cut to look at Cavendish. "Who is she?"

Duncan tipped his head. "Trooper Jenny Cavendish. My partner."

Stanley looked Duncan up and down. "You dress better in this job."

The Confluence grapevine would have passed news of his transfer to Criminal Investigation. "Thank you. Can I see Eddie?"

"Wait here." The slot closed.

Cavendish stepped back to take another look at the building. "His voice goes with the description you gave me."

"That was his friendly tone."

"What does he sound like when he's mad?"

Duncan studied the thick clouds overhead, which promised more snow later. "You don't want to know."

It wasn't long before the door opened. "Come in, quick." Stanley, dressed in his usual tight black t-shirt and black jeans, waved them in. "It's frickin' cold out, and I'm letting out all the heat."

The two troopers hurried inside. It was like stepping from a freezer into a sauna. Within seconds, Duncan felt the sweat beads popping out on his forehead. "Jesus, Stanley. You must have the thermostat set to eighty in here." He unbuttoned his coat and took it off.

"Eighty-five, actually. Eddie likes it hot." Stanley led them down a corridor.

Cavendish took off her winter jacket. "Your heat bills have to be ridiculous."

Stanley grunted. "Don't bother me. I don't pay them." He led them into an office crammed with a desk and filing cabinets. Piles of paper occupied every flat surface. "Here they are, Eddie."

Behind the desk sat a fat man who didn't look the least bit fazed by the heat. His red hair was slicked back. Despite the temperature, he wore a black suit tailored to fit his bulk with a bright white shirt and black tie. A stogie was clamped between his teeth. He removed it. "Trooper Duncan. I haven't seen you in forever. How are you?"

"I'm good, Eddie. This is my partner." He tossed his coat on a chair.

"Trooper Jenny Cavendish. Yes, Stanley told me." Eddie's brown eyes crinkled with mirth. "I swear, Duncan, how is it every time you show up here, you've got a different attractive woman with you? Don't they get jealous?"

"Just lucky, I guess. Jealousy isn't an issue. I'm only dating one of them."

Stanley took up his post in the corner, arms crossed over his massive chest.

"Trooper Cavendish, a pleasure." Eddie puffed on his cigar. "How long have the two of you worked together?"

"Since he came to Criminal Investigation. What, six months now?" She glanced at Duncan.

"More or less." Duncan wiped his forehead.

Eddie focused on Duncan. "I'm sure you didn't drop by to make introductions. To what do I owe the pleasure?"

"We found the body of a man who'd been shot, execution style." Duncan wished he could take off his jacket and tie, but suspected even stripping to his skin wouldn't help with the oppressive warmth. "In his basement, we found traces of cocaine and heroin. His bank accounts show a suspicious amount of cash."

Eddie spoke around the stogie. "Drug dealer?"

"That's the theory, but we don't know definitely yet."

Cavendish hadn't moved. The heat had to be killing her, too, but aside from perspiration at her hairline, she didn't show it.

"Does this dead man have a name?" Eddie asked.

Duncan laid a picture on the desk. "All the documents in his house, including a Pennsylvania driver's license, say Ellis Martingdon."

Eddie picked up the photo. "Fake?"

"License snapped clean when I bent it." Duncan pointed. "You recognize him?"

Eddie held the photograph under his desk lamp. "Never seen him. I haven't heard that name, either."

Cavendish broke in. "Excuse me, mister…"

The bookie eyed her. "Just call me Eddie."

She dipped her head. "I apologize, but since I'm meeting you for the first time, what is it you do here and how would you know our John Doe?"

Smoke swirled around Eddie's head. "I run a small gambling operation. Card games mostly, a couple of table games. I also make book on various sporting events." He set down his stogie. "I have a lot of contacts, Trooper Cavendish. They tell me things. Trooper Duncan knows me from living in Confluence. I've helped him out on occasion. In exchange, he refrains from hassling me or my clientele."

Duncan noted that Eddie had not yet called Cavendish by his pet nickname. He glanced at Stanley, who stood in his corner, statue-like. No reason to get nervous. Yet. Eddie couldn't like everyone, right? Cavendish had done nothing to provoke the bookie or his doorman, but Duncan rested his hands on his hips, which pushed his jacket back just enough to show off the Glock on his belt. "Eddie's information has never failed me."

Cavendish waved a hand. "Thank you."

Duncan took back the photo. "Have you heard any rumblings? New players in the drug game?"

Eddie spoke to Duncan but didn't take his eyes off Cavendish. "I have not. I can ask around. Discreetly, of course."

"We'd appreciate it." Duncan picked up his coat. "Oh, one other question. Who would be your pick for quality fake IDs in this area?"

"You don't really expect me to answer that, do you?"

Duncan glanced at his partner. "Come on, Eddie. We're not interested in busting someone for churning out a driver's license so a kid can buy beer. But the ID on our John Doe was quality goods. We need to talk to the supplier."

Eddie scratched his jaw. "I know a guy. I'll call him and see if he's open to a conversation. Within specific limits, of course."

"Naturally." Duncan slipped into his coat. "Thanks for the help. We can see ourselves out."

"In a second." Eddie tapped ash from the cigar and stuck it back in his mouth. "Trooper Cavendish, may I ask you a question?"

She shrugged. "Go ahead. I'll answer if I can."

"Aren't you a little warm? I see you took off your winter coat, but while my friend Duncan looks like he's ready to jump into a snowbank as soon as he leaves, you haven't shown the slightest hint of discomfort." He folded his hands across his belly.

Her gaze scanned the room. "Reminds me of the time I spent in Florida when I was in college. Have you ever seen an alligator, Eddie?"

"Not in the wild, no."

"They are very good hunters. When it's hot, they're either sitting still as a rock on the shore or swimming lazily under the water. I decided maybe they had the right idea." She gave a tight grin. "Turns out they do. If you don't jump around like an idiot, you don't get nearly as overheated."

Eddie's answering smile was sly. "They conserve their energy until it's needed. Is that what you're saying?"

"Pretty much."

Eddie gave her a long glance, gray smoke curling up to the air vents on the ceiling. "Thank you. Come back any time. Pretty."

Cavendish made a short bow. Then she shrugged on her jacket. "Coming, Duncan?" She turned and left.

Duncan shook his head. "You had me worried there, Eddie."

The fat man giggled. "I have to keep you on your toes, my friend. You lucky dog. You really do get all the pretties."

"Just call me when you find something." Duncan nodded to Stanley and left.

Chapter Nine

Once Duncan and his partner were back in the car, Cavendish reached over and turned the heater on full blast as soon as the engine started. "From sweltering to frigid. I'm gonna catch pneumonia." She rubbed her hands together in front of the vent. "I thought fat men hated the heat. What's his deal?"

"No clue. Maybe it's glandular." Duncan tossed his cell in the center console. "I didn't know you loved the heat so much."

"I don't. Florida was awful. Why do you think I came back to Southwestern Pennsylvania?" She blew on her hands. "Of course, this isn't much better. Temps so cold you turn to ice crossing a parking lot."

"If you'd wear gloves and get a more suitable coat, you wouldn't become a popsicle before you walked a hundred feet."

"Bite me." She leaned against the seat. "I hear San Diego is a nice place. Or Aruba. Warm, sunny, and breezy all year round. And the beach."

"I don't think California would agree with you. And I can't see you as a beach bum." His phone rang, but he did not recognize the number. "This is Duncan."

A tremulous female voice answered. "Trooper Duncan? This is Margie Allington. I don't know if you remember me."

Martingdon's neighbor. "Yes, Mrs. Allington. Is there something I can do for you?"

"I don't know. I was walking Sammy. He doesn't really like the cold. I think it hurts his arthritis. Dogs are just like people, you know. When we get old, the joints don't like these sub-zero days." She sighed. "Sometimes I think we'd be better off moving south, like my son says. But I've lived here so long. Who knows if I'd make friends, and maybe the change of scene would be worse for Sammy than the cold."

Duncan took a deep breath. The woman must have had a purpose in calling besides talking about her aging Labrador. "I understand. I'm a dog owner myself." Out of the corner of his eye, he saw Cavendish shake her head. "If you're looking for advice, I recommend talking to your vet."

"Oh, no. How silly of me." Sammy barked, and Allington shushed him. "I called because I found something, and I don't know what to do with it."

"What is it?"

"It's a gun. It looks big and black. Sammy and I are on our way home, and it's lying here in the storm culvert. Should I pick it up and take it to our local police?"

Duncan reached over and tapped Cavendish on the leg. "Do not touch the gun, ma'am. Where exactly are you?"

"About fifty yards from home. Are you sure?"

Duncan put the car in gear as Cavendish snapped on the lights and siren. "Quite sure. I know it's cold, but if you can stay where you are, we'll be there as fast as we can."

"Sammy's awfully uncomfortable, Trooper. I don't know if we'll be able to do that."

Of course. "Sit tight. I'll send someone to you. Do not leave that spot." He hung up and called for a uniformed officer to guard the scene.

Cavendish checked her watch. "It'll take us at least half an hour to get there."

"Then we better hurry."

They didn't speak as the car zipped over the roads, the bare trees flying by. A couple of times, Duncan risked passing other motorists on the narrow two-lane. Taking Sugar Loaf Road would be shorter in mileage, but he knew it would take at least ten minutes longer to drive because of the road conditions, so he went up Route 40, pushing the speed limit as much as he dared, given the icy weather and other cars.

When they turned onto RJ Lilley Drive, where Martingdon's body had been found, he spotted a marked state Ford Interceptor idling on the side of the road. He pulled to a stop behind it and killed the engine. "You see the gun?" he shouted as he exited the car.

McAllister got out of the driver's side of the Interceptor. "Oh yeah. I sent the witness home after taking her statement. That poor dog's paws were turning blue." She pointed. "I haven't touched it."

Duncan stepped over a pile of dirty snow and made his way over to where McAllister had indicated. Half-hidden in a snowbank was a black handgun. He took his pen out of his pocket and used it to lift the gun by the trigger guard. "Walther P22. Not too big, but I guess if you're not used to handguns, it might appear that way." He sniffed the barrel, but the weapon had been outside too long to have any residual scent. He handed the pen to Cavendish and pulled on a pair of nitrile gloves. He took the Walther back and checked the magazine and the chamber.

"You think it's been fired?" Cavendish asked, holding her hair out of her face.

"One in the chamber, eight in the clip. Could have been fired at least once. Twice if the shooter carried like we do." He inspected the gun. "It's clean. Someone took good care of it." He glanced at McAllister. "You dust it for prints?"

She shook her head, curls held in place by her campaign hat. "Nope. I took Mrs. Allington's statement and waited for you. I think you'll have a hard time getting anything off that grip. Plus, if the suspect is as professional as we think, he had to have wiped it down. Or worn gloves."

"Grip, yes, but maybe not the magazine." He made the weapon safe, bagged it, and filled out the chain of evidence. "What did the witness say?"

McAllister referenced her notebook. "She and her dog were coming home. He, the dog, didn't go berserk, but he wouldn't leave this area alone. She has one of those extendable leashes, so he was pretty far away."

"I hate those things." No dog should be on one, especially a big dog like a Lab. *You're not here to evaluate dog ownership.*

"Anyway, she said Sammy didn't leave this spot, even after she came up on him. She tugged him away, and that's when she saw the Walther." McAllister flipped the notebook shut. "She swears she didn't touch it. She pulled her pooch to safety and called you."

Cavendish knelt to inspect the ground. "Footprints are shit. Between the snow, the dog, and the people, the area's been pretty well trampled."

Duncan surveyed the landscape. The spot wasn't that far off the road. "Doesn't matter. Our shooter could easily have tossed the gun out of a car window." He turned back to McAllister. "Mrs. Allington didn't see this when she left home?"

McAllister waved her arm. "She was walking on the other side of the road on her way out. She also said she doesn't remember seeing a person around here or a car." She measured off the distance. "If a driver pulled up on the side of the road and rolled down the passenger window, this is an easy toss. Assuming it's our murder weapon, he had to have ditched it on the way back toward Route 40."

Cavendish came over. "No way of telling how long it was here?"

Duncan checked how far away the Victorian was. Not that far. "No. But if it had been here for long, I'm betting one of these people would have found it by now. It's a .22, so the right size for the murder. Ballistics can confirm." He walked back to the sedan. "McAllister, can you send me a picture of your notes?"

"Got it, Boss. You need anything else?"

"Go get warm. Thanks."

McAllister trooped off to her Interceptor. After a slight delay, she pulled away.

Duncan's phone dinged with an incoming text. The picture from the younger trooper. He bagged and tagged the gun. "Let's get this back to the lab."

Cavendish struggled up the gentle slope of the culvert and out of the snow. "Not before we stop at Dunkin'. I think my feet turned into ice cubes." She glared at him. "And if you make one crack about my boots, you're buying."

Duncan held up his hands. "Wouldn't dream of it."

* * *

By the time Sally made it back to the office, it was almost a quarter to three. "How's it going?" she asked as she checked for messages.

Tanelsa's gaze stayed glued to her monitor. "I feel like the tortoise."

"Excuse me?"

"Slow and steady wins the race." She checked the reference book at her elbow and continued typing. "What'd you learn from the PI?"

"Not much more than we knew." Sally reviewed her meeting with Gerald Harper. "Is there anything I can do to help you out?"

Tanelsa paused. "Not really. I'm in the zone. You thinking of taking a trip to Marsdale?"

"The sound strategy is to proceed like we agreed." Sally didn't have any messages or texts and she put the phone in her purse. "But it can't be bad to dig into this witness a little bit. If we wind up going back to trial, I'd like to have the option of calling him."

"Sounds good to me." Tanelsa flexed her fingers. "You head to Marsdale and let me know what you find. I'll stay here and keep on keeping on."

Sally slung her purse over her shoulder and headed back out to her SUV.

It took almost forty minutes to reach Marsdale, a sleepy town in rural Monongahela County. To say it had one stoplight, and a blinking one at that, might be a stretch, but it couldn't be much bigger than Confluence. Relying on GPS, Sally drove to the last known address for Kyle Palmer. She parked on the side of the street and headed to the house, skirting the clumps of slush.

A bleary-eyed man answered the door. "Can't you see the sign? No solicitors. I'm trying to sleep."

"I apologize, but I'm not selling anything." Sally held out her business card.

"I don't need a lawyer, either."

"I'm not offering my services. Did you ever meet the previous resident here, a man named Kyle Palmer?"

The man blinked. "Don't know no one named Palmer. House was empty when I rented it. Although."

Sally waited.

"The landlord did say something about the previous guy running out of here in a hurry. Paid the last two months of his rent in cash and left without explanation." He scratched his shoulder. "That mighta been the guy you're looking for."

"Your landlord is Ben Trippi?" Sally opened the Notes app and showed it to him. "Is that still his address?"

"What's Palmer to you?"

"He could be a witness in a murder trial."

"Oh." The man hesitated. "Yeah, I rent from Ben. He lives a few streets over."

"Thank you. Sorry to interrupt your nap." Sally went back to her car. She entered Trippi's address into the navigation system. Sure enough, it was two blocks down and one block over.

A man dressed in dark jeans and a parka, and wearing heavy gloves and a knit cap pulled over his ears was shaking a bag of rock salt over his driveway. He didn't turn as the silent SUV eased to a halt.

Sally got out. "Are you Ben Trippi?" He didn't respond, and Sally repeated her question, this time much louder.

The man jumped, a shower of crystals landing on the asphalt. He took out two wireless earbuds, which had been hidden by the cap. "Crap, lady. Don't scare me like that. That thing got stealth mode or something?"

"Electric." Sally approached him, but kept a healthy distance. "I'm looking for Mr. Trippi. He manages a rental property where a man named Kyle Palmer lived until a few months ago."

"That's me." Trippi thumped down the bag. "Let me guess. Palmer bailed on you, too."

"Not quite. Tell me, when was the last time you saw Mr. Palmer?"

Trippi squinted. "What's it to you if he doesn't owe you money?"

Sally pulled out another business card. "He's a potential witness in a murder."

He whistled. "You don't say. Good luck finding him. Last time I saw him was, shit, early summer?"

"I take it you didn't collect his rent in person."

"Nope." Trippi hawked and spit on the side of the road. "He usually mailed his rent in cash."

"Not an ACH bank transfer or through Venmo?" She stamped her feet to keep the circulation moving. The cold was not fun, but at least it wasn't snowing. Yet.

"Cash. Not even a check. I offered to set him up with an automatic payment, but he said no thanks. Guess he's the old-fashioned kind." Trippi spit again. "I think I was over there in May to look at a leaky pipe. Marsdale's a small town, so you think I'd see him around, but I rarely did. Kept himself to himself, if you know the type."

"I do." Sally made a note on her phone. "The gentleman who is living in the house now said Mr. Palmer left in a hurry."

Trippi snorted. "That's one way of putting it. In August, he paid the last two months of his rent. Left an envelope full of twenties in my mailbox with a note saying he wouldn't be renewing. I went over to the house two weeks before the lease expired. I have a form to fill out when a tenant leaves. I do an inspection for damages, that sort of thing. Palmer was gone. Everything was dusty, and I saw cobwebs in the kitchen. Place felt unlived in, you know?"

Sally mulled over his words. It meant Palmer could have left town earlier than she thought. Perhaps as early as August. "You didn't see him those last two months?"

"Nope."

"That means he could have left anytime between when he gave you the rent and when you went over two months later with your form."

Ben gave a slow blink. "I guess so. I assumed he'd stayed to finish out the lease, but yeah, he could have gone earlier."

It would be good cover. With the rent paid and a landlord with a reputation for not checking in unless called, no one would notice Palmer leaving. But he'd been working. At least, that's what Gerald Harper said. Sally was losing track of the timeline. She'd draw it out back at the office. "He didn't say where?"

"Not a blessed word." Trippi rubbed his nose. "Not to me, not to any of his neighbors. Just up and left."

Sally thought a minute. "Did you know the Wilson couple?"

"Yeah, and no one saw that coming either." Trippi took a tin of chewing tobacco out of his pocket and tucked a wad between his lip and gum. "Alec and Vivien were real nice, real quiet. They went to church regular; she volunteered with the school, he did taxes for some of us at a good discount. I would have said you couldn't meet nicer people. She could be a bit condescending, especially toward Alec, but they were good folks."

Sally started another note. "Did you know they were having marital difficulties?"

Trippi chewed his tobacco. "I remember seeing them at church and acting kinda stiff, like they were mad at each other. I didn't think anything of it. Most couples have at least one or two good fights in their marriage. But you could have knocked me over with a feather when she was murdered, and then they arrested Alec for it."

"You didn't know about her affair."

"Not until the trial." Trippi spat a gob of tobacco juice into a pile of dirty snow. "Funny thing, I never would have thought Alec would have the guts, you know? Some people, you can't see them as killers. Just goes to show every man has his breaking point."

Sally knew the truth of that. She'd seen it too many times in her professional career. "Alec told me he didn't know the man's name, Vivien's lover. Did it ever come out? Or were there rumors?"

Trippi rubbed his chin. "No one in Marsdale admitted to it. Some of us got the impression he mighta been from up in Pittsburgh, or somewhere closer to that. But that's not for certain."

She thought back to Alec's evasion around possible enemies. "Did you ever think someone might be after the Wilsons? Or even just one of them?"

"Funny you should say that." Trippi glanced around as if to check for snoopers. "Couple of times I saw guys in suits driving black cars visit. Generally, when Vivien wasn't around. Dark suits, dark cars. On TV, that would be the feds."

Sally stared at him. What about Alec Wilson would interest the federal government?

Chapter Ten

Duncan waited in the car while Cavendish ran into Dunkin' for a coffee. He kept the heater on high. The temperature was dropping, and he could smell snow in the air. With any luck, it would hold off until he was home, where he could build a fire and sit on the couch with Sally.

The passenger door opened, letting in a blast of frigid air. "I think my coffee froze between the store and the car," Cavendish said as she slid in.

"If so, Dunkin' needs lessons on the proper serving temperature." His cell phone rang. Caller ID showed Unknown.

"Is that right, Mr. Coffee Snob?" She popped the tab on the lid. "It's colder than a witch's you-know-what out there, and you won't lower yourself to get a hot drink."

He held up a finger, silencing her. Then, he slid his finger along the screen to answer the call. "Duncan."

Eddie's girlish voice was blunt. "Where are you?"

"Uniontown getting coffee."

Cavendish cautiously sipped and sent him a quizzical look.

"Perfect. Which one?" Eddie asked.

Cavendish slapped Duncan's arm. "Who is it?" she mouthed.

He placed his hand over the mic. "Eddie." He uncovered the speaker. "The one on Morgantown."

"The ID guy will be there in fifteen minutes. Call him Ralphie."

"Wait. How will I know him?"

"He'll recognize you. Duncan."

59

"Yes?"

"I had to talk fast to get him to agree to see you. Don't screw me on this." Eddie clicked off.

Duncan turned off the engine. "Guess I'm going to have to settle for mediocre coffee. The fake ID supplier will be here in fifteen." They got out and headed into the building. While he ordered, Cavendish grabbed a table with a good view of the front door.

"At least I can warm up." She wrapped her hands around the cup. "What does this guy look like?"

"Eddie didn't say. Only gave us a name: Ralphie. I doubt that's real." He sniffed the coffee. "According to Eddie, this guy will recognize us."

"It's one way of doing business." Cavendish sipped her drink. "Oh, come on. It's not that bad."

Duncan raised an eyebrow. "If you say so."

About twenty minutes later, a weedy young man in a black puffer jacket came into the restaurant. His thick brown hair hung to his shoulders, giving him the appearance of a brown-headed mop. His black jeans were tight, with a ragged hole in the left knee, and he wore black sneakers with neon green laces. He scanned the patrons.

Cavendish nodded to him. "Think that's our guy?"

The younger man caught sight of the troopers and jerked his head at the register.

"I believe so." Duncan set aside his cup.

Once the ID supplier had his order, he came over to the table. "Are you Troopers Duncan and Cavendish?"

"That's us." Duncan pointed at the orange plastic chair across from him. "Have a seat. You must be Ralphie."

He looked around again and sat. "You alone?"

"A CERT team isn't hiding in the bathroom, if that's what you mean." Cavendish eyed him. "What's got you so jumpy? It's a coffee shop, not a minefield."

Ralphie grabbed a handful of sugar packets, opened them, and dumped it all into his coffee. "You never know who's watching. A man in my line of

60

work has to be careful."

Duncan leaned back. "You're sitting at a table with two state troopers. I think you're safe."

"Yeah, well, no offense, but this wasn't my idea." Ralphie tried his coffee and added two more sugars. "Eddie vouched for you. Said you were cool. He's done me a solid more than once, so I'm repaying the favor. But don't press your luck. Got it?"

"Got it." Duncan's impression was that Ralphie would bolt as soon as he felt like it, so he didn't waste any more time. "Eddie said you're the best he knows if you need a quality ID."

"That's right." Ralphie fixed his gaze on Duncan.

"How long have you been doing it?"

"Not gonna answer that."

Duncan tried again. "Got a big client base?"

"Not answering that either." Ralphie glanced at his watch. "You're running out of time, pal."

"What will you answer?" Cavendish asked, her voice blunt.

Ralphie grinned. "Eddie said you had a question about one guy. I'll answer that one."

"All right." Duncan pulled the evidence bag with the broken fake driver's license out and slid it across the table. "Recognize him?"

"Never could fix the whole breaking issue." Ralphie studied it. "Yeah, I remember this one. Paid me five hundred dollars. He musta gone ballistic when you snapped it."

Cavendish stared at the skinny man. "He didn't flinch."

"Really?" Ralphie asked. "I find that hard to believe. Why not?"

"Because he's dead."

Ralphie whistled. "What do you know? He wasn't lying. Someone did want to murder him."

Duncan found the reaction interesting. "Mind telling me why you went straight to that? He might have died in a car accident." Most people flinched at the mention of criminal homicide. This man seemed to take it in stride.

"I suppose that could be so." Ralphie handed back the bag. "Two troopers could be looking into an accident. But you're plainclothes. That means detectives. Cops like you don't do traffic deaths, not usually. Besides, he told me he needed to disappear. There were some men who wanted him gone."

Cavendish leaned on the table. "Let's back up. What's his real name?"

"No clue." Ralphie seemed genuinely uninterested.

"You didn't ask?"

"It wasn't relevant." He gulped his coffee. "Here's what happened. I got a call from a buddy at the end of September. He said he had a fish on the line who needed a new license. But the customer didn't want to give a name. I said sure. We met, I took photos and said I needed a legit address for it to really be a good fake. He gave me one in Farmington. Then he asked how fast I could get it done. I told him a week. You can't rush a master, right?"

Every crook thought he was hot stuff, but in the case of Ralphie, he might be right. The license had been almost flawless. Duncan didn't doubt it would pass inspection from a cop on a traffic stop. "What did he say?"

"He got real upset. He said he'd double my fee to get it done in a day. I asked why the rush. That's when he told me some guys were after him. Said it was better for my health if I didn't know who." The forger held up his hands. "Who was I to argue? He came back the next day, said he was happy, and left." He nodded at the broken license. "How'd he snuff it?"

Cavendish answered. "Shot in the back of the head."

Ralphie seemed to consider her words. "And here I thought he was blowing smoke up my ass." He grabbed his cup and stood. "We good? I can't tell you anything else. Never got his name and he paid me in used twenties."

Duncan thought it over. "No one ever approached you or the friend who referred him to you, asking about this guy?"

"Not a whisper."

Duncan glanced at his partner, who gave a tiny shrug. "That's it. Thanks for your time."

Ralphie left without another word.

Cavendish drained her coffee. "What do you think?"

Duncan lifted his cup but set it aside. Being lukewarm wouldn't make the liquid inside taste any better. "We don't have any reason to doubt him."

"He's a crook. Don't they all lie like rugs?"

"But Eddie sent us to him, and Eddie has never steered me wrong." He stared at the line of customers at the register. "The victim gave Ralphie the address in Farmington, which means he either had the house already or had his eye on it. He was nervous, thought someone might be after him."

"Makes sense if he was busting in on someone's drug operation."

"But if he needed to disappear, it wasn't anyone from Farmington. You don't disappear in a town that small if that's where you're from."

Cavendish considered his words. "Fair enough. John Doe rented the house. We haven't talked to the landlord yet."

"Why don't we take care of that right now?"

* * *

After Sally left Mr. Trippi, she visited a few more neighbors, but none of them offered any new information. She went back to her SUV and checked the time. It was three-thirty. She plugged the address of Kyle Palmer's last employer into her navigation system. It was only twenty minutes away. She made a quick call to Tanelsa. "How's it going?"

"I'm chugging along. Learn anything useful?"

Sally told her partner what Ben Trippi had said. "Is there anything in Dave's files about the feds being involved with either Alec or Vivien?"

"I'd have to look again, but I don't remember anything off the top of my head. I'll check after I finish this section. Now, don't bother me. I'm almost done with the first draft." She hung up.

Sally drove to Mon Valley Contracting. The sprawling yard contained a couple of backhoes, a digger, a small bulldozer, and piles of rebar, metal I-beams, and lumber. She went directly to a squat cement building and entered. "Is this the main office?"

A husky man with a five o'clock shadow on his jaw looked up. He wore a faded blue-checked flannel shirt. He held the burnt-out end of a hand-rolled cigarette between stained and callused fingers. "Yes, ma'am. What can I help you with?"

She held out a business card. "I'd like to speak to the site manager. Or whoever is in charge."

He tossed the butt in a metal bucket half full of sand. "That would be me, I guess. At least, it is if you want to know what actually happens around here. If you want the sales pitch, I can't help you." He held out a scarred, dirt-streaked hand. "Charlie Scoggins."

She shook, her fingers engulfed by his calloused fingers. "I'm looking for a man named Kyle Palmer. He could be an important witness for a murder appeal I'm working on."

Scoggins sat. "The Wilson murder? Pull up a chair, Ms. Castle."

She dragged over a high-backed wooden chair. "Good guess."

He chuckled. "We don't get too many high-profile cases like that in Monongahela County. Least not that would bring a nice-looking lawyer in a good suit into my office. Why is Palmer a witness?"

"He may have information that could help Alec Wilson." Sally set her bag on the floor. "Unfortunately, he disappeared before the trial. We—my partner and I—would like to try and find him before we present our appeal."

"Good luck with that." Scoggins opened a drawer and removed a box of rolling papers and a small pouch. "Mind if I roll a cigarette? I won't light it, promise."

"Go right ahead."

"I say good luck because I heard Kyle did a runner." He pinched tobacco out of the pouch and made a neat pile on the paper.

"You heard right." Sally took out her notebook. "It's probably too much to ask, but do you know where he might have gone?"

"I'd like to help you, but I have no clue."

"When was the last time you saw him?"

Scoggins licked the edge of the paper. "September thirtieth at five in the afternoon."

She paused her writing. "That's awfully precise of you, Mr. Scoggins."

"Not hard to remember. That was the last day he clocked out. Didn't

64

come back for three straight days. When I couldn't reach him, I fired him." He set the newly made cigarette in the ashtray. "Not that he ever came back to find out."

Then, he had left Marsdale at the beginning of October. "How long did he work for you?"

He put his booted feet on his desk with a thunk. "About eight months, I think."

"Did you ever have any problems?"

"Kyle wasn't one of our skilled laborers. He was a ground guy. Did rough work, cutting, a little spot-welding, things you didn't need specialized skills for. Repetitive shit. He'd picked up enough knowledge to be useful, but not so much as he could really move up the ladder. But he worked hard, at least between the start and end of his shift. Never came late, never left early. Although he punched out right on time."

It tallied with what Tanelsa had found. "He didn't fight with any of the other men?"

"No more than usual. I mean, hell. Scuffles break out, guys get frustrated. Especially on a big job or if the schedule is tight." Scoggins scratched his stubble. "But no, I never heard more than the average complaints from anyone."

She wasn't learning anything. "What about after hours? Did he go out drinking with the crew?"

"A couple of times. I guess that was the only truly annoying thing about Kyle." He tipped his chair back to balance on the back legs. "He wasn't sociable. He didn't talk about any hobbies, didn't hang out with the guys, or bitch about his family. Close-mouthed. I think that bothered people more than anything. When you work like we do, you like to know the guys on your crew, understand?"

"I do." She paused. "This is going to sound odd, but did you ever see him with anyone suspicious?"

"Like how?"

"Someone he didn't seem comfortable with or didn't look quite right." She tried to figure out how to phrase the question. "We all meet people who make the hair on the back of our necks stand up because we instinctively know something's off. That's what I'm talking about."

Scoggins stared at the ceiling. "I get it. There was one guy. Right before Kyle quit, he got a visitor here. Tough guy, looked like a country boy imitating a big-city street thug."

"You have a description?"

"Not that tall, but muscled, looked like he worked out a lot. Dressed all in dark clothes. Black guy, one of those close haircuts. Lots of tats." He frowned. "Not the type of guy you generally see in these parts. Would've looked perfect on a city street."

Sally wrote this down. "Did Kyle look happy to see him?"

Scoggins laughed. "Not hardly. But he wasn't afraid either. Mad as hell. Marched him right back out the gates. He was half this guy's size, but Kyle didn't hesitate. It was the end of the day, so he didn't come back. I asked about it the next day, but Kyle blew me off."

She made a note. It wasn't much to go on, but anything might help. "Anything else?"

"Like I said, Ms. Castle. I'd love to be able to give you a clue, but I can't. Sorry." He let the chair come forward and took his feet from the desk.

She stood. "Thank you for your time. If you think of something, please call. You can talk to me or my partner, Tanelsa Parson." She shook his hand again and left.

Chapter Eleven

Duncan pulled into the driveway of a neat farmhouse on Route 381, also known as Farmington-Ohiopyle Road. A half-made snowman leaned to his right in the front yard.

Cavendish surveyed it. "He looks like he's going to fall into that sled."

"Everyone's a critic." Duncan was more interested in the house. The bare limbs of a tree, oak or maple, stretched over the brick front step. A black mailbox stood next to the steps, which matched the door and trim of the white house. The garage was open, allowing the view of a salt-encrusted silver Chevy Trax. Crowded around the SUV were two bikes, a set of in-line skates, and a small workbench.

As Duncan stood by the car taking inventory, a man appeared from around the garage, holding a snow shovel. "Good afternoon," Duncan said. "Are you Marcus Ford?"

The man slowed and gripped the shovel. "Who's asking?"

Duncan held out his badge wallet. "This is my partner, Trooper Cavendish. Are you the landlord at 79834 RJ Lilley Drive?"

Cavendish showed her own badge.

The man relaxed his hold. "Yeah, that's my name and my property. Why?"

"I'm sorry to have to tell you this, but your tenant, Ellis Martingdon, was found dead this morning. Shot."

"Son of a bitch." Ford ran a gloved hand over his head. "His rent's due next week."

Cavendish's expression didn't change. "I don't think he'll be paying it."

"How much of a mess is there?"

"Bloodstains on the carpet. Oh, and fingerprint powder everywhere. That's from us. We can give you the names and numbers of a couple of good cleaning services."

"Serves me right." Ford put the edge of the shovel on the ground and gripped the handle.

Duncan and Cavendish exchanged a quick look. "What serves you right?" Duncan asked.

"The guy was weird. Not the kind of person I normally rent to, but…" He looked off and focused back on the troopers.

"Tell me, what do you know about Mr. Martingdon?" Duncan took his pen and notepad out of his pocket.

"Not that much. He showed up in early October and said he'd seen the For Rent sign in the yard. He had a driver's license and paid the deposit and two month's rent in cash. I gave him the keys, my cell number, and told him to call if he had any problems." Ford's expression bordered on glum. "I guess I got his money for next month after all, but now I gotta list the place again. You sure it's him?"

"His license has that name, but did you know it wasn't a genuine one?"

Ford blinked. "No idea. Looked real enough to me."

Cavendish spoke. "You didn't run a credit check?" Her voice betrayed her disbelief.

Ford's cheeks, already red from the cold, took on a deeper hue. "I, um, no. As a matter of fact, I didn't."

Cavendish muttered, the words unintelligible.

"The house had been empty for almost six months. No one around here was interested." Ford appealed to Duncan. "When a guy showed up and wanted to move in immediately and had cash in hand, what was I gonna do? Say no?"

Duncan looked at the house, the newer SUV, and the off-road bicycles. "You needed the money. What do you do for a living?"

"I'm an electrician. My wife doesn't work. But she and the boys sure can spend." The landlord's voice held a bitter note. He threw a look over his shoulder. "You aren't going to tell her, right? That I didn't do the credit check? I'd never hear the end of it."

Duncan held up a hand. "Your secret is safe with me. Tell me, what was your impression of Mr. Martingdon? Did he give you any personal information, list a job on his rental application?"

"Hold on. I'll go get it." Ford laid down the shovel and disappeared inside.

Cavendish blew out an exasperated breath. "What kind of yahoo doesn't run a credit check on a prospective tenant?"

"Go easy on him." Duncan looked around the property again. "I don't see a truck, so he might work for someone. He said boys, plural. This is a nice house. If the wife doesn't have a job outside the home, and he's the sole breadwinner, I can see him being so desperate for money, he'd skip the formalities. But I bet he'll never do it again."

"Ain't that the truth." Cavendish hunched inside her jacket. "Why didn't you ask to go inside? My feet are turning to ice cubes again."

"Why don't you have warmer boots?"

Cavendish didn't reply.

Ford reappeared a couple of minutes later, a sheet of paper in his hand. "Here. I'd ask you in, but I don't think I want my wife to find out this kind of news from the cops." He handed over the contract. "Martingdon, or whatever the hell his name was, listed his profession as general contractor."

"Well, that part was accurate." Duncan examined the contract. It was fairly simple, filled out in the same neat handwriting as in the notebook. "May I keep this? I can make a copy and send back the original."

"No need. Not like he'll be renewing. I suppose I should call Laurel Mountain Insurance and cancel his policy. Or will you do that?"

"I'm sure we'll contact them as part of our investigation, but yes. You need to call them." Duncan folded the paper. "Did Martingdon ever call you for anything?"

"Nope. If he was a contractor, he might have been able to fix any minor issues."

"You never knew about any visitors? Never got complaints or anything as the landlord?"

"None." Ford picked up his shovel. "Which is a little surprising. I think he expected trouble."

Cavendish, the cold apparently forgotten, gave him a sharp look. "Why do you say that?"

"He got a phone call when he was signing. On a flip phone, of all things. He got real agitated and said, 'It doesn't matter. They won't be able to find me here.' I asked if there was a problem, but he brushed me off." Ford shrugged. "Maybe it was unrelated to his murder, but I guess there was a problem after all."

It was probably just as good John Doe hadn't said anything, or this poor guy might have been killed, too. Duncan held out a card. "If you think of anything else, please give us a call. Good luck with your wife."

Ford's answering smile looked sick. "Thanks."

The troopers headed back to their car. Inside, Cavendish cranked the heater up as soon as the engine started. "Flip phone. Bet I know what that sounds like to you."

Duncan put the car in gear and backed out. "Burner. Mr. Doe should have stayed in general contracting."

Cavendish, who'd been blowing on her hands to warm them up, paused. "You think?"

* * *

Sally pulled into a convenience store and checked the clock. Four o'clock. Her cell phone dinged with Jim's text tone. **Meet at Whiskey and Rye at five?** She thought a moment, then sent back **See you there**. It would take a little more than an hour to get to the distillery near the Troop B headquarters in Eighty Four. Lunch had been a long time ago. She needed something to sustain her until she got there.

Inside, she grabbed a bottle of unsweetened iced tea and a bag of mixed nuts. She headed to the counter.

The rough-looking woman behind the register rang her up. "Six forty-seven." She looked out the window and brushed her frazzled blond hair off her face. "That your SUV, the electric one?"

The surly tone in the woman's voice made Sally hesitate. Was she annoyed about losing a gasoline sale? "Yes. I bought it a week ago."

"You don't see many of those around here. We don't have a lot of charging stations." She barked a laugh. "You must be new in town. I don't remember hearing about any house sales in Marsdale."

"I'm visiting. I live in Confluence."

"What are you doing way over here?"

"Research. I'm a lawyer." Sally knew she should get on the road, but maybe this woman knew a little small-town gossip that would help. "Do you know the Wilsons? Alec and Vivien? I'm working on his appeal."

"Who doesn't know them? That conviction was a crock." The woman leaned on the counter, all surliness gone. "I sold Alec Wilson gas all the time. Never woulda thought he'd go round the bend and murder his wife. Now, his wife cheating on him? That I can believe. What a bitch."

Jackpot. "I'd heard a rumor about the affair. It was true then?"

The cashier's eye gleamed. "Oh yeah. Brought him in once, didn't she? Fancy-pants from Pittsburgh, wearing a suit and everything. She tried to pretend the guy was an associate of her husband's, a fellow accountant, but I could see the way they looked at each other. If they weren't doing the horizontal tango, I'll eat that wasabi-flavored beef jerky hanging next to you. And that stuff's horrible."

Based on the lurid packaging, Sally was sure the woman was right. It seemed this lonely cashier could be a gold mine. "I also heard Vivien was planning to leave her husband. Isn't that why they say he killed her?"

"Oh, that was her plan, all right. Surprised the shit outta me. I guess she'd had enough of bullying poor Alec. But it wasn't gonna happen." The woman leaned in and dropped her voice to what she clearly thought was a conspiratorial whisper. "She was in here one day talking to herself. All worked up. He can't do that to me, and what am I gonna do now, and I'll show that bastard. I'm gonna tell her. I think she got dumped." The cashier nodded.

Tell "her." A wife? Possibly. If Vivien's lover was a married man, and she threatened to blow up his marriage over the affair, would he have tried to shut her up? For Sally, it depended on the marriage. "Did you tell this to the cops?"

"Didn't ask, did they?" The other woman scoffed. "Worst police investigation ever, in my opinion. They had their man in poor Alec, and they weren't gonna look any further. But you listen to me." She stabbed her finger on the counter. "I went to high school with Alec. If they'd given out an award for Least Likely to Lose His Shit and Go Off the Rails, Alec would have won it. There's no way he killed his wife. Not like they said."

Sally pulled a twenty out of her wallet. "You called Vivien a bitch. Why?"

"Because she was." The woman looked thrilled to have a captive audience for her story. "Now, if the murder had been the other way, I'd say Vivien was guilty no doubt. Although violence wasn't her style. Manipulation, that was Vivien's game. She could play someone like a fiddle and make him dance to whatever tune she wanted. Alec was a nice guy in high school. Not one of the jocks, always had a kind word. By the time Vivien was done with him, he was so withdrawn and miserable, it made me sad. I asked him why he didn't leave her. 'I won't find anyone else,' he said." She slapped the counter. "I ask you, does that sound like a man who has the balls to stab his wife?"

It didn't, but that didn't mean anything. "The jury didn't agree."

"Yeah, because those Uniontown people didn't know shit. If Alec had been tried here, my money would have been on a hung jury at the very least." Her gaze sharpened. "Wait. You said you were working on Alec's appeal? For the murder?"

Sally put her wallet back in her purse. "Yes."

The woman opened the cash register. "It's on the house. Alec's a good guy. You take my word. He didn't do it."

"No, I'll pay. But keep the change." Sally handed her the twenty and walked back to her SUV. It wasn't that simple. She couldn't stand in front of a judge and base her appeal on the opinion of a convenience store clerk.

But why had no one ever looked into Vivien Wilson's affair?

Chapter Twelve

Duncan shed his coat and stood by the table he'd claimed in Whiskey & Rye. He had a clear view of the door, so he'd see Sally when she arrived. He turned to his partner. "You owe me a drink." He'd wanted to stay and do more work, but they'd reached a point where they needed the reports. That would take time. Might as well grab some food while they waited.

She put her hands on her hips. "How do you figure that?"

"You said you'd get the first round if I found a witness. I found three."

"Oh, come on." She tossed her head. "Two of them weren't helpful, and the third was barely so."

"Hey. That's your fault. The quality of the witness was not part of the deal." He spotted Sally at the door and hailed her.

She rushed up and gave him a quick kiss. "Sorry, I'm late. The drive from Marsdale took longer than I thought, especially since the snow is picking up."

"No worries. We just got here." Duncan kissed her again, a little longer.

"All right, you two," Cavendish said. "Get a room or take a seat."

Duncan didn't look at his partner. "You're just jealous." Sally's cheeks were flushed from the cold, and her eyes glowed. For a moment, he regretted saying he'd go out for drinks.

"Damn straight." Cavendish shook out her hair. "Duncan, the usual? Sally, they've got a nice red wine here. Want a glass?"

Sally took off her long coat and threw it on the extra chair. "I'll have what he's having." She jerked her thumb at Duncan. "It's been a day."

"Three single malts, coming up." Cavendish headed for the bar.

Duncan frowned. "You don't usually drink whiskey. Is everything okay?"

"As much as it can be." She rubbed his shoulder. "I'm fine. I'll tell you when Jenny gets back with the booze. That way, I only have to relive the torture once."

They sat. It didn't take long for Cavendish to reappear with three tumblers, one of which included ice. "Sorry, Sally. I didn't know if you liked it on the rocks or not. You said what he's having, so I got it neat."

"That's quite all right." Sally took the glass and sipped. "That hits the spot."

Duncan took his own drink. "What happened? If you can tell us."

Sally waved her hand. "Nothing secret. You know about the appeal. I told you last night."

Cavendish looked puzzled, so Duncan said, "Sally's taken on the Wilson murder. He's appealing."

His partner made a face. "That shitshow. Good luck."

"I take it your opinion is the same as Jim's." Sally rotated her glass.

"I'm sorry, but someone over in Monongahela County screwed up. That poor bastard might be guilty as sin, but the procedure was inexcusable, and the judge never should have allowed his statement to stand." Cavendish shook her head and stared into the amber liquid before taking a drink.

"We're working on it." Sally, in what Duncan was sure was broad terms, gave the low down on the appeal and her day's activities. "The guy, Palmer, is gone. Puff of smoke. I can't find a trace of him." She looked at the troopers. "You two know as well as I do that it's almost impossible to successfully disappear these days."

Duncan agreed. "They ask someone to water the plants, use a debit or credit card. Some little screw-up."

"They get caught on CCTV buying Corn Nuts at a 7-Eleven." Cavendish drank. "Always something stupid. You say it's been a month? Give it time. This guy will make a mistake sooner or later."

"That's the thing. I don't have time." Sally stared at the whiskey. "I have five days. Ugh. What was I thinking?"

"Relax. You and Tanelsa will get it done." He patted her arm. "Cavendish and I know how you feel though." He recapped their day and the failed quest for the identity of their John Doe.

Sally whistled. "Talk about deep cover."

"Tell me about it." Cavendish leaned on the table. "This guy went all in. Fake license, car registration, rental agreement, all the utilities, everything."

The three looked at each other.

Cavendish slumped back. "Oh, don't even tell me. No, can't be."

Sally paled and stared at her whiskey.

Aw, hell no. Duncan held out a hand. "Sally, got a picture of your missing witness? Kyle Palmer, right?"

Sally dug in her purse and passed him a photocopy of a Pennsylvania driver's license. Then she buried her face in her hands.

Duncan laid the picture half of the broken fake license next to the photocopied picture. It was clearly the same man. He slid the items to his partner. "Meet Kyle Palmer, aka Ellis Martingdon."

Sally muttered a steady string of expletives from behind her hands.

Cavendish examined the two pictures. "Shit. Good for us, but sorry, Sally. What does this mean for your case?"

For a moment, Sally didn't speak. Then she sat up, drank the rest of her whiskey in one gulp, and stood. "I need a refill. Anyone else?" When she didn't get a response, she walked off.

Cavendish sat, mouth slightly open. "I didn't know she drank whiskey. Or could swear like that."

"Well, as she said, it has been a day." Duncan watched his girlfriend snake her way through the crowd to the bar. Sexy as hell, smart, and could toss back a good single malt like a pro. No wonder he loved her.

* * *

Over three hours later, they sat at the table surrounded by empty glasses and the ruins of several appetizers.

Sally picked at the last of the fried cheese sticks. "I mean, honestly. What are the chances?"

Cavendish squeezed the mangled remains of a lemon wedge over her glass of water, but very little came out. "Too bad we all wasted a day. If only we'd been in touch with each other sooner."

Duncan dipped a thick-cut french fry into the last of the ketchup. "What, are we going to start checking in with each other every time we catch a case? Yes, knowing this hours ago would have been nice. We didn't. Moving on."

"At least T and I never planned on making Palmer the linchpin of our appeal." Sally swirled the melted ice in her glass. "I want another whiskey."

"I told you, you're cut off."

"And I told you, I'm not that much of a lightweight. Besides, it's been hours, and I've been eating."

"No." Duncan had made her switch to water when they'd decided to order food. She hadn't been happy—and didn't bother to conceal it—but gave in when he told her if she didn't, she'd have to leave her SUV behind and come back with him tomorrow to get it. And then drive to Uniontown.

Cavendish emptied her glass. "Frankly, you shocked the hell out of me, Sally. I didn't know you were a whiskey fan."

"Only when stressed." Sally rested her chin in her hand. "I think this counts."

"Enough with Debbie Downer, you two." Duncan clapped his hands. "What do we know?"

Sally straightened up. "Kyle Palmer lived across the street from the Wilsons. He was on Dave's witness list, so he must have known something that could help clear Alec."

"Didn't you say he volunteered to testify?" Cavendish asked.

"According to Alec, yes."

"That makes zero sense to me." Cavendish pushed away a plate of chicken wing bones.

Sally drank off the remaining water in her glass. "What do you mean?"

Cavendish pointed at her. "Kyle Palmer lived like a man on the run. He paid his bills in cash. He left Marsdale under cover of dark, or so it seems. He completely reinvented himself under a fake name. ID, rental agreement, utilities, car registration, the works. Why the hell would a man who is doing all that *volunteer* to get into a witness box for a high-profile murder trial?"

Sally opened her mouth, closed it, and frowned.

"Cavendish is right. It doesn't make sense. But we only have Wilson's word that Palmer volunteered." Duncan went in for another fry.

"Or—" Sally drew out the word. "Try this. Dave is hounding Palmer, thinking he must have seen something. To get Dave off his back, Palmer agrees to testify, knowing it'll never happen because he's leaving town. Palmer blows out of Marsdale in the dead of the night, Dave's out a witness, Palmer's problems are solved. He gets Dave off his back and anonymity."

There was silence. "I like it," Cavendish said.

"But what drove Palmer out of town?" Duncan asked. "He wasn't having problems at work. It doesn't seem like anyone was threatening him. Damn it. I need to talk to Pete Adams." He glanced at Sally. "You've got that look again. What's going through your mind?"

"Palmer. I don't think him leaving was as spur-of-the-moment as we think. He'd been laying the groundwork for two months. At the end of September, something happened to make him jump." Sally's gaze went from Duncan to Cavendish. "Are you sure he was killed over drugs?"

Duncan popped the last stuffed mushroom cap in his mouth. After he swallowed, he said, "Drug residue was found at the scene. The logical explanation is Palmer was trying to break into the market. Whether he started that in Farmington or Marsdale is unclear. But he could have been killed for other reasons. We're not ruling anything out yet." He watched her.

She dropped the remainder of the cold cheese stick. "I get that you don't think Palmer would testify considering his situation, and maybe you're right. But what if someone *thought* he was going to take the stand? What if Palmer wasn't killed because of drugs but because of Alec and what someone believed he was going to uncover? The killer thought Palmer knew more than he did. Goodbye, Mr. Palmer."

Cavendish took Sally's lemon wedge. "Possible." She squeezed the fruit and was rewarded with a thin trickle of juice.

Duncan didn't like Sally's expression. "There's more, isn't there."

She sighed. "I'm not sure I trust Alec Wilson."

"What makes you say that?" Cavendish asked.

Sally hesitated, almost certainly thinking about how much she could disclose without violating her ethics. "I've asked some very straightforward questions, ones that shouldn't be too difficult to answer. He won't do it."

"Such as?"

"Who was his wife's lover? Did she have any enemies? Does Alec?" She stared at Jim. "I need the police report. These are things that should have been asked. I want to know why they weren't."

"Looks like we both need to talk to Chief Adams." Duncan rubbed his face. "I'm bushed. Are we done here? We should leave before they throw us out."

"I think so." Sally surveyed the ruins of the food and drink. "We really made a mess, didn't we? Perhaps an extra tip is in order."

"Good talk, though." Cavendish stood, dusted her hands, and pulled a twenty out of her purse. "Come on, you two. Pony up."

Duncan and Sally added their contributions.

Cavendish grabbed her jacket. "We should do this more often."

Duncan helped Sally into her overcoat, and she pulled her hair clear of the collar.

She faced them. "Yes. But next time, I'm not driving. I don't like being limited." She kissed him. "See you at home." She left.

Cavendish followed Duncan to the parking lot. They'd dropped the state car at headquarters and drove their private vehicles to the distillery. "Sally and I need to go drinking more often. She's a blast."

Duncan watched Cavendish get into her car and leave. Let the two of them go out together? If that happened, he'd better stay home so he could pick them up.

Perhaps with bail money.

Chapter Thirteen

Sally stood at the sink and brushed her teeth. She bent over and spit. After the conversation earlier, she was more determined than ever to get her hands on the police file for the Wilson investigation. That would tell her what the cops had done, and not done, at the time of Vivien's death. The evidence they'd found, conclusions they'd drawn. She could hear Tanelsa's voice in her head. Their job was to present the appeal. But if they won, what then? What if the case went back to trial? Tanelsa had said she was also not satisfied with the official record. What if they needed to continue? Shouldn't they be prepared?

She rinsed and reached for the mouthwash. The whole idea was ridiculous. If someone had killed Kyle Palmer to prevent him from testifying, that meant the person also wanted Alec Wilson convicted for his wife's murder. She finished and stood in the doorway.

From the bed, Jim stared at her. "I can almost hear the wheels turning, Sally. Say it."

She drummed her fingers on the doorframe. "Do you honestly think that police chief will let me see the file on the Wilson arrest?"

"Pete Adams? If it were his case, maybe. But he's the chief over in Vance Township. He wouldn't have had anything to do with a county PD investigation. Unless the case happened on his patch, which it didn't."

"He must know someone in the county police department."

"Most likely, he does. No guarantee they'll share with you."

Why was he being so difficult? "Then can you get it?"

He sighed. "Sally, we've had this conversation. Just because I'm state doesn't mean I can stomp over someone else's business. Mon County has their own police department, and quite a good one."

She snapped off the bathroom light. Jim lounged in bed, reading a magazine, both dogs at his feet. When she'd started spending the night regularly, they'd bought a king. Two adults and a large canine did not fit on a queen mattress. Adding Pixel in October added to that need.

He set aside his magazine. "You aren't happy with me, are you?"

She climbed into bed and snuggled down under the comforter. Pixel humphed as she wedged her feet under him, but then settled again. "Please, Jim? Just ask him. Unofficially, of course. Did the county guys ever look into any suspects for Vivien's murder except Alec?" She was asking a lot. She knew that. But based on what Dave had handed over, the answer was no. Officially, that is. She needed the water cooler gossip.

Jim closed his eyes and sighed. Then he looked at her, hazel eyes showing glints of gold. "I'll give him a call in the morning. No promises."

"Thank you."

"You know the chances of these cases being connected is one in a million, right?"

Sally closed her eyes and inhaled the clean smell of Jim's soap and scent. "There's a million-to-one chance of getting hit by lightning, too, but it happens."

Jim laughed and brushed hair off her face. "You have a wild imagination, Sally. The simpler, and more probable, explanation is the one we talked about earlier with Cavendish. An unsub killed Vivien Wilson. Or her lover or her husband, take your pick. Palmer disappeared because of his drug activities. It's pure coincidence that Palmer was a potential witness for Wilson."

Sally jabbed him in the ribs. "Since when are you a believer in coincidences?"

"Ow." He rubbed his side. "You got me there. But they do happen." He lay down. "Tomorrow. I know I said I'd help you move, but I don't know if I'll make it. Depends on what happens with the case."

"I understand. We'll work it out." She kissed him. Then again. He raised up on his left arm, cupped her face with his right hand, and returned the favor, deeper, stronger. Her stomach tightened. Many people, including her sister, thought she was crazy leaving Uniontown for the "backwater" of Confluence. But she'd go to the moon for the man next to her.

Jim got out of bed and herded the dogs to the door. "Sorry, boys. We need a little space. And some privacy."

Pixel and Rizzo went, although reluctantly. They just didn't understand.

Chapter Fourteen

Duncan called Chief Pete Adams the next morning, as promised. The chief didn't answer his phone, so Duncan left a message with the department secretary, a competent-sounding woman named Nancy, who swore she'd let her boss know "the minute he gets in." Duncan checked the time. Eight o'clock. If Adams was the kind of cop Duncan thought he was, he had been at his desk for at least an hour. But Duncan also sensed that arguing with Nancy was an exercise in futility.

When he got to his desk, Cavendish was already hard at work. He set down the oversized travel mug of coffee he'd brought for her. "You're here early."

"A rolling stone gathers no moss." She lifted the cup in thanks. "I expected you at least thirty minutes ago."

"I had to wait for the coffee to brew at home." He flipped the top of his own cup open. "And I had to make a phone call."

"To whom?"

"Chief of police over in Vance Township." He took in her expression. "Monongahela County. I want to pick his brain."

"What would the chief of a tiny township in the middle of nowhere know that could help us?" Cavendish returned to staring at her monitor.

"You don't know until you ask." He sorted through the paperwork on his desk. "Besides, Chief Adams has friends in the county PD. I did a favor for him recently. I hope he'll do one for me in return." The piles on his desk held nothing important. "I assume you're already hot on the trail of Kyle Palmer."

"Correct. I've filed all the requests for standard background. Financials, job history, credit. I've been running his name through NCIC and NLETS."

"And?"

"Nothing."

Duncan thought of the weapons found at the scene and the drug residue. "That's odd. Of course, without convictions, there wouldn't be any official records."

"I thought the same." She leaned back and drummed her hands on the arms of her chair. "The guy who found the body. Rosen. He was carrying some heavy firepower."

"Legally registered. But I see your point. He was expecting trouble."

"From Palmer or someone else?"

"Good question." He swirled his coffee. "What about the gun we found on the side of the road yesterday?"

"It's a ghost gun. No serial number, no way to identify it." She held up a hand. "Still waiting on ballistics. There weren't any fingerprints on the grip, but there was one thumbprint on the magazine. I'm running it now."

Damn it. "Then we know about as much about Kyle Palmer as we did Ellis Martingdon."

She rocked her chair. "Until the requests come in, yup."

＊ ＊ ＊

Sally arrived at her office, her travel mug and a box of pastries from a local bakery in hand. She set the box on the table.

Tanelsa came in five minutes later. "Holy sugar bomb. Are you expecting small children?" She took off her coat and selected a frosted doughnut. "Not that I'm ungrateful, mind you. Lisa's on a health food kick. If I have to eat one more bowl of plain granola for breakfast, I'll scream."

Sally waved at the box. "I figured we'd need the boost." She paced back and forth. "I have news."

"Good lord, woman. Stay still. How many of these have you had already?"

"One, but this is my third cup of coffee. I've been up since five, thinking about the Wilson appeal. There's news."

"You're cut off. Let me get my caffeine. Try not to climb the walls." Tanelsa disappeared to go to the coffee machine. She returned a couple of minutes later with one of the communal mugs. Steam curled off the top. "Now, slowly and calmly, tell me what you know."

Sally recounted what she'd learned about Kyle Palmer the night before while she was out with the two troopers.

"Well, shit." Tanelsa picked out a second doughnut and put it on a napkin. "There goes that angle."

"I don't think it matters." Sally peered into her travel cup. Where'd her coffee go? "I need a refill. Hold on."

"I told you, no." Tanelsa grabbed her mug. When Sally headed for the box of sugared goodies, her partner turned her around. "You don't need sweets, either. Why doesn't it matter?"

Sally's insides were jittery. Her nerves buzzed like she'd touched a battery with her tongue. Coffee had never done this to her. Of course, she wasn't quite used to what Jim made, either. "I don't think we should include him for the appeal. Don't even bring it up. How far did you get yesterday with your edits?"

"Pretty far." Tanelsa set down her cup and picked up a stack of printouts. "I'm polishing the prose and found two additional references, cases that went about the same. I think arguing that Miranda should have been read immediately is a losing approach. Both by Wilson's account and the police records, everything talked about at the scene was very standard. What happened, where were you, all that jazz. But look again at the transcript once things moved to county headquarters." She handed it over.

Sally chewed her lip as she read. "I see what you mean. They started asking the same things in different ways. There's only one reason to do that."

"They were trying to trip him up." Tanelsa ripped her first doughnut in half and dipped it in her coffee. "By now, they're at police HQ. I'm guessing an interrogation room. Two cops. You and I know how this game is played."

The police had almost certainly been unfailingly courteous. Alec Wilson could leave at any time, but it would be so much easier to get it cleared up that night. "You said you've got precedents?"

Tanelsa nodded while she finished off the half-pastry. "I need to fine-tune the language a little more. I don't want to call the judge a dumb-ass, but I do want to make it clear it was a mistake."

"Yes, let's not call the person on the bench a dumb-ass. That won't help." Sally put the paper on her desk. Her heart was still beating twice as fast as it normally did. At least, that's what it felt like. But her thoughts were returning to a somewhat normal state. "I think we should look into Vivien's background."

Tanelsa, in the process of dunking the second half of her doughnut, paused. "Why?"

"Let's say we win the appeal." She took one look at her partner's face. "Correction. We're going to win the appeal."

"Damn straight."

"What then?"

Tanelsa shrugged, mouth full.

"What if the appeals judge declares a mistrial? The DA is certainly going to refile charges. Dave is still in the hospital." Sally stared at Tanelsa.

She swallowed. "So?"

"We're the logical candidates to take over, aren't we?"

"Oh, no. Don't you go down this road." Tanelsa stepped around to her chair and sat. "We've got one job, Sally. One."

She came over to lean on the desk. "Be real. Would you be comfortable handing this over to a stranger?"

"Your buddy might be back on his feet by then."

"In a week? After a triple bypass?" Sally knew Tanelsa wouldn't necessarily be swayed by sympathy. After all, she didn't know Dave Sturgess. But there was one argument she wouldn't be able to resist. "It's a paying client, T. Dave would be eternally grateful. I know he would. So grateful, he might give us the majority of his fee for the new trial."

"I thought he told you the client had emptied his bank account the first time around."

Sally waved off the words. "I know Dave. He would find a way to get his money. He doesn't do freebies. Anyway. This one case would guarantee we'd finish the year in the black."

Tanelsa grumbled.

"It makes sense. You know it does." Sally waited. "You said yourself the investigation is full of holes. Let's plug them."

Tanelsa fiddled with her second pastry. "What do you propose we do?"

Gotcha. Sally returned to her desk. "We're going to find out who killed Vivien Wilson."

"Just like that, huh?"

Sally booted up her laptop. "Don't worry. I know a guy." Or rather, Jim did.

* * *

Duncan whiled away an hour doing random internet searches for information on Kyle Palmer. There wasn't much. The man had almost no social media footprint. His name popped in a couple of local police blotter mentions, usually in connection with bar brawls or similar small-time crime. In a couple instances, other names were mentioned. Duncan wrote them down for later reference. Chances were slim any of them would provide a useful lead, but investigations had broken on that kind of thing before.

He looked over at Cavendish. "Any word from ballistics?"

She stared at her computer screen. "If there had been, I would have told you." She made a face. "No wonder insurance costs so damn much. Bunch of legitimized thieves."

"What prompted that non-sequitur?"

"Oh, some local outfit being investigated by the feds for fraud."

"Who?" Duncan wasn't really interested in the answer, but the conversation was better than staring at the surface of his desk, or reorganizing his paper clips, while he waited for something, anything on Palmer.

Cavendish scrolled up. "Laurel Mountain Insurance. I've never heard of them."

"Neither have I." That wasn't true. "What was that name again?"

Cavendish repeated it. "Why do you care? You don't have a policy with them, do you?"

"No, but I've heard it recently." Where? He grabbed his phone to text Sally. **Where did Alec Wilson work?**

Her response came in about a minute. **Laurel Mountain Insurance. Why?**

Duncan stared at the screen. "Send me a link." He replied to Sally, **They're in the news. Sending info to your email.**

Cavendish complied. As soon as he got it, he skimmed the story. He'd assumed that Laurel Mountain only provided insurance, but they also offered financial advice, including a selection of managed investments. He forwarded the link to Sally's work email. Then he sat back.

"Are you going to share with the class?" Cavendish snapped a rubber band in his direction. "What about some podunk insurance company is so fascinating to you?"

"Not to me, personally." Duncan skimmed over the story again. "But this is where Alec Wilson worked. The guy Sally is writing the appeal for."

Cavendish's face was blank. "So?"

"Sally said Wilson is hiding something." He tapped the screen.

His partner clearly wasn't making the connection. "He killed his wife because his employer was committing fraud? Talk about a stretch."

"What if Vivien knew something? Maybe she overheard a conversation or saw some papers he brought home." Duncan stretched. "This might have no bearing on anything. But knowing Sally, I think she'd want to find out."

Cavendish snapped her fingers. "Palmer's landlord, for the house he was living in when he was shot. He said the insurance was through Laurel Mountain."

He blinked. "Right. We were supposed to contact them about Palmer's death."

"If they provided renter's insurance, Palmer would have had to sign something, even as Martingdon."

Which meant someone at Laurel Mountain had seen Kyle Palmer and knew he was living under a false identity.

Chapter Fifteen

S ally read the story about Laurel Mountain Insurance and their legal woes aloud. "How interesting."

Tanelsa stood by the whiteboard in the conference room, where they'd sketched out as much as they knew about Vivien Wilson. "Not sure I follow."

Sally closed her laptop lid. "Everybody assumed Alec's motive in killing his wife was the affair. What if it was something else?"

It took a moment, but Tanelsa's eyes eventually showed understanding. "Vivien knew something about the fraud."

"Maybe. That widens the suspect pool." How much did Alec talk about work at home? According to what he'd told Dave at the beginning of his trial, Vivien didn't work at the same firm, so she wouldn't have been involved. But what if she'd learned something from her husband, and the culprit felt threatened? If Alec had been involved in the fraud, it also gave him another motive. True, the state couldn't compel spouses to testify against each other. But there would be nothing to stop her from voluntarily talking to a federal investigator if she knew something or thought she did.

"Did the police explore that avenue?"

"There's nothing in Dave's files to indicate they did."

"Yet another miss on their part. It's like the Keystone Kops. I can't believe Dave didn't exploit this."

Sally couldn't either. It wasn't like her friend to be so sloppy. She didn't want to call him out, though. Ineffective counsel was a solid reason for appeal, but in light of Dave's health issues, she didn't want to pile on. Hell, it was possible he'd been feeling, and ignoring, signs of his heart attack all along. No wonder he wouldn't have done his best work.

She picked up her laptop. "I'm going to go talk to Alec again. If we both go, maybe he'll finally come clean with what he's been trying to avoid."

"No, I think you should do it alone." Tanelsa turned back to the board. "He's never met me, so he may clam up. You might have more luck. I think I'd rather stay here and see what I can dig up about Vivien. If we're going to paint a picture that says her husband wasn't the only person with motive, I think we need to know more. Especially the name of this high-flying lover of hers."

"We'll trade stories when I get back." Sally put her computer on her desk and grabbed her coat. She texted Jim a quick note of thanks and headed for the county jail.

Once there, she waited in the same plain room where she'd met Alec before. Eventually, a guard brought him in, fastened Alec's shackles to the table, and gave the standard instructions for when it was time for Alec to return to his cell. Then he left.

Sally surveyed her client. Jail time left a mark on any person, even a night or two. Alec Wilson had been in there for months. Compared to the pictures of him from the beginning of the trial, he looked like a man suffering from a terminal illness.

He ran his fingertips over the scarred tabletop. "You must have news if you're here."

"I do." She brought him up to speed, including Kyle Palmer's death. As she spoke, she watched him closely.

News of the murder obviously shook him. "Kyle is dead? No wonder he didn't show for the trial."

"He was killed recently. The question of why he disappeared and solving his murder is not our problem."

Alex leaned forward, forehead furrowed. "But he was a witness for me."

Sally could tell he was confused. She took out her pad. "Do you know why Dave was going to call him? What his testimony would be?"

Alec's thin shoulders twitched. "He was supposed to give evidence that would prove I wasn't at the house when Vivien died. I didn't see him that night, though. Could be he saw me. Dave said Kyle was going to say that he'd seen someone else, as well." He drummed his fingers. "But he skipped town. Doesn't him being dead hurt my chances?"

"We're not using that. I told you. For an appeal to be successful, we have to show the judge made a mistake. Our argument is all about the Miranda warning, or lack thereof, and showing the trial judge made an error when he denied Dave's motion to suppress."

"Then why bring it up?"

She clicked her pen. "It might be helpful in the future. You never know. But that's not everything I want to talk about right now."

He blinked twice and pulled back. "It's not?"

"Your employer, or former employer, is under investigation by the federal government. Did you know that?" She watched him.

The reaction was immediate. His gaze shifted, so he focused on his hands. "Of course. The whole office knew."

"What did you know about the fraud?"

"Not that much." He picked at his cuticles. "I wasn't very high in seniority, you understand."

"Did you talk about it at home?"

"Vivien was never interested in my job."

"But did you have friends over, maybe called someone?" He was definitely nervous. "It could be she overheard you talking."

"Even if she did, why is that important?" Alec shot a quick look at Sally.

"Because if she knew something that could send someone to jail, or solidify the case against the company, that's another motive for the murder. We need to be prepared." She didn't mention the person Vivien could have identified might be him.

That got a reaction. He jerked his head up. "Vivien didn't know anything about my job or the people I work with, okay? Drop it."

"It was just an idea." Sally held up her hands. "Tell me, what does an actuary do?" She knew, of course. She wanted to hear him say it.

He relaxed a little. "I'm a statistician. The insurance industry runs on risk probabilities. Like, young men between the ages of eighteen and twenty-five are more likely to be in a car accident, that kind of thing. The level of risk affects how much you pay for insurance. I'm the person who helps analyze the data and create those tables."

"I didn't think the SEC investigated the insurance industry."

Instantly, the tension returned. "Laurel Mountain did other things as well. Investments. I don't know anything about those."

"Tell me." Sally leaned forward. "Did the SEC question you at all?"

Alec swallowed, his Adam's apple moving up and down. "Guard!" He stood. "You were hired to present my murder appeal, Ms. Castle. Which has nothing to do with my job. I don't want to talk about that. I'm sorry." The guard entered, unlocked the handcuffs, and led Alec out.

Sally remained sitting. Alec didn't care to know the name of his wife's lover. He wasn't interested in the investigation at his employer. Either Alec Wilson was the most incurious man on the planet, or he was hiding something.

* * *

Duncan's desk phone rang at nine-thirty. He listened for a moment, thanked the caller, and hung up.

Cavendish didn't look over from her monitor. "What's the word?"

"Ballistics confirms the gun we found is a match for the one that killed Palmer."

"They find anything else?"

"That thumbprint on the magazine? It matches a guy named Lucas Jones. He's in the system from an armed robbery charge five years ago."

She tapped on the computer. "That would be a long time for a print to last." She tapped a few more keys. "Well, shit."

"What?"

"Jones is still a guest of Washington County. There's no way he could've shot Palmer."

"Maybe not, but he's linked to that gun. He might know who else could

92

have used it." Especially if he'd given it to someone before he was arrested.

She picked up the phone. "You got anything on those other names associated with Palmer?"

Duncan read his notes. "One in prison, confirmed. One no longer in the area. Another one deceased."

"Cause of death?"

"Heart attack. Live fast, die young, as the saying goes."

Cavendish made a face. "That it?"

"There's a guy named Gus Lamb who might be worth checking out. He's mentioned in a couple of the same blotter reports I found, the ones that mentioned Palmer. He was arrested in at least three of them." He grabbed his phone. "I'll call my buddy in Vance Township again."

Cavendish's phone rang, and she picked it up. From the conversation, Duncan decided it was someone at the Washington County Correctional Facility. He dialed Chief Adams's personal cell, which went to voicemail. He then called the Vance Township police department.

"I'm sorry, Trooper. As I said when you called earlier, the chief is out on the road." Nancy's voice held a note of exaggerated professionalism, the kind people used when they are stretched thin but trying to maintain their calm. "He'll call you back when he has time."

She'd said he wasn't in yet, but Duncan decided not to mention that. "Can you make a guess as to when that will be?"

"No, I can't." The secretary didn't sound old, but Duncan was willing to bet she didn't tolerate any nonsense.

"I appreciate your help, both of you. Let him know if he can look into his records and see if he has any information on Kyle Palmer, or a man named Gus Lamb, he'd be doing me a big favor. I don't need a dissertation. Only the high points." *He shouldn't mind, either. I've done the same for him in a far less official capacity.*

"I'll pass the message. Goodbye." She hung up, the trill of the phone in the background.

"Thank you," he said to the dead line.

Cavendish finished her call and grabbed her winter jacket. "Who was that?"

"The secretary. I get the impression she thinks I call too often."

She shot him a quizzical look. "How many times have you called today?"

"Twice, and that may be one time too many." He shrugged into his overcoat and slipped his phone in his pocket.

"You need to charm her." Cavendish grinned.

"She's doing her job. I'll have to wait my turn. Meantime, we have people to see." He selected the keys to a car. "They expecting us at the jail?"

"The red carpet should be rolled out and waiting." She zipped her jacket. "I wonder what kind of story Mr. Jones is going to spin for us."

With their luck so far, probably one full of bullshit.

Chapter Sixteen

Sally went back to the office, still mulling over Alec's strange behavior. Did the fraud issue really not connect to his conviction? Because the identity of Vivien's lover sure did. In her experience, prevarication was the sign of a problem. Alec might not be explicitly telling her lies, but he wasn't being completely honest, and she wanted to know why. Preferably before it blew up in her face.

Tanelsa leaned out of the conference room. "There you are. How'd it go?"

"Very strangely." As Sally hung up her coat, she recounted her conversation with their client.

"I don't get it." Tanelsa tugged at her earlobe. "There is no reason not to talk about his employer's problems. And what cuckolded man doesn't want to know the guy his wife is running around with?"

"It makes me think there's more to the story than we, or Dave, were told." Sally sighed. "Did you get the background on Vivien Wilson?"

Tanelsa beckoned. "In here."

The conference room looked like a paper-filled explosive had gone off. Stacks of printouts covered the table. On the whiteboard, Tanelsa had written a bullet list of data. "You can read through everything, and you definitely want to, but the board has the highlights." She pointed. "Vivien and Alec have been married almost eight years. She graduated from Carlow with a degree in marketing. She worked from home as a freelance consultant for various companies throughout the region and a few in other states. Most of her clients came through a couple of firms she had relationships with. Some were word-of-mouth referrals."

Sally skimmed through the pages. "What kind of marketing?"

"Digital stuff, a lot of social media consulting, helping companies build their brand." Tanelsa tapped the board. "She must have been good, because she worked on a steady basis. The past few years, she cleared six figures."

Sally put aside the educational background and looked for the financials. "She was the breadwinner."

"She and Alec kept separate checking accounts." Tanelsa pushed over a stack. "Looks to me like they divvied up the bills. She paid the mortgage. He paid the utilities. It evened out."

"Joint credit?"

"Nope. Everything was separate. In my opinion, that's where it gets interesting."

Sally looked up.

Tanelsa went to the board. "The year before she died, that would be two years ago, Vivien went in the hole. The mortgage got paid regularly, but her bank balance was routinely low, and she maxed out a couple of her cards. Then, bam." She tapped the marker on the board. "In February of last year, she got a big influx of cash. All the cards were paid off, and she was in the clear."

"Where'd the money come from?"

"No clue." Tanelsa picked up a bottle of Diet Coke and drank. "Cash deposit."

Sally riffled through the papers. "How much?"

Tanelsa swallowed. "Twenty-five thousand dollars. Enough to pay off the debt and a little cushion."

"Was it a gift, a loan, money from Mystery Man? Alec found out about the affair summer of last year. They could have been together much longer."

Tanelsa shrugged. "No records at all."

Sally sat and perused the bank information. It all looked simple. There were regular deposits from the various companies Vivien worked for. Other deposits were attached to individual names. Those must have been Vivien's private customers. The large deposit Tanelsa mentioned was exactly what she said, cash. "Do we have Vivien's client list?"

"I don't think so." Tanelsa shuffled some paper around. "Maybe the cops have it. She did run an LLC, so I guess we can try to get a subpoena for those records."

If Jim's contact came through, perhaps the client list would be part of the case file. Sally stared at the board. Tanelsa had already written the date of the cash deposit with some questions underneath it: *Gift? Lover? Family? Lottery?* "Did she win the lottery?"

Tanelsa grinned. "I don't think so. It's up there for giggles."

Sally got up and went around the table. "Why do I get the feeling Alec didn't know about this? If they were running separate finances, the only way he'd be clued in to a problem is if she didn't pay the mortgage, and you said that was always taken care of."

Tanelsa, mouth full of soda, nodded.

Sally wrote one more possibility under the note about Vivien's debt. *Loan?*

Tanelsa frowned. "There aren't any records of her getting a loan."

"Not from a bank." Sally took out her phone. "There are other places. Not as public, but the repayment terms can be a bitch." She thumbed a text to Jim. **Need to talk to Eddie. Can you make that happen?** Then, she went to a blank section of the board and drew a line. She headed the column with the word Suspects. "So far, we have the Mystery Man. Who is he? If the affair was about to become public, what would it cost him?"

"Would he kill to keep it secret?" Tanelsa tapped her bottle. "We need his name."

"I'm working on that. Second, did Vivien get a shady loan to pay down her debt?"

Tanelsa drummed her fingers on the table. "Think the cops have that info, too?"

"If they don't, Jim has a guy. I've already asked to talk to him." Sally wrote some more. "Why is Alec so determined not to give us these facts? I can't shake the feeling it might be related. We won't know until we find out what he's hiding."

"Sally, I hate to say this, but,"—Tanelsa crossed her arms—"have you given any weight to the thought Alec Wilson might be guilty?"

"I have." The idea had occurred to Sally as she left the jail earlier that day. "There is no doubt the police screwed the pooch on this one. However. That doesn't mean they didn't get the right guy."

"Only that they did it in the wrong way."

"You said it." Sally dropped the marker into the board tray. It was not something that gave her a warm fuzzy feeling, the idea that she might be working to help a man who had brutally murdered his wife. But this was why she'd gotten into defense law. It wasn't only about defending the innocent. It was about making sure the prosecution played fair. Because if they, and the cops, got to bend the rules any time they felt like it, even if the defendant was guilty, what happened when an innocent person was caught in a bind?

Her cell phone sounded Jim's text tone. **Waiting on a message from Eddie. Will ask if he'll talk to you and let you know.** "We can't let that derail us. Let's keep pushing forward with the appeal presentation. Meantime, I'll work on getting a look at the original police investigation file and looking into the possibility Vivien got herself into a mess with a loan shark or something similar."

"And if we find out Alec is guilty?" Tanelsa leaned on the table.

Sally stared at her for a moment. "Let's deal with that later, shall we?" She walked out of the room. It was a possibility she wasn't ready to face.

* * *

When Duncan and Cavendish arrived at the Washington County Correctional Facility, they checked their weapons with security. One of the guards led them to a sterile room with a metal table, four uncomfortable chairs, and a camera hung in one corner. "We'll be watching in case he gets rowdy," the guard said, jerking his thumb at the camera.

Cavendish unzipped her jacket and sat. "Do you expect trouble?"

"With the inmates, you never know." The guard shrugged. "Jones is pretty quiet, but better to be prepared. Someone'll bring him in shortly." He left.

Duncan paced the room. "I hope their definition of shortly isn't the same as my doctor's office."

Cavendish placed a notepad and pen on the table. "Relax. We got a little time. Sit."

He shrugged out of his overcoat, unbuttoned his jacket, and sat. "Sorry. This one has me antsy for some reason."

"It'll be fine."

They waited for about ten minutes until another guard finally brought in a slight man with dark hair and dark eyes. He was covered in tattoos, including the fingers of each hand. "Sorry for the delay," the guard said. "Mr. Jones picked today to become slightly uncooperative." He gripped the prisoner's arm and guided him to the table.

Jones yanked away and sat. "I got it, man. Sit and talk to the suits. I know the drill."

The guard eyed him. "You want me to stay?"

Cavendish waved him off. "Between the two of us, I think we can handle Mr. Jones."

The guard looked like he wanted to say something but left.

Jones watched him, then turned his attention back to the troopers. "I been here for five years. Nobody but my mama comes to see me. All of a sudden, two state cops show up. What's the deal?"

Duncan pushed a picture of Palmer across the table. "Do you know this man?"

Jones barely glanced down. "No."

Cavendish pinned the photo to the table with a finger. "Take a good look."

Jones glared at her but complied. "Never seen him before in my life."

Duncan produced another picture. "What about this gun?"

This time, Jones's eyes barely flickered. "Don't know about no gun."

"You sure about that?"

"Yep."

Cavendish leaned forward. "You oughta know about this one."

Jones's expression conveyed boredom, his voice flat. "Why's that?"

"It has your thumbprint on the magazine."

He waited for a few beats. "Ain't mine. Five-oh framing me. Got a piece? Blame it on the brother in jail."

Cavendish didn't move.

Duncan folded his hands on the table. "Mr. Jones, you were arrested quite some time ago, and you've been here ever since. You must think we're stupid if you truly believe we are framing you for a crime that happened forty-eight hours ago."

Jones turned to him, a flicker of curiosity in his eyes. "What crime?"

"The man whose picture I showed you? He was murdered. Yesterday. In Farmington, in Fayette County."

Jones picked at his chin. "No shit."

Cavendish tapped the table. "One more time, the gun. Do you recognize it? We know the shooter wasn't you. But don't play us and say that a ghost gun just happens to have your thumbprint on the magazine. Or insist we put it there. Trooper Duncan and I would have to be five kinds of dumb to frame a man in county lockup for murder. And whatever you and your *brothers* think, we aren't that clueless."

Jones turned the photo of Palmer around. "I'm telling you straight. I don't know this white dude."

Duncan took a deep breath and exhaled. "I believe you on that, seeing as he lived in another county for all the years you've been here. Tell us about the gun."

"Police took my piece when I got busted."

The troopers waited. Duncan knew that unless Jones said something, they were wasting their time. But science didn't lie. Jones may have used a different gun in the armed robbery incident that landed him in prison, but he had handled the ghost gun at least once. Or at least its magazine.

Cavendish blew out a disgusted breath. "This is a waste of time. We might have put in a good word for Mr. Jones here, considering he'd have helped with a homicide. Clearly, he's enjoying Washington County's hospitality so much, he doesn't care." She stood.

"Wait." Jones squinted. "What kind of word?"

"That you'd been helpful." Duncan tilted his head and watched the man across the table process the words. "Don't misunderstand. We, meaning Trooper Cavendish and I, can't do a damn thing about your situation. But

100

we can talk to the folks in charge and let them know of your assistance. Or lack thereof. It's your choice. Maybe that makes a difference to your living arrangements. Maybe it doesn't. But hey, it's more than you have right now."

Jones rubbed his chin. The gothic letters on his right hand spelled *hell*. He reached out his left hand, where the letters spelled *cats*, and picked up the picture of the ghost gun. "This ain't for certain, you dig?"

"Nothing's for certain in life but death and taxes." Cavendish sat, folded her hands, and set them on the notebook.

"You got that right. At least the death part." Jones tossed back the photo. "I had a gun looked like this. Got one of those kits from the internet. You know, one that gives you all the pieces so you can make your own. No serial numbers."

Exactly what this is. Duncan kept his face still. "Go on."

"I hid it before I got pinched. But my friend, Elijah, he knew where to find it. He's on the outside. Could be you should talk to him."

Cavendish wrote a note. "Elijah got a last name and address?"

Jones eyed her. "Munk. Last I knew, he livin' in Uniontown. Don't know exactly where."

"He a petty thief, too?"

"Nah, bitch. Elijah's a big dude. Don't know if he was telling the truth, but before I got sent down, he claimed he had a job with a major player. Heroin." Jones waved his hands. "I don't play with drugs. Those brothers'll shoot you for looking at them cross-eyed, you dig?"

Cavendish glanced at Duncan, the question in her eyes. *Anything else?*

Duncan stood and buttoned his jacket. "Thank you, Mr. Jones. You've been very helpful."

"We got a deal, right?" Jones leaned toward him. "You gonna put in a good word for me?"

"Don't worry." Cavendish got up and went to bang on the door. "Guard! We're done." She faced the prisoner. "We'll tell them you played nice."

Duncan didn't think it would do any good, but they had promised.

* * *

Outside, it had begun to snow. Duncan cleaned off the car while Cavendish started the engine and defroster. When he finished, he got in the passenger side.

Cavendish held her notebook in front of her. "Next stop, Elijah Munk?" she asked.

Before Duncan could answer, his phone rang. Caller ID showed Unknown. "Yeah, Eddie."

"I have the information you asked for. Be here at two."

"Got it." Duncan paused. "Mind if I bring Sally? I believe she has questions of her own. She thinks you might be helpful."

Eddied laughed. "Of course. I always like seeing Pretty Prime."

"Pretty Prime?"

"The first one, the one I know is your favorite. Mine, too. See you then." He ended the call.

Duncan shook his head and tapped out a text to Sally. **Eddie willing to meet at two. Pick you up at your office?** It was around eleven now. He'd have time to work on finding Elijah, get to Uniontown, then out to Confluence.

Sally's response was quick. **Sure thing. See you then. And thanks.**

Duncan set the phone in the console.

Cavendish sent him a quizzical glance as she pulled out of the facility parking lot. "Who was that?"

"Eddie. He has something for us." Duncan rubbed his hands together and watched the windshield wipers swipe back and forth, removing the water left by the fat flakes as they melted against the glass. "Sally asked to go. Guess she has something of her own to check into. We have to go into Uniontown anyway, so you can drop me at her office."

Cavendish nodded. "Copy that. But what am I going to do while you talk to Eddie?"

"I guess that depends on if we find Elijah."

She made the turn that put them on Route 40. "I hope Eddie turns the

102

thermostat down for her. Otherwise, you may want to let her get changed into a sundress or something before you head out."

Chapter Seventeen

S ally set her phone on the conference room table. While Tanelsa continued work on fine-tuning their presentation, Sally swept up all of her partner's work and clipped it neatly together. Then she dumped out every sheet of paper in Dave's files and spread them over the table's surface. She'd gone through the records with an eye to making the appeal. Now she was studying everything with a different objective.

Just who killed Vivien Wilson?

She'd drawn the timeline of that night based on police records, Alec's statements to Dave, and her talks with him. It appeared straightforward.

Everything was consistent: Alec and Vivien had had a major fight that afternoon over Vivien's infidelity. Alec got to the bar around five. The bartender corroborated his statement that he'd left in an Uber shortly before nine. From there, things got murky.

Alec claimed to have been drunk when he left the bar. He tried to get into the house, but couldn't because it was locked. He'd been too drunk to look for the spare and instead gone walking to sober up. The bartender who'd been working at the time Alec had left said he appeared inebriated, thus the call for the ride. The man had started his shift after Alec arrived, so he couldn't testify as to how much Alec had consumed earlier. When the police located the bartender who'd been serving earlier, he had no specific recollection of Alec being drunk.

It pained Sally to think her client could have exaggerated his level of drunkenness. But the fact remained that the police hadn't administered a breathalyzer test until hours later, at which point Alec was under the legal limit. Observation was not necessarily reality.

That was the first inconsistency.

In his official statement, Alec said he returned to the house somewhere around eleven. At that point, he'd found the door open and Vivien in the kitchen, dead and bloody.

According to the police report, Alec had initially claimed to have entered the house upon his arrival the first time, something he denied later when questioned at HQ.

Which statement was true?

Next, Sally combed through the documents provided during the discovery phase of the trial. Alec's clothing had been covered in his wife's blood. Again, his assertion was that he'd tried to determine if she'd been alive. But since the time of death could have been as early as nine o'clock, it could also have been spatter from repeatedly stabbing her.

The only real mention of Vivien's lover in the police reports was the description of her argument with her husband earlier that day. There was no evidence they'd ever looked for him. It seemed they'd zeroed in on Alec Wilson and let everything else go by the wayside. The initial canvass of the houses in the neighborhood made mention of Kyle Palmer, but only that the man had refused to say anything and had shut the door in the officer's face.

"What were you going to say on the stand, Kyle?" Sally murmured to herself as she read the police reports for the fourth time. "Or were you going to testify at all?" Jenny had been right the previous evening. A man on the run didn't volunteer as a witness in a high-profile murder case. She leaned over and picked up her phone to make a FaceTime call. "Hey, Dave."

"Sally. How's it going? You're going to be ready come Monday, right?"

She was encouraged by the color on his face. "I'm going to do my best, as always. You're looking better."

"I'm ready to get out of here, but the docs are being cautious." He shifted his pillows. "You didn't call to discuss my health. What can I do for you?"

"Tell me about Kyle Palmer." She sat and propped her phone against a pile of papers so she could take notes.

"What about him?"

"He's on your witness list. Why?"

"He was one of Alec's neighbors. At least, he lived across the street. According to the materials I got from the Monongahela County PD, he refused to talk to them the night of the murder." Dave stared at the ceiling. "But he'd been home, that much is known. I went back to him. I said he had to have seen Alec that first time and could be able to back up Alec's story."

"That he'd gone to his house, couldn't get in, and left."

"That's correct."

Sally scribbled some notes. "Did Palmer ever say that? Explicitly?"

Dave's face creased in puzzlement. "What do you mean?"

"Did he tell you, 'Yes, I saw Alec, and I'll take the stand and testify to that'? Or anything to that effect?"

"Let me see." He thought. "Not in so many words, no. But I wore him down. He said he'd testify for Alec. That had to be what he was going to say."

"I'm not so sure." She told Dave what she'd learned about Kyle, his disappearing act, and his re-emergence in Farmington with a new identity.

Dave paled. "He's dead?"

"As a doornail. Dave, here's the thing. A friend of mine in the State Police doesn't think it's likely he'd agree to be a witness if he was trying to disappear." She paused. "I have to agree with her."

"What are you saying, Sally?"

"I think he sold you a bill of goods, my friend. He needed you off his back, so he told you what you wanted to hear." She watched her friend's expression droop. She hated to be the bearer of bad news, but sometimes, that was the way it had to be.

"You think he disappeared so he didn't have to perjure himself?" Dave asked.

"No, I think he did it for his own reasons. Nothing to do with you or Alec Wilson." She paused. "I'm sorry, Dave."

"I was sure he would back up Alec's alibi." Dave's eyes had a haunted look. "All you needed to do was stand up in court and present the appeal, Sally. Why are you doing this?"

She spread her hands. "Bad habit. I wanted to make sure what I was presenting was solid. Once my partner and I started digging in, questions cropped up. It's a lot of he said-she said, and that leaves me wondering."

Dave was silent for several moments. "My God. If that's true, and no one can back up Alec's statement, do you know what that means?"

"I sure do." It meant there was no way to prove Alec Wilson hadn't sold his lawyer a bill of goods.

* * *

Duncan made a quick call to headquarters. Then he plugged Elijah Munk's address into his GPS. "I asked someone to check Elijah's record. He has quite a sheet."

"Drugs?" Cavendish clicked her seatbelt.

"That, misdemeanor larceny, misdemeanor assault, auto theft, and extortion. He's been in and out of prison for the last twenty years."

"Not a nice man."

"That's an understatement."

They arrived at their destination an hour later. It was a shabby two-story house. The steps leading to the wide front porch rose from the sidewalk. Overgrown evergreen bushes flanked the steps on either side and cheap planters, now empty, showed where someone had tried to add a spot of color with summer annuals. The stairs were swept free of snow, the porch clear of furniture and garbage.

Duncan rang the bell. He loosened his Glock in its holster, just in case Elijah became aggressive. Behind him, he heard Cavendish do the same.

But the person who answered the buzz was not Elijah Munk. Instead, a tiny woman with a cloud of fluffy white hair and a wizened face opened the door. She wore a dark purple velour tracksuit and peered at him through trifocals. "Yes?"

Duncan held up his badge. "Is Elijah home?"

The woman glanced at Cavendish, who also held out her identification, then looked back at Duncan. She gave a snort of disgust. "What's that boy

107

done now?"

"I'm not sure he's done anything, Missus…?" Duncan gave her a questioning look.

"Munk, Georgia Munk. I'm Elijah's mama." She shivered. "You all want to come in? It's mighty cold out there, and these old bones ain't what they used to be." She turned and trotted off.

Duncan opened the door. "You first."

Cavendish put her hand on her sidearm and entered.

The inside of the house was clean but worn. The furniture was covered in lace doilies and upholstered in fabric right out of the 1970s. The carpet was threadbare, but there wasn't a speck of dust or a crumb to be seen. The tables were solid wood and of a style not seen in decades. The most modern pieces were a flat-screen TV and a recliner covered in tweed.

Mrs. Munk came out of the back room holding a tray with a teapot, some cups, milk, and a sugar bowl. "Can I get you something to drink? You look like you're half frozen. Especially you, young lady." She peered through her glasses at Cavendish.

"No, ma'am, thank you." Duncan's gaze flitted around the room.

"He ain't here. You can relax." Mrs. Munk set the tray on the coffee table. "Sit down and take a load off. If I know Elijah, he's been running you ragged. How long you been looking for him?"

Cavendish sat on the couch while Duncan seated himself in the matching arm chair. "Not very, actually. Will he be back soon?"

"Gawd, I hope not. I threw his body outta here last month. Haven't seen him since." Mrs. Munk sat and poured herself a cup of tea. "You sure you don't want nothing?"

"I'll take a cup. Sugar, no milk, please." Cavendish reached out a hand to accept the tea. "Why'd you give him the heave-ho?"

"Because I warned him. Stop bringing those ruffians you call friends around here. I'm a God-fearing woman, Miz…what was your name?"

"Jenny Cavendish. My partner over there, the one who doesn't like tea, is Jim Duncan." Cavendish gave him a sly smile.

"Jenny. My, what a pretty name. Much better than what girls is calling their babies these days. I don't think half of 'em are real names at all." Mrs. Munk poured a splash of milk into her cup. "Elijah never did like his name, but his daddy and I told him it's a strong one. It has meaning. Jim. I take it that's a nickname for James." She fixed a beady eye on Duncan.

It was like talking to his grandmother. "Yes, ma'am."

She nodded. "Another strong name. May God protect. You follow Jesus, don't you?"

"Um, yes." Duncan wasn't sure how to get the conversation back on track. He shot a look at Cavendish.

She held her hand over her mouth and set down her teacup. She rubbed her hands together. "Mrs. Munk, have you seen your son lately? Say in the last couple of days?"

"No. Told you. I told him to pack up his things and leave. Until he got himself right with Jesus, he wasn't welcome in my house. His blessed father, God rest his soul, woulda beat him proper, the kinds of people Elijah brought to this house. Too bad he died before he could pound some sense into our son's brain." Mrs. Munk sipped. "With a pretty name like Jenny, you surely walk with Jesus."

"Yes, ma'am. Methodist born and raised." Cavendish smiled.

"But no ring yet. What's holding you up?"

Cavendish sighed. "It's hard to find a good man these days."

The old woman nodded sagely. "Too many men not right with God. Not like my Nate. Lord rest his soul."

"Amen."

Duncan focused on his notebook. *I've stepped into the Twilight Zone.* "You've mentioned these friends twice. Do you have any names?"

"Not that would help you. Benny, Slim, Big George; they were all the same." Mrs. Munk sipped. "Boys who thought money was the way to happiness. Being one with the Lord, that's the right path. Couldn't tell any of them that, no more than I could tell Elijah."

"Did you hear them talk about how they got their cash?"

"I didn't want to. But I know." She gave him a knowing stare. "Drugs, theft, robbery. All against the Ten Commandments. And don't tell me there ain't no Commandment against drugs. You know what I mean." She shook her finger at the troopers.

Cavendish's expression stayed solemn. "You're absolutely right, ma'am."

Mrs. Munk nodded in satisfaction. "Elijah went to Sunday School. He oughta known better. He had the flashy clothes, the big chains, expensive shoes. Didn't have a job. I watch television, Mr. Duncan. I know where that kind of money comes from, and it's nowhere good."

She was right about that. Duncan continued. "One of Elijah's friends, a man called Lucas Jones, said Elijah might have some information about a gun used in a recent murder. Did Elijah leave any of his things behind we could take a look at?"

"I'm sorry. I wish I could help you. But he took everything. Well, he left that poster of Jesus with the children we gave him when he was twelve." She sighed. "But all his clothes, shoes, his stereo, all the CDs with that noise they call music, he took all of it."

Cavendish pushed her own notebook across the table. "I know you said you don't have names. But we sure would appreciate it if you'd write down what you can recall. You never know what could be helpful."

The old woman stared at the paper. "I don't think I will. I know what happens when two White cops go looking for Black young men."

Cavendish held up her right hand. "I swear, we only want to talk to them."

"Ma'am, you let us into your house," Duncan said. "That's a sign of trust, isn't it?"

"It's a mark of politeness and hospitality. We learned that from Abraham." Mrs. Munk fixed him with a bright eye, like a bird eyeing up a fat worm. "The Bible says to welcome the stranger. No, Mr. Duncan. You two seem like right nice folk, but I'm sorry. You still the police. You want to find my boy and his friends, you're gonna do it the hard way. You won't learn nothing from me."

A sleek black cat appeared, seemingly from nowhere. It sniffed the visitors, then rubbed against Duncan's leg. It leapt into his lap, purring loudly, and headbutted his hand.

Duncan obliged by stroking it. Rizzo and Pixel were going to be very unhappy when they smelled him that night.

Mrs. Munk watched him. "Old Bess, she likes you."

"Seems so," Duncan said. He was not much of a cat person, but the animal seemed friendly enough.

Cavendish picked up her tea. "Mrs. Munk, I understand your hesitation. Frankly, if I was in your place, I'd think twice myself. But we're after a murderer. We're not saying that's Elijah. But he may have important information. Your cat seems to like us, and animals are good judges of character. You sure you can't help us out?"

The old woman thought a moment. "No. I'm sorry, but I gotta do right by my blood. Like I said, you two seem like good people. But what happens if I give you names and the next police officer who comes looking isn't so nice? No, I won't have that on my conscience."

The two troopers exchanged a look. Duncan knew they were beaten. The woman might be friendly enough to invite them for tea, but she wasn't going to give up her son. Or his friends. He gave Bess one last scratch and stood. "Thank you for the tea. We'll show ourselves out."

Cavendish drained her cup before she set it down and followed Duncan to the door.

Mrs. Munk trotted after them. "You both take care. And stay warm. Jenny, I'd give you a coat if I had one. That one looks a mite thin for air this cold."

Duncan grinned. "I've been telling her the same thing, ma'am."

Just then, a hot rod, engine roaring, sped by the house. Mrs. Munk shook her head. "Young people and their cars. And trucks. Why's it all got to be so fast? And loud? Like that boy who picked up Elijah when I made him leave. What a mouth on him. If I'd have been his mama, I'd have washed it out with soap. Him and his truck, making noise and swearing worse than a sailor."

Duncan paused on the steps. "Truck? Do you remember what kind?"

"I don't know anything about that. It was big and black. Noisy. He had the stereo up so loud, my windows shook."

Cavendish tipped her head toward the unmarked Ford. "Once again, thank you for the tea." She headed for the car.

Duncan followed. There were a lot of big, black trucks in the area. It didn't necessarily mean anything.

Then again, whatever he'd told Sally, he wasn't a big believer in coincidences.

Chapter Eighteen

Duncan navigated the slush-filled streets of Uniontown. "You remember any of those names?"

"I'm writing them down now, for what it's worth." Cavendish recited as she wrote. "Benny, Slim, Big George. The old lady was right. Not much to go on."

"Better than nothing." He glanced at her out of the corner of his eye. "You lied to that nice woman."

"About what?"

"Going to church. Since when?"

She pointed at him. "I said nothing about attending services. I said I was raised Methodist, which I was. Besides. What do you know about what I do on my days off?"

"Fair point. Apologies."

She put her notebook and pen back in her purse. "I haven't been to church in at least fifteen years. But that's still not what she asked."

Duncan decided—wisely, he thought—to say nothing.

"Are you going to make your meeting with your CI?" She nodded at the clock.

It was just after one. "It might be tight, but yeah. I'll swing by Sally's office. You take the car back to HQ. See if you can attach real names to those street monikers."

"When did Mrs. Munk say she tossed her son out?"

"Last month. What are you thinking?"

She shrugged. "Might be a wild goose chase, but I'll see if there's any traffic cams or anything else on that street that might have caught the truck. If the driver picked Elijah up that night, chances are good he's been around before."

"Good call. We might get lucky." He pulled to the curb in front of the Castle & Parson office. He put the car in park and left it running for her. "I'll let you know how things go with Eddie. Depending on what happens, I'll either see if Sally can drop me back at HQ or maybe you can come get me. Or something."

"Copy that. Good luck."

Duncan went inside as Cavendish pulled away and drove off. Inside, Tanelsa and Sally were studying a whiteboard in the conference room. The board was covered in notes. "You ready?"

Sally started. "Is it time already? Shit. Let me get my coat."

He made a circle in the air with his finger. "Time's a wasting, and Eddie won't be happy." He nodded at Tanelsa. "How are the kittens?"

"Kittenish." She made a face. "We can't get them to stop climbing the draperies. It's driving Lisa batty."

"I don't have experience, but I hear scratching posts are wonderful things."

"We have two of them. They're still climbers, especially hers." She rolled her eyes. "At least this has cooled her jets on the whole 'let's have a baby' thing."

Duncan laughed. "Which was the point, right?"

Tanelsa grinned.

Sally reappeared, coat on. She pulled her hair from under her collar. "Who's driving?"

He pointed. "You. Cavendish dropped me off. I'm pretty sure you know where you're going."

They headed out. Duncan climbed in and clicked his seatbelt. "Onward, Jeeves."

Sally pulled the SUV out of its space. "Keep it up, buddy, and I'm never driving again."

* * *

114

Sally didn't say much while she drove to Confluence. She was too wrapped up in her thoughts. She wasn't sure what she hoped to learn from Eddie, but with any luck, it would be something that would kickstart her stalled case. Perhaps stalled was the wrong word. She had the facts and records from the first trial. She and Tanelsa were making steady progress on their analysis. She just couldn't shake her gut feeling that there was more to Vivien's murder than met the eye.

Jim must have sensed her mood because he didn't say much either. He spent the drive buried in his notes, occasionally muttering to himself about guns, convicts, and fake IDs. None of it made a lot of sense. Of course, if he'd meant it to, he would be talking to her about it.

He didn't look up until they reached the Confluence town limits. "We here already?"

"Time flies when you're having fun." She turned down the snow-caked road that led to Eddie's place of business.

"How's the charge? You need to plug in?"

"Relax. I've got plenty of juice. If you think I'm going home and walking to Eddie's, you're nuts."

"Good. Because my boots are in my Jeep."

Moments later, she parked in Eddie's immaculate parking lot. A delivery truck was at the side, idling while Stanley supervised the unloading of several boxes.

Jim lifted his hand in greeting. "Restocking the bar?"

"Gambling is thirsty work." The hulking doorman kept his eyes on the men, going back and forth. "Careful, you blockhead. Drop that box, and you'll owe him a new shipment. And that isn't rotgut you're carrying."

The delivery man adjusted the box in his arms and staggered into the building.

Stanley wore a disgusted expression. "It's hard to find good help." He nodded. "Hello, Ms. Castle."

"Stanley. Haven't I told you before? Call me Sally." It amused her that while Eddie called her by a nickname, his doorman-slash-bodyguard was always formal in his speech.

He shrugged. "Habit." He focused on the unloading. "Door is unlocked, Duncan. He's expecting you. You know your way."

"Thanks." Jim took Sally's arm and led her to the door. "After you."

The sudden temperature swing took Sally's breath away. She'd been here before, but never in the winter when the heat was on. She shrugged out of her coat. "Likes it warm, doesn't he?"

"Cavendish said the same thing. Sorry. I forgot to warn you. This way."

Eddie was in his office, a cigar clamped in his teeth as usual. He was poring over a sheet of numbers and looked up as they entered. "Pretty! It's been too long. Give an old man a kiss. How are you?"

Sally leaned over the desk and kissed the proffered cheek. She was sure the man had a rough side, but he was a dear. At least to her. "Not bad, Eddie. You?"

"Huffing along, as you can see. How's private practice? Duncan told me you hung out your own shingle."

"It's interesting." She draped her coat on the back of a chair. "Mind if I sit?"

He gestured. "He also said you needed to talk to me. What can a tired old bookie like me do for a ravishing attorney such as yourself?"

"Flattery will get you everywhere, Eddie." She glanced at Jim, who sat next to her after shedding his overcoat.

"Ladies first," he said, sitting back and resting his right foot on his left knee.

Sally thought for a moment. "Hypothetical situation. I'm in debt, a lot of it. I need to pay it off quickly. I'm looking for the money, fast, and I'm not averse to a source that isn't picky about my credit history and will be, shall we say, discreet. Where do I go?"

Eddie clasped his hands across his vast stomach. "How much?"

"Twenty-five thousand."

He eyed her. "This isn't hypothetical. And we're not talking about you."

"Correct, but it's for a case. I can't say much more." She hesitated. "The borrower lived in Monongahela County, but I don't know anyone there. I do know you."

"You figure I might have contacts." Eddie's contralto voice held a note of amusement. "You think a lot of me, don't you, Pretty? What makes you, either of you, think I give a damn what happens in another county?"

She shrugged. "Knowledge is power. Yeah, you've got a little fiefdom here in Confluence, but if I know you, your ear is always open to something that may help you down the road. Or hurt you. You'd want to be able to steer clear."

He took his stogie out of his mouth and examined it. He tapped off the ash and set it on a beaten copper plate. "Too true. Well, I have good news and bad news."

She'd expected the answer. "Go on."

"If your borrower is looking for money, quickly, in Fayette County, I'd have no problem hooking her up. The application process might be easy, although the terms would be strict, and she wouldn't want to fall in arrears. But it could be done."

"The bad news?"

"I don't know anyone personally in Monongahela County. But"—he held up a plump finger—"my bankers here at home might. How fast do you need the information?"

"The sooner, the better."

"Shocking." He pushed a sheet of paper and a pen to her. "Write down a number where you can be reached. I'll make some calls. Can you tell me the borrower's name?"

"Vivien Wilson." Sally scribbled her cell number.

Eddie's thin eyebrows went up. "The woman who was murdered over in Marsdale?"

"You've heard of her."

"Pretty, I don't live under a rock. I'd be very surprised to find someone in Southwestern Pennsylvania who hasn't heard of that one." He tilted his head, a curiously bird-like movement for a man his size. "What's your interest in the matter, Pretty? Her husband was convicted."

"He's appealing. I'm filling in for his attorney during the process."

"Ah." He scrutinized her, expression unreadable. "Does his wife's finances have anything to do with his appeal?"

"Not directly, no."

"Then why the interest?"

She schooled her expression and met his gaze. "I don't think I care to say right now. As I said, knowledge is power."

Eddie merely laughed.

Chapter Nineteen

Duncan watched as Sally and Eddie went back and forth. There was a time when she'd been a little hesitant in front of the fat man. Not now. In fact, he'd noted an uptick in her level of confidence since she'd left the Public Defender's office. It wasn't that she hadn't been sure of herself before. But being out on her own, calling the shots, suited her. He hadn't thought it possible for her to be more attractive.

He'd been wrong.

Eddie puffed his cigar, sending a cloud of foul smoke toward the air vent. He turned his attention to Duncan. "You meet with Ralphie?"

"I did. It wasn't quite like getting blood from a stone, but he wasn't eager to talk. What did you tell him?"

The bookie spread his hands. "The truth. I did my best, Duncan. I can't help it if every criminal in the county doesn't trust you like I do."

"I have a name for my John Doe." Duncan consulted his notes. "Kyle Palmer. Also formerly of Mon County."

Eddie tapped a thick spot of ash into the copper dish. "Don't you people stay home? What's wrong with right here?"

"My area got a little bigger when I moved to CIS. Anyway." Duncan waved away a tendril of smoke. "As far as I can determine, Palmer doesn't have much of a record over there, either. I'm working on that. Were you able to find out anything on this end? Even without a name?"

"Precious little." Eddie laid the stogie aside and handed Duncan a sheet of paper covered in handwriting. "You don't get to keep this. Take your own notes. Bottom line is this. Unless Martingdon, or Palmer, or whatever his name is, wanted to stay a bit player in drugs, he'd be up against some stiff competition. In fact, I think he'd have had a better time of it if he'd stayed away."

Duncan scanned the sheet. All the names were familiar, except one. "Who is Ryan Ellis?"

"A true up-and-comer." Eddie clasped his hands. "There have been several candidates to fill the hole left by Aaron Trafford last year. Ellis seems to be the guy who came out on top. Word is he's the man to beat if you want to get into the heroin trade in these parts. He's not the only source, not by any means. But he's the name that comes up most frequently."

"I thought you didn't get involved with drugs, Eddie." Sally swung her leg slightly, a small frown on her face.

"I don't," Eddie said. "It's bad for my business. Brings too much heat. Which is why I like to know who to avoid. Mr. Ellis is one of those people I'd rather not associate with."

Duncan wrote the name, along with the others on Eddie's list, in his notes. "Did you find any links between Ellis and Martingdon-slash-Palmer?"

"Direct? No." The bookie gave him a shrewd look. "But this isn't Los Angeles or New York. I did hear a rumor that a new supplier was trying to undercut Ellis. I didn't get a name, but it could very well have been your murder victim."

"Do you know if Ellis is only local? Or does he have operations in other counties?"

Eddie spread his hands. "I didn't dig that deeply."

No matter. Duncan put that on his list of things to ask Pete Adams. "What about other rackets? Did you come across the name Martingdon associated with anything else?"

"Not me, but hold on a minute." Eddie cupped his hands around his mouth. "Stanley! Are you out there?"

After a moment, the doorman came into the office. "Keep your shirt on. What's up?"

"Tell Trooper Duncan what you said to me this morning."

Stanley wiped his face. "About a month ago, maybe a little more, I was visiting my cousin over in Uniontown. He works as one of those people who searches for deadbeats who have run out on their bail."

"A skip tracer," Duncan said.

"Yeah, that. Anyway, I was at his office waiting for him to close up so we could go get a beer when this guy comes in. A stranger to both of us."

Duncan waited. He wanted to hurry the story along but knew Stanley would tell it in his own way.

"He says he's looking for a potential witness who left in a hurry. He had a picture, said the name was Palmer. My cousin, he shows the photo to me 'cause he knows I work for Eddie and maybe I'd know something about it. It was the stiff, Martingdon."

"You didn't think to mention this before?"

"Hey, the last time you were here, you called him Martingdon." Stanley sounded bored. "I stood in the corner like I always do when you and that other cop were here last time, so I didn't see the photo. If I had, I would have said something. You want to hear the story, or you want to criticize me?"

"Stanley, be nice," Sally murmured.

"Whatever you say, Ms. Castle." Stanley dipped his head. "Eddie had a printout on his desk this morning. That's when I saw the picture, and I put it together. Far as I knew, you were looking for a different guy. I told Eddie about my cousin, and he said I should tell you when you got here. Now I have."

Duncan thought over the doorman's words. "This guy who visited your cousin. Do you think he was one of Ryan Ellis's crew?"

"No, too well dressed. He had on a suit, a nice one. I pegged him for an FBI agent, like you see on TV, but he wasn't. He works for those folks in Washington who oversee investments and stuff." Stanley pointed at the desktop. "Like I said, I didn't put it together when you first came because of the different names, but as soon as I saw the picture from Eddie, I knew the suit was looking for the same guy."

Duncan looked at Eddie. "What else do you know about this?"

"Only what Stanley told you. I'm not big enough for the federal government to hassle. You'd know about any investigations in the county at that level far sooner than I would." Eddie puffed the cigar back to life. "Judging from your expression, this is news to you."

"Yes, but that's not surprising. Unless the government needed help from the PSP, they could be here and gone without my knowing it." Duncan looked back at Stanley. "Don't suppose he gave a name, this well-dressed stranger."

"Not out loud, but he did give my cousin and me his phone number." Stanley pulled out a plain white business card. "Keep it."

"Thanks." Duncan read it. Agent Ned Gaskell, Securities and Exchange Commission. What did the SEC want with Kyle Palmer? He slipped it into his pocket. He and Cavendish would look into this later. He stood. "You hear anything else—"

"I know where to find you." Eddie reached out to take Sally's hand and kissed it. "Good to see you again, Pretty. Keep that guy out of trouble, will you?"

Stanley held Sally's coat, and she slipped it on. "I'll do my best."

* * *

Sally stepped out of the balmy interior of Eddie's place and was assaulted by the difference in temperature. She pulled her coat tight around her throat. When she had shown up, she hadn't expected an instant answer. But Eddie would come through. He always did. He was reliable that way. Plus, he liked her, so she was sure he'd go the extra mile to find the information she needed.

From behind her, Jim cursed softly. "I'm going to buy that man a fleece blanket and make him turn the temperature down when I visit. I feel like I walked from the tropics smack dab into the North Pole."

She laughed. "You can try. I don't think he'll change, though. You get what you needed?"

"Sort of. As usual, I have more questions than I had before I got here." He hustled over to her SUV. "Hurry up and turn this thing on, will you?" He had his hand on the door handle when his phone rang. "It's Pete Adams. Hold on. Yeah, Chief. Thanks for calling me back." He walked off to the corner of the lot.

She beeped the doors open and slid inside. She started the engine and turned on the heat. Her phone chirped with Tanelsa's text tone. **Where are you?**

Sally peeled off her gloves so she could type better. **Just leaving Eddie's in Confluence. Why?**

Three bubbles. **Get back here, stat. I've got info on Vivien, and we're going to have a very important visitor from the SEC soon.**

Sally stared at the screen. The SEC? Why?

Jim got into the SUV. "I hope you're free for lunch tomorrow."

"I think so."

"Well, you'd better be." Jim reached up and pulled down his seat belt. "We're meeting Chief Adams and a buddy of his at a place called Parson's Roadhouse over in Vance Township at noon."

"Parson's? I wonder if Tanelsa is running a separate business behind my back."

He shook his head. "Very funny."

"Also, we? I thought you were going to look into things. You can't go without me?"

He fixed her with a look. "Sally, I said I'd make the introduction. You have to do your own dirty work. I have a case, remember?"

"Right." She once again studied the text conversation with Tanelsa. Should she tell Jim? Could she?

"What I'm not entirely sure about is why the SEC would be looking for Kyle Palmer."

If Tanelsa had been around, Sally might have made a different decision. But she could trust Jim's discretion. "Maybe because they want to talk about Alec Wilson, too."

Jim narrowed his eyes. "Wilson? That doesn't really shock me, I guess." He took in her expression. "You didn't read the story I sent?"

"I did, but let me read it again." She went back to her email and found the message. She clicked the link and read. "Now I see why the SEC is going to be at my office when I get back."

"Wilson never said anything to you about this?"

"No. Makes me wonder if he's the whistleblower or the crook." She put the SUV in gear and pulled out of the parking lot. "I don't suppose Jenny can come get you from Uniontown, can she? If I'm expecting a visit from the feds, I really don't want to drive an hour out of my way."

"I texted her after I got off the phone. She's going to meet me with what she has on Elijah Munk."

"Pretty inconvenient."

"It's my own damn fault for not having my own vehicle. Head up Route 40. Feel free to be a little flexible with the upper end of the speed limit. Back to the matter at hand." He took out his notebook. "I think the SEC was less interested in Kyle Palmer personally than what he might have been able to say about his neighbor."

Sally frowned. "You think so?"

"I do. If I'm investigating someone, I talk to friends, neighbors, acquaintances. I don't see why the feds would do it any differently." He gazed out the window, then faced her. "I think I need to explore a connection between Wilson and Palmer. Cavendish and I need to interview your client."

Sally knew Tanelsa would not like that, but she didn't see a way around it. "Today? I don't know what this guy from the SEC wants."

"Not today. You're busy. I'm busy. Plus, we have plans later."

"We do?"

An amused glint appeared in Jim's eyes. "We're meeting at your apartment to work on the move. Remember? Six? You said you'd order food."

Right, the move. "Got it. It slipped my mind. Yes, I'll order something. Preference?"

"Only that if you order pizza, get mushrooms and onions." He wagged a finger at her. "Don't forget. I don't want to be hauling boxes by myself."

"Check. I'll ask Tanelsa to remind me." She wished Alec had been more forthright about whatever the government wanted, because she knew in her gut this was part of what he'd been holding back.

God, she hated when clients did this to her.

Chapter Twenty

Duncan gave Sally a quick kiss and jumped out of the SUV in the parking lot of the Panera, where he was meeting Cavendish. Sally had taken his advice about the speed limit to heart and made good time from Confluence to Uniontown. "See you later."

"With bells on."

He closed the door and banged on the roof, and she drove off, the only sound the swish of the tires through the slush. "I will never get used to that."

"Get used to what?" asked Cavendish from behind him.

He hadn't heard her walk up. "The whole electric vehicle thing. Cars make noise."

"Looks comfy, though." She jerked her thumb in the direction of the state Ford. "Wanna get in our not-so-comfy car and figure out our next move?"

"No, I want to go and get a snack while we plan what's next. I'm hungry and dinner is a few hours away yet."

"Whatever you say. I can always eat."

They went inside. Duncan got a coffee and a bear claw. They snagged a table in a corner, where he filled his partner in on everything they'd learned at Eddie's.

Cavendish paused, a spoonful of butternut squash soup at mouth level. "The SEC? What the hell? I thought Palmer was in the drug scene, not securities fraud."

"I don't think he's the one the SEC is after." Duncan tore off a bit of pastry. "If anything, the feds wanted background into Wilson. I've asked Sally for an interview with her client."

"Yeah, good luck with that."

"I think she'll play along." He wiped his fingers. "It'll be supervised, of course. I wouldn't expect anything less. But she'll let us talk to him." He gulped some coffee. "What have you got on Elijah and Ellis?"

"As far as Ellis goes, only what I had time to find. He has a sheet as long as your arm, mostly drug-related stuff. Been quiet for the last six months. At least we haven't caught him." She passed over a printout. "He does seem to be up there as far as the pecking order goes in Fayette County. I wouldn't go so far as to say he runs things, but it's damn close."

"Do you think he'd view a new supplier as a threat?"

"It's a definite possibility. And he's got a charge from ten years ago when he shot a guy over a bad deal. Didn't kill the victim, but it shows me that he's capable of it."

He ripped off another piece of the bear claw. "Me, too. Got a location on him?"

"Last known is right here in Uniontown. Well, over in Uledi, just outside the city limits."

"What about Elijah?"

"He's playing hard to get. Figuratively speaking." She slurped up some soup. "Using the street names Mrs. Munk gave us, I looked at his past convictions and arrests and was able to get a couple of real names. Benjamin Frawley, James 'Slim' Cooper, and George Kinsey. Of the three, Frawley was picked up for armed robbery last month and is doing a stint in the Fayette County prison system. Cooper is MIA. Kinsey's last known is the thriving metropolis of Oliphant Furnace."

Duncan finished his bear claw, deep in thought. "Frawley may be our best bet. He may not know exactly where Elijah is, but he could give us a lead."

"If he's feeling cooperative."

He snapped a lid on his coffee. "Why don't we go find out?"

* * *

Sally got back to her office slightly after four. "T! Where are you?" She hung

127

her overcoat on the coat tree by the door.

"In the office," Tanelsa said. "With a visitor."

Expecting a man in a suit, Sally was taken aback to see a woman sitting with Tanelsa. She had soft brown hair and brown eyes and was dressed in dark jeans and a ruby-red turtleneck sweater. Her hands were wrapped around a steaming cup of coffee. There wasn't a wedding or engagement ring on her left hand, but she wore a silver signet, maybe a class ring of some kind. She looked to be in her mid-thirties, about the same age as Vivien Wilson. "From your text, I was expecting someone else." She extended her hand. "My name is Sally Castle. I'm Tanelsa's partner."

"Laura Richards," the woman said in a soft voice. "Viv and I were college roommates."

"Our other visitor is due between four thirty and five." Tanelsa got up and pulled Sally to the corner. "I was able to contact Ms. Richards while I was assembling some background on Vivien. She was kind enough to come in. She's got an interesting story."

Sally held out an arm, and they returned to the table.

Tanelsa retook her seat. "Sorry for the interruption. Do you mind going back to the beginning since we didn't get very far? It'll be better for us to both hear it at the same time."

"Sure." Laura sipped her coffee. "I told you Vivien and I were college roommates at Carlow. We stayed friends after graduation. I was a bridesmaid at her wedding to Alec. I thought they were the perfect couple, you know?"

"I gather that changed." Sally pulled a pad close to her and clicked open a pen.

"It was about a year, more like a year and a half ago. Time sure does fly. Anyway." Laura gave a nervous giggle. "Vivien and Alec were going through a rough patch. I guess he'd been spending a lot of hours at work. Or that's what he said."

"Did Vivien suspect an affair?" Sally asked.

"No." Laura drew out the word. "We met for coffee, and I asked. 'He wouldn't look at a woman if she danced naked in front of him, and that includes me," she said. She wasn't sure what it was, but she knew it had something to do with his job. Not in a good way, either. He's an actuary. A stats guy. Suddenly he was spending a lot of time at the office after hours, being all secretive and stuff. He got all defensive when she asked him what was going on."

Sally thought again about the SEC investigation and the fraud. Was Alec looking into it? Or was he part of it? "Go on."

"This particular day, though, she was all bubbly. Vivien. She'd gotten her hair cut and a fresh manicure. She was wearing this beautiful silver pendant. I asked if Alec had given it to her, a make-up gift. She laughed and said the hell with him. She was tired of weaklings, and she'd found a man who knew how to treat her right."

"She was having an affair," Tanelsa said.

Laura nodded and took a drink. "She didn't say it in those exact words, but I'm not stupid, Ms. Parson. I warned her to be careful, but Viv always did have a reckless streak. I told her to find out what Alec was up to, and then she could make her move. Then again, I'm not surprised she was ready to cut him loose."

Sally glanced at her partner. "Why not?"

"I told you I thought they were the perfect couple. That was at first." Laura shook her head. "I don't mean to speak ill of the dead, or my friend, but Vivien had issues. She needed to be in control, all the time. It wasn't so bad with me, but she ran Alec ragged."

"What do you mean?"

"Okay, so one time when they were dating, some guy came on to Vivien. It was college bar talk, right? He said something; she gave it back to him. It was an inappropriate level of flirting, if you ask me. Alec came out of the bathroom and caught the tail end. He told Vivien to knock it off."

Tanelsa raised her eyebrows. "What did Vivien say to that?"

Laura twisted her signet ring around her finger. "She laughed at him. Alec, I mean. She told him just because they were dating didn't mean she couldn't have a little fun. He ought to be grateful she didn't dump him. She was always doing things like that."

"Putting him down?" Sally wrote down the incident in her notes.

"Yes. Viv could be mean. Alec was a nice guy. But nothing he did ever seemed good enough." Laura held up a hand. "But then, other times, she'd fawn all over him. He worshipped the ground she walked on. That was clear. Most of the time, things were good. But the longer they dated, the more Alec seemed to, I don't know, pull into himself. He didn't want to go out. His friends from college drifted away. He talked about how lucky he was to have Vivien, but he didn't act like it." Laura shifted in her chair. "I spoke to Viv once about it and asked if she was worried he'd get fed up and leave. She brushed it off. She said Alec was too wussy to do anything like that, and she had him under her thumb."

Vivien sounded even more like a classic emotional abuser. Sally thought of her client. Years of living with a woman like that would explain his lack of confidence, his withdrawal, and his inability to make decisions. How long could a man live like that?

No, she couldn't think that. Not right now.

Tanelsa's voice broke her interior dialogue. "Did Vivien mention the man's name? The one she was sleeping with?"

"Dom. That's all she said." Laura finished her coffee in a single swallow. "I told you. I'm not dumb. Through talking to her, I gathered he was from Pittsburgh, successful, and had ambitions in politics. But no, she never gave me a last name."

Sally glanced at the clock. Four thirty. She needed some time with Tanelsa to talk this over before the man from the SEC arrived. "Thank you, Ms. Richards." She stood. "We appreciate you coming in."

Laura followed her lead. "Anything to help Viv. She was my friend, whatever she did." She paused. "If I can do anything else, please call me. In the meantime, I'll try and think if she ever mentioned Dom's last name or any details that might help you find him."

Tanelsa led her to the door and once again thanked her for coming in.

Sally stared at her notes. A successful man in Pittsburgh named Dom. There were probably a dozen of those. If she was lucky.

Chapter Twenty-One

C avendish was able to snag a parking spot close to the Fayette County courthouse, which fronted the county jail. Duncan got out and hustled to the jail entrance. Someone needed to open a coffee shop across the street. That way, he could have had Sally bring him right to where he needed to be instead of having to detour to Panera.

Inside, they checked their weapons with security and showed their IDs to the guard at the door. "We're here to see Benjamin Frawley," Duncan said.

Another guard led them to an interrogation room. "Wait here. Someone'll bring him down in a bit."

Cavendish stomped her feet and rubbed her hands. "Shortly. In a bit. Why can't someone say, just once, 'We'll get him immediately'?"

"Relax and sit." Duncan pulled out a chair. "And quit being such a baby. It's not that cold in here."

"Says you." Cavendish dropped into the seat next to him. "The man who grew up in this tundra."

Duncan ignored her. If he'd known he would be at the jail anyway, he'd have pressed Sally harder to get a meeting with Wilson. Oh well. Rome wasn't built in a day. Why should a murder case be?

It took about ten minutes for yet a third guard to escort Frawley into the room. The guard pushed him down into a chair and secured him. "Holler when you're done," he said and left.

Duncan took a moment to assess the man across the table. His first thought was that people had to have a hell of a time describing him. He was completely unremarkable. No birthmarks, tattoos, or scars were visible on his arms, neck, or face. His dark blond hair was cut short, but not flashy. There were no holes from ear or nose rings. His eye color hovered somewhere between blue and green, and his build could only be described as average. In short, a witness to any crime committed by Frawley would give a sketch artist a picture that would fit hundreds of other men in Southwestern Pennsylvania.

Which had to mean he got away with a lot of crimes.

He stared at the two troopers. "You gonna tell me what you want, or are we just gonna look at each other?"

Cavendish took the lead. "You know a man named Elijah Munk." She offered it as a statement, not a question.

"And?"

"When was the last time you saw him?"

Frawley let loose a laugh that sounded like a mule braying. "You've gotta be kidding me. Elijah doesn't come to see how I'm doing or bring me care packages."

Duncan laid his notebook and pen on the table. "We can check the visitor logs if you insist on being difficult. Want me to call the guard and ask him?"

Frawley licked his lips. "What do you want with Elijah?"

"To ask him some questions. It's a little complicated, and I'm not prepared to go into it with you. Let's say he may have information we need and leave it at that."

"About what?"

Cavendish examined her fingers. "A murder."

Duncan knew Frawley's rap sheet included nothing more serious than armed robbery. The casual mention of homicide had the desired effect.

"I haven't killed anyone." Frawley's gaze switched between the two cops.

Duncan held up his hand. "We know that." At least, they assumed so. "We're not interested in you. Only what you know about Elijah. Where is he?"

"And don't give us his mother's address because we've already been there," Cavendish said, not looking up from her nails.

A cunning gleam came into Frawley's eyes. "What's in it for me?"

"Quite honestly? Not much. You'll get a gold star for cooperating, which might help if your parole comes up or the question of early release for good behavior. Or it might mean shit. I don't know." Duncan could have lied, but he wasn't in the mood. The bear claw hadn't been enough. He hadn't eaten since breakfast, and he was hangry. "We have other people we can talk to. If you're telling us this interview is over, have a nice three to five." He pushed himself up.

"Wait." Frawley held out his cuffed hands.

Duncan sat.

"Okay, yeah. I've seen him. Elijah. About a month ago, right after his old lady threw him out." Frawley focused on Duncan. "He wanted to know if he could stay at my crib, since I'm obviously not using it right now."

Cavendish looked up. "What did you tell him?"

"Why wouldn't I let him? As I said, the place isn't doing me any good." Frawley drummed his fingers on the table. "I told him where to find the spare key and said not to let the landlord catch him smoking weed."

Duncan waited for a long minute. "And?"

"And what?"

Cavendish blew out a breath. "The address?"

"Oh, right. It's a duplex over in Lemont Furnace." Frawley rattled off the address. "I don't know if he's still there, or what. But that was the last time I saw him, I swear."

Cavendish called for the guard.

Duncan stood. "Thanks for the info. You've been a big help."

The guard came in, and the troopers headed for the door. "Wait," Frawley called out. "What about my gold star?"

Duncan sighed and squeezed his eyes shut.

Cavendish saved him from making a snarky answer with one of her own. "We'll put it on your permanent record."

Back outside, they got into the state car. "You want to head to Frawley's, see if Elijah is there?"

The honest answer was yes, but Duncan looked at the dashboard clock. "I can't. It'll take an hour to get back to HQ. I gotta get my car and drive back here to be at Sally's by six. It's almost four-thirty now, and that's two hours of driving. Actually, I should call her and cancel. This comes first. She knows that." He looked at her.

"No." Cavendish put the car in gear. "I've got it. Just once, put Sally first. She's under a lot of pressure herself, and the move has to happen. But do her a favor and grab a chocolate bar or something. Hell, I have power bars in my desk."

"She's ordering dinner. I'm already doing her a favor by abandoning you to spend my night hauling boxes." He rubbed his face. Food couldn't come soon enough.

"That's the wrong attitude and more evidence you need to eat, pal. She's moving in with you. If she was getting a new place of her own, that would be doing her a favor." Cavendish crossed her arms. "You may be the primary, but I repeat. I got this. Go."

"Okay, I misspoke. But really. I'm not that cranky."

Cavendish didn't answer. Given her propensity for smart-aleck comebacks, that was a response in and of itself.

* * *

After Laura Richards left, Sally took some time to add the information they'd just learned to the whiteboard. Then, she joined Tanelsa in getting ready for their next visitor.

"I don't think we should talk to whatever-his-name-is in here," she said as she swept up some papers.

"Agent Ned Gaskell? I agree. We'll use the table in the office." Tanelsa followed her back to the main space where their desks were. "What was the date on that story Jim sent you?"

Sally consulted her phone. "A month ago."

"You think this is what Wilson is hiding from us? That the feds are looking for him?"

"I think it's part of it. I wish we had time to talk to him first." Sally checked her watch. "When did Agent Gaskell say he was coming?"

CHAPTER TWENTY-ONE

The bells at the door jangled.

"Right about now." Tanelsa tugged her jacket straight and faced the door.

Ned Gaskell fulfilled every TV stereotype of a federal agent. Dark suit, white shirt, dark tie, buzz cut hair, spit-shined shoes. The only things missing were the sunglasses and the gun under his jacket, which made sense. One, it was winter and two, he was from the Securities and Exchange Commission, not the FBI. "I'm looking for Tanelsa Parson and Sally Castle. We have a meeting at five. I realize I'm early."

Sally took a step forward and held out her hand. "I'm Sally Castle. This is my partner, Tanelsa Parson. It's quite all right, Agent Gaskell. My boyfriend would say early is on time, and on time is late."

"He'd be right." Gaskell looked around. "Where should we sit?"

Tanelsa nodded to the small table in the corner. "Right here. Our conference room is full of privileged information. Hope you don't mind. Coffee?"

"Not a problem, and no, thanks. This late in the day, the caffeine will keep me up all night." He unbuttoned his coat and sat.

"We have decaf."

Agent Gaskell held up a hand. "That's okay. You ladies are already doing me a favor by meeting late in the day. I don't want to keep you longer than necessary."

The attorneys sat across from him. Sally sized him up. "What can we help you with?"

He looked around. "Mr. Wilson isn't here."

"No." Tanelsa smoothed her skirt. "You tell us what you want, and we'll decide whether a meeting is advisable. At this point, we don't know if you're looking at him as a suspect or a witness."

"Fair enough." He crossed his legs and folded his hands. "Do you know anything about Laurel Mountain Insurance?"

"We know Alec Wilson worked there. We know they are under investigation for alleged securities fraud." Sally shrugged. "That's about it."

"Then let me give you a little background. The president of Laurel Mountain, one Alexander Nelson, is indeed under investigation. Laurel

Mountain offers a few investment vehicles. In addition, Mr. Nelson owns a couple of other small investment firms. These are behind shell companies, but we've traced them to him. I won't go into details, but we believe Mr. Nelson is engaged in a Ponzi-style scheme that interlocks all of these investments."

Sally didn't know a lot about finance, but thanks to Bernie Madoff, she was familiar enough with both Ponzi and pyramid schemes to know what Agent Gaskell was talking about. "Do you believe Alec Wilson was involved?"

"We aren't sure." He uncrossed his legs and pulled a notebook out of his jacket pocket. "Early this year, Mr. Wilson contacted us, saying he had information about the scheme. His boss was unaware of his call, or so he said."

Tanelsa steepled her fingers. "This is December. What took you so long?"

Gaskell smiled, showing teeth with a small gap between the top two front ones. "We first had to determine if there was any credibility to the claim. The SEC isn't going to launch a full-scale investigation into something that might be an employee with a grudge. Then, we had to figure out what his role was, informant or participant-turned-witness. Once we had found enough evidence to pursue this further, Mr. Wilson was, shall we say, otherwise occupied."

The murder trial. "You didn't want a man accused of killing his wife as a witness," Sally said.

"We tried to make our case without him. Yes, the optics aren't good if you have to rely on a felon. Also, one of our agents did try to contact Mr. Wilson, but his attorney, a David Sturgess, rebuffed us when we couldn't offer any assistance with the murder trial in return."

The feds weren't going to get involved in a local case, especially not the SEC. Sally didn't blame her friend for trying to solicit some help for his client, but she completely understood why Gaskell had declined. "What changed?" she asked.

"We need Wilson, after all." Gaskell consulted his notes. "We've built up a lot of circumstantial evidence, but it's that. Circumstantial. We need something more concrete if we're going to bring Nelson to trial. Wilson claimed to have hard details. Names, dates, amounts. The nail in the coffin, so to speak."

Tanelsa's expression stayed inscrutable. "What does our client get out of it? You said you can't help with his murder trial. I understand. But given the situation, you can see where his priorities have changed."

"I do. And you're right. We can't do anything about his wife's murder." Gaskell closed his notebook. "But some of the information we have leads us to believe Wilson was a participant in the scheme. Being convicted of murder in the Commonwealth of Pennsylvania will not keep us from pursuing a federal charge of securities fraud."

Sally saw where he was going. "But cooperating with you just might."

He inclined his head.

Sally and Tanelsa exchanged a look. "All right. We'll talk it over and confer with our client. What's the best number to use if we want to reach out?"

He held out two business cards, one to each of them. "My cell number is there. Call me any time, and we'll set something up." He stood. "Thank you, ladies."

Sally escorted him to the door. Behind her, the phone rang, and Tanelsa answered it. "Question for you. What's the SEC's interest in Kyle Palmer?"

Gaskell's expression didn't change. "I don't know who that is. Good night." He walked out.

Sally watched him go. *Bullshit.*

She returned to the office. Tanelsa stood there, hand still on the phone. "You look like you've seen a ghost," Sally said.

"That was the county jail," Tanelsa replied.

"Is something wrong with Alec?"

"You could say that." Tanelsa blinked and faced her. "Someone tried to kill him with a shiv in the exercise yard this afternoon."

Chapter Twenty-Two

Sally's thoughts were in overdrive. The last time she'd spoken to her client, he hadn't mentioned feeling threatened. Now, someone had stabbed him? The attack felt like it had come out of nowhere.

Unless it hadn't, and she'd missed something.

She'd called the jail, but there was nothing for them to do. Alec was in the infirmary and sedated. It would be morning before he was able to tell them his version of what happened. She went to the conference room.

Tanelsa followed her. "What did you think of Agent Gaskell?"

"He's a smooth operator. I believe him when he says they tried six ways from Sunday to make this case without Alec."

Tanelsa went to the whiteboard. "I heard you ask about Palmer."

"That's where I don't believe him. The guy who works for Jim's CI specifically said Gaskell was looking for Kyle Palmer."

"You know how backward that sounds, right? That you don't trust a federal agent, but you do believe a criminal?"

"Stanley and Eddie have proven themselves. I don't know why Gaskell'd be looking for a small-time drug dealer, but he was. And it has to do with this Ponzi scheme. What, I don't know. That'll be Jim's problem." Sally leaned on the table. "We need to go back to the beginning. Pull everything apart."

"Agreed." Tanelsa spread out their files. "When does Jim meet with that police chief?"

"You mean when do I meet with him? Tomorrow, noon. Jim's making me do the talking." Sally made a face.

Tanelsa grinned. "Serves you right. He's your man, not your go-fer. Do you think we'll get anything we don't already know?" She waved at the piles of paper.

"I hope so." Sally twisted up her hair to get it out of her face. "These are all the reports from the officers who ran the investigation. Jim told me that Chief Adams is bringing another person to this meeting tomorrow, but I don't know who it is. Hopefully, that'll give us a new angle."

Tanelsa turned back to the board. She cleared a section and wrote. "Fact: Vivien Wilson was brutally murdered. Fact: her husband denies doing the deed, but his story is shaky at best."

"Fact: Vivien Wilson was having an affair with a man from Pittsburgh who may have found her suddenly inconvenient." Sally came up beside her friend. "First name, Dom. The convenience store clerk told me she was talking to herself about being used. Did she threaten to expose the affair and ruin his career and/or marriage?"

Tanelsa kept writing. "Fact: Alec has information about this Ponzi scheme. Is he complicit? We don't know. But what if his boss, this Nelson guy, found out and threatened Alec? He refused to keep quiet, and Nelson kills Vivien as payback. Or as a threat. Keep quiet or else."

Sally nodded. "But in that case, why not kill Alec? It would make more sense."

Tanelsa thought a moment. "What if that was the plan? But when the killer showed up, Vivien saw him. She had to go because she could identify him. He ran before Alec got home."

"Possible." Sally rolled the idea around in her head. Definitely possible. "Maybe Palmer also knew something. Did Alec talk to him? Or did Palmer see the killer? We don't know. I can ask Jim." Later. But not too much later. They were on a deadline.

"Fact: Vivien was deep in debt and looking for a non-bank way of getting money." Tanelsa stepped back.

"Did we ever find out why?"

"I did. Turns out she'd taken a loan for her business. She overextended herself."

139

It made sense and at the same time, it didn't. "Why not just make the payments on that loan?"

Tanelsa lifted a shoulder. "Without asking her, which is impossible, I don't know. Maybe having such a big liability against her was hurting her credit, and she wanted to pay it off fast. Or she was in danger of losing her company. That might have driven her to look for fast cash. What did Jim's CI say?"

"Eddie's working on it. She wasn't in Fayette County, so he doesn't have anything for me yet, but he's asking around."

Tanelsa tapped the marker against her chin. "I can't believe your buddy didn't think of any of this. There are a ton of suspects other than Alec here."

"I've been through his notes. While you and I do have more detail, I think he tried. I don't have the trial transcripts. But really. All the prosecution would have to do is keep hammering on the fact that no other people were seen that night, and no fingerprints, other than Alec's, were found at the scene. Speculation is great, but at some point, you have to back it up." Sally looked at the board, covered with notes, the papers, and put her hands on her hips. "Well, we may not know who killed Vivien Wilson, but I am sure of one thing, T."

Tanelsa laid the marker in the tray. "What's that?"

Sally picked up the first pile. "It's going to be a long night."

* * *

Duncan arrived at Sally's apartment a little after six. The place was locked and dark, but he had a spare key, so he let himself in. The first thing he did was change into jeans and a sweatshirt. Then he checked his phone. No message from Sally. He thought about texting her, then stopped. She had probably detoured for dinner. He'd get started, and she'd be there.

An hour later, he'd gone from mildly annoyed to seriously disgruntled. "Where the hell is she?" He picked up his phone for the umpteenth time. Still no message. He'd texted her at six-thirty, asking where she was. This time, he also called. It went straight to voicemail. "Hey, I'm at your place.

I'm famished, so I'm going to order something. Don't bother calling me. Just get here."

Something turned out to be Chinese, which he ate while sitting on the floor since they'd gotten rid of her dining room furniture the other day through an online advertisement. He cracked open the fortune cookie. "Plans are about to change," he read. "Yeah, well, no shit." He checked the time. Seven-thirty. Still no Sally. Not a call, not a text.

Now, he was angry. He'd joked about being a moving service. If something had come up, she should have called him. Or texted. Or something. He had work to do. He could be questioning a suspect or running down a lead. His finger hovered over her name in his Favorites list. No, he wasn't going to do it. In his current mood, he'd say something he'd regret. His father had always cautioned him about acting out of anger. Duncan had ignored that advice once with Sally. The result hadn't been disastrous, but it hadn't been pretty, either.

"But don't think we won't talk about this later." He got up, threw the empty containers in the trash, and grabbed the next box.

* * *

It was close to midnight when Sally got to Confluence. She pulled into the garage and plugged in her SUV. Then she closed the door and headed for the back of the house. The smell of wood smoke drifted through the air. She and Tanelsa had worked for hours, sifting through every scrap of paper, writing copious notes for both the appeal and the future. They'd agreed that the job had morphed from simply presenting someone else's work. They needed to be ready for any and all questions. As for what came after the appeal, Alec Wilson might not want to hire them, but it didn't hurt to be prepared.

She noted the lights on in the front of the house. And the fire was still going. That was nice of Jim. She'd thought the place would be cold and dark when she arrived. But he had stayed up. She let herself in and tapped snow off her boots. She was in the process of hanging up her coat when she froze.

It was a Tuesday night. Why was Jim up this late?

"Hello?" she called as she walked through the kitchen. Pixel and Rizzo clattered in to greet her. "Hey, boys. Good to see you, too. Where's the boss, huh?" She kept her voice down in case Jim had banked the fire and gone to bed, leaving the fire for her so she could relax.

No such luck. "I'm in here." His voice came out of the living room.

Sally went out, the dogs trailing her. "Hey there."

Jim sat on the couch, his feet up, something wedged behind his back. A tumbler of whiskey rested on a coaster by his right hand. "Well. Look what the cat dragged in." He checked his watch. "You're a little late."

"Sorry about that. T and I were mired in this Wilson case. You would not believe where it's gone."

He stared. "I don't mean coming home. We had plans. At six. At your apartment."

Six. Her apartment. She closed her eyes and groaned. "Oh, my God. The move. Jim, I am so sorry. We talked to Vivien's friend from college, then an agent from the SEC came, and with everything going on, it completely left my brain."

"I called. I texted."

"I turned my phone off. We were concentrating. I am so, so sorry."

He got up and hobbled to the fire.

She watched him. "Why are you moving like that? Is something wrong?"

He poked a log, sending up showers of sparks. "Oh, around eight, I forgot the first rule of lifting heavy objects."

"What?"

"Lift with your legs, not with your back."

She clapped her hands over her mouth. "Did you hurt yourself? You did. Oh my God. Jim, I am—"

"If you say you're sorry one more time, I'm going to have Rizzo and Pixel push you into a snow bank." He dropped back onto the couch. "Thank God the fire was laid, and I always keep wood stacked. I could add logs from my knees."

"Is it bad?" Her voice sounded tiny to her ears. How could she have forgotten? She heard her sister's scolding voice in her head. *Because you lost track of things, like you always do.* Think, Sally. Think!

Jim leaned back and closed his eyes. "I don't believe so. I pulled a muscle. I took some ibuprofen. The whiskey helps." He sipped.

"What can I do?"

He threw a beanbag at her. "Put this in the microwave for a minute and heat it up."

She hastened to follow instructions. When it was done, she took the fabric sock, which now smelled faintly of popcorn, and placed it behind his back. "There?"

"A little lower." He let out a breath. "That's the spot." He opened one eye.

"You should have called again. The office line, not my cell."

"It wouldn't have been a good scene. I was pretty pissed off, Sally. I left Cavendish to come help you. We could have done one more thing, and I put it off because I promised you I'd be there."

"I know. I blew it." She sat and laid her head on his shoulder. She felt the tension go out of him as he relaxed.

"Was it at least worth it?"

"We did more work on the appeal, and we have new information." She told him about their meeting with Laura Richards and Agent Gaskell. "Stanley gave us his card, Gaskell's. Why'd he lie?"

"He's a fed. Who knows? I'll call him tomorrow. I want to know why he was looking for my victim." Jim took another sip. "Did you talk to Tanelsa about us interviewing Wilson?"

"No, but you may have to wait a bit for that." She told him about the attack on Alec. "We'll get it done as soon as he's up to it. T may not like it, but I owe you for tonight."

He grunted. "Someone attacked him? Why?"

"It could be a grudge, something that happened in the prison. But."

"The timing is pretty convenient. Sounds to me like you better call Agent Gaskell tomorrow and find out what he's keeping from you. After you talk to the guards and make sure it isn't an inmate-to-inmate argument."

"I will. What's the plan for tomorrow? The meeting in Vance Township?"

He arched an eyebrow. "I'll be at your office at eleven, sharp. We'll head out to see Adams and his friend for lunch. I'm driving."

"Are you sure you want to go together? I could meet you there." She lifted her head. "You'll have to come all the way back to Uniontown."

"Absolutely. That way, I know you won't forget about me again. I moved your boxes. I'll be damned if I'll do your investigating."

Ouch. But she deserved the jibe. "Is there anything left at my apartment?"

"Plenty, including all the stuff you're giving away. And what I did get is still in the Jeep, so we'll be taking your vehicle tomorrow." He finished his whiskey. "Bank the fire. I'm going to hobble upstairs."

"Are you sure I can't do anything else for you?" She poked the logs and pulled the screen and glass doors on the fireplace shut. The wood would burn out by morning. The dogs were sacked out on the rug, but she wasn't worried about them. They were smart enough not to get burned.

Jim grabbed the banister. "Not tonight. Ask me again in the morning. Someone has to empty my Jeep. Just remember, lift with the knees."

"Not with the back. Got it." Something told her she'd be doing a lot of lifting for the next few days. She deserved that, too.

Chapter Twenty-Three

The first thing Sally did after Jim dropped her off at the office on Wednesday morning was make coffee. It was going to be a long morning, and she needed fortification. The second was to call the county jail and speak to the warden. By the time Tanelsa arrived at eight-thirty, she had her notes in order. She stood up as soon as her partner appeared. "Don't bother to hang up your coat."

Tanelsa complied. "Where are we going?"

"Over to the jail." Sally handed over the information she'd compiled. "I already spoke to the warden. Here's the story. At around four-thirty yesterday, most of the inmates, including Alec, were outside for exercise. Alec was standing off by himself, as usual. Another inmate came up to him, they spoke, and the guy used a shiv to stab Alec in the side."

"How badly is he hurt?"

Sally fastened the last button on her coat and went outside. She waited for Tanelsa, then locked the door. "Thankfully, the attacker had crappy aim. And Alec turned at the last minute, so the blade missed any major organs." She tugged on her gloves. "We'll walk. It's not far."

Tanelsa looked around. "Where is your car?"

"Jim has it. You coming?"

Tanelsa opened her mouth as if to ask a question, then shut it and fell in beside Sally.

Thank you for knowing when to say nothing. "The guards questioned the person they believed was the other inmate, but he denied being involved. Said he wasn't even in the yard at the time. A search of his cell turned up nothing."

"Did Alec argue with him? Hard to see that happening. The guy is a wimp." Tanelsa's breath fogged in the cold morning air. "Wait. They don't know it was this inmate?"

"No. He was careful to keep his face away from the camera. Alec claims he doesn't know his attacker. That is, he gave them a name, but he only *knows* him because it's another inmate. They aren't friends, and they don't hang out together. As much as prison inmates do that kind of thing. The warden tells me Alec isn't social." Sally hurried along the sidewalk. The gray stone of the courthouse loomed in front of her. "But the first guard on the scene, who was watching the yard at the time of the incident, says the two definitely talked before the attack."

"And the guard didn't see the inmate either?"

"He says he didn't. He was busy watching the rest of the yard and didn't pay much attention to what he thought was a casual interaction."

"They must have detained the second guy." Tanelsa handed over her purse and phone to the security guard at the county jail entrance and walked through the metal detector."

Sally followed suit and retrieved her purse and bag. The phones would stay behind until they left. "Everyone was focused on Alec in the immediate aftermath. By the time they caught up to the alleged attacker, he was in the weight room. He swears he was there the whole time. But he was alone, so no one can back up his story. There's CCTV, of course, but it's not great quality. It shows a guy in the gym. They're trying to clean it up."

"Surprise, surprise."

They went straight to the infirmary. Alec was in the far bed, eyes closed. Sally stopped the nurse on duty. "Is he sleeping?" She tilted her head in his direction.

"I doubt it. He spends most of his time that way. Not a talker." The nurse looked the two women up and down. "You his lawyers?"

"Yes." Tanelsa showed her ID. "Has he given you any trouble?"

"Not a bit," the nurse said. "I assume you'll want some privacy. Follow me." She led them down the ward to Alec's bed, drew the curtains, and left.

Sally waited. "You can stop pretending to sleep." She introduced Tanelsa. Alec opened one eye. "I didn't know it was you."

"Sure you didn't." Tanelsa set down her purse on a chair. "What the hell happened?"

"Don't know." Alec fiddled with the covers. "He just came up to me in the yard and stabbed me."

"That is weaker than the story my nephew gave my sister about why his science project wasn't done." Sally crossed her arms. "Why does the SEC want to talk to you?"

Alec said nothing.

"Dude, I am done playing games." Tanelsa's voice was tight. "We did you a favor taking this appeal."

Sally bit her lip. In truth, they'd done Dave Sturgess the favor. But maybe if Alec felt obligated, he'd open up.

Tanelsa continued. "Since then, you have stonewalled us at every turn. You don't know who your wife was sleeping with. You don't have any enemies. Your wife doesn't either. You can't tell me it's a coincidence the feds show up, and hours later, some homeboy sticks a shiv in you. We should walk away. You know that, right?"

He looked up. "But you won't, will you?"

"Alec." Sally sat in the second chair. "We know about the Ponzi scheme. We know you contacted the SEC with information. Why won't you tell us what's going on?"

He fixed Sally with a hopeful stare. "Are they going to help with my trial?"

"No. They have no interest in a state murder charge, and honestly, they have no influence, either." Sally watched him. "But that's not the point. *You* called *them*. Why?"

He sighed. "It doesn't matter. I can't do anything, and it was dumb to think I could."

"It might." Tanelsa moved her bag and sat. "Have you ever considered that Vivien was killed to threaten you? Or maybe she knew what was up, talked, and that's why she was murdered."

"Vivien never took any interest in my work."

Tanelsa pressed. "But did you ever mention the scheme in front of her? Maybe she overheard you on the phone?"

Alec hesitated. "I don't know."

Sally caught her partner's eye. "Rewind. What started it all?"

Alec laid back. "I don't work in that part of the business. But I have friends who do. Last April, one of them mentioned an uptick in the number of clients investing in one of the products. Performance wasn't spectacular, so she didn't quite understand it, but it was the boss's pet project. She gave me a brochure on it. The details were in the 'too good to be true' category. I started looking into it on the side."

Tanelsa was taking notes, so Sally focused on the questions. "Go on."

"Around mid-May of last year, I got an email that I think was supposed to go to the boss, Alexander Nelson. It happens all the time since our names start with the same three letters. You start typing, autofill gives you the wrong name, but you're busy so you don't notice. Anyway, this email was about the same investment. The way the person was talking about it, all I could think of was it sounded like a great Ponzi scheme. I went to Zander. He brushed me off, said it wasn't something I'd understand, and to delete the email and go back to my statistics. Instead, I picked a night when I knew he wouldn't be there, stayed late, and searched his office. I found enough to know he was up to no good. He had a ledger showing cash flows and it didn't quite match the official marketing and reporting information. It took me almost three months to put everything together, but eventually, I called the SEC."

"What happened then?"

He shifted on the bed. "I got what I'm pretty sure was a canned response saying they'd look into it. A few months later, someone called me, but by then, Vivien had been murdered, I was arrested, and, well, you can figure it out."

Sally didn't have to. She'd heard it from Agent Gaskell. "In all this, did you ever talk about it to Vivien?"

"I don't remember. I might have." He closed his eyes.

Tanelsa stopped writing. "Could she have found anything in your personal papers?"

Alec gave a tiny shrug. "Maybe. My briefcase doesn't have a lock. I leave it in my office at home. If she got curious, it'd be easy for her to open it." He opened his eyes. "Do you really think that's what happened? She found something out, and someone killed her to keep her quiet?"

Sally answered. "We don't know, but it's a possibility." If Vivien couldn't get the money she needed from a loan, blackmail would work. "Did you know why Vivien needed money?"

He exhaled, sounding weary. "Something about her business. She wouldn't give specifics. She said it was too complicated for my little brain."

Communication didn't seem to be one of the strong points in the Wilson marriage. "One more question. Did you ever talk about this to Kyle Palmer?"

Alec gave her a blank stare. "Kyle? The guy who lived across the street?"

"Yes."

"I don't recall a conversation with him that wasn't small talk. You know, the weather, the Steelers, that sort of thing. Kyle didn't invite confidences. I can't imagine I would've talked to him about something this big." Alec frowned in thought. "Doesn't mean I didn't, but I don't have any memory of it. Why?"

"He was murdered recently."

Alec's eyebrows shot up. "I didn't do it."

Sally held up a hand. "You were in jail, Alec. You've got the perfect alibi. No, that's not what I'm implying. The SEC was looking for him as well. It has to be about this Ponzi thing."

"That's insane. He didn't know anything. He couldn't."

Tanelsa pointed at him with her pen. "You don't know that. Marsdale is a small town. It's very possible you said something you didn't think was important, but it got him suspicious, and he went off on his own. You were a little preoccupied at the time. How do you know what he was doing?"

Alec pressed his lips together.

"The state trooper investigating Palmer's murder wants to talk to you," Sally said. She didn't look at Tanelsa. "I think you should."

"No. I'm not talking to the cops. That's what got me convicted in the first place."

Tanelsa shot Sally a warning look but said nothing.

"This time will be different. Tanelsa and I will be with you. Troopers Duncan and Cavendish only want to talk about Kyle Palmer."

Alec gripped his blanket. "No way. They twist everything. Cops, I mean. I do this, and I'll wind up being convicted of killing him, too."

Tanelsa stood. "Sally, a word, please?"

Inwardly, Sally groaned. She knew that tone. Tanelsa wasn't happy. She followed her partner to the end of the ward.

Tanelsa faced her. "What the hell are you thinking? Did Jim put you up to this?"

"He asked, in a professional capacity, if he could interview Alec with us present. It's for his investigation." Sally wouldn't let herself be cowed by the stern look in Tanelsa's eyes. "Alec's not even a suspect. He has nothing to lose."

"He has nothing to gain, either." Tanelsa tapped her fingers on her arm. "What does Jim think he's gonna learn? The guy's been in jail."

"T, the SEC had a reason to look for Palmer. I told you I knew for a fact they were doing so, which means Gaskell lied to us yesterday." Sally paused. "Tell me that doesn't make you curious."

Tanelsa's face made it clear she was arguing with herself. "Yes, but we don't care about Kyle Palmer."

"Playing nice doesn't hurt us. Jim will owe us a favor." She took a deep breath and mustered up her courage. "I kinda screwed up with him, too. I was supposed to go help move last night. Instead, I stayed with you, left him on his own, and he threw out his back."

Tanelsa groaned softly. She looked down the ward at their client, who watched them intently from his bed. "Oh God, help me. I warn you, Sally. If this blows up in our faces...." She let the sentence trail off.

"It won't." Sally wanted to add "I promise" but knew that was tempting fate. She went back to their client. "You need to do this, Alec. I can't say it's going to help you, but it won't hurt."

He glowered at them. "You both better be there."

CHAPTER TWENTY-THREE

"We will." Sally bit her lip. "One more thing."

"Yeah?"

"Who was your wife sleeping with?"

Alec snorted. "You never let up, do you?"

"It's her superpower," Tanelsa murmured.

He darted a look at them. "Dom Rossi, all right? He lives in Pittsburgh. After I found out, Vivien and I got into a big fight about it, yelling and stuff. I asked why and all she said was the guy was going to be a big deal since he was already rich and was sure to be elected to the Pennsylvania legislature. She died a few hours later. Happy?"

Not really, Sally thought. But the information might help.

Chapter Twenty-Four

Duncan had an ulterior motive for driving Sally's SUV to work. The Toyota had heated seats, which his Jeep did not. Despite taking another dose of ibuprofen before he left home, he looked forward to the comfort of the heat as he drove.

He was at his desk, re-reviewing statements from Palmer's neighbors in Farmington, when Cavendish arrived. "Morning."

She did a small double-take. "I didn't think you were here. I didn't see your Jeep."

"I drove Sally's SUV."

"I don't think I want to know why." She set down her travel mug. "How'd the moving go?"

"You don't want to know that, either." He swiveled his chair to face her. "What did you do last night?"

"I came back here. While you were playing moving-man, I decided to do a little more work." She beckoned him over. "After we left, Palmer's phone records came through."

Duncan pushed his chair to her desk. "He had a burner and no landline in Farmington."

"Records from before he left Marsdale. Cell and house." She gave him a quizzical look. "You okay? You're sitting a little stiff."

"Tweaked my lower back. What's in the records?"

Cavendish accepted the explanation, but from her expression, she suspected there was more and chose to let it slide. "Surprisingly boring. Nothing popped out at me until about a month before he left town."

Duncan took the paper. "What happened then?"

"He made two phone calls to Agent Ned Gaskell. I don't think Palmer spoke to him. It looks like the calls might have gone to voicemail."

"Gaskell had to have been looking for information about Wilson, and Palmer contacted him. You know, the old leave your card in the door routine." He scanned the lists of numbers. "Did you call Gaskell?"

"Left a message. But there are a few other tidbits."

"Such as?"

She pointed. "Those two calls were to Dominic Rossi. Who is he, you may say. Well, Mr. Rossi is from Pittsburgh. He's a wealthy man, dabbles in business, but it's his wife who has the money. He's also taking a run at a seat in the legislature."

"Long conversations." He made a note to have a chat with Rossi. "Got an address to go with this number?"

"Right here." She tapped her phone. "Palmer also made a series of calls and texts to Gus Lamb. Again, before Palmer left Marsdale."

"Isn't that the guy known as Dinky?"

"Correct. Did you know that good ol' Gus was arrested for attempting to rob a bank in Brunswick?" Her eyes twinkled. "There was a second suspect. Got away, but the description is awfully familiar."

"Kyle Palmer."

She tapped the end of her nose. "When the cops picked up Lamb, he was standing on the sidewalk, cussing a blue streak. The officers saw a car driving away at a high rate of speed."

"Palmer was the getaway driver?"

"That's a good assumption. Lamb never said. The case fell apart. The robber shot out the CCTV, so there was very little footage, and no one positively identified Lamb. He was released. But." She held up a finger. "Palmer beat it before Lamb was back on the streets. I don't think Dinky would be very happy if he was left standing on the sidewalk and got arrested while his so-called partner drove off at the first sign of trouble, do you? I think he'd be very interested in finding this unknown driver."

"I think you're right." Not thinking, he stood up and immediately sucked in his breath. The over-the-counter painkillers weren't cutting it, but the last thing he had time for was a doctor's visit.

"Seriously, are you okay? You're moving worse than a ninety-year-old man with rheumatoid arthritis." Cavendish narrowed her eyes. "Did you forget to lift with your legs?"

"Leave it alone." He consulted the clock. "I'm meeting with Chief Adams up in Vance Township around noon. I'm sure he'll have the lowdown on this bank robbery, as well as anything else Palmer might have been up to."

Cavendish looked like she wanted to pursue the subject, but she didn't. "We're racking up quite the to-do list."

Duncan's phone buzzed. He took it out and looked at the text from Sally. "Add one more thing. We have to go to Uniontown and talk to Alec Wilson."

"When?"

Duncan slipped on his winter coat. "Right now."

* * *

Duncan and Cavendish drove separate vehicles to Uniontown. He wasn't sure how long this interview would take. Neither driving back to HQ, which would be an hour out of his way, nor stranding his partner appealed to him. Once at the jail, they checked their weapons with security and waited to be escorted to the infirmary.

"Did you know he was attacked?" Cavendish asked in a low voice as they followed the guard.

"No. Sally didn't mention it." *Of course, I didn't give her a chance to, either.*

"She must have found out last night. You didn't hear the call while you were moving boxes?"

He sighed. "Sally never showed last night. She got distracted at work and, well, let's just say the evening didn't end the way I thought it would."

Cavendish winced. "I'm sorry. The moving man crack was supposed to be a joke."

He waved his hand. "Don't mention it. Seriously. Sally feels guilty enough on her own. She didn't make a peep when I commandeered her SUV this morning."

"I hope you aren't going to hold this over her head. It happens to us, too."

"I know, and I've already forgiven her. But those heated leather seats sure felt good this morning." He grinned.

Sally and Tanelsa waited for them at a bed at the end of the infirmary. After everybody exchanged greetings, Sally spoke. "Trooper Duncan, Trooper Cavendish. For the record, Mr. Wilson has agreed to speak to you about the murder of Kyle Palmer of his own volition."

From the expression on Wilson's face, Duncan doubted the decision had been entirely his. "Understood. As you know, we have no interest in his wife's murder or his pending appeal."

Cavendish broke in. "We're also sure you and Ms. Parson will shut this conversation down faster than a health inspector closes a roach-infested restaurant if we get into potentially incriminating water."

Tanelsa's answering smile was tight. "Good. We all understand each other."

Sally brought over two chairs. "Would you like to sit? This could take a while."

Duncan read the mute apology in her eyes. "Don't mind if I do." Beside him, Cavendish sat in the other chair. The two lawyers remained standing. Duncan removed his notebook and a pen from his pocket. "Mr. Wilson, I'm sorry to hear about the incident in the yard and I hope you're doing as well as can be expected. Thank you for talking to us."

Wilson shifted on the bed. "Whatever. Ask your questions, please."

Duncan dipped his head. "I understand Kyle Palmer was your neighbor in Marsdale. How well did you know him?"

"We weren't buddies, if that's what you were asking." Wilson moved again. "We said hello if we saw each other out or around town. I knew he worked general construction, and that he wasn't married. I saw his truck in his driveway. I figured he liked Budweiser because I saw the empty cases on garbage day. He knew enough about football to talk about it, but I don't think he was a rabid fan. No banners or flags in his yard."

"About as well as a modern neighbor knows anyone, in other words."

Cavendish made a note. "Ever have any problems with him?"

Wilson shook his head. "Nope. He didn't have loud parties, didn't have a lot of visitors, none of that. There were times if I hadn't seen his truck, I wouldn't have known he was home."

"Did you ever talk about work?" Duncan asked.

"We did such different things." Wilson glanced at Sally, who nodded. "I worked in an office. He did manual labor. There wasn't a lot of common ground."

"You never complained to each other about a rough day on the job, anything like that? A bad day is a bad day."

"You're asking if I ever talked to him about the SEC investigation into the Ponzi scheme." Wilson again shot a look at Sally. "As I told Ms. Castle and Ms. Parson, I honestly don't remember. They've told me it won't hurt my appeal to tell you this. I'm the one who contacted the SEC in the first place. I may have mentioned something to Kyle in passing. There were a few weeks where it was pretty tense in the office. The calm before the storm, if you get my meaning. But then I got a little distracted with other things."

He meant with his wife's murder, Duncan was sure of it. But he'd said he wasn't interested in that, and he meant it. "Could there have been any communication between him and your late wife?"

Wilson tensed. "I thought you weren't going to ask about her."

Tanelsa laid a hand on her client's arm. "Trooper, just to clarify. You are asking if there was any communication between Mr. Palmer and Mrs. Wilson regarding the Ponzi scheme at Laurel Mountain Insurance?"

What does she think I'm asking about? Duncan took a moment to study the two attorneys and their client. Wilson had clearly become agitated at the mention of his wife. Almost excessively so. He could be gun-shy, considering his past experience. But Sally and Tanelsa would have offered him reassurance in that area. With two capable attorneys present, there was no way he'd get sideswiped again. Why would a simple question of his wife talking to another man set him off?

Unless he was hiding something.

That is not your case. Focus. His back throbbed, a dull ache. Sitting in this god-awful chair was not helping.

Cavendish spoke up. "We told you earlier. We're not interested in the homicide. It's a simple question. Assuming Mrs. Wilson might have known something, is there any chance she and Mr. Palmer might have talked?"

Tanelsa leaned over and whispered in Wilson's ear. He answered. She straightened up. "Marsdale is a small community. You know what that's like, Trooper Duncan."

He did.

"Mr. Wilson doesn't even know how aware his wife was of what was going on at his office. He admits it is entirely possible his wife and Mr. Palmer ran into each other, talked, and she told him enough to make him curious."

"Are we about done?" Wilson asked. "I'm getting pretty tired."

Duncan and Cavendish exchanged a look. The interview hadn't resulted in a lot of solid information, just a lot of maybes. Was it worth continuing?

The nurse bustled over. "Time's up, people. This man may be a prisoner of the county, but he's also a stabbing victim, and he needs his rest. I have to ask you all to leave." She pointed at Sally and Tanelsa. "That includes you two. You get a couple of minutes to wrap it up, then out."

Duncan and Cavendish stood. He wanted to pursue the details of the relationship between Wilson and Palmer. Regardless of what they wanted to ask, they weren't going to have the opportunity to do it. Not right now.

* * *

Sally and Tanelsa followed Jim and his partner out of the jail but lagged behind the two troopers, who were also involved in a quiet conversation. "I hate to say it, but I have no idea how that went."

"Neither do I." Tanelsa kept pace beside her. "I don't think they got what they wanted. But Alec was a little too antsy for my liking. This should have been a no-stress conversation."

"He didn't get that way until they mentioned his wife."

"That's a bad sign for a man who insists he's innocent."

Sally concurred. She'd defended a lot of people, innocent and guilty alike. This one puzzled her. Not in a good way, either. She pulled out her phone.

"Who are you calling?" Tanelsa asked.

Sally held up a finger. "Yes, I'd like to speak to Alexander Nelson, please. I'll hold."

Tanelsa's puzzled expression cleared. "Laurel Mountain Insurance?"

Sally nodded.

"Zander Nelson," a deep male voice said.

"Mr. Nelson, my name is Sally Castle. I'm temporarily representing Alec Wilson, and I'd like to meet with you."

"On the advice of my attorney, I have no comment." Nelson ended the call.

Sally stared at her phone. She hadn't even said what she wanted to talk about. Something was off.

Tanelsa rubbed her gloved hands together as the breeze played with a loose strand of hair. "What did he say?"

"He hung up on me."

"Because that's not suspicious at all."

Ahead of them, the troopers stopped and turned around. The sun had come out, offering no warmth, but a dazzling light reflected off the small piles of snow. Jenny put on a pair of reflective aviator-style sunglasses. "Your client got a little worked up at the end. Hope he's okay."

Out of the corner of her eye, Sally could see Jim's intent look, but she focused on his partner. "He's not had a good experience with the police on that front."

"Hmm." The other woman's expression was unreadable, considering the mirrored glasses. She turned to Jim. "It's quarter to eleven. What do you want to do?"

He stretched and winced. "I think Sally and I should get on the road. Sure, we might arrive early, but that's no problem. My understanding is this Parson's Roadhouse is a restaurant, so we can grab lunch and wait for Chief Adams and his buddy."

Jenny grinned. "Ms. Parson, I had no idea you were in the food service business."

Tanelsa's expression was sour. "I'm already done with that joke, thanks."

Sally faced her partner. "When you get back to the office, start looking for Dom Rossi."

"You got it," Tanelsa said.

Jim and Jenny exchanged a look full of meaning.

"What?" Sally asked.

Jenny shrugged, dug her keys out of her pocket, and faced Jim. "Not our case, not our problem. Go ahead and tell her." She waved at Sally, then continued talking to Jim. "I'm heading back to the barn. Gonna call Gaskell and see if he's willing to talk. I'll also see what I can dig up about our other leads. Text me when you're on your way back." She strode off toward her car.

Sally crossed her arms. "Tell me what?"

Jim rubbed his chin. "Where'd you get the name Dom Rossi?"

Sally bit her lip. "I shouldn't say."

"Right, from your client. We know a Dominic Rossi was in contact with Kyle Palmer. We aren't sure why yet. Just watch your back, okay?"

"Do you have any concrete evidence it's the same man?"

"No, but what are the odds there are two separate guys with that name, and both of them are connected to a homicide?" He gave her a knowing look.

"In other words, Palmer might have known that Mr. Rossi and Vivien were canoodling on the side and tried for a spot of blackmail." Tanelsa nodded. "Which means Rossi might be a killer."

Sally watched Jim. "It's not only Palmer. If Rossi is really on a trajectory upward, and Vivien threatened to dump their relationship on the front page, he may not have appreciated it." She hesitated. "Thanks for the tip."

"No charge. Let's go. The cold is not helping my back." He headed for Sally's SUV without a backward glance.

Chapter Twenty-Five

Duncan and Sally arrived at Parson's Roadhouse a little before noon. Not quite as early as Duncan would have liked, but it would do. Given the presence of a marked Vance Township Explorer, Chief Adams felt the same way about being on time. Or he wanted to claim the high ground since this was a meeting with an unknown person—namely Sally. The Explorer was parked next to a dark sedan with county plates, which could only be an unmarked police car. Clearly, Adams had brought a friend.

"You ready for this?" Duncan asked as he waited for Sally to retrieve her briefcase from the back of the SUV.

She closed the liftgate. "As I'll ever be. You said Chief Adams is easy to work with, so I'm not expecting problems."

He nodded toward the unmarked county sedan. "I get the feeling you'll be talking to someone unexpected."

They entered the restaurant. A woman with purple hair greeted them. "Hi there. My name is Tiffany. Sit anywhere. I'll be with you in a moment."

Duncan scanned the room. "I'm looking for Chief Pete Adams."

"You must be the guests he mentioned. He and Detective Baronick are at the bar."

While Tiffany was speaking, Duncan spotted his fellow LEO. "I see them. Thanks." He walked over, Sally trailing. "Adams, good to see you again." He held out his hand.

"The feeling is mutual." Adams shook, then jerked his thumb toward the man next to him. "Trooper Jim Duncan, Detective Wayne Baronick of the

Monongahela County PD."

"I've heard all about you," Baronick said.

"Only the good parts, I hope." Duncan summed up the new guy. Typical of most detectives, Baronick wore a dark suit with a white shirt. His teeth, however, were as white as those of a TV anchorperson.

Baronick flashed a smile at Sally. "Who is this?"

Duncan stood aside so Sally could offer her hand. "Sorry. Chief Adams, Detective Baronick, this is a colleague, Sally Castle. She's a defense attorney and the one with the questions about the Wilson homicide."

Baronick's grin got wider. "My lucky day. In my line of work, I don't get to eat lunch with such an attractive companion often. You're a definite upgrade over Pete, Ms. Castle."

She shot Duncan a look, then focused on Adams. "I thought I'd be talking to you."

"Change of plans." Adams leaned against the bar. "I know a little about the Wilson case, but Jim said you wanted the inside information. So I brought Wayne along. Being with County, he knows more about the details than I do."

Baronick extended an arm. "Why don't we go get a seat and leave these two guys to their business? This way, Ms. Castle." He walked off.

Sally raised her eyebrows but followed.

Duncan watched her go. "Is your friend a ladies' man or something?"

Adams laughed. "I'm not sure that's the right description. Wayne is a cocky son of a bitch in everything he does. But make no mistake. He's a damn good cop. Just don't tell him I said that." He pushed off the bar and grabbed a file off one of the seats. "Let's get a table. Too bad we're both working. The beer isn't bad." He sat at a four-seat table, positioning himself to see the door.

Duncan did likewise. "How's Zoe?" He grabbed a menu. He'd met Adams's wife, the Monongahela County Coroner, when they'd come to Confluence looking into a cold case. He liked her, and he thought she and Sally would get along. At the same time, both were strong, independent women. Who knew what kind of trouble they could get into if they were together.

"She's good. Busy, as always. Thanks again for your help this past fall."

"Don't mention it. Happy to be of service."

Adams tilted his head. "You look like you're moving a little gingerly."

"Pulled a muscle in my back." Duncan stared at the laminated sheet. "What's good?"

"I've always found the burger and fries a solid choice."

"Go with the local recommendation. That's my philosophy."

Tiffany came over and set down wrapped sets of utensils. "What'll it be?"

Adams held up a finger. "Cheeseburger with fries, and I'll have coffee."

Duncan handed back his menu. "Same."

"And Tiffany, one bill."

She nodded.

"Not necessary, but thanks." Duncan shrugged out of his coat. As he did, he checked on Sally. Detective Baronick was all smiles, clearly trying to win her over. Sally looked amused, but she was playing along. Duncan briefly wished he was sitting closer so he could listen in on the conversation. But he had his own questions to ask. He pointed at the folder. "That the information I asked for?"

"Yep." Adams pushed it forward. "Not a lot, but all I could find. You said Palmer was living under a fake name when he was murdered?"

"He was." Duncan opened the folder. Inside were a few police reports, some from the Marsdale PD. There wasn't much on Palmer or Gus Lamb. "What's the summary?"

Tiffany delivered two steaming mugs to the table. Adams took his and sipped with caution. "Precious little. I have nothing on either man in the Vance files. One of my officers used to work in Marsdale. I asked her to check with them."

"And?" Duncan took the second cup. A beer drinker, and Adams preferred black coffee. He was a man after Duncan's own heart.

"Again, very little. Palmer had no record. A couple of the people Abby—that's my officer—spoke to remembered him as being on scene for a couple of cautions, fights that were broken up, that kind of thing. But he was never an involved party."

"That doesn't surprise me. He didn't look like the kind of guy who'd come off well in a bar fight."

Adams took a drink. "That goes along well with the description Abby had for him."

"That he's a wallflower kind of guy?"

"Not exactly. The term Abby used was *sneaky*."

Duncan took out his own notepad and pen. "What does she mean by that?"

Adams shrugged. "You know the type, I'm sure. The kind of person who is always around the edges of trouble, but never in the middle. Doesn't cause problems directly, but always seems to be on the fringe of the situation."

"Yeah, I know what you're talking about." Duncan thought about the victim's house. "Any problems with drugs?"

"According to Abby, no." Adams took another drink. "There was never a hint of anything major until the botched bank robbery with Dinky Lamb."

"Stupid nickname. Let me guess. He's anything but small."

"Isn't that always the way?" Adams laughed. "Lamb looks like a guy who might have played on the defensive line for a college football team. You know, if he'd ever been the scholarly type, which he isn't."

Duncan paged through until he found Lamb's rap sheet. "Busy boy, but small potatoes. Why'd he try bank theft?"

"He's stupid." Adams nodded at the paper. "Here's what I understand. Dinky was small time. He got the idea that he could up his game by holding up the bank in Brunswick."

"Which probably isn't as big as a branch of PNC in Pittsburgh."

"Hardly. Anyway, he was smart enough to know he needed a partner. Enter, allegedly, Kyle Palmer. According to gossip on the street, Palmer had done the planning and had been the lookout and getaway driver while Dinky was the muscle." He paused. "Only two problems with that."

"Which were?"

"No one at the scene could identify Palmer. He wasn't on the bank's CCTV, what little of it there was before it was shot out, and he wasn't anywhere in the vicinity. That could be proven."

Duncan thought. "And the second?"

"Palmer had an alibi." Adams nodded at the file. "He produced statements from two different people that he was miles away at a work site at the time of the robbery."

"Hard to argue with that." Duncan made a few more notes. "My understanding is Dinky wasn't convicted."

"Nope. Case fell apart. One of the witnesses was proved to be lying. None of the other bank employees could positively identify Dinky, only a big guy with a gun wearing a mask. As I mentioned, there wasn't much on the security tapes and none of it conclusive." Adams sat back. "Without more evidence, the prosecution declined to refile after the initial case was dismissed."

"That's all interesting, but it doesn't answer my question." Duncan closed the folder. "Why would Palmer leave town so suddenly, and why did he put so much effort into the new identity?"

The chief didn't budge. "Have you seen Dinky's mug shot?"

"No."

"If a man that large was threatening me—and by everything I've heard, he was none too happy with Palmer—I'd leave town in a hurry."

"Got a last known for Dinky?"

Adams pointed. "It's in the file. He left for your neck of the woods."

Duncan riffled through the paper until he found Lamb's address. It was at the south edge of Uniontown, which wouldn't have put him far from Farmington. Despite Palmer's efforts, had his alleged bank robber buddy found him? "One more thing. Ever come across a guy named Ryan Ellis?"

Adams thought a moment. "Name doesn't ring a bell."

Tiffany came back and set two plates, each with a sizzling cheeseburger and crisp, hot fries on the table. "Enjoy."

Duncan took a moment to check on Sally. She was leaning forward, pen and pad out, her expression intent. Baronick was no longer smiling. By the body language, Duncan surmised a verbal duel was taking place at the other table.

Adams squirted ketchup on his plate for his fries. "What's wrong? You

164

look troubled."

"It's Sally." Duncan took the ketchup bottle. "I know that look. It's the one she trots out when she knows the witness is trying to wriggle out from the spotlight. I'm wondering if I should go give your buddy a hand before she draws blood. Figuratively speaking, of course."

Adams picked up his burger. He threw a quick look at the other table. "Relax and eat your lunch." He refocused on his food. "Wayne's a big boy. He can handle himself."

Chapter Twenty-Six

Sally sized up the man across from her. Detective Baronick had escorted—there was no other term—her to a table across the room from Jim and Chief Adams. Whether this was to prevent eavesdropping or to get her on her own, she wasn't sure. Maybe both. He was handsome, no doubt about it. His teeth were so white, they had to be veneers, and he made sure to smile frequently, showing them to their best advantage. Within five minutes, Sally decided three things. Wayne Baronick was good-looking and good at his job.

And he knew it.

She removed the case file from her briefcase, along with a legal pad and pen. "Detective Baronick."

"Please call me Wayne."

"Wayne." She dipped her head. "As Chief Adams most likely told you, I have a few questions about the murder of Vivien Wilson and the trial of her husband, Alec."

He held up a hand. "Why don't we order lunch first?" He held out a laminated menu. "I always find food helps the conversation."

"If you insist. I don't need a menu." Her stomach did feel neglected. She looked up at the purple-haired waitress. "Bacon cheeseburger, side of fries, and a ginger ale, please."

Wayne gave her an appreciative look. "The usual, Tiffany. Thanks." He waited until the woman left, then added, "I'm impressed. I expected you to order something healthy. No beer?"

"I'm working." Sally waved around the room. "It doesn't look like the kind of place you come to for a grilled chicken salad or seared salmon. Besides, I'm hungry."

He laughed.

"May I ask my questions now, Detective?"

He sat back. "I told you, call me Wayne."

She studied her notes. "I don't recall your name from the original investigation or the trial records. Were you the primary detective on the case?"

"I was not."

"Any reason I can't talk to him? Or her?"

He eyed her. "Detective Fullbright is no longer with the Monongahela County police. He took a position with the Allegheny County department not long after Alec Wilson's conviction."

From his tone, Sally gathered the move was not entirely voluntary. "Did you fire him? Mon County, I mean. Not you personally."

"No. He left on his own."

"Was he encouraged to leave? Maybe because his procedure in Alec's arrest was, ah, lacking?"

His eyes narrowed. "You don't expect me to answer that, do you? Are you going to tell me why you took over representation from Mr. Sturgess?"

That was answer enough. He knew Dave's name, which meant he'd read up before the meeting. "He had a heart attack and asked me to step in." She pretended to read her notes. "I've read the trial records and what my predecessor obtained from the prosecution via the discovery process. You knew Vivien Wilson was having an affair, yes?"

"We did."

"And you had to have her financial records, which showed she had been in a considerable amount of debt. Which was suddenly paid off."

"We knew. Is there a question here?"

Sally looked up. "Did you ever seriously look into either of these situations? For example, did you know her lover was a man named Dominic Rossi?"

He hesitated. "We did not."

"Where did the twenty-five thousand dollars come from? The cash she used to settle her debt."

"We didn't determine that either."

She laid down her pen. "Why not? They both seem like logical avenues of investigation. If you had, you would have learned that Dom Rossi is a wealthy man from Allegheny County with hopes of winning a seat in the Pennsylvania legislature next fall. I don't think it would help his image if the voters learned he had a torrid affair with a married woman, especially considering the fact he is also married."

Wayne did not respond.

"Admit it. You never looked beyond Alec Wilson, did you? Not only was your procedure slipshod, you failed to follow some basic avenues of possibility because you had your man." She used air quotes around the last words.

Wayne wasn't smiling now. "Why do I feel like I'm being cross-examined?"

She fixed him with what Jim described as her look. "I don't know, Detective. Why do you?"

He leaned forward, hands clasped on the tabletop. "Can we talk off the record?"

None of this would be admissible in court. Sally sat back. "Sure."

"You're right. Fullbright's procedure was a bit...sloppy. I wasn't involved with the investigation. I assure you that had I been, it would have gone differently."

She was certain he spoke the truth.

"You are also right in that we never looked for the lover, and we didn't dive into her debt or how she paid it off." He cocked his head. "Life isn't a TV show, Ms. Castle. We don't run around spending time and money just for the hell of it."

"Trust me, I'm well aware of that."

The food arrived and there was a pause while Tiffany set down plates and glasses. "Enjoy," she said and walked off.

Wayne continued. "If you've read the original files and the trial records, you know a few things. One, Alec Wilson was extremely angry about his wife's infidelity. *Incensed* I think is a good word. They'd argued about it."

"I know. I'm also aware that Vivien was not the most loving of spouses."

"Good." He ticked off points on his fingers. "Alec was on the scene. Procedure or not, he made conflicting statements to us. That he went in the house when he arrived home, which he later denied. He said he was drunk, but there was no one who could confirm that. Not for a fact. By the time we tested his BAC, it was within the legal limit. Going by his story, it should still have been high."

Sally knew all that, too, but she held her tongue.

"We found him in the kitchen, kneeling over his wife's body, covered in her blood. His fingerprints were on the knife. Yes." He held up a hand. "It was from his kitchen. You're going to say, of course, his fingerprints were on it. That he was kneeling over her because he was in shock. But the fact is that the more we pressed him, the weaker his story looked. We canvassed the entire neighborhood. No one else was seen that evening, not at the Wilson house, not on the street. While we found fingerprints belonging to unknown parties in the house, they weren't on the knife. Just Wilson and his wife. If it had been wiped, we wouldn't have found anything." He picked up his burger. "No, Ms. Castle, we got the right guy. Give me a chance to do it again, and trust me. That case will be airtight." He took a bite.

Sally believed him. She'd talked to a lot of cops over the years. Wayne Baronick wouldn't fumble the ball. "One more question. During the course of your investigation, did you ever learn anything that made you think Vivien Wilson knew details about the fraud at her husband's company?"

He wiped his mouth. "The thing the SEC investigation is looking into?"

"That one."

"No." He watched her. "Are you thinking someone at Laurel Mountain Insurance killed her to shut her up?"

"The thought had occurred to me." She took a bite of her cheeseburger. It was juicy and delicious, one of the best she'd ever had. Although there was that saying about hunger being the best sauce.

Wayne looked like he was rolling her words around in his head. "Interesting possibility. But would that kind of killer stab upwards of thirty times?

I'd think it more likely once or twice. Or she'd have been shot. Plus, as I said, there were no strangers seen in the neighborhood that evening and no unknown prints on the murder weapon."

"Did you check traffic cams or anything like that?"

He laughed. "I see you haven't been to Marsdale, Ms. Castle."

"Please, you can call me Sally."

He grinned, showing a hint of the veneers. "It's a small town. No CCTV in a residential neighborhood, and no one on the street has one of those fancy video doorbells."

"Then someone could have been there."

He nodded. "Okay, yes. It's possible. But I'm not feeling it."

They ate in silence for a couple of minutes. Finally, Sally set her burger down and swiped a fry through some ketchup before popping it in her mouth. After she swallowed, she said, "I'm sorry for the cross-examination thing, Wayne. People tell me I can get carried away."

He waved her apology away. "You can make it up to me by letting me take you to dinner tonight. Do you have plans?"

"No, but I would have to clear it with my boyfriend."

"Damn, I knew you were too good to be true." He tilted his head. "On the off chance he'd say yes, who's the lucky guy?"

Sally picked up another fry. "Him." She nodded toward the table where Jim and Chief Adams sat and enjoyed the look of chagrin on Wayne's face.

Chapter Twenty-Seven

Duncan eased into his overcoat. "I really wish you'd let me cover lunch. You're the one doing the favor this time."

Adams accepted the receipt from the cashier. "Don't mention it. Next time I'm in Uniontown, it's on you." He put his wallet away. "Zoe said ice, twenty minutes on, twenty minutes off, on your back. Ibuprofen as needed. But if it isn't better by Monday, you might want to call your doctor."

"What's it like, having a medic on call?"

The chief laughed. "Sometimes convenient, sometimes a pain in the ass." He turned as Baronick and Sally walked up. "Ms. Castle. You get everything you need?"

"I did. And please, it's Sally."

"Only if you call me Pete." He shook her hand again. "One of these days, we'll all carve some time out of our schedules and get together. I think you and Zoe would get along."

"I'd like that." Sally's phone rang. She looked at the caller ID. "I have to take this." She stepped away.

Baronick watched her go. "I have never been grilled like that in my life, on or off the stand."

Duncan could only imagine. "She's very dedicated to her job."

"She must make your life interesting."

"It's never dull, that's for sure."

Sally came back. "I hate to say this, but I have one more question for you, Wayne. And maybe you as well, Pete."

The two men exchanged a look. "Yes?" Baronick asked.

"Are either of you familiar with Owen Zigler?"

Baronick gave a low whistle. Adams said, "The loan guy?"

"Shark is more like it," Baronick muttered.

Sally slipped her phone into her purse. "I take it the answer is yes."

Adams crossed his arms. "Why do you want to know?"

Sally hesitated. "It's relevant to Vivien Wilson's death and her husband's appeal. I can't say more than that."

"Excuse me." Baronick pulled out his phone and walked away.

"I think you ruffled his feathers." Adams leaned on the counter. "Wayne is right. Zigler is a loan shark, but we've never been able to hang a charge on him. He has a reputation of being willing to get dirty when his customers don't pay."

"He does his own kneecap breaking?" Duncan asked. In his experience, men like Zigler had goons to do the hard work for him.

"Surprisingly, yes. He's a one-man shop. He uses an ebony wood walking stick with a silver handle. You think it's an affectation. Until he cracks you with it." Adams nodded at Sally. "I gather you want to talk to him."

Sally buttoned her coat. "Want to? No. Have to? Unfortunately, yes."

"I advise against that."

"I don't have much of a choice." She glanced at Baronick, who was still on the phone. "Where does Zigler live?"

"He does business out of Brunswick." Adams ripped a sheet of paper off a pad by the register and wrote. "Here's the address. I suggest you don't go alone."

Sally accepted the paper with thanks. She faced Duncan. "Mind if we stop in Brunswick on our way home?" She didn't wait for a response and walked out of the restaurant.

Baronick came back. "You're going with her, aren't you? I don't need to tell you to stay alert." Suddenly, he laughed. "She really does keep you on your toes, doesn't she?"

Duncan rubbed his chin and sighed. "You have no idea."

* * *

172

While Sally drove to the address Chief Adams had supplied, she told Jim about her aborted attempt to talk to Zander Nelson.

"Didn't say a word, huh?" Jim looked at the map on his phone. "Perhaps I should make time while we're here to talk to Mr. Nelson."

"What makes you think he'll say anything to you?"

Jim put his phone away. "He might not. Then again, I have a badge, and I'm investigating a murder, not a Ponzi scheme. He might think he can play me for a sucker and say something that would help both of us." He pointed at her. "But you need to stay in the car this time. I mean it."

He'd said that before. It rarely happened that way. Sally would worry about that later. They arrived, and she parked on the street near Owen Zigler's place of business. She was out of the SUV and on the sidewalk before Jim got out.

"Sally, hold up." He eased out of his seat and laid a hand on her arm. "Let's talk about this. You heard what Pete Adams said."

"I'm not alone. You're here."

"I'm not exactly at my best right now." He lowered his hand. "Why do you have to see him today?"

"Because if he has information about Vivien Wilson, I need to hear it."

"I'm going to play devil's advocate." He crossed his arms. "You've been hired to present an appeal. What does Zigler have to do with that?"

He had a point. "Jim, I tried to stick to the one job. I did. Sure, Tanelsa made a few stylistic modifications to the language, but my intent was to do the one job." She paused.

"What happened?"

"I told you. I started looking at the facts, and they didn't add up. It wasn't only the contested Miranda warning. There were red flags all over the place." She began to enumerate them. "They didn't look for Vivien's lover. They didn't dig into her debt. No one even gave a second thought to the possibility that Vivien's death might have had something to do with whatever was going on at Laurel Mountain."

"Wilson said they didn't talk about it."

She gave him a look of disbelief. "Come on. There's a lot you and I don't discuss in detail. We still have a general idea of what's going on with our jobs. I bet you can tell me how many cases I have pending right now."

He thought a moment. "You're right. Next question. Why now? Send Zigler a subpoena and talk to him in court."

She put her hands on her hips. "Are you serious? Do you really think a man like this is going to obey a court order? Odds are he'd laugh, rip it up, and throw it in the garbage." She held up a hand. "Then yes, I get the cops to haul his ass in. More wasted time."

"It's not a waste. You just said why it's necessary."

She bit her lip. "But I don't have time to go through the hoops. Listen, please."

He lifted an eyebrow.

"Pennsylvania gives you thirty days after sentencing to file your notice of appeal. Those thirty days are up on Monday. It's now midday on Wednesday." She took a deep breath. "If Alec wins this appeal, it is very likely the original proceedings will be declared a mistrial, and the prosecution will refile charges. Wayne didn't say it in so many words, but I could read between the lines. With Dave still in the hospital, it's likely Tanelsa and I will have to take over. I need to know what I'm dealing with."

He watched her face. "What did Baronick say, exactly?"

She didn't answer.

"Ah, so he thinks Wilson is guilty, despite the botched Miranda warning." Jim shifted position. "Do you believe him?"

"I think he's very good at his job. He wouldn't say it if he didn't think it were true."

Jim's hazel eyes held her gaze. "But do *you* believe him?"

"I honestly don't know. I don't want to. But there's so much missing from the original investigation." She waved at the building. "I know this is headstrong and maybe a tad unwise."

"A *tad?*"

"Okay, more than that." She tried to smile. "But you're here. You're armed. It's the middle of the day in a moderately busy neighborhood. He's not going to kill me now, is he?"

Jim said nothing for a couple of moments. Then he loosened his gun in its holster. "All right. I once told you I'd always have your back, and I meant it. But this time, it's going to cost you."

"How much?"

"When I meet with Nelson, promise you'll stay in the damn car." He pointed at her. "No promise, and we don't go inside to see Zigler."

Shit. One look at Jim's expression and she knew he meant it. He could be just as stubborn as she was. He rarely did it with her, but she knew this was one time she'd either have to knuckle under or he'd stop her. Physically, if necessary, bad back and all. She held up her hands. "Okay, promise. Can we go in now?"

He held out an arm. "After you."

She wouldn't break her vow. She'd stay in the SUV while Jim interviewed Nelson. That didn't mean she wouldn't try to get Jim to give her any relevant information on the way home. He might well refuse.

But she'd try.

* * *

Sally opened the door to the building. The interior looked much like any other office, with a small reception area. There was even a ficus tree and a chair for visitors. The receptionist, however, looked nothing like what Sally would expect to find in a legitimate business. He was bulky, with a shaved head and dark eyes. His suit wasn't tailored, but the bulge under his left armpit was obvious.

She cleared her throat. "Good afternoon. I'm looking for Owen Zigler."

The guard rose. "You got an appointment?"

"No, but I'm not here to talk about money. I need to ask him a few questions." She held out her court credentials.

He squinted at the card. "What kind of questions?"

"About a client of his. Vivien Wilson."

The man growled and put his hand on the gun.

Jim brushed his jacket aside to show off his own weapon and held out his badge with the other. "Let's not make a scene, shall we? Ms. Castle only wants to talk. No need to get belligerent."

A man emerged from the back. "Stand down, Charlie." He took in the scene with a cool gaze. "I couldn't help but overhear. Ms. Castle, is it?"

Sally nodded. "That's me."

The man in front of her was urbane, dressed in a nice, understated gray suit, black shoes, and a blue shirt with a ruby-red tie. His dark hair was neatly combed, parted on the side. He appraised her through cool gray eyes. "Are you here to accuse me of being involved with Mrs. Wilson's death?"

She glanced at Jim, who stood stock-still, his hand still on his sidearm. She could feel his tension like a physical force. "No. I represent her husband, Alec. I have questions that do not seem to have been asked in the original police investigation."

Zigler looked her up and down. Then he beckoned. "Come back into my office. You can bring your police escort if you wish, but I have no plans to hurt you. It wouldn't help my business, you understand."

Sally felt the unspoken "yet" in the air but followed, reassured when Jim fell in behind her.

Zigler's office matched the outer room, understated and with a surprisingly corporate atmosphere. She sat in one of the upholstered chairs in front of a solid wood desk. There weren't any windows, but lamps in the corners provided ample light.

Jim took up a position behind her, his gun still readily accessible.

Zigler gave them a faint smile. "I did mean it, you know. May I get you something to drink? A glass of water?"

Sally shook her head. "No, thank you."

Jim didn't speak but gave a sharp, negative head motion.

Zigler resumed his seat. "Vivien Wilson. What would you like to ask?"

Sally folded her hands in her lap. "I have reason to believe she got a loan from you, a significant one. Twenty-five thousand dollars. Is that correct?"

"It is." Zigler sat back, fingers steepled in front of him.

"Had she paid it back or started repayment?" Another question Sally knew the answer to, but the loan shark's reaction would tell her as much as his words.

"No on both counts." He didn't move.

"Was she supposed to have done so?"

Zigler smiled faintly. "You're wondering if she got behind on her payments, and I took action. Is that it?"

Sally lifted her chin. "Did you?"

"Here's the thing, Ms. Castle." He sat forward and traced a pattern on his blotter. "My primary concern, in any business transaction, is to get my money back. That is very hard to do if the borrower is dead. Now. I do not have the powers of a regular bank. I can't put a lien on your house or garnish your wages if you fall behind. I have to rely on...other methods."

Jim made a sound in his throat.

Zigler's smile broadened. "I see your police friend knows what I'm talking about. If Mrs. Wilson had been found with a broken kneecap or arm, yes, you'd have reason to suspect me. But murder? Not my first option."

Sally weighed his words. "You said first option. Then you admit there are circumstances where it might become necessary. For example, if the borrower indicated she was going to contact the authorities? Would you risk a trial or cut and run?"

He laughed. "Touché, Ms. Castle. While I've never found it necessary, I admit that I might have to take more direct actions in extreme circumstances. But trust me. They would have to be *very* extreme. That was not the case with Mrs. Wilson. Yes, she was having difficulty with her repayment. It was nothing that couldn't be worked out. With time." He eyed her. "As it is, I had to write her off as a loss."

"Is it possible your employee got carried away?" Sally asked.

"I don't hire people who can't obey simple instructions. I also handle my own affairs. I learned that lesson a long time ago."

She pointed over her shoulder. "Is the man out front one of your collection agents?"

"Charlie?" Zigler laughed. "Oh, heavens no. He doesn't have the finesse needed for collections. Affinity for violence, yes, but I've told you. That's a last resort. No, you have to sweet-talk recalcitrant borrowers first, and

Charlie isn't much of a conversationalist. I told you. I prefer the personal touch. We've had a lovely talk, haven't we? Not a hint of unpleasantness. Nine times out of ten, that's what is needed."

She snuck a look at Jim. He stood stiffly, but whether that was tension or pain, she couldn't tell. His face gave nothing away. "One last question. Where were you on October fourth of last year, between five and eleven at night?"

The question elicited a peal of laughter from the loan shark. "Really, Ms. Castle. That was well over a year ago. I don't keep a calendar." He held up a hand. "Please don't bother to ask me about Charlie. I don't watch his movements. At least not that closely and not when he isn't running an errand for me."

Sally fought to stay cool. "Let me recap what you're saying. Vivien Wilson did indeed borrow a sizable sum of money from you, she had not paid it back, and it is *possible* you took steps to remedy that situation. And that things may have gotten out of hand as a result."

"You must be desperate, Ms. Castle. Alec Wilson was convicted by a jury of his peers. End of story. Now." Zigler stood and buttoned his jacket. He consulted a tasteful and surely expensive wristwatch. "I have real business to conduct. Can you show yourself out, or do I need to call Charlie?"

Jim stepped back, not a trace of discomfort on his face. "We know the way. Sally, let's go." He held out a hand, his other not far from the gun on his belt.

She rose and went without argument. Had she learned any facts? None beyond what she already knew.

But she didn't need to prove Owen Zigler was guilty to do her job. As far as she was concerned, however unlikely it was, Zigler was more than capable of murdering Vivien Wilson. Sally's one reservation was the method. Based on the interview, Sally thought Zigler would have been much more cold-blooded.

Unless he was trying to frame Alec.

Chapter Twenty-Eight

Duncan got back in the SUV with a sigh of relief. The meeting had not gone as badly as he'd feared. True, it was unlikely Zigler would have done anything with a state cop present, but the possibility was always there.

Sally consulted the navigation screen and made a turn. "Were you that worried?"

"How do you know I'm not simply glad to be sitting down on your nice heated seats?" He fished the tube of ibuprofen from his pocket and shook out three caplets.

"Different tone." She pointed. "Be careful you don't ruin your liver."

"Thank you, Dr. Castle. But you're thinking of Tylenol." He washed the pills down with the last of his now cold coffee. "It's been eight hours. I'll be okay. I have Zoe's word for it, and she used to be a paramedic. Are you satisfied with the results of the meeting?"

Sally seemed to weigh the question. "No. I mean, I get it. You don't murder a person who owes you money. At least a man like Zigler doesn't. If he killed every customer who fell behind on her payments, he'd be out of business. I suppose it's possible he'd kill a customer's loved one, but Alec isn't the one who's dead."

"You're right about that."

"But maybe something happened to make it an acceptable loss. I don't know, and Owen Zigler didn't give me any reason to dismiss the possibility." She turned into the parking lot for Laurel Mountain Insurance. "Do you think you'll be long? If not, I'll keep the engine running and the heat on."

"I hope it won't be a lengthy conversation. Why don't I text you?"

She shrugged. "I should probably do that anyway, so I don't freeze to death out here while I wait."

He paused, hand on the door. "No last-minute plea to accompany me?"

She held up her hands. "I promised. I can call T and get a status update."

Duncan eyed her, but she gave a winsome smile and pulled out her phone. He got out of the car. Outside, he took a deep breath. If anything, the muscles in his lower back felt tighter and more painful than last night. Maybe he should call his doctor now. Except he had a case to solve. He could tough it out until this was done. Or at least until next week. He wouldn't get an appointment quickly anyway.

Inside, he stopped at the desk nearest the door. Showing his badge, he asked, "Is Alexander Nelson in?"

"Oh." The young woman's face paled. "Um, he asked not to be disturbed."

"Is he meeting with a client or something?"

"No. He just doesn't want to be bothered."

Duncan put away the badge wallet. "Unless he's with a customer, I'm afraid I'll have to insist."

The young woman opened her mouth, then closed it. A splotch of color appeared on each cheek. She got up and went to the back of the room. She opened a door and leaned in. A minute later, she came back, followed by a forty-ish-year-old man with prematurely gray hair dressed in a dark suit. She went back to work without a word.

The man did not extend his hand. "Are you the state trooper?"

"I am. Trooper Jim Duncan. I'd appreciate a few minutes of your time."

"On the advice of my attorney—"

"I got it." Duncan held up a hand. "I'm not here about your SEC troubles, Mr. Nelson."

Nelson blinked. "You're not?"

"That's not my circus. I have questions about another matter."

"What?"

"The murder of a man named Kyle Palmer."

Nelson was silent for a long moment. "I don't think I'm familiar with that name."

"I'd rather not have this conversation in front of your employees." Duncan gestured to the room. "Is there somewhere we can talk privately? Maybe your office?"

Nelson hesitated. "I suppose so. Heidi, this time, I really don't want to be disturbed. Understand?"

Heidi nodded.

"This way." Nelson led Duncan to the office in the back and closed the door. "Now, Trooper. Have a seat, if you wish, although I can't imagine this will be a long talk. But you insisted. I repeat: I don't think I know Kyle Palmer."

Duncan sat in a plush leather chair and took out his notebook. "You don't think or you don't know? Marsdale isn't a big town, Mr. Nelson."

Nelson took refuge behind the desk. He folded his hands on the blotter. "He's not a Laurel Mountain client."

"That's not what I asked. Do you know him?" Duncan held out his phone to show Palmer's picture. "I have a photo here if you need to refresh your memory."

Nelson barely glanced at it. "I don't know him."

"Alec Wilson did. They were neighbors."

"I haven't talked to Alec in quite some time. Not since before his wife's murder."

"Wilson never mentioned him? He never stopped in for a quote?" Duncan watched the other man for tells. "You're the only insurance company in town, aren't you? In fact"—Duncan consulted his notes—"you provided renter's insurance for the apartment Palmer rented. Do you have an office in Farmington?"

Nelson's lips barely moved. "We do."

"Wouldn't Mr. Palmer have had to stop in to sign a policy?"

A brief pause. "Yes."

Duncan sat back. "Then maybe you know him as Ellis Martingdon."

"Sorry, no."

Duncan thought a moment. "Do you go over to Fayette County often?"

"No, I have a branch manager." Nelson consulted his watch. "Is that all?"

Duncan's gut said Nelson was lying. "Sorry to bother you. I guess I'll stop and talk to your manager over in Farmington. Good day." He half rose.

"Wait."

I knew it. Duncan lowered himself. "Yes?"

"I forgot until a second ago. Yes, I knew Kyle, but only slightly. He stopped in here to price a car insurance policy last year. He couldn't afford the premiums." Nelson ran his tongue over his lips. "I hadn't seen him in a long while. I understood he'd moved."

"He did." Duncan didn't elaborate on Palmer's new identity. He rose again. "Thank you for your time. I'll see myself out."

"I'm glad I was able to save you a trip. I'm sure you want to move as quickly as possible on a murder case."

Duncan repeated his thanks and left. Outside, he held up a finger in Sally's direction and called Cavendish.

"What's up? You headed back?"

"Yes, but I want you to look into something. Got a pen?"

"Hold on." It sounded like Cavendish was rummaging in a drawer. "Go."

"Look up the address for Laurel Mountain Insurance's Farmington office. Go pay them a visit and see if Palmer ever stopped in."

Cavendish muttered as she repeated the instructions. "Got a lead?"

He told her about the conversation with Nelson. "He seemed rather intent that we not go to that office. I want to know why."

"I'm on it. See you in about an hour?"

"Yes." Duncan ended the call. Then he got into the toasty warm SUV and sagged into the leather seat. "Let's go."

"You get what you need?" Sally put the SUV in drive.

"Maybe. Cavendish is looking into something." He eyed her. "Want a tip?"

She shot him a look. "Always."

"Get a quote on a new insurance policy for this car. I suggest Laurel Mountain Insurance in Farmington."

"But I don't—" Sally broke off. "Thanks. I might do that."

"No charge." He leaned back into the seat and closed his eyes.

* * *

Sally drove for half an hour through swirling flakes of snow while Jim dozed in the passenger seat. On the one hand, she really wanted to talk to him. On the other, she knew his back was hurting more than he let on. Other people couldn't see past the "tough guy" cop exterior, but she had been around him long enough to catch the minute tightening around his mouth when he moved and the undercurrent of discomfort in his voice. She would finish her move by herself. No way would she let him pick up another box.

On cue, he opened his eyes and rubbed his face. "Where are we?"

"About thirty minutes out."

He looked around. "Is that your water?"

"Yes, but help yourself. I haven't even opened it."

He twisted off the cap and chugged. "Sorry I fell asleep on you."

"I think you earned it." The snowfall was light but steady under light gray skies. Her wipers kept pace, but it was the kind of weather that brought several inches by nightfall. She focused on the road but risked a glance at Jim out of the corner of her eye. "I'll do the rest of the move on my own. Maybe Tanelsa can help me. Or I'll hire someone, which I should have done in the first place."

"Don't be ridiculous. You can't hire anybody before Friday." He took another drink. "You know I'm not holding a grudge. Shit happens."

"I still feel guilty."

"Well, stop it." He set the water bottle down and pulled out his notebook. "You say Wilson hasn't talked to you about the SEC thing?"

"Not much." Since Jim wasn't investigating the fraud and the topic had nothing to do with Alec's murder appeal, she went on. "T and I met with Agent Gaskell. He confirmed that Alec was the one who reported the Ponzi scheme at Laurel Mountain. The feds never followed up with him because he was hip-deep in a murder trial. They wanted to try and make the case without him."

Jim reached for the water again. "Could they?"

"After our meeting, I don't think so. A man convicted of murder doesn't

183

make a great witness, but...." She trailed off.

"Better than none at all." Jim put his notebook away. "It'll be interesting to see what the Laurel Mountain Insurance manager says about Palmer. It's the one point of contact."

"Mmm." Sally thought about her next question. "If I ask you for an opinion, would you give it?"

"Depends on what you want, but probably."

She concentrated as a car driving too fast for the conditions passed her. "Why would a judge deny a motion to suppress a statement made without the suspect having been properly Mirandized?" She didn't look at him, but his silence told her he was considering the question.

"Couple of different reasons," he finally said. "The defense argument might not have been strong enough. Maybe the prosecution convinced him, the judge, that Miranda didn't apply. I mean, it's an argument, right? Both sides weigh in."

"It is." She hesitated. "Could the judge be on the take?"

"Sure. You're talking about the denied motion in the Wilson trial. Who was the judge?" Jim tipped the water bottle to take a drink.

"Judge Holtz."

Jim choked and sprayed water over the dash. "Sorry." He wiped it up with his coat. "If you asked me to name the judge who is the least likely to be crooked, I'd say Holtz, hands down. The guy practically has a stick up his ass." He paused. "Have you ever argued a case in front of him?"

Sally nodded. "A couple of pleas. One case where the prosecution withdrew the charges due to lack of evidence. He didn't have a sense of humor or anything, but he was okay."

"You wouldn't get a good picture from that." He drank again. "You're familiar with the phrase judge-shopping, right?"

"Of course."

"Holtz was a favorite among troopers in the Uniontown barracks who were looking for a sympathetic judge when writing search warrants. I imagine he still is." Jim screwed the lid back on the bottle. "I know he signed off on more than one warrant that would have been denied by anyone else.

184

Judges are supposed to be impartial, but Holtz definitely has a reputation for giving the prosecution and law enforcement the benefit of the doubt."

Sally gripped the wheel. She knew of the practice. She hated it but was realistic enough to understand why it happened. In a perfect world, defense counsel would win that argument every time. But the world wasn't perfect. "In other words, Judge Holtz believes that if a defendant is in front of him, that person must have done *something*, so he sides with the state every time."

"That's going a bit far. Let's say Holtz has a very generous interpretation of probable cause and leave it at that."

"Did he ever sign any of your search warrants?" She couldn't keep the accusatory note out of her voice.

"Yes, but I hope you know me better by now." His voice sounded sober. "I always try to make sure my affidavits are clean and supported by facts."

"I'm sorry. Knee jerk reaction." She risked another glance in his direction. To her relief, she couldn't detect any anger in his expression.

"Apology accepted. What did Baronick tell you?"

"That they got the right guy. He didn't come out and admit it, but I get the feeling he wasn't thrilled with how it all happened, either. Regardless, he was quite certain Alec Wilson is guilty." She thought again about Wayne Baronick. He *was* a good cop. She felt it in her bones. He'd made that statement not out of arrogance or hubris, but with the simple conviction of a good investigator. "He's sharp. At least, that's my impression. I also got the feeling he knows he's good."

"According to Pete, he is. Not that Pete would tell Baronick that. And yes, confidence is not his weak spot." Jim grinned.

"Then you don't believe Holtz was on the take or, say, involved in the Ponzi scheme and wanted Alec out of the way?"

"I won't say it's impossible. I will say I think it's unlikely. Personally, I think Holtz is a jerk. That doesn't mean he's bent." He paused. "It also doesn't mean he wasn't wrong. When he denied Dave Sturgess's motion, I mean."

It was a small consolation, but not much. Because even if Alec's statement to the police should have been inadmissible, he could still be guilty.

Chapter Twenty-Nine

Duncan thought about Sally's question as they pulled into Uniontown. He understood why she'd asked. In her mind, it was crystal clear: The motion to suppress should have been granted, and any competent legal mind would see that. Therefore, if a judge's decision allowed the statement to stand, that judge must have an ulterior motive.

Duncan was not ashamed of his profession. When he'd worn the gray uniform, he'd done so with pride. He believed every word of the Call of Honor. He was also not stupid or naïve. He'd had the good luck to serve with many honorable men and women over his nearly fifteen years on the job, both those in uniform and on the bench. He'd also known some less-than-perfect examples. People like Corporal "Golden Gary" Sheffield, who valued politics and ladder-climbing over true service, or Judge Holtz, who had a definite prosecution bias visible in his actions, if not his words.

Fortunately, Duncan had never served alongside any truly corrupt or malicious troopers. What Georgia Munk said was true, though. Black men had good reason to distrust law enforcement. Duncan could only hope that if he ever found himself in a situation where the rights of the accused came second to getting an arrest, he'd have the integrity to do the right thing.

Sally broke his train of thought. "Are you sure you want me to drop you off in Uniontown? I have enough time to take you somewhere."

"No, thanks. Cavendish texted and said she would meet us." He gathered up his things. "What's the plan for tonight?"

"What do you mean?"

"There's still stuff at your apartment. The Jeep is full, but if you can fit two

186

large dogs in this technological marvel, I'm sure it can handle a few boxes." He held up a hand. "And don't give me that 'I'll do it myself' bullshit."

Her answering smile was weak. "How about we not promise to meet at a specific time, and we'll play it by ear? You've got a murder to crack. I have that appeal to run through. Tanelsa has made enough tweaks that I want to make sure we've got our presentation down pat. I'll text you." She pulled into the parking lot of the Panera.

An unmarked state Ford waited nearby, billows of white exhaust streaming in the cold air. Duncan leaned over and gave Sally a kiss. "Deal. Good luck. Remember, I love you."

"I love you, too. Tell Jenny I said hi."

"Will do." He got out of the SUV, closed the door, and knocked on the roof. He watched as Sally pulled away, then headed over to the Ford and slid into the passenger seat. "Afternoon." The seats were not nearly as nice as Sally's car and the ibuprofen had barely taken the edge off the pain in his back. Perhaps he had done something more serious than pull a muscle.

Or maybe he needed to slow down, rest, and spend a few hours on his couch with a heating pad. No, ice. Zoe Chambers-Adams had said ice. Fat chance of that happening. Sally might have a point about the boxes, though.

"You look like something the cat dragged in," Cavendish said as she handed him a cup of coffee.

"I take back everything bad I ever said about you." He accepted it with gratitude.

"You damn well better, or we'll have words, buster."

"Did you go over to Laurel Mountain?"

She put the car in drive. "I haven't had the chance yet. I did swing by Frawley's duplex in Lemont Furnace. Someone is living there. Someone with a black Ford Raptor."

The big black truck. Duncan glanced at the clock. Three-thirty. "When does Laurel Mountain close?"

"According to their social media page, five." She checked traffic and turned out of the parking lot. "I'm thinking Elijah first, insurance second. We're already running the risk of Elijah disappearing again. Laurel Mountain isn't going anywhere."

"Agreed."

Even with the deteriorating road conditions because of the snow, it took less than fifteen minutes to arrive at the duplex. There was nothing remarkable about it, except for the single slush-and-salt spattered truck at the curb.

Cavendish parked behind it. She held her thumb and forefinger a quarter inch apart. "You sure you're okay to do this? You look this close to collapse."

"I'll be okay, as long as I don't have to wrestle or chase him. If he does a runner, let him go. You're sure that's Munk's truck?"

"I ran the plate last time I was here. It's his. At least if we lose him, we've got something for a BOLO." She unsnapped her seatbelt. "Let's do this."

"I thought Mrs. Munk said someone picked Elijah up."

"She did. But he could've easily loaned it to a buddy that day. Or it was a different truck."

They approached the house. Duncan loosened his Glock and stood off to the side as Cavendish rapped on the door.

"Elijah Munk. Pennsylvania State Police. Open up." Nothing. She knocked again. "Come on, Elijah. We know you're in there. We just want to talk."

The door opened to reveal a man roughly three inches shorter than Duncan. Even dressed in jeans, boots, and a T-shirt, Duncan could tell there wasn't an ounce of fat on his body, which showed evidence of long hours at the gym. His hair was cropped short, and his dark brown eyes focused on Cavendish. "You got ID?"

Cavendish flipped open her badge wallet. He opened the storm door and leaned forward as though inspecting the identification. With the sudden strike of a snake, he shoved the door wide, knocking into Duncan. He stumbled backward, which set off a searing pain in his lower back.

The man he assumed was Elijah rushed outside and muscled Cavendish aside. But she managed to hook her foot around his ankle and sent him sprawling into a pile of snow. Before he could recover, Cavendish scrambled over, knelt on his back, and pulled his arms around. "You okay?" She threw the question over her shoulder to Duncan.

He gritted his teeth. "I should have anticipated that. Sorry."

"No worries. As long as you're still standing, and I don't have to call an ambulance." She pulled out her cuffs and snapped them around the suspect's wrists.

Elijah twisted. "Lemme go. I ain't done nothing."

"Get up. You're Elijah, right? Hasn't anybody ever told you not to use a double negative?" She nudged him toward the car. "Is anyone in the house with you?"

"I'm alone. Where are you taking me?"

"See, that's the thing. We wanted to have a friendly talk. We could have done this at your place. By charging out and assaulting an officer of the law, now we're going to the Uniontown booking station." She opened the rear door of the Ford sedan and guided him inside. Then she turned to Duncan. "You should go home. Seriously. We'll hit Laurel Mountain tomorrow. I'll question this punk and fill you in later."

"I'll be okay once we get to Uniontown." He held up his hands. "I'm fine as long as I don't move."

Cavendish circled the car. "Yeah, because that's what we have. A nice, sedentary job. You are a stubborn SOB. Anybody ever tell you that?"

He exhaled, the worst of the pain ebbing with the action. "Many times. On second thought, I'm going to stay here. I'll freeze the scene myself, get a search warrant by phone, and see what's inside. I'll figure out how to catch up to you."

Cavendish didn't respond, but her look of disapproval said volumes. She got into the car and drove off.

Duncan pulled out his phone and called in to start the affidavit process. His gut told him time wasn't on their side.

* * *

After leaving Jim, Sally headed to her office. "T, I'm back." She went into the main area.

189

Tanelsa was on the phone, repeating "uh-huh" as she scribbled notes. "Thanks for the update." She hung up.

"Who were you talking to?"

"The warden up at the county jail. I got more details on Alec's stabbing." Tanelsa stuck her pen in the holder. "You first. Was it a worthwhile trip?"

"I think so." Sally pulled her chair over to Tanelsa's desk and filled her in on what Detective Baronick had told her.

At the end, Tanelsa snorted. "Of course, he's sure they arrested the right man. He can't very well say anything else, can he?"

Sally tapped her thumbs together. "No, but I got the feeling this was more than the Blue Line closing around one of their own. Face it: Alec has the magic triangle. Means, motive, and opportunity."

Tanelsa pointed to the conference room, where the whiteboard was still covered with notes. "Plenty of other folks with motive. Means? She was stabbed with her own damn knife. Anyone with her could have used it."

"Anyone *with* her. So far, that's just Alec." Sally loosened her hair and shook it out. "What did the warden say? Anything new?"

Tanelsa picked up her notes. "No. They examined the CCTV of the yard. They saw the attacker. He walked up to Alec. They talked for a few minutes. You can see the other inmate move to block the camera, then walk away as though nothing had happened. Alec flinches, and a moment later, he collapses. Security swarmed in, and that was the end of it."

"What was the weapon?"

"Would you believe a toothbrush? The assailant had filed the end to a point."

Sally drummed her fingers on the arm of her chair. "Who is the inmate?"

"That's the kicker." Tanelsa sat back. "They aren't sure."

"You've got to be kidding me."

"Not in the slightest." Tanelsa rocked in her chair. "The guards on duty say they saw a guy in a prison uniform walk up to Alec. His hair was dark and cut short, but he kept his face turned away. There were too many people in the yard for the guards to be watching every single person all the time, and the area was crowded. Lots of prisoners out taking advantage of half way

190

decent weather. By the time the guards saw how badly Alec was injured, the attacker had fled the scene."

"Don't they have video from the yard?"

"They do. But all they can really see is a medium-sized White guy with dark hair come over, talk for a bit, and walk off. Like I said, he kept his face away from the camera, so that tells us he knows where they are in the yard. That could be anyone who's been an inmate for more than a few days. Prison officials can't see any identifying numbers on his uniform. And while the video isn't the worst in the world, it also isn't military satellite-grade quality."

"The guy had to have blood on his clothes or something."

"They detained and questioned every inmate who was known to be in the yard at the time of the incident. They got a shit-ton of denials, and nobody's prison duds had blood on them."

"Alec gave them a name. What does that person say?"

"He insists he was in the weight room the entire time and wasn't even outside. He repeated that story six ways from Sunday. When asked about being alone and working without a spotter, he said he wasn't bench-pressing and didn't need one."

Sally blew out a breath and slapped the chair. "This is ridiculous. The inmate is lying. I suppose Alec could be, too, since he doesn't have a great track record for telling the truth. I don't know why he wouldn't be honest this time, though."

"Maybe he's scared."

"Of what?"

"Maybe this other inmate has friends." Tanelsa tossed her notepad on her desk. "Alec's safe in the hospital now. But eventually, he'll be released. He might be afraid of another attack."

"That's insane." Sally scoffed. "They'll put his assailant in solitary. Or they could even put Alec there for his own safety."

"Assuming the suspect was working alone."

The statement stunned Sally into silence. "If this wasn't an inmate argument, there's only one reason Alec would be attacked."

"To shut him up. Permanently."

The two women looked at each other. Sally stood.

"Where are you going?" Tanelsa asked.

Sally slipped into her coat. "The jail. It's time that man stopped messing with us and came clean." She headed for the door.

* * *

After Cavendish left, Duncan returned to the house. Standing was uncomfortable in the extreme, but sitting on the concrete porch wouldn't be much better. A cheap lawn chair, the folding kind with an aluminum frame and vinyl webbing, leaned against the house. He unfolded it and sat. Legally, he couldn't begin the search until the authorization came through. He might as well rest up.

Fortunately, it didn't take long for the warrant approval to arrive. He went inside, shut the door, and dropped onto the couch. He took a moment to sit and wait for his back muscles to return to something resembling their normal state of being. When Elijah had thrown open the door, Duncan had twisted so he could grab the support that held up the porch roof in an attempt not to land on his ass in the snow. He should have taken the fall. He doubted Elijah had seen him. It was more likely that Elijah had been trying to make a break past Cavendish. Duncan had been collateral damage.

After a couple of minutes, the stiffness in his back had reduced enough that he felt ready to wriggle into a pair of nitrile gloves and start work. He didn't think it would take very long. Frawley didn't seem to have a lot of possessions and Elijah hadn't brought a lot of his own.

Duncan started in the bedroom. An oversized duffel bag overflowed with clothing, none of which looked big enough to fit a six-foot-tall, muscular man like Elijah. Frawley's? The guess was confirmed when Duncan opened the drawers, which contained an assortment of dark jeans, cotton shirts, socks, and underwear. It looked as though Elijah had dumped out his friend's possessions and taken over, rather than live out of a bag. Duncan ran his hand through the clothes. Nothing.

Next up was the bathroom. Aside from a water-stained plastic shower curtain and a mirror that had seen better days, the only things there were a bottle of men's body wash, a towel, a washcloth, toothbrush and paste, and a shaving kit in a leather bag. A popular brand of men's deodorant and body spray nestled next to a five-bladed razor and a can of shaving cream.

The second bedroom was almost empty. The bed was unmade, and the naked mattress displayed stains that Duncan didn't want to think about the origins of. There was an empty chest of drawers beside a closet that held only a few bent metal hangers.

The kitchen was slightly more promising, although it looked as though Elijah ate out a lot. The fridge contained only beer, half a gallon of milk, and a piece of cheese that had turned into a science experiment. A single box of dry cereal was on the counter, and a bowl and spoon were on the drying rack beside the sink. Piles of junk mail covered the table. There was also a calendar. Today's date was circled with the notation "PGH INTL AA2789 7PM." It must be an arriving flight. Duncan pulled out his phone and searched. Sure enough, American Airlines Flight 2789 was scheduled to arrive from Miami tonight at seven. "I don't think you'll be making your pickup, Elijah," Duncan said. Who was coming in from Miami? Everything else looked untouched.

He hit pay dirt in the freezer. A plain spiral notebook listed what looked like inventory written in simple code. Columns of letters, maybe shorthand for drugs, next to a column of numbers preceded by a plus sign. Another column of numbers had a dash in front of them. Amounts in and out? A third column had dollar amounts followed by a slash and either the mark for ounce or gram. Duncan paged through the book. He'd bet the next round at Whiskey & Rye it was a record of inventory in, out, and maybe the street value per unit.

Stuck behind the last page of the book was a piece of paper that had a brown stain covering half of it. Duncan sniffed. Beer. On it was written an address. 79834 RJ Lilley Drive.

Kyle Palmer's address.

Chapter Thirty

It was nearing four when Sally and Tanelsa arrived at the infirmary of the county jail and asked to speak to Alec. A security guard sat nearby, watching a video of the interior.

"We don't usually do visiting hours after three," the nurse informed them.

Tanelsa opened her mouth, but Sally laid a hand on her arm. "We're Mr. Wilson's lawyers. We were here earlier. It's imperative that we speak to him."

The nurse sighed. "I'll see if he's willing to talk to you."

"No, you won't," Tanelsa said, voice sharp. "You will inform Mr. Wilson that we're here, and he's going to see us whether he wants to or not." She pointed at the screen. "And turn that off. This is a privileged conversation."

The guard tapped the monitor. "No sound. Injured or not, we keep an eye on all the inmates. We won't be able to hear you, but if anything goes wrong, I'll see it."

The nurse's disdainful expression left no doubt as to her feelings, but she disappeared. A moment later, she returned. "You can go in."

Before Tanelsa could retort, Sally intervened. "Thank you."

Alec was in the same bed at the end of the ward. No other inmates were currently patients. "What do you want now? I told you everything before."

Sally set her briefcase on the floor. "Alec, playtime is over. Who stabbed you?"

He glanced at Tanelsa, then back at Sally, before focusing on his hands. "I told the warden who it was."

"Yes, and he insists he was in the weight room. Either he's lying, or you

194

are." Tanelsa sounded like she'd reached the end of her rope. "So help me God, if it turns out to be you, I will walk out that door. I told you before I would. I wasn't kidding then, and I'm definitely not now."

"Tanelsa put it a little more bluntly than I would have, but she's not wrong." Sally leaned forward. "You have to throw us a bone here, Alec. We aren't magicians. Even if you win this appeal, it is very likely the DA will refile charges, and you'll be back on trial."

He looked up, startled. "That can happen?"

"Yes." Sally let that sink in.

He swallowed, his eyes wide. The phrase *deer in headlights* described him perfectly. "Where do you want me to start?"

Tanelsa sat down and took a legal pad and pen out of her bag.

"Tell us about Vivien. You said before her lover was Dom Rossi. Is that Dominic Rossi from Pittsburgh?"

"The one and only." Alec lay back. "Last year, Vivien and I, well, it wasn't good. I was working a lot. She was, too. Or so I thought. She spent a lot of time in Pittsburgh over the summer. Working with a new client, she claimed. I was distracted at work for those months with the Ponzi thing. I told you about that. But I came home one night, must have been the end of September, and he was at the house. Rossi. I recognized his picture from the paper. Vivien claimed it was a business meeting, but it didn't look like any business I was familiar with." He closed his eyes. "I couldn't get it out of my mind, so I searched her phone. Vivien's passcodes are always her birthday. I've told her not to do that."

"I'm guessing you found proof." He had been lying. Sally failed to find any satisfaction in having her suspicions confirmed.

"Oh yes. They'd been texting. The notes were pretty clear as to what they were about. I didn't know what to do at first." He slumped. "Then, in the middle of September, Rossi showed up at the office. He taunted me, saying how pathetic it was I couldn't keep my own wife satisfied. I wanted to punch him in the mouth. I told Vivien she needed to call it off. That Rossi was just playing with her. She refused, said she wanted a divorce. She was ready to go public and claimed Rossi was as well. We bickered for a couple of weeks.

The night she died, well, that was the high point. Or low point, depending on your perspective."

Sally, however, had fixated on his earlier statement. "Wait. Rossi was at Laurel Mountain? Why?"

"To rub things in my face, I guess." Alec shrugged. "Or maybe Colonials just stick together."

Sally looked at Tanelsa, who seemed equally caught off guard. "Do you think Vivien was right? About Rossi?"

"No." Alec's response was swift. "The man is running for state office. He is married. His wife is loaded. Why would he divorce her? He'd get nothing, and Vivien certainly wasn't going to compensate for that. And his political career would be in the shitter. Judging by the people I know in Marsdale, folks are still mostly conservative in rural Pennsylvania."

Finally. A perfect motive for murder. Rossi had a lot to lose if Vivien went public with the affair. "All that is good. Did you know Vivien was in debt?"

"No, but it makes sense. She was short-tempered that spring, more than usual. A lot of bills came to the house stamped second notice. That's what they do for unpaid stuff, right?" Alec smoothed the covers. "Suddenly, they stopped. I asked her about it, and she brushed me off. She told me I'd imagined it all, and everything was fine. I kind of lost track of it, to be honest. I was too worried about work and then the affair."

Sally made a note to look at Vivien's phone records again for a connection to Owen Zigler. "I'm glad you brought up work. You told us before about what happened with the SEC. Think hard. Did you ever talk about it with Vivien?"

He scrunched up his face. "I...I don't think so. She knew I was stressed, but I remember not wanting to drag her into it. I thought she wouldn't take me seriously and would laugh. The way she always did when I tried to do something. But now that I think back...."

Sally waited. When he didn't continue, she prompted him to go on.

"It had to be summer. July or August? I was still looking into the Ponzi angle, since I hadn't heard from the SEC, but I hadn't found out about her affair yet. One night, I left my office to go to the bathroom. When I came back, she was there, standing at my desk. I asked what she was doing and she, I don't know, jumped a little, I guess. She said she'd come in to tell me dinner was ready and was wondering where I'd gone. I told her she had no business going through my papers and she insisted she hadn't, that she'd only been in the office for a few seconds. She said something about how it didn't matter, that I couldn't be involved in anything important, given how low my position was in the company." He twisted the bedsheets. "I had no reason to disbelieve her, but now…I don't know."

This might be the connection Sally was looking for. "If she had snooped, do you think she would have gone to your boss?"

"She hardly knows him. Why would she do that?" Realization dawned on his face. "Oh my God. You said she was in debt. Do you think she blackmailed Zander? Is that why she's dead? She told him she knew about the Ponzi scheme, and he killed her?"

"I don't know. It's another possibility."

He stared at her. "I do know who she absolutely would have told. Dom."

"What does her paramour have to do with it?" Tanelsa asked.

Alec looked at her. "I told you. He wants to go to Harrisburg. One of his talking points is weeding out corruption. If he could expose a big scandal like this, he'd be a hero. The common man taking on the companies exploiting John Q. Public." He reddened. "Plus, it was an opportunity for them to make fun of me. That I thought I could actually do something about it, whatever *it* turned out to be."

Sally and Tanelsa stared at each other. They'd come looking for more evidence against one alternative suspect for Vivien's murder. They were leaving with an additional option. They were incredibly lucky.

Or it was all incredibly convenient.

"Final question," Sally said. Should she push her luck? "Who really stabbed you? Don't give us this nonsense about the other inmate, whatever his name was. You know, the guy who swears he was lifting weights."

He slumped. "The guy who attacked me was Brian Kolchak. He's a guard at the jail."

That took Sally by surprise. "A guard? Why?"

"No clue. You'd have to ask him. He works the eight-to-four shift. You've probably missed him, but I'm sure you can get his address." He looked from Sally to Tanelsa. "I'm not lying. I have no idea why he'd do that and even less of a clue why he'd wear a prison uniform to do it."

To say Alec Wilson had not been entirely truthful would be an understatement. But one look in his eyes and Sally knew this time, he was telling the truth.

Chapter Thirty-One

Duncan's solution to his problem of how to get to the Uniontown booking station was simple. He called the local State Police barracks and asked for a ride. After the uniformed trooper dropped him off, he took the bagged evidence from Elijah's house and went in search of Cavendish. He found her in the bullpen area, chatting with one of the Uniontown patrol officers.

She broke off her conversation when he walked up. "How'd it go?"

"Not bad." He told her about his findings, in order of importance.

"Well, if he's the muscle for Ellis, Lucas's so-called major player, no surprise about the drug information." She tilted her head. "He had the address, huh? You think he was the guy Palmer was running from?"

"I'm not sure. I think if that was the case, I'd have heard about it when I met Pete Adams for lunch today. But he'd never heard of Ellis, which tells me they weren't operating in Mon County. If that's the case, Palmer would have run to them, not away, when he moved." He checked his watch. How could it have only been four hours since his last dose of ibuprofen? Could you take Advil more frequently? "I find it more likely that Palmer was escaping from his alleged botched bank robbery partner, this Gus 'Dinky' Lamb, and ran afoul of Ellis here in Fayette County."

"That reminds me." She snapped her fingers and pulled out her notebook. "We can cross Ellis off the list. He was arrested this morning in Miami. They caught him buying a shipment of Colombian cocaine in a DEA bust. He's been there for two weeks."

The flight noted in Munk's papers. "Ryan Ellis might not have pulled the trigger, but Elijah could have been acting on orders."

"True. But we're not going to have much luck convincing the DEA to send Ellis here for questioning on a murder rap. Not when they've got their hooks into him." She flipped her notebook shut. "It's almost five. Too late to go to Laurel Mountain. It'll take you fifteen minutes to walk to the car."

"I told you, I'm fine. Just a little stiff from riding in a patrol car." He sold the lie for all it was worth.

Cavendish crossed her arms and raised her eyebrows. She wasn't buying the story. "I saw you walk in here. You look worse than my grandpa. I say we talk to Elijah and call it a day. Besides, don't you and Sally have more moving to do? Not that you're in a condition to lift anything heavier than a jewelry box."

"Ha, ha." He pulled out his phone. No message from Sally, so he sent one to her. **Hey, you working late? Or should we try to get some work done?**

The bubbles indicating she was responding appeared almost immediately. **I'm fried. Might as well do a little mindless labor. But you are forbidden from lifting anything. Give me until five-thirty.**

"I've got some time. Sally can't get me for another forty-five minutes." He slipped his phone into his pocket.

Cavendish tapped the desk she had been leaning on. "Then let's go talk to Elijah Munk."

They were seated in an interview room when one of the Uniontown cops led Elijah inside. He was still cuffed, his face expressionless, but his dark eyes betrayed a spark of curiosity.

"Have a seat." Cavendish gestured to the empty chair. "You weren't very nice to us earlier, Elijah."

His voice came out in a deep bass. "Nothing to talk about."

Duncan took out a picture of the ghost gun. "We beg to differ. Does this look familiar?"

"It's a handgun."

Duncan watched the suspect. They might have been discussing the weather for all the interest he showed. "It belonged to your buddy, Lucas

Jones."

"He's in jail."

"We know that," Cavendish said. "Funny thing. He told us *you* knew where he'd hidden this gun."

Elijah switched his heavy-lidded gaze to her. "Did you find my fingerprints on it?"

Neither trooper answered.

Elijah smiled, his teeth very white against his dark skin. "Didn't think so. What's the big deal about that gun?"

Duncan shifted a smidge but still masked his physical discomfort. "Someone used it to kill a man."

"Oh? And that interests me how?"

Cavendish pounced. "Because we found his address in your buddy Frawley's duplex. You know, the one you've been living in." She set down the evidence bag with the calendar. "Along with this. By the way, don't worry about picking up your boss. The DEA is giving him a room tonight. And for several nights to come, I expect."

Elijah didn't flinch.

The man was either a stone-cold killer, or he didn't know Kyle Palmer was dead. "This is the murdered man. Do you recognize him?" Once again, Duncan pulled up the picture on his phone and showed it.

Elijah looked at the picture but remained silent.

Duncan tried again. "Witnesses saw your truck the night of the murder. What business did you have with Kyle Palmer?"

Again, no response.

Cavendish leaned on the table. "Come on, Elijah. We can put you on the scene. We know you had access to this gun. Palmer was trying to bust in on the drug scene, take business away from your boss. Why don't you talk to us? It'll be a lot easier on you. If Ellis sent you to pull the trigger, why not roll on him? He's not going to come home anytime soon, not if the DEA has anything to say about it. Why not play ball with us?"

Elijah gave a slow blink. "Fine, I'll tell you something."

Duncan took out his notepad.

"I want a lawyer."

Well, shit.

* * *

The minute Sally picked Duncan up, he could tell she was distracted. Her mumbled hello, a kiss that felt like an afterthought, and the abstracted look in her eye told him that she might physically be in her old apartment, but her mind was miles away.

He stood in her kitchen, phone in hand. "Pepperoni, sausage, sardines, spinach, kale, and pickles?"

She didn't turn around. "Yeah, that sounds good."

He laid down the phone. "Sally, are you even listening to me?"

"Of course I am." She faced him, box in hand. "What did you say?"

"I listed some of the most disgusting toppings for a pizza, and you didn't even blink."

She gave a half-hearted grin. "Sorry. My mind is still at work. Just the usual is good."

He walked over to her. "I ordered twenty minutes ago. Wow. You really are checked out. At least when it comes to this." He gestured at the boxes littered around the apartment.

"Oh, God. I'm sorry. It's just…I can't seem to focus on anything." Tears welled in her eyes. Unchecked, they leaked out and ran down her cheeks.

Duncan grabbed the box. "Give me that."

"No, you can't. Your back."

He tugged it out of her hands and let it drop on the floor. "Talk to me."

She dashed a hand across her eyes. "Jim, I had no idea what I was getting into. When Dave asked me to present this appeal, I thought *no problem, easy,* and now it's such a mess." She started crying in earnest.

Sally never did this. He'd seen her in a lot of scary situations: a gun to her head, tied to a chair by a deranged stalker, and standing next to him as he faced down a killer. Never had she burst into full-fledged tears. "Why are you crying?"

"It's what happens when I'm frustrated. And angry." She wiped her cheeks, but the waterworks didn't stop. "I'm both right now."

He had no idea what was going on with the Wilson case, but it had to be awful. "Come here." He folded her into his arms. He'd been told over and over, mostly by his ex-wife, that he sucked at this part of relationships. Everything he could think of to say sounded lame, so he held his tongue and let her cry. He stroked her hair, feeling his shirt growing wetter and wetter.

After a few minutes, she pushed away. "I think I still have access to the laundry room if you want to throw that in the dryer." She wiped her nose on her sleeve.

He lied. "I barely feel it." He pulled her over to one of the larger boxes. Then he pulled his handkerchief out of his pocket. "Here."

She laughed and dried her cheeks. "I've told you before. You are such an anachronism. Seriously. I don't know a single man, other than you, who still carries a cloth hankie."

"Blame, or thank, my father." He debated sitting on another box but chose to remain standing. "Can you tell me what's up?"

Haltingly, she told him about what she'd learned over the past three days. He knew she was leaving a lot of details out, but he heard enough to know it truly was a shitstorm of a case. At the end of her recitation, all he could say was, "Wow."

"Yeah." She sniffled one last time and wiped her eyes. "The worst part is not knowing for sure. I may very well be working on an appeal for a man who killed his wife. I've had clients in the past who were guilty, but my role was to ensure they got a fair trial. This time, I may be freeing a murderer."

"You can't quite wrap your head around that."

She nodded, tears making her green eyes more intense than usual.

He stared at his hands. He was a cop. They both wanted the same thing— justice—but they came at it from different ends. This was not his area. But if he didn't say something, he'd hate himself. "I may be in over my head here, but you need to listen to me."

She looked up.

"You've always said the guilty deserve the same rights under the law as the innocent. Your job is to protect those rights. Do you really believe that?"

"Of course I do."

"Then you aren't freeing a killer, even if Alec Wilson is indeed guilty. Which you still don't know for sure."

She watched him.

"You've said it before. The appeal isn't about setting him loose or getting him off the hook. It's about making sure it's done the right way. If he was convicted because of a statement that shouldn't be admitted, his rights were violated. That only means the prosecution will have to try again and do it better this time." Duncan paused. "You spoke to Wayne Baronick. If Wilson wins his appeal, do you think Baronick will let it go?"

He could see the wheels turning in her head. Finally, she spoke. "Not in a million years."

"Okay. You do your job. Let Wayne do his."

She bit her lip. "You're a good boyfriend. You know that?"

He chuckled. "Tell Tish that. She didn't think I was so great."

"Her loss." Sally stood and hugged him tightly. "And I'm not going to tell her shit. Because you're mine now, and I have no intention of letting you go anytime soon."

Chapter Thirty-Two

Sally arrived at her office early on Thursday morning. She was bone-tired after all the moving, especially on top of the emotional upheaval she'd been working through. Thank God for Jim. He hadn't carried a lot of boxes the previous night, but he'd handled a far more important job with his typical dependability. He'd kept her from flying apart.

Despite getting in before eight, she didn't beat Tanelsa. "What's this? Early bird catches the worm?" Sally asked as she hung up her coat. "We either have to stop coming in at this hour or tell management to adjust the HVAC. It's freezing."

"That's what coffee is for. To warm us up and get the juices flowing. I spent most of last night assembling a bio of Dominic Rossi." Tanelsa got up and beckoned. "Come see."

"Caffeine first."

A couple of minutes later, Sally entered the conference room, hands wrapped around a steaming mug. "Lay it on me."

"Right." Tanelsa picked up a sheaf of paper but stopped when she took a hard look at Sally. "Are you sick? Did something go wrong at the apartment last night? Lisa could pack her wardrobe in the bags under your eyes."

"I'm fine." Sally waved her hand. "At least I am now. Last night, not so much. Jim had to glue me back together." She gave Tanelsa the highlights of the evening. "I didn't sleep that well."

Her partner pursed her lips. "Don't fall apart on me now. I may have rewritten parts of that appeal, but you're the one who needs to stand up in court and do the talking."

"Why me? You're more than capable."

Tanelsa shook her head, not a strand of her dark brown hair out of place. "It's not about ability. Yes, I'm a damn good attorney. That's why you brought me on. But you are the heart and soul of this outfit." She held up her hand. "Don't argue with me. I give you grief about your flights into idealism, and yeah, I talk a lot about paying the bills. It's necessary. But you are the energy that drives this place. Don't ever doubt that. I wouldn't have come here for anyone other than you."

Sally stared. She'd always assumed Tanelsa's decision to leave the public defender had been based on logic, not emotion. "T, I'm flattered."

"Look at me, getting all mushy." Tanelsa set her shoulders and shook the pile of paper. "Point is Jim's right. We have a job to do. Let this Baronick guy deal with finding the evidence to convict. If it exists. Now. Where was I?"

Sally was touched by the unexpectedly soft side of her partner, but she was smart enough to let it go when Tanelsa made it clear it was time to move on. "Rossi's background."

"Dominic John Rossi. Age forty, married to Sylvia, lives in Pittsburgh. Graduated from the University of Pittsburgh. Sylvia, by the way, is loaded. She definitely brought the money to the relationship." Tanelsa sipped her coffee. "Dominic announced his candidacy for the Pennsylvania State Senate earlier this year. He's considered a fringe candidate, but hey, stranger things have happened than a complete unknown getting elected to public office, right? Also, he has a town hall here in Uniontown later this morning. Convenient, huh?"

"Where else in Fayette County would you hold such a thing? Flat Rock? You'd get three attendees." She swiveled her chair back and forth as she thought. "You wouldn't think a man with a rich wife and political aspirations would start an affair, much less one with a married woman."

"But that's exactly what he did. At least, allegedly. I went back to Laura Richards and pulled a few more details out of her. Looks to me as though they, Vivien and Dom, were an item for almost three months before Alec found out." She pointed at a new column on the whiteboard with a summary of the details.

Sally stared at the writing. "You say they met in June of last year. Where?"

Tanelsa skimmed her notes. "The annual summer get-together at Laurel Mountain Insurance. Company anniversary or some such thing." She gave Sally a sharp look. "What are you thinking?"

"Two things." Sally considered the remaining liquid in her mug and set it aside. "Why would Dom Rossi be at a company party for Laurel Mountain? He doesn't work there. Is he a part-owner? Silent investor?"

"I didn't find anything like that."

"Then how does he know Zander Nelson well enough to get invited to an event for a company he isn't involved with?"

Tanelsa thought a moment. "Good question."

"The other thing is the timing." Sally went over to the board and tapped it. "June. That's a month after Alec said he called the SEC with his suspicions about the Ponzi scheme. Coincidence?"

"Ain't no such thing." Tanelsa sat on the conference room table. "Sharp catch. See? Told you that you were the key to this place. What are you thinking?"

Sally surveyed the wall of words. So much data. Was this how cops felt looking at a murder board? If so, no wonder Jim sometimes felt as though he was running uphill over ice. "That we need to ask Mr. Rossi about his affair with Vivien Wilson. And his relationship with Zander Nelson at Laurel Mountain. Too bad the chances of us getting to see him without a court order are somewhere between slim and none."

"Hold that thought." The expression on Tanelsa's face was downright gleeful. "Let's crash his event. It's public. He won't be able to ditch us. Not easily." She scanned the table, grabbed a piece of paper, and held out a flyer.

Rossi's town hall was scheduled for ten-thirty. "What time is it?"

Tanelsa consulted her watch. "A little after eight."

Plenty of time. "I'd tell you to dress up, but you always look fabulous." Sally slid off the table. "I hope you're good at pressing the flesh. We're going to a town hall."

* * *

When Duncan arrived at the office, he had barely gotten his overcoat off when Cavendish accosted him. "We have a visitor," she said. "Conference two."

"Who is it?" He followed her.

"Ned Gaskell from the Securities and Exchange Commission."

At least they wouldn't have to spend time tracking the federal agent down. Duncan hurried behind his partner, compiling the list of questions to ask, starting with, "Why were you looking for Kyle Palmer?"

Gaskell sat at the table, paper cup in front of him, seemingly at ease. He looked up from the notebook he had been studying as the troopers walked in. "Morning. Sorry to drop in unannounced." He stood and extended a hand.

Duncan shook and immediately sized up the man in front of him. Almost six-foot tall, dark hair in a close, but not quite military, cut, dark eyes, perhaps in his forties. His black suit did not hide the evidence of regular gym workouts. No sitting behind a desk, abhorring fieldworkfield work, for Agent Gaskell. The sharp gaze told Duncan that his visitor was performing the same evaluation.

Cavendish must have noticed as well. "Please tell me you two can get along, and we're not going to start a TV-trope pissing match over whose authority trumps whose. Otherwise, I'm going out for breakfast."

Gaskell laughed. "My apologies. Occupational hazard, and I'm sure you both understand. The need to automatically take stock of who you're speaking to." He resumed his seat.

Duncan followed suit. "If I'd known you were coming, I'd have brought better coffee."

Gaskell waved a hand. "It's hot, and it's caffeine. That's all I require. Don't go thinking it's better at my office because it's not. Station house brew is the same all over."

"What can we do for you, Agent Gaskell?" Cavendish asked as she took a seat next to Duncan.

"Please, call me Ned. What can you tell me about the Palmer homicide?"

The troopers exchanged a look. Duncan laid his pen and notebook on the table. "Before we say anything, what's your interest?"

Gaskell hesitated, pulled up a sound file on his phone. "This." He played it. The recording was of a man's voice, slightly nasal, but clear. "Agent Gaskell, my name is Kyle Palmer. I know Alec Wilson. I know about your investigation into Laurel Mountain. I have information you might find useful. Please call me back at 724-555-8364." When it finished, Gaskell sat back. "Now, we could parry back and forth about how much each of us should divulge about our respective investigations. Frankly, I find that type of exchange boring and counterproductive. Hollywood and the media like to make hay out of how agencies at various levels don't get along, but I have nothing but respect for local LEOs. So why don't we cut the bullshit and go straight to the heart of it?"

Duncan found himself taking an immediate liking to Gaskell. He was the type of guy you could enjoy a beer with. "Sounds reasonable to me." He proceeded to give the highlights of the murder investigation to date. "Prior to leaving Marsdale, Palmer did not have a record. Not the best reputation, but no major run-ins with the police."

Gaskell tapped his thumbs together. "Aside from the suspected involvement in the bank heist."

"An allegation with no actionable evidence." Cavendish sat back.

"What we still don't know," Duncan continued, "is why he was living in Fayette County under an assumed identity. Especially one he'd taken so much care to build. That tells me he was running from something serious." He pointed at the recorder. "When did you get that call?"

"Back in August. The message touched off, maybe not alarm bells, but warning signals for me. I wanted to check into Palmer before I contacted him. Learn more." Gaskell took a drink. "By the time I reached out, he'd disappeared. House empty, phone disconnected, and no one knew anything."

Damn. Duncan rubbed his chin. "That's what we've learned. I was hoping you might shed some light on why Palmer up and left."

"Wasn't because of me." Gaskell leaned back and crossed his legs. "What has Alec Wilson told you about my investigation?"

"Not much." Cavendish flipped through her notes. "We know he had evidence of fraud at his workplace and called you. But we were concerned with the homicide, so mostly we were just interested in whether he told Palmer anything, especially knowledge that would get him killed."

Duncan thought a moment. "Was Wilson right? I mean, did he really uncover financial shenanigans at Laurel Mountain?"

Gaskell seemed to be deciding how much to say. "He was. That's part of what took me so long to get back to him. Was he a whistleblower or a participant? Because if it was his scheme, maybe he contacted the SEC in an attempt to shift the blame elsewhere. Unfortunately, by the time we had enough evidence to move forward, he'd been arrested for his wife's murder."

"Then he had nothing to do with the Ponzi deal?"

"Undetermined, but between us? I don't think so." Gaskell drained his cup. "Without going into boring details, we have enough to arrest Zander Nelson. But we also know Nelson wasn't working alone. The identity of the other partner is still a mystery. Our hope is that we can get Nelson to roll if we dangle incentives in front of him." He tossed the cup in the wastebasket.

"Palmer didn't have any information on him when he died?" Gaskell asked.

Cavendish shook her head. "If your name hadn't come up in a conversation with an informant, we'd never have suspected the connection."

What were they missing? Duncan re-read his notes. "What about the name Dominic Rossi? Ring any bells?"

Gaskell sat forward and clicked open a pen. "Who is that?"

Duncan gave him what the PSP knew of Rossi's background. "Palmer called him, twice. Why, we don't know. Rossi hasn't called us back. No incoming calls to Palmer, so we can only assume the two men never connected."

"And he was having an affair with Wilson's wife?"

"That's what Wilson tells us." Cavendish drummed the table. "But we don't know how or if Rossi connects with Laurel Mountain. It could be a completely different deal."

Gaskell scribbled the name. "Another thing to ask Mr. Nelson. I'm headed there next." He pocketed his notebook and pulled out a business card. "Thanks for the coffee. Needless to say, if you learn anything that you think could be of use, please holler."

"Likewise." Duncan walked the agent to the door. "Good luck with Nelson. I almost feel special that you stopped here first."

"Not too special, I hope." Gaskell shrugged into his coat. "You were on the way."

Chapter Thirty-Three

Duncan and Cavendish watched through the window as the taillights on Gaskell's car disappeared down Route 40. A gentle snow had started, the flakes dusting all the cars in the lot. "Smart ass," she said. "Do you think he meant it? He only stopped because we were along his route?"

Duncan grabbed the keys to an unmarked Ford. "I think he'd have come to see us eventually. What, are you feeling slighted?"

"It's more that I don't know if I should feel that way. If you're going to insult me, go on and do it."

They'd gotten their coats earlier. Duncan opened the door, and a swirl of cold air hit him dead on. It was going to be one of those days when he wished headquarters had covered parking. He was sure his back pain, which had subsided to a nagging ache as long as he didn't move suddenly, flared at the thought of clearing off his Jeep at the end of his shift. "Come on. We have our own investigation to work, remember?"

Cavendish tugged on her gloves. "How can I forget?"

Duncan drove to the Fayette County satellite office for Laurel Mountain Insurance. Located along the main drag in Farmington, it was a small brick building that looked like a repurposed house. Inside, Duncan showed his ID to the receptionist. "We're looking for the office manager."

"Michael Spencer," she said. "He's in the back office. Go on through. This place isn't big enough for an intercom. I just saw him in the kitchenette, so I know he's free."

They followed her pointed finger to a medium-sized office filled with office furniture that looked like it could have been purchased at any general supply store. No plush chairs or solid wood desks for this place. Michael Spencer looked on the young side for an office manager. Somewhere in his early thirties, his most prominent features were the round wire-rimmed glasses he wore and a pair of ears that were slightly too big for his head. He looked up at the knock. "Can I help you?"

Duncan introduced himself and Cavendish. "Sorry to bust in on you. The woman out front said it was okay."

"Oh, yeah, no problem. I don't have any appointments for a while." Spencer blinked. "Why don't we go to the kitchen? The chairs are better. At least that's my opinion."

For a moment, Duncan thought about refusing. But Cavendish nudged him, and he read the admonition in her stern glance. "If you wouldn't mind, that would be great. Normally, standing is fine, but my back and I haven't been on good terms these past couple of days."

"Sure thing." Spencer led them to a bare-bones kitchen. An IKEA table with four plain wooden chairs was in the center of the room. The white refrigerator was of a style that Duncan hadn't seen in stores in years. A microwave took up the corner of the laminate counter, and a drip-style coffee pot sat between it and the sink.

Duncan sat, trying not to look too grateful to be off his feet. "You don't even get a one-cup coffeemaker, huh?"

Spencer snorted. "Are you kidding? I had to bring the Mr. Coffee from home when the first one broke. Mr. Nelson is such a cheapskate. The fridge is from a scratch-and-dent place. Gwen, she's our receptionist, had to buy the microwave. She got this table and chairs off social media marketplaces." He pulled over a chair for Cavendish, then took his own seat. "Enough complaints. How can I help you?"

Was Nelson cost-conscious or was something else in play? "Business looks a little slow. What kind of insurance do you sell here? I mean, is it all homeowner's insurance or auto, or something else?"

"We keep the lights on." Spencer adjusted his glasses. "We don't do auto coverage. We offer homeowners, but most of our customers are renters. At least, the landlords refer their tenants to us. A tenant is always welcome to get their own insurance, of course."

No auto? That's at least one lie from Nelson, Duncan thought. So much for his tip to Sally. Hopefully, she hadn't yet acted on it.

"Or go without?" Cavendish peeled off her gloves but elected to keep her coat on.

"Oh, no. Well, I guess there might be landlords who aren't very good businessmen and who wouldn't make you get insurance, but it's a pretty standard requirement these days." Spencer pushed his glasses up again.

Duncan had thought he was chilled from being outside, but no, the thermostat was definitely set low. Come to think of it, the woman at the front desk had been wearing a thick fleece pullover. Nelson was stingy with the heat, as well. "Do you offer investments?"

"Not here. I'm not qualified to give financial advice. That's a completely different certification. It's only insurance." Spencer got up and got a canister of coffee from the cabinet. He fussed with the Mr. Coffee and started the brew cycle. Then he sat again. "I apologize for the cold. Company policy states the thermostat stays at sixty-seven. The cost of natural gas is through the roof."

Cavendish raised her eyebrows. "Nelson doesn't sound like a great boss. I understand the need to keep costs in check, but doesn't he know how cold it is in December around here?"

Spencer's fair skin flushed. "He's not, but I haven't been here long. I only passed my insurance exam about a month ago. Hopefully, after I work here for six months or so, I can go somewhere else."

Duncan could read into what Spencer didn't say. Somewhere that treated its employees better. Wait, a month ago? "Did you work here before you passed your test?"

"You can't sell insurance without a certification." The smell of the coffee filled the air. "My hiring was contingent on passing, but I didn't actually start until the day after I got my results."

Duncan shot a look at Cavendish, who looked as perplexed as he felt. "Did you provide a policy to a man named Ellis Martingdon?"

"That name doesn't sound familiar. Hold on." Spencer got up and left.

Cavendish leaned over. "Martingdon moved to Farmington three months ago. This guy can't be the first manager."

Before Duncan could answer, Spencer returned. "I'm sorry, yes. Mr. Martingdon did have a basic renter's policy from us. He signed it back in September."

"Great." Duncan made a note. "Who was the office manager before you? We need to speak to him. Or her."

Spencer blinked again. "What do you mean?"

"Who would Mr. Martingdon have bought the policy from?" Cavendish spoke slowly. "Since you said you couldn't sell before your certification."

"Oh, I get it. There wasn't a manager before me." Spencer set down the folder he held. "Mr. Nelson managed the office personally before I was hired."

* * *

Sally sat at her desk, re-reading the dossier Tanelsa had built on Dominic Rossi. The more times she did, the less she liked the man. At first blush, it was a rags-to-riches story. Dom Rossi came from working-class stock in Pittsburgh. He'd gone to Central Catholic High School courtesy of grants and by the sweat of his parents' brows. After high school, he attended Pitt, where he earned a business degree and graduated without honors, but not by the skin of his teeth, either.

He'd married his college sweetheart, Sylvia Donaldson, a couple years after graduation. Her father owned his own company, some sort of health insurance brokerage firm, and she'd brought the cash to the relationship. His first job had been as a manager for his father-in-law. Tanelsa had written "prenup?" next to that paragraph and underlined the word three times. Sally had to agree. No woman in her right mind would have neglected that detail before tying the knot. And if Sylvia didn't, Sally was pretty sure daddy-dearest had. Especially since Sylvia was his only child.

Rossi had put out feelers for a campaign run about two years ago. He didn't just want to be a mere state representative, though. His goal was a seat in the state senate. He had no experience and no political background. No one locally had been interested in backing an unknown candidate with no connections, so that must have been what drove him to look at other districts. He bought a parcel of land in the Laurel Highlands and started his campaign. If it worked in U.S. Senate races, why not for the Pennsylvania legislature?

What he did have was piles of his own—or rather his wife's—money. Money that, assuming the existence of a prenuptial agreement, would be in jeopardy if Vivien Wilson went public with their affair. Never mind what the news would do to his goals. Voters were becoming more progressive all the time, but Sally knew the district Rossi was campaigning in. People there still liked their elected official to keep his pants zipped. At least in public.

While Sally was ruminating on this and formulating her list of questions, her phone rang. She picked it up. "Oh shit, it's the jail."

Tanelsa's head jerked up.

Panicked at the thought of a second attack on Alec, Sally tapped the green button. "This is Sally Castle."

Alec's anxious voice came over the line. "Ms. Castle, thank goodness I got you. I was afraid you wouldn't answer or something."

Sally felt her blood pressure tick down as she motioned to Tanelsa to relax. "No, I'm here. What can I do for you, Alec?"

"I thought of something this morning. You said Vivien owed a lot of money?"

"Yes, why?"

"About two months before her murder, a man came to the house. I opened the door, and he asked to see her. She appeared before I could get his name, and she hustled him away. I mean, thinking back, she was really mad. She slammed the door behind them, but not before I heard her ask why the hell he'd come to the house."

Had Alec really just remembered this tidbit? Sally pawed through Dave's records but didn't find what she was looking for. "Hold on a second." She muted her phone. "T, look for any records of conversations between Dave and Alec. I want to know if he ever mentioned a visit Vivien got before she died, one that made her angry."

Tanelsa immediately got up and started looking. "On it."

Sally unmuted the call. "Sorry about that. This man. What did he look like?"

"Not very interesting. He was maybe as tall as me or a little taller. Dark hair. He couldn't be that much older than I am, I don't think." He paused. "I didn't know him, but he kinda reminded me of a shark."

The description was eerily similar to Owen Zigler. "Good to know."

"Does it help?"

"Maybe. Facts never hurt. Are you still in the infirmary?"

He hesitated. "They discharged me this morning. The warden said I'm going to solitary because of what happened. Not that I did anything, but they don't want me wandering around the general population, I guess."

"That's fairly standard. Has Brian Kolchak come back to work?"

"I haven't seen him. But I wouldn't, right? I guess unless he's the one they sent to escort me, but you talked to the warden yesterday, didn't you?" Alec sounded nervous. "Should I be scared?"

"No, they know what's up. I highly doubt every employee of the Fayette County Department of Corrections is corrupt." All the same, Sally made a note to follow up on the whereabouts of the guard who had stabbed her client. "Listen. I'm working some new leads in your case. You sit tight and keep your head down."

"I don't have anything else to do." He hung up.

Tanelsa came over, hands full of paper. "I can't find anything. Not one word about a strange man visiting before Vivien's death."

The two women stared at each other. Sally desperately wanted to believe their client. But he'd told so many lies already, she didn't know what to believe anymore.

* * *

Duncan gritted his teeth as he listened to Cavendish mutter all the way into

Uniontown. "Why are you so pissed off?" He glanced at her. "People lie to us all the time. It's a cliché. Everybody lies. Why not Zander Nelson?"

Her expression turned even more sour. "I don't know. Because I'm cold? Maybe I wouldn't be so irritated if it was summer. Or it could be this guy just gets under my skin in a special way. Whatever. The fact remains that he knew exactly where Kyle Palmer was, and he denied it, looking, as my grandmother would have said, as though butter wouldn't melt in his mouth. It should have immediately set off my cop radar, and it didn't. Of course, did you see the condition of that branch office and what he does to his employees? Nelson probably lies about everything. Maybe that's why I didn't notice."

"Or you're right, and you're frozen solid."

Her answering look could've dissolved a six-foot-thick snowbank.

Duncan held up a placating hand. "Relax. We'll check on Lamb and go back to Nelson. I'll give you first dibs on blistering the skin off him. Does that make you happy?"

Cavendish groused some more, but her expression turned slightly mollified. "It'll do, I guess."

It was not quite nine thirty when Duncan parked in front of the address he had for Gus "Dinky" Lamb, which turned out to be in a surprisingly middle-class neighborhood. The houses weren't fancy, but they weren't run-down either. Most were a shade of white, blue, or gray, modest square buildings with snow-covered front yards behind sidewalks that homeowners had cleared and sprinkled with ice melt. The cars were what Duncan would expect to find in such an area, a collection of Chevys, Fords, and Dodges, mostly mid-sized sedans a few years old, with several trucks thrown in for good measure. A lime-green Dodge Caliber, the roof and hood dusted with the previous night's snowfall, occupied the driveway at their destination. It made Duncan wonder, not for the first time, why large men drove small cars. "If the robbery had been successful, I'd say Dinky could be spending his share. This is a nicer neighborhood than I'm used to for suspected felons."

"But not on his ride, if the Caliber belongs to him." Cavendish ran the plate. "Yep, it's his. At least we know he's home." She studied it. "Didn't you say this guy is big?"

"That's what Pete Adams told me."

She pointed. "Then what's with the clown car?"

"I wondered the same thing." He turned off the engine and put his hand on the door handle.

"Hold it." Cavendish laid her hand on his shoulder. "How likely is Lamb to get frisky?"

The question puzzled him, but he answered. "Not very. Least, I wouldn't think so. Unless, of course, he's guilty of murder, and he tries to run for it."

"Uh-huh. That's what I was afraid you'd say." She chewed her lip. "Maybe we should call for backup."

Now, he was really perplexed. "Why? You and I have handled stuff like this before."

"Yeah, when you were operating at your peak." She held up a hand to forestall a response. "Shut up. Jim, I can see the pain lines around your mouth. You've been popping Advil like clockwork for the past two days. Face it: You're hurting. You'll put yourself, and me, in danger with your stubbornness. I thought you were smarter than that."

He sagged against the seat. She was right, and he said so. "If we knock with a phalanx of uniformed cops at our backs, don't you think that's more likely to make him freak out, not less?"

She considered his words. "You might have a point."

"How about this. If he runs, we let him go. No chase. A man that size, and in that car, can't outrun pursuit, and he certainly can't beat the radio." It occurred to Duncan that he sounded like his nephew, bargaining for ice cream before dinner instead of after. "If we don't threaten him, maybe we can have the conversation, leave, and come back if necessary. With that posse of uniforms."

Cavendish unfastened her seat belt. "Deal. But if you break it, so help me God, you'll be buying every round at Whiskey & Rye through this time next year. *Capisce?*" She got out and strode to the front door.

Duncan followed. *Dinky, don't you dare make a liar out of me.*

Cavendish pushed the doorbell while Duncan took up position behind her and used the wait time to make sure his Glock was easily accessible. She had reached for the buzzer again when the door opened.

Duncan's first thought was that Adams had undersold Dinky's true size. The man wasn't the size of an NFL linebacker. More like an offensive lineman. He was easily three hundred pounds, but it wasn't flab. This was a man who, if he chose, would be almost impossible to move without the assistance of heavy machinery. "Who are you?" he asked in a moderate voice.

Cavendish held out her ID. "Pennsylvania State Police. Are you Gus Lamb?"

Lamb glanced at Duncan, who showed his own badge.

"That's me. What do state cops want me for? I ain't done anything." He scowled. "Is this about that damn bank robbery? They dropped those charges. If that's what you're here about, I'm calling my lawyer. I still got his number."

A stiff breeze blew through the yard and Duncan felt the chill through his heavy wool coat. "That both is, and isn't, why we're here, Mr. Lamb. Do you mind if we talk inside?"

"As a matter of fact, I do." Lamb came outside and stood on the concrete steps. He was so big the wind probably gave way before him. "Something I learned from the last run-in I had with police. Don't never let a cop into your crib without a warrant. Don't suppose you got one of those, do you?"

Cavendish held out her empty hands. "Fresh out at the moment. But my partner is right. This isn't really about the bank robbery itself. It's about the man you were allegedly with. Kyle Palmer."

Lamb's eyebrows lowered. "That asshole? Haven't seen him in months." He turned to go inside.

Duncan spoke before that happened. "I take it you aren't on good terms with Mr. Palmer. Why's that?"

Lamb stopped and turned. He spoke slowly, as though he were talking to idiots, not police officers. "Because he's an asshole. I gotta have a reason? Is it against the law to think a guy's a prick?"

"No, but when the man in question has been murdered, it tends to make people like us curious as to why you feel that way."

Lamb didn't move. "He's dead, huh? Guess he was a dick to the wrong person. Don't have anything to do with me."

The wind picked up again, but Cavendish didn't budge. "You said it's been months since you saw Kyle?"

"That's right."

She took her phone out of her pocket, scrolled to a photo, and held it out. "Then, if I tell you he was living barely a twenty-minute drive away from the very spot we're standing on, that would be a surprise to you?"

Lamb's right eyelid twitched. "Yeah, it would. I don't want anything to do with him. You got anything else you want to talk about?"

Cavendish studied her phone.

Duncan gazed at the erstwhile bank robber, who stood like a boulder in front of his closed door. The house was shut up tight, blinds down. There was nothing in plain view that would justify a warrant or even taking Lamb into the warm confines of a nearby police station. Nothing except that eyelid twitch and that could as easily be from the snow or wind as from telling a fib. "No, that's it. For now. Although, there is one thing. Where were you last Sunday night into Monday morning?"

Lamb waited before answering. Trying to remember or coming up with a story? "I went to Pittsburgh to see my mother. She's old. We have a family dinner every weekend. I stayed over Sunday night since she's kinda frail at her age. She needed some of my dad's things taken to the curb. He died six months ago, so I been helping her get rid of all his shit."

That would be an easily verifiable story. They didn't even need to get the mother's name and address from her son. "Thank you. Stay warm."

Dinky didn't answer and went inside. He shut the door, and they heard the snap of the deadbolt as it slammed home.

The troopers headed back to their car. Inside, Duncan immediately turned on the engine and put the heat on high. "Did you do what I think you did?"

"Take his picture? Sure did." Cavendish clicked her seatbelt. "Head back to Palmer's. His neighbors would have to be blind to miss a strange man that big walking down their street."

"A man that big driving a bright green car. No one's mentioned one of those." He pulled away. It should be a slam dunk. Then again, he'd never been that lucky. Although there was a first time for everything.

Chapter Thirty-Four

Dom Rossi's event was scheduled for ten-thirty that morning at the building on the corner of South Gallatin and E South Street. Sally arrived early enough to get the lay of the land, but not so much that someone on Rossi's staff would ask her to leave. At least not without causing a scene, and Sally was betting that was the last thing Rossi wanted.

The event hall was half full when she arrived. The majority of the attendees looked like retirees. They'd be the ones able to attend a rally early on a Thursday morning. And more likely to vote. There were a dozen or so men in their forties or fifties, some wearing shirts or ball caps touting "clean coal" energy. That was one rail on Rossi's platform, which was sure to play well in Fayette County. Rounding out the crowd were a few younger men, millennials perhaps, all in jeans, flannel shirts, and Carhartt jackets. From their conversation, they were out of work and wondering how Rossi would deliver on his promises of jobs for all.

Sally kept to the back of the room. A table off to her left held three enormous coffee urns, all of which had lines. Baskets of wrapped snacks took up another table. Food and caffeine. Two ingredients of a successful political event. She cast her gaze over the group. It wasn't a big crowd. Dom Rossi, who would presumably be wearing a high-quality suit and tie, should stand out like a tropical parrot in a flock of ravens. Where was he?

Sally and Tanelsa had debated the best time to corner Rossi, before or after he spoke. Ultimately, they decided on before, which was Sally's preference. Tanelsa had opted to stay at the office and see what else she could find on

Owen Zigler. "If you've seen one political rally, you've seen them all," she'd said. That left Sally to question Rossi. She didn't have the luxury of listening to an hour of empty promises designed to woo voters. Besides, if she caught the man before he got comfortable, he might let something important slip.

A disturbance near the door caught her attention. It was the candidate himself, trailed by a man who had to be an aide. Dressed in an immaculate gray suit, white shirt, and red power tie and flashing a thousand-watt smile, he worked the gathering like a pro. From his expression, he was immensely interested in whoever was in front of him, young or old, working-class or professional. Just like an experienced politician. Or a really good actor.

Of course, Sally mused, it could be argued those were the same thing.

She angled her path to intercept Rossi before he reached the stage. He finished shaking hands with an elderly woman and turned to find Sally in his path. "So glad you could come. It's a pleasure to see a young professional here. What's your name?" He held out a hand.

Sally gripped it. His skin was warm and dry, but the grip lacked strength. "Sally Castle, of Castle & Parson."

"Sounds like a law firm."

"It is."

He gave her what he clearly thought was a dazzling smile. His teeth might even have been whiter than Wayne Baronick's, and that was saying something. "What kind of law? Are you here to learn about my plan for helping struggling local businesses?"

"Criminal defense."

The skin around his eyes tightened. "Fascinating. As your state senator, I want to serve all my constituents' needs. What can I do for you in Harrisburg?"

She withdrew her hand. "In Harrisburg? To be honest, I'm not sure. But I think you can help me right here in Uniontown."

"How so?"

"I believe you know my client, or rather his late wife. Vivien Wilson."

There was no imagining the flash of panic in Rossi's eyes. His smile faltered for a millisecond, but then he pasted it firmly back into place.

"Wilson? Oh, that poor woman who was murdered in Monongahela County. Her husband was convicted. Life without parole? That's not enough. When I'm in Harrisburg, I'll lobby to reinstate Pennsylvania's death penalty for such cases." He tried to move on.

His aide, a young man in an off-the-rack suit, attempted to shoulder her aside.

Sally didn't let him. "I'm against capital punishment, but that's beside the point. How well did you know Vivien Wilson?"

Again, the hitch in the practiced politically motivated open expression. "Only as well as anyone who reads the paper."

"I've been told it was much better than that. And, of course, you met Alec."

"Never saw the man. Excuse me."

Again, the aide attempted to nudge Sally away without looking like he pushed her.

She easily stepped around him. "Sure you did. Because you know his boss, Zander Nelson. At Laurel Mountain Insurance. Alec remembers seeing you at a company picnic in the summer of last year. And he met you in the office a couple of months later. He knows you were sleeping with his wife. Why'd you do it? You're a married man with a political future. Seems like a risky decision."

Rossi froze. He glanced around. Most of the crowd had fallen away. He let the fake friendliness leave his expression. "He's mistaken. Anyway, it doesn't matter. Alec Wilson is going to jail for a very long time. I'm afraid convicted felons don't have much credibility."

"He's appealing his conviction."

"He's going to lose."

"No, he's not." She held his gaze in a silent battle of wills. She wondered if it was the first time anyone had said no to him.

After several beats, Rossi plastered the broad smile back on his face. "You're out of your depth, Ms. Castle. Alec Wilson is going down. Be careful you don't go with him."

Sally masked the frisson of apprehension that went down her spine. "Is that a threat?"

"Advice. You enjoy the rest of the event. Get a cup of coffee and mingle. You might learn something." He ducked around her and thumbed the screen on his phone. He touched the screen and held it up to his ear as he walked away.

This time, Sally let him go. She'd pushed her luck far enough.

* * *

Duncan's phone rang while he waited in the drive-thru line at Mickey D's, where he'd stopped so Cavendish could buy a midmorning breakfast sandwich. Caller ID told him it was Gaskell. "Ned, what can I do for you?"

The SEC agent didn't bother with small talk. "I'm at Laurel Mountain Insurance to talk to Zander Nelson."

"What's he got to say?"

"Nothing. He's dead."

Duncan reached over and tapped Cavendish on the knee to get her attention. "Hold on. Let me put you on speaker so my partner can hear." He tapped the icon and held the phone in the palm of his hand. "You said Nelson's dead?"

Cavendish raised her eyebrows.

Gaskell's voice was slightly distorted by the speaker but still clear. "Shot through the head. Apparent suicide, but the local cops aren't convinced."

Duncan inched the car forward. "Badly staged scene?"

"No, it was done quite well, actually. I'm no homicide investigator, but the LEOs say it looks good." Gaskell must have covered the phone because his voice got muffled, but then he came back. "Killer only made one mistake. Nelson's a lefty, and he's shot through the right temple."

Cavendish was scribbling notes. "Either the shooter didn't know, or he made a mistake. Could it be the actor who shot Palmer?"

Duncan's thoughts had gone to the same place. "When did this happen?"

"I'm getting the impression it was several hours ago, but not last night. The coroner lady refuses to be more specific. The firm doesn't open until eight, so it would have been before the other employees were here."

Based on Duncan's previous meeting with Zoe Chambers-Adams, he knew she wouldn't give details until she'd done an autopsy. Regardless, the killer was long gone. Duncan lifted his gaze to meet his partner's. "We appreciate the news, Ned. I assume Mon County PD is on scene? I know a guy there. I'll give him a call later."

"Wait. That's not the only reason I reached out."

Duncan's finger had been hovering over the *end* icon. "It's not?"

Again, Gaskell's voice became muffled. "Detective Baronick wants to talk to you."

"Jim." Wayne sounded tense. "Where's Sally?"

Why would he want to know? "Work."

"Are you sure?"

Dread knotted Duncan's stomach. He nodded to Cavendish, who pulled out her phone and texted. After a moment, she said, "She's at Dominic Rossi's town hall meeting in Uniontown."

Duncan didn't know why, and he didn't care. "Did you hear that? What's up?"

"It might be nothing. But we found a note on Nelson's desk. The impression of one, at least. Someone wrote Sally's name and underlined it a bunch of times. From the dent in the paper, he was pressing pretty hard when he did it. We're assuming the shooter took it with him." Wayne paused. "Do you know what she's doing over there?"

"No clue. You had lunch with her. She does what she thinks she needs to do for her clients. And she doesn't tell me everything, often because she can't." Duncan hit the siren for a single whoop. The car in front of him moved, and he swung out of the line, food abandoned. It was a mark of Cavendish's concern that she didn't complain.

Baronick continued. "Like I said. Might not mean anything. But you should check in with her if you can."

"Already on it. Thanks." Duncan ended the call as Cavendish flipped on the lights and siren.

Chapter Thirty-Five

Sally stayed at the town hall for about forty-five minutes. By then, she'd had her fill of political double-talk and heard enough promises she knew would be almost impossible to fulfill. To make it worse, Rossi had begun to repeat himself, which made his vague assurances sound worse.

She murmured apologies to the people in her row and ducked outside, where she inhaled deep lungfuls of crisp, clean air. Not that the meeting hall had been particularly stuffy. But she felt the need for cleansing breaths after listening to so much bullshit.

As she walked down the sidewalk toward her car, she could hear the faint sound of a siren. Fire or police? She sniffed. If it was fire, it wasn't close. She couldn't smell smoke. Police sirens in a city were common enough that they didn't cause her alarm.

After another few steps, she stopped and shivered. It was cold, but the sensation wasn't that. Someone was watching her. The back of her neck prickled, and she gripped her purse strap. She was the only person on the sidewalk. The building she'd just left was quiet, the snow-covered yard unbroken by footprints. A string of parked vehicles lined the street, drivers absent. They most likely belonged to attendees of the town hall.

The sensation of unease grew, along with the volume of the sirens. She instinctively knew someone scrutinized her, biding their time. Where was he? She stopped next to a rust-splotched pickup truck and scanned the building on the opposite side of the street. All the windows were covered by slatted blinds. There was no visible reason for her unease.

Three things happened in quick succession. The side mirror of the pickup exploded. A dark sedan, with flashing lights behind the grill and siren wailing tore around the corner and screeched to a halt behind the truck.

And the sound of a gunshot split the air.

* * *

Duncan scrambled out of the car as soon as he slammed it into *Park* and tackled Sally. Both of them landed in the snow beside the truck. His back immediately let him know he'd pay for his heroics later, but at that moment, it didn't matter. "Stay down!" He pulled his Glock from its holster and dropped low behind the minimal cover of the pickup. "Cavendish, talk to me."

"I'm calling for backup." Her voice rang out crisp and no-nonsense. "Shots fired, corner of South Gallatin and East South. Officer needs assistance."

Sally struggled to get up. "Jim, what the hell—"

"I said stay down." He spared her a brief glance. "Are you okay?"

"My ass is wet and getting wetter. Was that a gunshot?"

"Yes." Duncan's gaze raked the building across the street. Based on the broken mirror and his high school knowledge of physics, the shooter had to be on an upper level. All the windows looked closed, blinds down. He patiently scanned each one, tensed for a second shot. There. Second floor, third from the left. It looked closed, but the blinds moved ever so slightly in response to the wintry breeze. They would only do that if the window was open. The muzzle of a rifle protruded from them, but in a flash, it disappeared.

Their target was not a pro. A true sniper wouldn't let himself or his weapon be seen.

He felt Sally come close, not touching, but crowding as close as she dared. "Don't move," he said. "This truck isn't great cover, but I don't know where the shooter is right now."

"Aren't you afraid of losing him?" she asked.

"We very well might, but I have no idea if he's still there, what kind of firepower he has, or if there is more than one. Neither Cavendish nor I can go in alone, and I'm not leaving you." He didn't look at her. "What are you doing here?"

"I came to hear Dominic Rossi's traveling dog and pony show. He's got about as much chance of that pile of slush surviving winter of getting elected, but he's giving it his best shot. Why a businessman from Pittsburgh with a rich wife thinks he can connect with the voters down here is beyond me, but hey, politics makes strange bedfellows and all that." She paused. "Why are *you* here? You and Jenny came in with your pants on fire."

"Cavendish, where's that backup?"

"Two minutes out," she called from her own spot, where she'd taken cover behind another car a little farther up the street.

He shifted. God, his back hurt. It didn't matter. Until they cleared the scene and verified the shooter was gone or they took someone into custody, Sally's safety mattered more than his personal comfort. He shot her another look. "Why did you come alone? Last I heard, Rossi was on your list of suspects for Vivien Wilson's murder."

"It doesn't look like it now, but there are at least a hundred people in there. I think I'm okay. I get that I have a history of being a little headstrong, but I'd like to think I've put my days of confronting murderers behind me. I thought I proved that last month." She bit her lip. "You haven't told me why you're here."

He adjusted his grip on the Glock and continued his scan of the building. "Zander Nelson is dead."

"What? When?"

"Early this morning, or so they think. Supposed to look like a suicide, almost definitely murder. Wayne Baronick called me because they found your name at the scene." He gave her the details.

"That doesn't make any sense. I never talked to Nelson. I tried, but he hung up on me. I don't know anything. Why would he come after me?"

"We don't know."

"Is this person the same one who shot Nelson?"

"We don't know." He wished he had a better answer. He'd seen the fear in her eyes. He wanted to hold her and tell her she was safe. But he couldn't. Not yet.

Her voice was shaky. "What now?"

"We wait." He continued to scan the street. Behind him, he heard a door open and the sound of a crowd. "Cavendish, keep those people inside."

"Everyone back in the building." Cavendish snapped. "You, keep the attendees in the building until you get the all-clear from me."

The noise retreated.

Cavendish used the cover of the parked cars and came over. "See any movement?"

"I saw a flutter of blinds and what I think was a rifle muzzle on the second floor. Gone now, but I can't tell if our shooter is still there." He shifted slightly, setting off new complaints from his overtaxed muscles. "Where the hell are the unis?"

In response, three Uniontown black-and-whites turned onto the street, sirens wailing. They came to a halt between the pickup and the brick building from which the suspect must have fled. Each car disgorged at least one officer.

Duncan snapped his fingers at the nearest one. "I've got a civilian here. Probable target. Uninjured, but stay with her and make sure she keeps her head down." He turned to Sally. "I hear you've moved even a toe, I'll lock you up for the duration. Got it?"

She nodded, still pale and shaky.

Cavendish gripped her Glock. "You sure you don't want to stay with her?"

"No." Duncan gritted his teeth. "Let's go."

The rest of the group approached the building cautiously, making the most out of what little cover was to be had. Two of the uniformed officers hunkered down to cover the front door. Duncan, Cavendish, and the others ran around to the back. The door was wide open, a clear set of footprints through the snow leading away. "You, follow those prints and see where they go. Don't mess them up." Duncan nodded at one of the uniforms.

Cavendish approached the back door in an angled position and checked inside. "Looks clear. Going in." She slid through the opening.

One by one, Duncan and the remaining Uniontown officers followed. Methodically, they cleared each room before proceeding to the second floor. "In here," a patrolman called.

Duncan had been right. It was the window he'd noted from the street. The room held only a chair and a table. A .22 rifle rested on the floor where it had been discarded. It was a Ruger, a common gun in Southwestern Pennsylvania, not a sniper's weapon. Then again, the distance hadn't been that great. The shot didn't require a high level of accuracy. Any half-decent hunter could have made it. But since it had been discarded, Duncan figured the chances of the gun yielding any evidence were low.

"We'll clear the rest of the building, but I think he's in the wind." Cavendish nodded at the uniformed officer, and they left.

Duncan holstered his Glock and snapped on a pair of nitrile gloves. He examined the rifle. They could get a serial number, which would tell them where it had been sold and to whom, but if it had changed hands, the info would be next to useless. Pennsylvania gun laws didn't require licenses for long guns. The shooter hadn't left any other evidence behind. No bottles, candy wrappers, or cigarette butts. They'd dust for prints, but Duncan was willing to bet they'd come up empty.

Cavendish re-entered the room, her own weapon back in its holster. "This place is stripped bare. Find anything?"

He held up the rifle. "Just this. The case is in the corner. Nothing else. He was clean." He stepped over to the window. "The angle up here is shit. We're not dealing with a professional. He'd have had a better shot from ground level."

She clicked her tongue. "Same shooter who capped Nelson?"

"Depends on when he was killed. It's an hour's drive from Marsdale to here. If Nelson died in the last couple of hours, no. If Baronick is right and the time of death is early this morning, maybe." The suicide had been well staged. This second shooting was sloppier. But it might be easier for an amateur to fake the circumstances of Nelson's death.

Cavendish looked at the label on the side of the case. "Artwell Guns & Ammo. That's right here in Uniontown."

"They probably sell fifty of those in a month. But yes, we should check it out." He heaved himself to his feet. Now that the adrenaline had ebbed away, he could barely move. He sucked in his breath.

It didn't go unnoticed by his partner. "You still with me? Or did you finally push it over the edge?" She stood aside as a crime scene team entered the room and began their routine.

"I'm hanging in there. By my fingernails, but I'll take it easy once we're done." He gritted his teeth as he walked down the stairs. *This one is easy,* Sally had said. *All I have to do is stand up in court and read. Piece of cake.*

Famous last words.

Chapter Thirty-Six

Sally didn't even try to dissuade Jim from accompanying her back to the office. For one, she didn't think it was possible. Also, the incident had shaken her more than she wanted to admit. Even with a bad back, his calm, solid presence wrapped a sense of security around her like nothing else could. Which meant Jenny Cavendish came as well.

The minute they walked through the front door, Tanelsa dashed out of the office. "What the hell happened? I heard it on the scanner. Are you hurt?" She swept her gaze over Sally and the two troopers before coming back to rest on Sally.

"I'm fine. Minor grazes to my palms and a cold, wet ass." She cleared off two chairs so the visitors could sit.

"Can I get you anything?" Tanelsa asked.

"Dry pants. Even sweats are fine." Sally took off her coat. Jim eased down into a chair, but Jenny stayed standing.

"I wouldn't say no to a cup of something hot." Jenny tossed her gloves on the table.

"Same." Jim took a bottle of ibuprofen out of his pocket and shook out three capsules.

Sally bit her lip. "T, do you have any of those Vicodin left from your oral surgery last month?"

He gave her a sharp look. "I'm not taking someone else's drugs."

"But—"

"I said no. End of discussion." He looked around. "Are you going to make me dry swallow these things?"

234

Jenny cleared her throat. "Ms. Parson, how about I give you a hand with those warm beverages?"

Tanelsa gave her a grateful look. "Sure. This way." She hurried off, Jenny in her wake.

Sally grabbed an open bottle of water from her desk. She handed it over and sat next to him. "Why do I have the feeling you're lying to me?"

He swallowed the pills. "I'm no worse than I was this morning. Physically, that is." He shifted to face her and brushed hair from her cheek. "I'm more worried about you."

She tried for a laugh. "Nothing doing. This wasn't nearly as bad as last winter, when I was zip-tied to a chair by a lunatic waiting out a snowstorm. Come to think of it, you turned up in the nick of time for that, too."

"I think this incident trumps that one." He cupped her face, his eyes intense.

"Nah. Piece of cake. I've been in tighter situations. I—"

He kissed her. Intensely, the way he only did when they were alone. Behind his passion, she could feel other, more tightly controlled emotions. She realized he'd been scared, maybe more than she had been. For her, because of her? It wasn't clear. A little of both, maybe. But she hadn't seen this side of him since he'd burst into that flimsy trailer a year ago. The side he kept well-covered in front of everyone except her.

She touched his cheek. "Hey, now. Is that proper behavior while on the job?"

He let loose a phrase he rarely used and leaned his forehead against hers. "If I hadn't been there. If the shooter had been even the slightest bit competent. Shit. I don't even want to think about it." He folded his arms around her.

She let him. She closed her eyes and soaked in his warmth, his scent. At that moment, she didn't have to be strong and brush it off. Someone wanted her dead.

She shuddered as the last of her adrenaline left her body.

They sat like that for a long moment. A slight cough broke through. It was Tanelsa. "Do you two need to use the conference room? I can cover the whiteboard. I hear all the time how a brush with death makes people horny.

Wouldn't blame you if you wanted some privacy."

Sally pushed away and met Jim's gaze. She tried to put all her thanks and reassurance into her eyes. "No. We're all set for company."

He squeezed her hand. The moment was over.

Tanelsa held out a mug. "Sally, drink this. Hot chocolate. You're still half in shock. The sugar should help."

Jenny appeared. "Everybody good? We ready to move on?" She handed a mug of cocoa to Jim.

Jim shifted his focus to Tanelsa. "Did you hear anything else on the scanner?"

"Nope. My brain kind of shut down once I realized the address was the same place Sally went to." Tanelsa sat on her desk. "What the hell happened?"

Sally sketched in the details, trying to make it sound less serious than it was. She looked at Jim. "Baronick didn't say anything?"

"Not more than what he told me."

Tanelsa whistled to get their attention. "Anyone want to clue me in?"

Duncan did so in as few words as possible. "You said you've never talked to Nelson. Not in depth."

Sally refused to let go of his hand. "Not beyond that one time."

"Did you call anyone else associated with Laurel Mountain?"

"No. We've been focused on the appeal." She looked at the two troopers. "You're sure it has to do with them?"

Jim ran his hand through her hair, which had come loose. "It does appear to be the connection." He spoke to Jenny but kept his gaze on Sally. "What came of those footprints?"

"Nothing." She leaned against the wall. "They ended at the sidewalk, which had been shoveled. Print is from a standard work boot, men's size ten."

"Only about a thousand or so pairs of those around these parts." He blew out his breath. "Sally, I don't suppose I can convince you to go home for the day."

She tried to read his thoughts. He was concerned, no doubt about it. But he had to know her answer. "I have work to do."

"I'd rather you did it from Confluence. Anybody gunning for you is likely to go to your apartment here in Uniontown. Rizzo is a lousy attack dog, but he's a great alarm. Just in case someone does find you."

"My place is here."

His hazel eyes darkened. "I can't sit inside your door this time and keep you safe."

He was talking about last winter when he'd spent the night on her couch after her panicked call for help. "I know. You've got a job to do. I promise I'll keep in touch."

He pressed his lips to her forehead. Then he stood and picked up his overcoat. "You left Rossi at the town hall?"

"Yes, but he can't have anything to do with the shooting. He was inside the building with a hundred witnesses." She watched him button up.

"True, but he's now involved with two dead guys. One murder, one staged suicide." He grabbed his cup. "That's a little too much random death for my taste. Just because he didn't pull the trigger doesn't mean he can't lead me to who did."

Sally watched them get bundled up. "You already have a killer to find. I'm sure the Uniontown cops will figure out who shot at me."

He kissed her again. "You stay with Tanelsa inside. Text me when you leave. Stay away from the windows."

The no-nonsense tone of his voice scared her more than the gunshot. "I will. I love you. But Jim, you can't find both this shooter and the guy who killed Palmer."

"I love you, too. Stay safe." He looked straight in her eyes. "As for the rest? Watch me."

* * *

As soon as Duncan got in the car, he pulled out his phone and made a call to a friend in the Uniontown police department to arrange for an unmarked unit to keep an eye on the Castle & Parson office.

Cavendish pulled away from the curb. "I thought you told Sally you couldn't protect her?"

"You weren't listening. I said I can't do it personally. You and I have stuff to do. But after what just happened, if you think I'm leaving her without someone watching the door, you're out of your mind."

She lifted a hand. "I don't blame you. Where to?"

"Panera."

"I think you've had enough coffee and pastries."

He shifted. "I'm not looking for food. There's too much crap swirling around this case. We need to clear the water so we can focus."

Once inside, Cavendish bought a bagel sandwich while Duncan claimed the table in front of the fireplace. He laid out a pad of yellow legal paper he'd snagged from Sally's office. He preferred a whiteboard, but this would have to do. "I thought you said you didn't need to eat?"

Cavendish sat. "Now, who's not listening? I said *you* didn't. I didn't get my snack earlier. Let's get to it. What do we know?" She took a bite.

Duncan wrote Kyle Palmer's name in the center of the paper. "Here's what is provable. Palmer was shot in the head on Monday. We know he left Marsdale in a hurry last September and had gone to a lot of effort to create a new identity."

"Which is why I still don't get why he volunteered to testify in the Wilson trial."

"I doubt he had any intention of doing so. But he was on the witness list, so that's another provable item." He wrote Alec Wilson's name and drew a line to Palmer.

Cavendish took another bite and swallowed. "We also know Palmer was horning in on Ryan Ellis's turf here in Fayette County."

"No, we don't." Duncan tapped the paper. "While there was drug residue found at Palmer's home, we don't have any hard evidence he was making a play for Ellis's customers. They could have had a business arrangement. Or it's not even from him and has been sitting in the basement for months."

"He went on the run, but then got into the drug trade?"

"Remember, with a new identity. My guess is he wanted to move up in the crime world, and he reinvented himself."

CHAPTER THIRTY-SIX

She nibbled a stray piece of bacon. "Who would be able to tell us?"

"Possibly Elijah Munk." He drew a line from Ellis to Palmer with a question mark and wrote Elijah's name. "Do we consider it fact that Palmer and Dinky Lamb were partners?"

Cavendish thought a moment. "I think there's enough circumstantial evidence to say yes. There's definitely bad blood there. Why? The only thing that's come to light is this botched bank robbery, when Palmer left Lamb to take the fall. At least, that's the assumption. I also don't buy that it's a coincidence Lamb is living within spitting distance of his old friend."

"Fair enough." Duncan twiddled the pen. "But I'm not sure I can get behind him as good for the murder. Lamb didn't go to jail. Yeah, it was inconvenient to be arrested, but nothing else happened to him. If Palmer had been beaten up, sure, I'd look at Lamb. But he was shot in the back of the head. Dinky didn't strike me as that kind of guy."

"Agreed." She crumpled up the sandwich wrapper. "I wouldn't strike him from the list, but he's not a top suspect."

"That brings us to another thing we're certain of. Zander Nelson." Duncan wrote the name and a line. "Nelson sold Palmer his renter's policy, which means he knew Palmer under both identities. And knew exactly where to find him. I'm surprised Palmer didn't bolt again right then and there."

"But that would mean Palmer had to know about the Ponzi scheme."

"Correct, and that's the third thing. Fourth? I've lost track." He wrote Dom Rossi's name and connected it to Palmer. "We have Palmer's phone records, and he called Rossi. To talk about what? The two have no connection except—"

"Zander Nelson."

Duncan drew a line between Nelson and Rossi, then another between Rossi and Wilson. "We know Rossi was having an affair with Vivien Wilson."

"Which started not long after her husband called the SEC with his suspicions." Cavendish twirled a loose strand of hair around her finger. "Try this on for size. Rossi was a partner in the Ponzi scheme because he needed money for his campaign. He got close to Vivien Wilson to find out exactly how much her husband knows."

"I thought Rossi's wife was financing him?"

Cavendish let her hair go. "Do we know that? Or are we making another assumption?"

It was a decent idea, but how did Palmer play into that? "Adams described Palmer as sneaky. He lived across the street from Wilson. Maybe he saw Rossi coming out of the house late at night. Could be he even saw a little kissy-feely between the two. Knowing Palmer's personality, what do you think he'd do?"

"He saw an opportunity. He reached out to Rossi and said, 'I know what you're up to.' He was talking about the affair, but Rossi thought he knew about the scheme. Because here are two more facts." She grabbed the pad and wrote. Then she pushed it back. Rossi's name was connected to Sally and Wilson. "Someone stuck a shiv into Alec Wilson. And someone took a shot at Sally today." She tapped Rossi's name. "Who better to try his hand at murder than someone who's killed at least once? Twice, if you count Nelson."

Duncan stared at the page. Maybe not a man who was facing marital ruin and a political loss. But someone who was facing time in a federal jail? Heck, yeah.

*　*　*

Sally watched out of the front window as the unmarked Ford pulled away. Then she returned to her desk.

Tanelsa studied her. "Are you sure you don't want to go home? I mean, you were shot at barely an hour ago. It's okay to take the rest of the day off."

"I'm fine." Sally brushed off the concern. "Jim thinks I'm safe enough here as long as I stay inside with you. I'll definitely be more productive." She opened her laptop.

"If you're sure."

"I am." Sally opened the file on Alec Wilson. "Where are we for Monday?"

Tanelsa took the hint and became all business. "As far as the appeal, I think we're solid. I made a few last refinements to the language. The document should be in the cloud for you to review. As long as you don't have major changes, we did it. We crafted a solid appeal in less than five days."

"To be fair, we did have a head start. But yes, that mission's accomplished." Sally clicked and opened it. "Are we set for any surprise questions?"

"I think so. I don't know what judge denied that motion in the first place, but he, or she, was insane. Or on the take."

"I asked Jim about that. He said this judge is known for a bias in favor of the prosecution and law enforcement. I'm willing to leave it at that. We've got enough on our hands without taking on judicial misconduct."

"Amen, sister." Tanelsa clicked her pen repeatedly. "But aside from the appeal, there are a couple things that bother me. Alec is stabbed while he's in jail. Oh, did I tell you they found a prison uniform in the trash?"

"You did not." This could be important. "Whose trash?"

"The jail's. And it was outside the cell block, so inmates wouldn't have access. Lends weight to Alec's claim that his attacker was actually a guard."

"If he ditched the uniform right after the incident, he could have blended right back in. A guard would know exactly where the cameras are. No wonder he disappeared." Sally mulled this over. "Did they find any helpful evidence on it?"

"Like DNA? Not that they told me. But." Tanelsa arched an eyebrow. "The guy Alec fingered? Brian Kolchak? He hasn't been to work since the incident."

Sally made a note of that. "We need to track him down."

"The cops will do it."

"Of course they will. But when? They have a lot on their hands right now."

"You're insane. And you'll do it yourself if I don't go with, won't you?"

Sally said nothing.

Tanelsa scribbled a note. "The other thing is now you've been shot at. Why? What were you doing that was so threatening, and who felt at risk?"

"I'd just left Rossi's town hall. I said I knew he'd been involved with Alec's wife. He brushed me off, and I left."

"Is that all?"

Sally thought back. Had it only been a couple of hours ago? It seemed like forever. "He denied ever seeing Alec. I said that wasn't true, because he'd been at Laurel Mountain twice that we know of, and he knew Zander Nelson."

"What did he say to that?"

"That Alec was mistaken. Wait." Sally snapped her fingers. "Colonials stick together. That's what Alec meant. Nelson and Rossi were college classmates. The Colonials are the athletic mascot at Robert Morris."

Tanelsa caught her lower lip in her teeth. "But I thought Rossi graduated from Pitt." She tapped on her keyboard. "Yep, here it is, in his bio on his website. Degree in business from the University of Pittsburgh."

Sally's instincts screamed she was right. She logged into one of the databases they used for research. After a couple of minutes, she had what she was looking for. "Dominic Rossi may have graduated from Pitt, but he spent two years at RMU first." She tapped again. "He was there at the same time as Zander Nelson. They would have been in the same graduating class with the same field of study."

"RMU isn't so big you wouldn't know a guy in your year and major. Especially considering business schools often have specific clubs and shit." Tanelsa dropped the pen on her desk. "That's lie number one."

Where there was one, there were usually more. Sally searched for a number and picked up the phone.

"Who are you calling?" Tanelsa asked.

"Sylvia Rossi."

"Think she'll talk?"

"No harm in trying." The line rang three times before it was answered. "Hello, Mrs. Rossi? My name is Sally Castle. I'm a defense attorney in Uniontown. I have a couple of questions about your husband, if you are willing to give me a few minutes of your time."

"Ex-husband." Sylvia's voice dripped with scorn.

"Excuse me?"

"Perhaps I should have said 'soon-to-be' ex. I filed for divorce at the beginning of this month."

Sally scribbled "divorce" on a sheet of paper and held it up to Tanelsa, whose jaw dropped. "I assume that means you'll be pulling your financial support from his campaign?"

Sylvia gave a harsh laugh. "What support? I never gave Dom a nickel for that hare-brained idea. Where he got the money, I don't know. But it wasn't me."

But hadn't Rossi said something about that? Or had everyone assumed that was the case? "This is a rather personal question, and feel free to tell me to mind my own business, but are you leaving him because of his affair with Vivien Wilson?"

"Oh, hell no. Dom's never been able to keep it in his pants. I knew that when I married him."

"Then why did you? Marry him, I mean."

"Men aren't the only ones who need arm candy, Ms. Castle." The amusement came through clearly. "Besides. Being married freed me up to pursue my own interests without prying eyes."

Sally wasn't sure why the woman was being so forthright. Could she be that bitter? Sally definitely didn't want to know what Sylvia meant by her "own interests." Whatever the reason, the information was helpful. "Then why divorce him?"

"This stupid campaign. His opponent has dug up every woman Dom has ever slept with, including the murdered one. He doesn't realize it, but he's the laughingstock of Pittsburgh. By extension, that means I am, too. The clueless wife who can't keep her husband satisfied."

"And you don't like it. Is that the reason you're willing to talk to me?"

Sylvia paused, and it sounded like she was taking a drag on a cigarette. "I don't like being laughed at, Ms. Castle. I told him years ago. Do whatever you want. But don't you dare embarrass me, or you'll regret it. Well, he has. Time to pay the piper." She hung up.

Tanelsa rose, put her hands on her desk, and leaned forward. "What did she tell you?"

Sally summarized the call. "If the money didn't come from Sylvia Rossi, where did it originate? And why won't Rossi admit to knowing Zander Nelson?"

"I don't have to think hard for an answer to those questions."

Sally didn't either. She'd bet the outcome of Alec's appeal that Nelson and Rossi had been in the Ponzi scheme together. Sally grabbed her phone. She needed to tell this to Jim. Now.

Chapter Thirty-Seven

Duncan made a call to see if Elijah Munk was still in custody while Cavendish took care of the warrant application for the gun store sales records. Elijah wasn't at the jail. He'd been arraigned, posted bail, and released earlier that morning.

"Warrant in progress for the gun records." Cavendish hung up. "I arranged for Uniontown detectives to serve it so we don't waste any more time. But the store owner only has paper files. It'll take them a day, or more, to get through it all."

Of course. "Head back to Elijah's house. Might as well see if he's there." Duncan pocketed his phone but pulled it out again as Sally's text tone sounded.

Nelson and Rossi were college classmates. Wife divorcing Rossi. Never financed him.

He stared at the words. He sent back a quick thanks. "Get a load of this." He told Cavendish about the text.

"Well, that's interesting." Cavendish tapped the steering wheel. "You think Rossi and Nelson were in bed together on the Ponzi?"

"I think it's a good possibility. But let's focus on Elijah."

They were in luck. As Cavendish pulled to the curb, Duncan spotted Elijah lugging a black trash bag to the garage. Duncan got out of the car. "Afternoon. I see you're none the worse for wear."

Elijah tossed aside the bag. "No thanks to you. You all got an alarm or something? A little radar blip that goes off to let you know where I am?"

Cavendish came up. "Nothing that fancy. We made a telephone call and

245

an educated guess."

He hawked and spat. "What you want now?"

"Same thing we did the first time." She put her hands on her hips, the right one close to her Glock.

Duncan made a placating gesture. "We got off on the wrong foot. We want to know about Kyle Palmer, also known as Ellis Martingdon. That's it." Of course, if Elijah had shot him, they'd address that later.

"I told you, talk to my lawyer." Elijah flipped them off and headed for the house.

"Hey, wait a minute." Duncan tried a jog, but quickly changed to as quick a walk as he could muster. "You might not want to play hardball with us."

Elijah paused. "Yeah? Why not?"

"Because your boss got pinched by the DEA. It's only a matter of time before they show up here." Duncan watched Elijah's face for a sign of interest. "To them, you're small potatoes. Heck, you might even be able to flip on Ellis and get off scot-free."

"You're not helping yourself."

"Let me finish." Duncan took a breath. "You won't be able to fluff off the feds the way you're trying to do to us. They'll get you to talk about Palmer, his role in the trade, and your role in his murder."

A flash of worry appeared in Elijah's eyes before he schooled his expression. "If I had a role."

Cavendish, who had moved closer, crossed her arms. "Elijah, if you talk to us now, maybe we can slip that information to the DEA. They might still get you for the drugs, but that'll be less than a murder charge."

"All we want to know is whether Palmer was in competition with Ellis or if there was something else going on." Duncan waited.

Elijah was silent for what felt like forever, but finally spoke. "We didn't know his name was Palmer. Only the other one, Martingdon. He came to Ryan a few months ago. Asked if we needed a sub-contractor. Said he had experience."

Out of the corner of Duncan's eye, he saw Cavendish take notes. He focused on the man in front of him. "Palmer worked for Ryan Ellis?"

"Kind of. Trev gave him a cut as a trial. Said if the dude did okay, they could talk."

"Then the black Raptor that was seen the night he died was yours?"

"Yeah. I went to make a pickup. He'd done good. I told him Ryan would be in touch."

Cavendish broke in. "He lied to you. He didn't have any experience. He did general contract labor in Mon County before coming here."

Elijah's face split in an amused grin. "Shit. We knew that. Ryan figured, what the hell? It put another layer between him and the customer. He wasn't gonna give this guy the percentage he was asking for. If he got busted, no one would believe a baller like Ryan would use a flunky like Palmer."

No honor among thieves. Or drug dealers. "You went to Palmer's. You picked up the money. Then what?" Duncan asked.

"I left." Elijah shrugged. "Not like we were gonna hang out and smoke a joint, you know?"

"Why did you leave the gun behind?"

The big man's shoulders moved up and down. "He said he needed a piece. For protection. I knew the gun wasn't traceable. With Lucas locked up, seemed like a good idea. Get it outta my hands."

Duncan had to agree. The last thing Ellis would want to do was give his lackey something that could rebound to him. "When did you leave?"

Elijah's forehead furrowed. "Midnight? One? Late. Real late."

The story tallied with what the witnesses had said. "And he was alive?"

"That's what I said." Again, Elijah spat. "I'm not denying I would have capped him if he'd been short or playing games. But he had the money, and it all added up. No reason for me to pop him."

It explained the residue in the basement. And the truck. "One more thing." Duncan glanced at Cavendish.

Elijah huffed and rolled his eyes. "Now what?"

"Did you see anyone else while you were there? Either when you arrived or when you left?"

"Not at the house. Passed a car as I was leaving, but I didn't pay it any attention."

Cavendish perked up. "You didn't even notice what it looked like?"

"Nope." Elijah sounded bored, like he was about to end the conversation. "Some redneck with a busted headlight. We done?"

Duncan nodded, and Elijah went inside. "That went about as well as it could have." He walked off to the car. "Let's find out what our other suspects drive."

"DMV records won't tell us if one of them is driving a padiddle." Cavendish slid into the car.

Duncan followed. "Nope. But we'll know what we're looking for when we show up to inspect it."

* * *

Sally worked until one-thirty. With the appeal done—at least mostly done—she could address a few things that had been put off, including returning a couple of phone calls, scheduling a meeting with a new client for after the first of the year, and catching up on the last couple month's worth of expense reports and financials so she could have everything to their accountant by the end of January.

She looked over at Tanelsa. She was at her desk and wore an expression of dissatisfaction. "What's going through your mind?"

"That I need to stop editing this appeal before I ruin a thing of beauty. Now I'm changing things for the sake of changing them." She sighed and closed her laptop. "But I don't have anything else to do. I can't get the whole Rossi-Vivien-Nelson thing out of my head."

Sally knew how she felt. "How about a field trip?"

"Where?"

Sally pointed at her computer screen. "To look for our missing prison guard. Brian Kolchak. I have his address here."

Tanelsa raised her eyebrows so high they almost met her hairline. "Are you out of your mind? That's your idea of a field trip? I told you. Let the cops handle it. Especially after this morning."

"Let me rephrase. I don't really want to talk to Kolchak. I want to chat up

248

his neighbors. He lives in an apartment complex over on Collins Avenue. I want to know if anyone has seen him, what his habits are, has he had visitors, has Dom Rossi been there...you know. Snooping." Sally held up her hands. "If Kolchak is home, we'll leave. I promise."

Tanelsa stood and grabbed her purse. "I'm going to hold you to that." She looked outside. "We have company."

Sally stretched to look over Tanelsa's shoulder. A Uniontown black-and-white idled not far from their office. "No, I have a babysitter."

It took several minutes to convince the officer she needed to leave her office. In the end, the uniformed officer insisted on following them to their destination.

Tanelsa shot her a smug grin. "At least we'll have backup in case we run into trouble."

Not long after that, they reached the apartment on Collins. "Kolchak lives in 304." Sally scanned the building. It wasn't impressive. A five-story block of yellow brick. Most of the windows were covered by curtains. A few showed potted plants or Steelers flags. The walkway had been shoveled, and the line of industrial-grade trash cans along the side of the building stood as straight as soldiers at arms. There wasn't any detritus or abandoned children's toys to be seen. Either the inhabitants were very orderly and didn't have kids, or maintenance was on their toes.

"Do you want to go floor by floor?" The sky was overcast, but Tanelsa shielded her eyes anyway. "What's our spiel?"

"As close to the truth as possible. We're attorneys investigating the stabbing of our client at the Fayette County Jail." Sally had decided that on the way over. "Kolchak may be a witness, but he hasn't been at work. Blah, blah. You get the picture. And yes, we might as well start at the bottom and work our way up."

Some residents didn't answer their knock. Sally left business cards with a note on the back wedged in the door. Those who were home seemed to know Kolchak by sight, including that he worked at the jail, but nothing more.

When they reached apartment 303, they got lucky. "Yeah, I know Brian," said the middle-aged woman who answered. She wore an apron over a faded Pirates T-shirt and leggings that did not flatter her wide hips. Her mousy brown hair was pulled back in a low ponytail, but loose hairs straggled over her forehead. "What a pain in the ass. Even if he is a witness, good luck getting him to say anything. He'd probably slam the door in your face just because he could."

Tanelsa opened the Notes app on her phone. "You don't have a high opinion of him. Why? Missus...?"

"Dennison. Ginny Dennison." She brushed the hair away from her eyes. "Brian has a pretty high opinion of himself. He doesn't need me inflating his ego."

"What makes you say that?" Sally asked. "Does he cause problems in the building?"

"Not exactly. It's more like he acts like he's doing us a favor by following the rules. You know, put your trash in the cans. Sort your recyclables. Don't track water or snow through the entire building." She shrugged. "He has no problem telling us we're out of line, but he won't own his screw-ups."

"How so?"

"For example. If the super has told him once, he's told him a thousand times. Carry his rifle in a case, not out in the open. Does he listen? Not on your life."

Sally perked up. "He has a rifle?"

Ginny snorted. "To hear Brian talk, he's the best Big Game Hunter since Ernest Hemingway. My late husband was a hunter. Brian isn't bringing down anything bigger than a white-tail with a regular old .22. Not that I think half his stories are even close to true."

It was the same caliber rifle found after she'd been shot at. "What kind of stories?"

"That he was an Army sharpshooter, can hit a buck at five hundred paces, even through the trees, that kind of thing." Ginny waved a hand. "All a bunch of bullshit, in my opinion. He doesn't even drive a truck, for God's sake. He's got an old Honda Accord with one headlight burned out. You can't haul anything in that."

"Interesting." Sally looked over at unit 304. "I take it he's not home right now."

"Nope. Don't know where he is. I suppose he's at work."

"He's not." Tanelsa broke in. "That's why we're looking for him. He hasn't been in for two days. When was the last time you saw him?"

Ginny blinked. "Really? I didn't think that man did anything except work. Let me see." She paused. "I definitely saw him Tuesday night because he'd parked in my spot. He does that, too. Add it to his list of faults. I think I saw him Wednesday morning. I left early to babysit my granddaughter. Well, I saw his car. I assumed that meant he hadn't left for work yet, but I guess that's not necessarily true, is it?"

It wasn't, but since Kolchak had gone to work on Wednesday, it was possible. He had definitely arrived at the jail because his supervisor remembered talking to him. It wasn't until lunch that he was missed, along with his Honda. "Does he have a lot of visitors? Maybe this man?" She held out a campaign shot of Dom Rossi.

"Brian has the occasional friend over, but no, I don't remember seeing this one." Ginny took the picture. "He kind of looks like a guy Brian spoke to on the street a few days ago, but then again, not really. That guy wasn't as good-looking or put together as this one. Isn't this that Rossi fellow, the one who is running for the State Senate? What a shyster. I heard him speak last month. I didn't believe a word that he said, especially about finances." She handed back the picture.

Sally put it away. "That's an interesting word to use, shyster. What makes you say that?"

Ginny laughed. "My late husband was a banker. He followed all the big scandals, Madoff and that sort. Well, I heard Rossi's plans and thought my Oliver would call it a Ponzi scheme for sure. Typical politician. Rossi thinks we're all morons, like we can't spot a fraud."

Sally and Tanelsa exchanged a look. Ginny's description couldn't be a coincidence, could it?

Chapter Thirty-Eight

Outside, Sally started her Toyota and rubbed her hands while the heater did its job. "Remind me to look into Kolchak's background when we return to the office."

"So noted." Tanelsa tugged at her gloves. "Are we going back now?"

Sally thought of Jim's advice the previous day. "Not yet. Let's go to the Laurel Mountain Insurance office in Farmington."

"Why?"

"Zander Nelson wouldn't talk to me even before he knew what I was asking. I want to know why." She told Tanelsa about the visit with Jim.

"You think a branch manager will know?"

"Maybe."

"Let me ask you something." Tanelsa twisted so she could look straight at Sally. "Why did you want to talk to Nelson?"

"To find out if he'd had any interaction with Vivien Wilson."

"Because if she knew about the scheme, he might have killed her." Tanelsa paused. "What makes you think some branch manager is going to know anything? It's not like Nelson would have gossiped with him. Vivien didn't live in Fayette County. What are the odds she visited here?"

Rats. Tanelsa was right. "I can't shake the feeling Dom Rossi is involved up to his eyeballs."

"Then what we need to do is connect Rossi and Nelson. After RMU."

Sally put the SUV in reverse. "We'd need a court order for Nelson's emails and phone records. There is no way we're getting those by end of day tomorrow."

"You never know. We might get lucky. Do you think Jim has them?"

"Doubtful. Besides, he can't share that kind of information with me." Sally drove away, thinking. "He'll have Palmer's as part of that investigation. If Palmer called both men, maybe that's enough for us. After all, the only reason Palmer would do that is because he knew something about the Ponzi scheme."

"And if he called Rossi and Nelson, that could be considered strong circumstantial evidence they were both involved."

It might well be. Now, the only challenge was getting Jim to tell her the details.

* * *

Duncan stared at his phone and Sally's text. **Need a favor. Not sure court order will come through in time. Did Palmer call both Nelson and Rossi?**

Cavendish parked in the lot at headquarters. "What's with that expression?"

He showed her the text.

She turned off the ignition. "What are you going to tell her?" She got out of the car.

Duncan followed, still focused on the phone. "I don't know. On the one hand, I shouldn't share details of an ongoing investigation."

"But you have in the past. On the sly. Don't deny it." Cavendish opened the door. "She's already put in the request. She'll get the answer, so you're not telling her anything she won't know. Eventually."

The interior warmth washed over him. What Cavendish said was true. But that didn't mean he should. And definitely not in a text. **Ask me later, when we're home.** He slipped off his overcoat and sat. He rubbed his face. Between the pain in his back and the frustration of the day, he wanted nothing more than to leave and spend the evening sitting in front of a roaring fire, beer in one hand, Sally in his arms, and the dogs at his feet.

"You look like hell." Cavendish, like all good partners, seemed keyed in to his mood. "Go home. There is nothing to do here I can't handle."

"Just one thing, and that's to follow up on Dinky Lamb's alibi for Monday." He pushed aside the discomfort and reached for his phone.

Cavendish shook her head but pulled out her notebook. "He claimed he was at his mother's for dinner, stayed the night, and didn't get home until late Monday afternoon."

Duncan pulled up information for Lamb's mother. "Let's give her a call." He dialed the Pittsburgh number. It rang four times.

A woman answered. "Hill District Police Department."

Duncan applauded the woman's spunk. Such an answer would run off most telemarketers. "Is this Mrs. Lamb?"

"This is the police."

"Ma'am, my name is James Duncan, and I'm a trooper with the Pennsylvania State Police. I know for certain I did not call a police department. But I bet you get a lot of hang-ups with that response."

"You know it." The woman didn't sound embarrassed. "State cops? How do I know it's you?"

He thought. "I'll give you my badge number, and you can call the Troop B HQ to verify. I'll give you ten minutes and call you back. How's that?"

She snorted. "Sounds like too much damn work. How about you tell me what the hell you want, and I'll hang up if I don't want to say nothing?"

"Fair enough. I'm calling about your son, Gus."

"He didn't do nothing."

Mrs. Lamb sounded like the polar opposite of Georgia Munk. "I didn't say he did. I'm calling to confirm a statement he made to my partner and me."

"He's right."

Duncan fought back a laugh. "Ma'am, you don't even know what he said. Are you sure you want to corroborate his statement?"

"'Course I do." She paused. "What did he say?"

Duncan put the call on speaker. Cavendish deserved to hear this firsthand. "That he visited you on Sunday and spent the night because you're in poor health, and he had to take care of you."

"Poor health? You wait until I get my hands on that boy. Let me tell you something, young man. And don't you tell me you ain't young. I got ears. You can't be more than thirty-five."

Cavendish clapped her hands over her mouth.

Mrs. Lamb was two years off, but Duncan wasn't going to argue. "I wouldn't dream of it."

"Good," Mrs. Lamb huffed. "I'm healthy as a horse. Doctor says I got years left in me. I'll probably outlive all my children, considering they're all overweight, got poor sleep habits, and can't stay out of trouble."

"Are you saying Gus is lying?"

"Only partly." Glasses clinked in the background. "He was here for dinner, same as every Sunday. Has to be, don't he? I sent him home with enough leftovers for the week. Otherwise, I'm not sure the boy would eat nothing but junk food. But he left early, around seven. Said he was gonna meet up with some friends down in Uniontown."

"Thank you very much, Mrs. Lamb. You have a good evening." Duncan hung up the phone.

Cavendish burst out in laughter. "Oh God. What a pistol. I bet she makes life interesting for her kids." She wiped her eyes. "I wish we could have interviewed her in person."

"It would be preferable, but we don't have time to drive all over Southwestern Pennsylvania."

She sobered. "There goes Dinky's alibi. If he left Pittsburgh at seven, he'd be back in plenty of time to be in Farmington by midnight."

Yes, he would. The problem was Duncan still couldn't buy the botched bank job as a motive. Unless there was something they didn't know.

* * *

Sally thought about texting Jim that she'd be late and staying in Uniontown to move more boxes. Then she remembered his concern from earlier and his insistence she stay with Tanelsa. She left work a bit early and headed home to make sure there would be a hot meal ready for him when he got to

Confluence. That, one of those reusable ice packs and a glass of whiskey. If he refused to take time off and see a doctor until the Palmer investigation was over, at least she could attempt to make his evening more comfortable.

The timer on the chicken-and-rice casserole had just beeped when he walked in the back door. "Something smells great." He kissed her before turning his attention to Rizzo and Pixel. "All right, guys. It's too damn cold, and my back hurts too much, to go romp in the backyard tonight. Go resume your naps."

The dogs genuinely looked as though the words had hurt their feelings. That lasted all of two seconds, and they returned to licking their lips at the scent of roast chicken.

Sally grabbed the ice pack from the freezer. "Here. I bought this from a pharmacy on the way home. And I poured you a whiskey."

"You are a gem." He pressed another kiss to her lips, this one with a bit more force. "Hold that. Literally. I'll be back."

He disappeared upstairs. When he returned, he wore his standard at-home relaxation clothes, a pair of PSP sweatpants and a Steelers hoodie. He grabbed the glass. "Thank you." He dropped into his seat.

Sally wedged the ice pack between his back and the chair. "I heard the advice from Chief Adams's wife. Twenty minutes on, twenty off."

"If you insist, nurse."

"I do. I'd have brought those Vicodin home if I thought you'd take them." She brought the casserole pan to the table.

"But then I couldn't enjoy this drink." He inhaled. "Thank you. Seriously. For all of it."

"It's the least I could do." She made sure the oven was off and sat. "Give me your plate." She dished up a generous portion and handed it back.

Jim took another sip of whiskey, then picked up his fork. "While I appreciate the concern, and I do think it's genuine, why do I also get the feeling you're trying to soften me up?"

"I'm not." She knew why he thought that. It wasn't like she hadn't done so in the past.

They ate for a minute. Then Jim said, "You back on track after earlier?"

CHAPTER THIRTY-EIGHT

"As long as I don't think about it, I'm good. How close was it?"

"If the shooter had been the least bit competent, we wouldn't be eating at home tonight."

She felt a tendril of cold snake down her spine, as though someone had dropped an ice cube down her shirt. "That bad?"

"It could have been." He studied her. "You still intend to present this appeal on Monday?"

"I've spent the last four days on it. Why wouldn't I?"

"Someone doesn't want you to. First they try to sideline your client, or worse. Then they take a shot at you directly." He dragged a slice of bread through the gravy on his plate. "Did you warn Tanelsa?"

"Of course. Not that I needed to. I think she was more freaked out than I was. Of course, that might have been shock talking." She pushed some chicken around. "I kind of still can't believe it happened."

He took another couple of bites. After he'd swallowed, he said, "The answer to your question is yes."

She looked at him, caught off guard. "What?"

"Did Palmer call both Nelson and Rossi."

"I didn't expect you to answer me."

He shrugged. "Cavendish was right. You have the request in. You'd find out." He took another mouthful, chewed, and swallowed. "What are you thinking?"

"We know Nelson was guilty, right?"

He thought. "If Agent Gaskell is telling us everything, I think that's a good bet."

"He and Rossi were partners. I know it." She told him about her interview with Ginny Dennison. "She specifically used the word 'Ponzi' when she described Rossi's spiel. That can't be a coincidence."

"That's less certain, but it makes sense." He picked at a piece of bread. "Palmer found out, somehow. He tried his hand at a bit of blackmail, and look where that landed him. Elijah told us he saw a car with a busted headlight the night of the murder. Rossi or Nelson?"

"Maybe neither." She told him about Brian Kolchak's Honda. "He's disappeared."

"We need to connect him to the others, but it's definitely something to look into." He wiped his fingers. "But what does this have to do with your client?"

"His wife was Rossi's lover. What if she found out about him and threatened to go to the cops? Or she asked for a piece of the action, which he didn't feel like doing." She picked up the empty plates and set them on the floor. Rizzo and Pixel leapt to their feet and licked the traces of casserole from them.

"Definitely motive. And he'd have means and opportunity, if he came to the house. The knife would be on the counter. But would he stab her like that?" Jim attempted to get to his feet.

Sally laid her hand on his shoulder. "Sit still, and I'll put your cold pack back in the freezer. Drink your whiskey. I'll clean up." She grabbed the silverware. "I think he could have. He'd be mad. Plus, it's an opportunity to get rid of the other threat."

Jim swirled the glass. "You mean Alec."

"Bingo." What better way to discredit your enemy than to put him in jail for murder?

Chapter Thirty-Nine

Sally arrived at her office Friday morning earlier than usual. An old prosecution colleague of hers called days like this Hail Mary days— the last day to make the adjustment that would nail the case. They were so close she could feel it. She'd read through their presentation in bed last night while Jim slept fitfully. Tanelsa's edits made a huge difference. They were going to be successful.

But then what?

"We go to trial. Again." Sally spoke to herself while she made coffee. "We'll be better prepared. Of course, a second trial means the prosecution will be able to revamp as well. It won't be an easy fight."

"It's a bad sign if you're talking to yourself."

Sally looked over her shoulder to see Tanelsa in the doorwaydoor to the kitchenette. "At least I'm not answering myself. Isn't that the real problem?"

"So they say." Tanelsa took down a cup and a pod of her favorite brew, dropped it in the machine, and pushed start. "You look like you got as much sleep as I did last night."

"I was reviewing the appeal. You did a great job on the revisions." Sally headed back to her desk. "What's your excuse?"

"I was thinking about Vivien. Why'd she have an affair?" Tanelsa followed, sat, and opened her laptop.

"Why does any woman? Because she's missing something in her life."

"But from all accounts, Vivien had Alec under her thumb. Anything she wanted, she got." Tanelsa laced her fingers and rested her chin on them. "Everybody has said the same thing. She wore the pants in that relationship.

259

What was she looking for that she wasn't getting at home?"

Sally frowned. "Maybe she was sick of Alec being a wuss. Or she got bored."

"That could be. But she didn't go searching for adventure."

Sally followed Tanelsa's logic. "When it came to her, she jumped. Rossi's not bad-looking. On the surface, he has money. He's an up-and-comer, a guy who seems powerful. That would be attractive to someone like Vivien, I think."

Tanelsa considered a moment. "I'm with you on that."

Sally continued. "According to everyone we've spoken to, *he* came on to *her*. Again, why? I've seen her picture. She was good-looking but not stunning. She wasn't charming, not based on what we've been told. She flirted right in front of Alec, passing it off as teasing, but it was cruel. No other word. Even her friend, Laura, said that. She wasn't rich or connected, so there was no way she could offer Rossi anything that would help him reach his goals."

"I see we reached the same conclusion."

"What'd Rossi see in her?" Sally asked.

Tanelsa tilted her head back and forth. "Are men usually attracted to cruelty?"

Sally didn't have an extensive dating experience, but enough to answer. "I don't think so. So the question is, did Alec become the way he is *because* of Vivien, or was he like that before? Remember, everyone we've talked to said he was a great guy."

They sat in silence. Finally, Sally spoke. "Dom Rossi does not lack confidence. Do you agree?"

"Without a doubt. Which takes us back to your question. Why did he go after her? If she was abusive, and *she* initiated the relationship, I'd say she wanted the challenge of a stronger man. But that's not what happened. By all accounts, she was perfectly satisfied until Rossi came along."

Maybe it was the lack of sleep, but Sally's mind felt sluggish. Men chose women for definite reasons. They had to "do it" for them in some way. Looks, sex, money, something. The lightbulb flickered on. "It wasn't about

Vivien at all. It was Alec."

Tanelsa pointed her finger. "Now you're talking. Rossi knew, probably from Zander Nelson, that Alec was sniffing around their scheme. How much did he know?"

"Rossi and Alec weren't friends. They didn't move in the same social circles. It would have looked weird, and probably made Alec suspicious, if Rossi had suddenly tried to be best buds. So he went through Vivien." Sally rubbed her temples. "Based on what we've been told, I think Vivien would have loved gossiping about her husband. 'Tell me about Alec, what a drip, he didn't really do that'...I can see Rossi encouraging her to talk. Vivien may even have said something about what a loser Alec was, thinking he'd found this big plot at work involving his boss. She wouldn't have believed him, and Rossi would have fed her disbelief." It made sense. "That brings us back to Rossi as Vivien's killer. He was sending a message to Alec. Leave it alone, or else. To top it off, Rossi frames Alec for the murder."

"That's where you lose me." Tanelsa got up and paced. "If you want to shut someone up, you go after *that* person. Threatening a loved one may work, but it's no guarantee. If the person knows you're responsible for the danger, now they've got more dirt on you."

"But they did go after Alec, in the prison yard." Sally nibbled her thumbnail. "Rossi realized he'd made a mistake with Vivien, or that Alec would talk anyway. Goodbye, Alec. Remember, we don't have to prove it, only raise the possibility."

Tanelsa played with a rubber band. "Then why take a shot at you?"

"We were going to spring Alec from jail. I was the one out in public asking the questions."

Tanelsa stopped. "But that can't have been Rossi. He was at the town hall."

"And it wasn't Nelson. He was dead." Sally raised her head. "We still can't find that guard. The one Alec claims did the stabbing."

Tanelsa snapped the rubber band, and it flew across the room. "Now Rossi is hiring assassins? Come on, Sally. This isn't a thriller novel. It's real life."

Sally ran her hands through her hair. Rossi had pulled out his phone immediately after they talked. At the time, Sally had thought nothing of it.

261

People were constantly checking their devices. Had it been more sinister? "I will tell you one thing. I think Rossi is right in the middle of everything. He talked to Jim's victim, he was friends with Zander Nelson, had an affair with Vivien Wilson. The man is a nexus if I ever saw one."

"Then we know what to do." Tanelsa leaned forward. "Let's see if there's a connection between Brian Kolchak and Rossi."

* * *

By the time Duncan arrived at headquarters, he'd already had two large black coffees in an attempt to get into a better mood. Sleep had been elusive the previous night. He couldn't get into a comfortable position, couldn't stay in one that was acceptable, and dozed on and off through the night. This morning, his back muscles felt tighter than ever. Getting dressed had been close to torture.

"You look like shit," Cavendish said when she saw him.

"I didn't sleep well."

"Your back?"

"No, this case." The lie fell from his lips. "This is all about the Ponzi scheme. I can feel it. But we can't prove it." He eased down into his chair.

Cavendish watched him, skepticism in her gaze. "I went back over the witness statements. No one saw a huge Black man or a lime green Caliber."

"We have to close the loop, but I think Dinky is out."

"Agreed. I've got a BOLO out on Kolchak and his Accord. I ran him through the system before you got here. He's clean. No wants, no warrants, no convictions." She pushed some paper across the desk surface.

He read it. "Middling credit history with a lot of credit card debt, average apartment, average car." He flipped the sheet. "He likes expensive stuff, doesn't he? I recognize some of these stores, and they aren't cheap."

"The car has a blown headlight, if Sally's witness can be believed."

"But also no obvious tie to Rossi or Nelson. This guy is as average as they come. What made him jump from prison guard to attacking an inmate?"

"If we can believe Alec Wilson." Cavendish took a drink of her coffee, grimaced, and threw it out in the can next to her desk.

There was that. "Oddly enough, I think we can this time." That didn't mean the man was telling the entire truth, but Duncan believed him about the guard. "What about the other inmate? The one who claimed to be in the gym?"

"Turns out he was in the gym." Cavendish sifted through the reports on her desk. "It was one of the things I followed up on last night after you left. The CCTV was terrible, but prison officials did find a witness. The guy in charge of the book cart. He saw his fellow prisoner at four forty-five, which was five minutes after Wilson was stabbed. Clean, no blood, and doing squats. He's off the hook."

Duncan shifted in his seat. Standing hurt, sitting was a bitch, and he'd taken the max dose of ibuprofen that morning. Lying flat on a hard surface might help, but he couldn't work his investigation from the floor.

"Do you think Wilson killed his wife?" Cavendish asked.

At first, the question felt like a non sequitur. He looked at her. "What does that have to do with anything?"

"Just this." She tapped her desk. "Seems to me we're working under a fairly big assumption. That Wilson is innocent, and his wife's death has something to do with this Ponzi thing, right?"

"Go on."

"What if we're wrong? What if Vivien Wilson died because she was an emotionally abusive bitch, and her husband snapped? Tragic, but not related to anything else. I got bored last night, so I dug up what was available. No argument that the lead detective screwed the pooch with the Miranda warning. And yeah, he should have at least ticked the boxes when it came to everything else. Her debts, her lover."

"Tunnel vision isn't always wrong. Is that your point?"

"Yes." She rested her arms on her desk. "Throw Vivien's murder out of the equation when it comes to Palmer. What do we have?"

Thinking helped divert Duncan's mind from his pain. "Who did Palmer call first? Rossi or Nelson?"

"Rossi. I had the same thought. With his campaign, he's a public official.

I double-checked. The first call was to his campaign office. He may have spun a tale about his old friend Dom and how he wanted to get in touch. Ten to one, a helpful staffer gave up Rossi's cell phone number." She shook out her hair and twisted the elastic in her fingers.

"Because the very first thing Palmer saw, the thing that made him suspicious, wasn't the Ponzi scheme. He saw Rossi leaving the Wilson house." This was why the pieces hadn't quite fit. It wasn't about the money, not at first. "All Palmer saw was a married man, who wanted to be a state senator, sneaking around with a married woman."

Cavendish continued the speculation. "He got in touch with Rossi and said something like 'I know what you did' or close to that. He was talking about the affair, but Rossi thought he knew about the investment game."

"It explains how Palmer got on the SEC's radar. They wanted to know why he was calling their suspect."

"Maybe Rossi said something that made Palmer suspicious, so he called Nelson. It's very possible that's who Palmer was running from. Not Lamb." She frowned. "But how did Rossi find him?"

"Palmer got his renter's insurance from Laurel Mountain, remember?" Duncan could sense the excitement building, that feeling when he knew he was close to the solution. "And Nelson was working there. Nelson called his buddy, Rossi, and bingo. Rossi arranged to get rid of the threat. He can't do it himself, though. Too risky."

"And that's where it falls apart." Cavendish pulled her hair back. "Rossi wasn't in Farmington that day. He has an alibi for Wilson's stabbing, for Nelson's death, and he didn't shoot at Sally. He may be a financial scumbag, but until we put him on a scene or connect him to Kolchak, we've hit a wall. So far, I've come up empty."

Damn it. With effort, Duncan stood up. "Let's do what we can do, and maybe we'll come up with an idea in the meantime." Stranger things had happened.

* * *

Sally opened her laptop to begin researching the investigation databases she subscribed to. Family connections, money, home ownership, criminal records were all at her fingertips.

Tanelsa broke her concentration. "I think we've got a problem."

"What now? I thought the appeal was solid."

"It is. This is for afterward." Tanelsa picked up a folder and came over. "Remember the interview transcript we read?"

"I think so. The one where they claimed Alec contradicted himself?"

"That's the one." Tanelsa laid down her file. "He did it with Dave, too."

Sally leaned forward. "I don't remember reading that. When?"

"It's in Dave's notes." Tanelsa tapped the page. "See where it's crossed out? The newer note matches what Alec told us. He forgot his keys, the door was locked, he was so drunk he forgot about the spare, and he went for a walk. But look underneath the scribbles."

Sally squinted at the nearly illegible text. "I see what you mean. He said he went inside, the house was empty, and he decided to take a walk."

"It's possible he made a mistake the first time. Memory is a funny thing and if he was inebriated on top of it, no wonder he didn't get the details right." Tanelsa perched on the edge of Sally's desk.

"Twice? Once, maybe. That night to the cops." Sally twisted a strand of hair around her finger. "The shock of finding Vivien, he's still a little buzzed. He fumbles the story. But he would have been stone sober when he talked to Dave." She picked up her phone.

"Who are you calling?"

Sally held up a finger. "Nichole, hi. Can I speak to Dave? Oh, no. Is he okay? I mean, relatively speaking? Right. No, it's not important. When you're able, and he's awake, give him my regards and tell him I'm pulling for him. Thanks. Bye." She tossed the phone on the desk. "That was Dave's wife. He had another heart attack last night. He's in the ICU, on a ventilator."

"Damn. Is he gonna make it?"

"Nichole said the prognosis isn't good. I wanted to ask him about this and see what he remembers, but that's not going to happen anytime soon."

"Does she know about our arrangement with Dave?"

"No clue, but I didn't think now was the right time to ask." Sally looked up at her partner. "We're on our own."

Tanelsa tapped her fingernails against the wood. "Too bad the bartenders can't tell us how drunk Alec actually was."

An idea occurred to Sally. "But the Uber driver can." She pawed through the file. "Where's the screenshot of the Uber transaction Dave submitted as evidence? Got it. Here's the contact information." She grabbed her phone again. When a man answered, she identified herself. "You drove my client home on the night of October fourth of last year. I know that's a long time to remember, but I have a question."

The man gave a short laugh. "Lady, he was arrested for first-degree murder. Shit yeah, I remember him."

"Good. I only want to know one thing. Was he drunk when you picked him up?"

"Depends on what you mean by drunk." The sound of a turn signal came over the line. The man must have been driving.

Sally hoped he didn't have a fare. "Was he impaired? Sloppy drunk or buzzed?"

"If he'd been pulled over, he'd have gotten a DUI, for sure. I could smell the booze on his breath when he leaned in to say hi." There was a pause. "But smashed? Nope. We had a nice chat about the Steelers and the World Series. He was talking clearly, walked up to the car without trouble, got in by himself, the works. He even complimented me on my ride, said he'd been thinking of buying one for himself. I drive an Acura."

Tanelsa leaned in. "When you let him off, did he go into his house?"

"I can't say. He definitely went to the door and was patting his pockets, like he was searching for his keys. I saw that. But I left before he opened the door."

They thanked the driver and hung up. "I don't like this," Sally said.

"Me, neither. You thinking what I'm thinking?"

Sally stood and grabbed her phone. "Only if you also think it's a good time for an impromptu visit."

Chapter Forty

Duncan stared out of the passenger window. There was a connection out there, and they were missing it. He knew it. Like the ache in his back, the thought wouldn't go away. It was always there, causing him grief. If only he had the time to stop and focus on it. Instead, they were on their way for a second interview with Dinky.

Cavendish pulled to a stop outside Lamb's house.

He peered through the slush-stained windshield. "Looks like his car in the driveway."

She turned off the ignition. "How do you want to play this?"

Duncan wished his answer could be that he would stay in the car while Cavendish handled the questioning. As long as he didn't move, he didn't hurt. But that was unprofessional. "We're pretty sure Dinky isn't a killer."

"That is so."

"Then all we need to do is let him know that we found out his alibi is bullshit, that we're not really interested in being hardasseshard asses, and he should just tell us where he was."

"Sounds simple." She opened the car. "Which means it won't be."

The troopers approached the house, their weapons at the ready. Without asking, Cavendish took the lead and knocked. "State police. Open up, Dinky. We know you're home. It's all good. We just have a few more questions."

It took a minute, but the door opened. Lamb wore sweats and socks, no shoes. He certainly didn't look like a man ready to take off running. "Aw, hell, man. What now?"

Cavendish held up her hands. "This can be a quick conversation if you want it to be. We called your mother."

Lamb's dark skin flushed. "What did you bother her for?"

"Because you gave her as an alibi," Duncan responded. "Did you think we'd take your word for it?"

Lamb mumbled.

"You hoped?" Cavendish pointed at him. "You're too funny. You had to know we'd check with her. Even the TV shows get that part right. Yes, you went to dinner, but you left in plenty of time to be in Farmington at midnight. By the way. Your mother is pissed that you think she's an invalid."

Lamb actually groaned.

"Here's the thing." Duncan tried to shift his weight to take as much pressure off his back as he could. "We're pretty sure you didn't pop your buddy Palmer. The pesky thing about police work, however, is that *pretty sure* isn't good enough for the reports. We need beyond a reasonable doubt. You tell us where you were and we'll leave you alone."

"What if it wasn't quite legal? You still gonna keep that promise?"

"You won't see us again." Duncan didn't say that depending on the crime, other law enforcement might come to pay a visit.

Lamb shuffled his feet. "My buddies and me, we go see a bookie at his place down in Confluence on Sunday nights. Bet on whatever sports are playing. It's winter, so football and basketball. We have a few drinks, eat, and shoot the shit. Don't ask me the bookie's name. He won't like it if I rat on him and send the cops in to bust him."

Duncan wanted to laugh. "Fat guy? Slicked-back red hair, smokes cigars, dresses well, has a bodyguard the size of a California redwood?"

Lamb blinked. "Yeah. You know him?"

"Eddie V and I go way back. It'll be easy for me to verify your story." Duncan raised a finger. "It'd better be the truth. Eddie will *definitely* not appreciate it if you used his name in vain."

Lamb made an X over his chest. "Swear to God, man. We was there until at least midnight, maybe later. I cleaned up on Sunday Night Football, so he talked me into staying for a late-night basketball game. Lost some, but still made out okay."

Cavendish tilted her head, the look in her eyes asking if they were satisfied.

"Take care, Dinky, and stay out of trouble. I recommend calling your mother and apologizing before you see her this weekend." Duncan jerked his thumb toward the state Ford.

Lamb muttered a response and shut the door.

On the way back to the street, Cavendish asked, "Do you believe him?"

"Easy enough to find out." Duncan made a call. "Stanley, it's Duncan. Checking on a patron of yours, Sunday night regular. No, just if he was there. Yeah. Big guy, Black, looks like a former footballer. Goes by Dinky. He was? Good. Thanks." Duncan ended the call. "Cross Lamb off the list. I don't think Eddie will be too happy being used as an alibi, but at least it was with me, not some stranger." He opened the car. "Poor Dinky. His mother is going to give him hell. So will his bookie."

"He's not going to jail for murder." Cavendish slid into the car. "I hope Rossi is at his campaign office here in Fayette County."

Duncan exhaled, waiting for the stabbing pain in his muscles to fade. "Why?"

She put the car in gear and pulled away. "Because there's a freaking storm coming this afternoon, and I do *not* want to be on the Turnpike when it hits."

* * *

After Sally returned to the office, she picked up her previous task and spent an hour building a profile of Brian Kolchak. Slowly, the picture came into focus. Kolchak was a man with Champagne tastes and a beer budget. He drove an aging Honda Accord, but he'd tried to get a loan for the purchase of much more expensive cars. He had credit cards for high-end sporting goods stores, used them frequently, and was often late with the payments, which dragged down his credit score. He was not married, not divorced, and had no children. He'd graduated from a local college by the skin of his teeth. "Kolchak reads like one of those guys from a bar with a cheesy pickup line. You come here often? That kind."

269

"Tell me about it. He has a pretty clean record, but I'd expect that since he worked in the prison system." Tanelsa rested her chin on her palm. "You can't get hired at the Department of Corrections if you're a felon. A few speeding tickets, one for blowing a stop sign. That's all I can find. He didn't go to college with Rossi. He grew up in a different town, so, no high school connection either. If Kolchak is Rossi's errand boy, Rossi must have a hold on him somehow. But what, I can't tell."

Sally stared at her screen. "Or they're family."

"Kolchak only has a sister, according to what I've found."

"They're cousins." Sally beckoned Tanelsa over. "Right here. I'm on a genealogy site. Rossi's father and Kolchak's mother are brother and sister."

Tanelsa rushed over. "Say what?"

Sally turned her laptop around. "Dom Rossi and Brian Kolchak are first cousins. Look."

Tanelsa's eyes flicked back and forth as she read. "Well, hot damn. This is it. You said Kolchak has expensive tastes. Wanna bet Rossi gave him cash under the table so it wouldn't show anywhere? Kolchak gets a taste of the high life. Rossi gets rid of a problem or two. Now we have to put Kolchak at the scene for the shootings."

"*We* do not have to do anything." Sally picked up her phone.

Tanelsa put her hands on her hips. "Wasn't that the point of this whole thing?"

"It was. But as you pointed out, we don't need proof. We need possibility. Now we focus on Monday." She tapped on her screen.

"What are you doing then?"

Sally finished her message and sent it. "Texting Jim. He and Cavendish will decide what to do with this information."

If they were right, Rossi had already taken a shot at her. She wasn't about to offer herself up as a target a second time.

Chapter Forty-One

Duncan heard Sally's text tone and immediately pulled out his phone. After the shooting, he wasn't going to put her off unless he was in the middle of slapping cuffs on a suspect. He read her message. "We have our connection between Rossi and Kolchak. They're first cousins."

Cavendish was driving but spared a glance. "How the hell do you know that?"

He shook the phone. "Sally. Unsurprisingly, she's rather interested to know who shot at her. Apparently, she and Tanelsa have been busy this morning." He tapped out a number.

"Should we take a detour?"

Duncan thought. "No. One, we don't know where Kolchak is. There haven't been any hits on the BOLO. Hold on." He turned his attention to the call. "Yes, it's Trooper Jim Duncan with the Pennsylvania State Police. I'd like telephone authorization for a warrant, please. Yes, I'll hold." A moment later, he'd provided the information required to get financials and phone records for Kolchak. Once he had the green light, he called the appropriate resources and made the requests. "I know it's a Friday morning, but the faster you can provide that, the better. Thank you."

Cavendish made a turn. "Think that will do any good? Or will they take their sweet time anyway?"

"You never know unless you ask." He made a second call to Rossi's campaign office but ended it before he identified himself.

"What was that about?" Cavendish entered the Uniontown city limits and headed toward the campaign office on West Main.

"I didn't want to announce our arrival and give him an excuse to leave." Duncan closed his eyes. He could hold it together for a couple more hours. "Here's hoping they thought the call dropped or something. Not unheard of in these parts."

"That might be true, but you need to work on your acting skills. You still sounded like a cop."

"Talk about the pot calling the kettle black."

Five minutes later, they cruised past the small lot near the office. "That Rossi's car?" Cavendish lifted her chin in the direction of a silver BMW sedan.

Duncan ran the plates through their car's computer. "It's his all right. He may have walked somewhere, but he's in the area."

Cavendish parked on the street, about twenty yards away. "Unless he caught a ride from someone."

When they entered the office, the first thing Duncan saw was Rossi talking to a young woman at the front desk. If Duncan was any judge of body language, Rossi was flirting, and the woman was slightly embarrassed and yet flattered at the same time. "Dominic Rossi, we're from the Pennsylvania State Police." Duncan held up his badge wallet. "We'd like a few minutes of your time."

Rossi didn't look impressed. "I'm rather busy at the moment."

"We can see that." Cavendish showed her badge, then put it away. "We're going to have to insist, seeing as it's related to a murder."

"Who died?" Rossi asked.

"A man named Kyle Palmer."

Rossi's eye twitched, but he stayed calm. "I don't know him."

"Funny. His phone records show he called you. Three times." Duncan watched for a reaction. It was slight, but he caught a tightening of Rossi's jaw muscle.

Cavendish took out her notes. "Is that the same way you don't know Alec Wilson?"

All trace of relaxation disappeared from Rossi's stance. "Him again? What is it with you people?"

Duncan knew the answer but asked the question anyway. "Who else asked about Wilson?"

"Some woman." Rossi waved his hand. "Sarah, Sammy. I don't remember."

His act was too practiced. Duncan didn't believe him for a second.

Cavendish put away her book and gave an insincere smile. "I can't speak to this woman, but we at the PSP are rather tiresome in that way. All these pesky questions in search of the facts."

"We tend not to stop until we're satisfied we have the right answer," Duncan added.

Rossi drummed his fingers on the desktop. "Fine. If this is what it takes to get you out of my hair, I can give you ten minutes. Angie, be a dear and make sure we aren't disturbed, will you?" He held out an arm. "This way, Troopers."

He led them to a conference room with a table surrounded by eight chairs. He unbuttoned his jacket and sat. "Tell me again. Who is this man who allegedly called me?"

Duncan noted he didn't offer any refreshments. He didn't want them staying, didn't think this would take long, or was plain rude. He sat. "Kyle Palmer."

This time, Rossi's expression remained blank. "You look a little uncomfortable, Trooper...?"

"Jim Duncan. This is my partner, Trooper Jenny Cavendish." Duncan nodded in her direction. "Mr. Palmer was murdered four days ago, very early on Monday morning."

"Very, very early," Cavendish added. "In what you might call the wee hours."

Rossi looked bored. "I told you. I never heard that name."

Duncan brought up a picture on his phone and held it out. "This is Palmer. Are you sure you don't recognize him?"

"Absolutely. You claim he called me?"

"He did. Long conversations, too." Duncan checked his notes. "Twenty minutes, ten, and fifteen. If you don't know him, why'd he do that?"

"Who says he didn't talk to my wife? Or one of my staffers?"

Cavendish folded her hands and set them on the table. "Because he didn't call your house or your campaign office. It was your personal cell number."

"I have no memory of those calls."

"Spoken like a true politician," Cavendish said.

Rossi laid a hand on the table. "Look. I respect the PSP. But we seem to be at a standstill. I say I never spoke to any Kyle Palmer. Could be someone else did using my phone."

"Mr. Rossi, please stop thinking we're stupid." Duncan swiped to close the picture. "You're a wanna-be elected official. I'm quite sure you don't leave your phone lying around for anyone to use."

"My staffers have the authority to answer it if I'm speaking." Rossi's answer was smooth. "You say Palmer called my number. Someone answered. For the third time, it wasn't me. What you really need is a record of a call *from* me to this dead man. Not to mention proof I made it. Judging by your questions, I don't think you have that, which means you don't have enough evidence to get a warrant for them." He placed his hands on the table. "I'm a very busy man. Now, if you'll excuse me." He pushed away.

"Mr. Rossi, we aren't done." Duncan grabbed the chair. "You said it could have been a staffer. Tell us more about your wife. How often does she answer your phone?"

Cavendish snapped her fingers. "There's an idea. Could be that's how she found out. Palmer told her."

"Who found out what?" Rossi snapped.

Cavendish's tone was sweet. "That you were sleeping with Vivien Wilson. No wonder your wife is leaving you. You naughty boy."

Rossi's eyes widened a fraction before he calmed himself. "You're delusional. My wife and I are just fine, thank you."

"No, you aren't." Duncan pretended to check his notes. "She's filed for divorce. She also told us she never gave you money for your campaign. Was the Ponzi scheme your idea or Zander Nelson's? By the way, he's also dead." It was a big bluff. But sometimes, those paid off.

Beads of sweat popped on Rossi's forehead. "I have no idea what you're talking about. What scheme? You'll have to ask Zander. Oh, wait. I guess he's not available."

Duncan put away the book. "Before he died, he talked to Agent Ned Gaskell of the SEC and spilled the beans. Did Nelson get cold feet and threaten to roll on you?"

"Zander committed suicide," Rossi snapped. "I heard it on the radio."

"You're going down, Mr. Rossi." Cavendish moved closer. "The only question is, will it be on federal fraud charges or double homicide? Palmer, Nelson. Whatever you heard, the cops in Monongahela County know he didn't kill himself."

Duncan pointed at her. "Don't forget Vivien Wilson. Triple homicide."

"That's right." Cavendish pretended to slap her forehead. "Did she threaten to talk to your wife? Spill the beans on your scheme?"

For a brief moment, it looked like Rossi would come back with a retort. Instead, he took a deep breath and brought out his politician's smile. "Troopers, I'm very sorry. But whoever told you these stories has fed you a steady diet of bullshit. You're correct. My wife and I are divorcing. I didn't want to make a big deal of it ahead of the election. But that's the only thing you got right. Now, if you'll excuse me, I have a campaign to conduct." He rose and took two steps toward the door.

"And a staffer to seduce," Cavendish said.

Duncan watched the other man take a third step without responding. "How's your cousin?"

Rossi stumbled a bit. He turned around. "What cousin?"

"Brian Kolchak. The one who works for the Fayette County Jail."

Cavendish nudged him. "Worked. He's in the wind, remember?"

"Right. Of course, if I'd stabbed an inmate, I'd run for it, too." Duncan watched Rossi like a hawk, searching for a sign of panic. There was nothing. "What did you offer him to kill Alec Wilson? You thought you were safe with Wilson in jail. Then there's an appeal, and you get word that maybe the SEC isn't averse to working with a felon after all. He has to go."

"Did you get Brian to take a potshot at Sally Castle as well?" Cavendish asked.

There was a heavy silence. Duncan knew they were on thin ice. Police were allowed to lie, but unless Rossi cracked, they had nothing, no proof. He knew it, and Cavendish did as well.

So, it seemed, did Rossi, because he didn't flinch. "I haven't seen or talked to Brian in ages. You two really should take this act on the road. It might play better as a comedy routine than it does for an interrogation. Have a nice day, Troopers. Please, take a flyer. And don't forget to vote Rossi for Change this spring in the primary." He left.

Duncan ground his teeth. *Well, shit.*

Chapter Forty-Two

Sally looked at the clock for what seemed like the millionth time that morning. It was slightly after twelve, although she swore the thing had stopped, and it was much later. But a check of her phone confirmed that the old-fashioned wall timepiece was correct.

Tanelsa didn't budge. "You got ants in your pants? Relax. He'll call you when there's something to say."

"I know, but I hate waiting. I want to corner Rossi and ask him myself. Did you hire your cousin to kill me?" She tossed her pen on her desk.

This time, the words got a reaction. Tanelsa fixed her with a glare and pointed. "And get yourself shot in the head? You make one move toward that door, and I'll tackle you. I swear I will."

"I said I *wanted* to, not that I was going to." She picked up the discarded pen.

"Good. At least you're showing some sense."

"I have to do something." Sally went and got her coat from the hall rack. "While we wait, let's go talk to Alec."

Tanelsa followed. Together, they set a brisk pace to the county jail.

Once there, they sat in the same room as they had previously while they waited for Alec to be brought up. Or maybe it wasn't the same room. Sally couldn't remember. They all looked the same. Bleak.

"The more I think about it, what are we doing here?" Tanelsa asked. "Does it really matter if Alec is guilty? We're going to present the appeal and represent our client to the best of our abilities on Monday. That's what's important."

Sally stared at the scarred table. "It does to me." She clenched her hands. "It won't affect how we do our job. I can defend a killer. But I want the truth. Don't you?"

Next to her, Tanelsa let out a breath. "Yes."

Moments later, a guard led a trembling Alec Wilson into the room. He licked his lips as the guard fastened his handcuffs to the table and left. They sat in silence for a long second. He finally broke it. "What is it? Did something happen? Do you want to go over Monday again?"

Sally smothered a sigh. She hated this. Why couldn't the man have been honest from the start? "Sort of. We want to review your statement from the night of Vivien's murder."

His expression betrayed his confusion. "I don't get it."

Alec's behavior struck Sally like that of a small animal caught in a trap. His eyes looked hunted and his body language furtive. "Humor us." She took out her notes. "Start with that afternoon."

He swallowed a second time, Adam's apple bobbing. "Vivien and I had a fight. About her affair. I went to the bar. I got pretty hammered, so they called an Uber for me. When I got home, I went into the house. Vivien wasn't there."

"Stop. You did it again." Sally pinned him against the wall with her gaze.

"I don't understand. You asked what happened." He was sweating now, shaking, and visibly uncomfortable. He shifted in the chair, unable to stay still, his gaze flitting from person to person.

Tanelsa rested her forearms on the table. "The flip-flop. It's what you did in front of the cops, one of the things that made them suspicious. You swore to us you never went in the house."

"Right, I didn't. You've got me all confused. I was so drunk, I...I have trouble remembering."

Sally shook her head. "No, you weren't. We located your Uber driver. He said you weren't so far gone you couldn't think. Buzzed, yes. Shouldn't have been driving, sure. But not falling-down sloshed."

"Why are you bullying me? You're just like her. Jesus, do all you women practice this?" Alec yanked on the cuffs, but he couldn't pull free. "Is it your goal in life to make a man feel like a child? I know what I did, like I know what was going on at work. Vivien laughed at me when I told her, did you know that? I thought I finally had something that would impress her, and she dismissed me like I was a delusional crackpot."

"We're not trying to belittle you, Alec. Honestly." Sally kept her voice gentle. "But these inconsistencies in your story are worrisome. The prosecution is going to bring them up. We need to have a response."

"There are other things, too." Tanelsa pulled the police report out of her briefcase. "We've spent this whole week looking into Vivien's lover. Her debt. Yes, there were other suspects. But forensics don't lie. No fingerprints on the murder weapon except yours and hers. No sign of forced entry into your house. No evidence another person had been there that night. No witnesses reported seeing strangers on the street. Just you and her. And lots of people who say she was an emotionally abusive wife. A person can only put up with so much before things get ugly."

He pulled on his shackles again, a panicked light in his eyes.

"Alec, listen." Sally reached out. "We're going to stand up in court on Monday and present that appeal. Your rights were violated when the cops didn't read the Miranda warning. Knowing the truth won't prevent that. But you owe it to us to be honest."

"Admit it. You killed your wife." Tanelsa's words were a statement, not a question.

"Yes!" He lowered his head so he could grab his hair in his fists. "Yes, all right? Satisfied?"

For a moment, Sally sat in stunned silence. She truly hadn't expected him to confess. Now he had and it was time to deal with the fallout. "Tell us what happened."

"We had a fight. About the affair. I did go to the bar, but yeah, I didn't drink as much as I said. Enough that I called for a ride, though. When I got home, she was still there. Vivien. She'd been going through my office, all the evidence I'd found on Zander. She taunted me, asked if I thought I was Harry Bosch or something. She said I was kidding myself. I wasn't man enough to be Bosch. Then she told me she was going out and I wouldn't stop her. I was so pathetic that I needed her to prop me up. I should be thankful she put up with me, and from now on, she'd do whatever she wanted." He paused. Tears welled up in his eyes, and he bent to rub his nose on his sleeve.

Sally had never met Vivien Wilson but was certain she wouldn't have gotten along with her. Sally never understood what drove one person to degrade another like that. If Vivien hadn't been happy, it would have been easy enough to get a divorce. *I guess some people just like the power they have over others.* Like tyrants. The problem was that the people who lived under tyranny had a habit of rebelling.

Next to her, Tanelsa passed Alec a tissue. "What happened next?"

"I grabbed a knife out of the block. I told her to stop. That I'd had enough, and she couldn't treat me like that. I said I'd get a divorce. She told me, 'Go ahead. I'll take you for everything you've got. I'm the wife, remember? What are people going to believe? That I abused you or the other way around?' I grabbed her. Pulled her around to face me. The first time I cut her, it was an accident. But then something in my mind, I don't know, broke. I stabbed her over and over and over. I couldn't help myself." He closed his eyes. "After, I was in shock. You know the rest." He rested his head on his hands, and his shoulders shook.

Sally and Tanelsa sat in silence. Yeah. They knew.

* * *

Outside, Duncan pulled his coat tight against a rising wind. He studied the sky and the lead-gray clouds. The air was heavy with the promise of snow. Cavendish was right. By this afternoon, the road would not be a good place to be. He looked over his shoulder. "You coming?"

"You didn't take a flyer." She held out a glossy brochure.

"I wouldn't vote for Rossi if he were the last man on the planet."

"Now, now." She read. "If he could pull off even a third of what he says, it'd be a miracle. Politicians."

"I don't give a damn about his empty promises. That man is behind at least two murders and the attempted murder of the woman I love. I want to lock his ass up and throw away the key." He pounded one hand against the other. "Vote Rossi for Change. What a crock of shit."

"I know." Cavendish's phone rang. She checked the caller ID. "Cavendish, go. Yeah. You did? Where? Did he say anything? You hold him, got it? Two counts of murder, one attempted. Call me back if he gets a lawyer." She hung up.

Duncan had only heard half the conversation, but he instantly knew what it was about. "Kolchak?"

"A sharp-eyed Turnpike patrolman spotted his car at the Valley Forge rest area. He's in custody out there. As soon as they told him he was wanted for questioning related to a murder, he sang like a canary. Still at it, apparently." She gave a tight grin. "Three guesses who hired him, and the first two don't count."

"Dom Rossi." Duncan turned to go back inside.

Rossi had resumed his flirting with the receptionist. He tried for a smile at the sight of the troopers but failed. "I thought I told you I was done talking."

Cavendish moved to flank him. "We have some new information. Your cousin, Brian Kolchak, was picked up by troopers near Valley Forge. He's telling a very interesting story."

Duncan stood on Rossi's other side. "You might want to come with us. Give us your side, as it were. Otherwise, your campaign will come to a screeching halt. It probably will anyway, but if you talk to us willingly, you might be able to end it with a little more dignity."

Rossi seemed to be weighing his options. "In that case, let me get my coat." He took a step, then pivoted. He grabbed a wheeled chair and shoved it into Duncan.

On instinct, he twisted to avoid the collision. His feet tangled in the chair's base, and he went down hard, his back exploding in pain. He tried to roll over and get up, but his body wouldn't respond. Any attempt to get to his knees, to even move an inch, set off a fresh wave of agony. He gritted his teeth. Above him and off to the side, he could hear the sounds of a scuffle and much swearing, some of it from Rossi, some from Cavendish.

Other voices joined the babble. From the jargon, it sounded like a

Uniontown patrol officer. Had the receptionist called 9-1-1? Duncan lay on the floor, willing his back to stop hurting. It didn't do any good. The tiniest movement started the cycle over again. He muttered a steady string of profanity under his breath. Cavendish was subduing a murder suspect, and he was stuck on his back like a stranded turtle.

She knelt beside him and put a hand on his shoulder. "Relax. Ambulance is coming."

"Did you get him?"

"We did. The receptionist, Angie, is a sharp girl. She called 9-1-1 almost immediately. We lucked out. There was a patrol car driving by."

"You said ambulance. Who got hurt?"

"You're joking, right?" Cavendish snorted. "It's for you, you idiot. Lie still."

"I don't need one. I—" He tried once more to get up, but the result took his breath away. He cursed again.

"All right, tough guy." She held him in place. It didn't take much.

Duncan waited for the pain to subside. If he didn't move, it didn't hurt so much. "You put me in an ambulance, and I will beat your ass. Just as soon as I can move again."

"Don't worry. I won't. I'll let the nice EMTs from the crew do that." Cavendish patted him, as though he were a small child. "If I let you walk out of here and hurt yourself even more, *Sally* will beat my ass. Fact is, I'm a lot more scared of her than you."

Duncan studied the perforated acoustic tile of the ceiling. Women.

Chapter Forty-Three

Monday, 1:00pm

Sally sat in the courtroom at the defense table, presumably studying her notes. Alec Wilson was beside her, Tanelsa on his other side. She and Tanelsa wore similar power suits without being matchy-matchy. Tanelsa was in black with a red silk shirt and her signature Louboutin shoes. Sally had chosen deep navy, with a white shirt and blood-red heels.

Between them, Alec looked a little rumpled in an off-the-rack suit. Not because it fit badly or hadn't been pressed. Ever since his admission to them, he'd projected a slightly defeated air. "What's taking so long?" he muttered.

"Stop worrying. We've done what we can. Now, it's up to the judge. She has a lot to think over." Sally needed to take her own advice. They'd presented their arguments that morning. They had been solid. Judge Monahan asked pointed questions, as she always did. Sally and Tanelsa had an answer for every single one, thanks to their preparation. The prosecution, a sharp young assistant District Attorney from Monongahela County, had offered a rebuttal. All they could do was wait.

Sally hated waiting.

The bailiff came in. "All rise."

Sally pulled Alec's elbow to get him to his feet. "Stand up straight," she said under her breath. She tugged her skirt into place. Out of the corner of her eye, she could see Tanelsa making similar adjustments to her clothes.

Judge Monahan took the bench. "You may be seated. I must say, you've given me a lot to ponder this morning. It's a Monday. I don't like to ponder on Mondays."

Not a great start.

"On the other hand, I also don't like shortcuts. I'm not talking about taking the back road to Grandma's house. I mean in procedure. In reviewing the defense's evidence, I think it's pretty clear there were several of them taken in this case." She peered over her rimless glasses at the prosecution. "In the case of Commonwealth of Pennsylvania versus Alec P. Wilson, I concur with the defense that an error of law was made in the original trial, and the motion to suppress should have been granted. I am declaring a mistrial in the original proceeding and dismissing the case without prejudice. Mr. Connelly, do you intend to refile charges?"

The ADA stood and smoothed his jacket. "I'll have to confer with my boss and the police in that matter, Your Honor."

"Very well. In the meantime, court's adjourned." Judge Monahan banged her gavel and left.

Sally wanted to sag into her chair, but that would be a bad look. Instead, she rose and offered Connelly her hand. He ignored it and made a beeline for a man in the back of the courtroom.

"What does that mean?" Alec asked. "I'm free to go? I can go home?"

"For the time being." Sally packed her papers in her briefcase.

His forehead creased. "What do you mean? She, the judge, said the case was dismissed, right?"

"Without prejudice." Tanelsa gathered her own material.

Alec looked from one to the other. "I don't understand."

Sally snapped her briefcase shut. "It means that while we were successful in arguing that Dave's original motion to suppress your statement to the police should have been granted, the prosecution can file new charges and go back to the Grand Jury for another indictment if they believe they have enough evidence to convict. In other words, you may be arrested again, and we'll have to do this all over."

Alec leapt to his feet. "But you'll defend me, right? Get me off? I'll figure out a way to pay you, I swear." He grabbed Sally's arm.

She looked at his hand, then his face. "We didn't 'get you off,' Alec."

He gulped and pulled his hand back as though he'd touched a hot stove.

Tanelsa slipped into her coat. "We corrected an error, which we needed to do."

Sally's attention was on the prosecutor. The other man, dressed in a dark overcoat, had turned around. She recognized Wayne Baronick. He gave a solemn nod in her direction. She returned the gesture. Then, he followed the ADA out of the courtroom.

They'd see each other again. Sally was sure of it. She faced her client. "If you wish to retain Ms. Parson and me for your defense, we will certainly do our best to protect your rights, same as we did here. However, whatever you decide, I'm going to offer you a piece of free advice."

Alec looked like he'd been smacked in the face, which probably wasn't far from how he felt. "What's that?"

"I know the man who will most likely be the lead detective in a second investigation. He's very good at his job." She hefted her briefcase. "If the prosecution offers you a deal, you should think about taking it. Because your chances of walking away next time are slim."

Chapter Forty-Four

Duncan relaxed on the couch, feet up on the ottoman, dogs sprawled on the floor in front of the fire. They'd given him good drugs in the ER on Friday, along with strict orders to see his doctor first thing Monday morning. The doc had diagnosed a severe lower back strain, given him muscle relaxers, and told him to take it easy for a week. The lieutenant, backed by Cavendish, had forced him to agree to take time off.

He'd talked to Cavendish after his doctor's appointment. Brian Kolchak claimed Dom Rossi had paid him to shoot Kyle Palmer and make it look like a drug deal gone bad. It turned out Rossi had helped Kolchak get the job at the Fayette County Jail years ago, a job he wasn't qualified for. When Rossi had called in the chips—and offered to give him an extra ten grand—Kolchak had agreed to stab Alec Wilson and take a shot at Sally. He'd planned to take the money and move to another state. The only murder Kolchak denied being involved in was Zander Nelson's staged suicide. That, he said, was all Rossi.

"What a dumb ass" had been Cavendish's judgment. "Like we can't arrest him if he lives in New Jersey or whatever. I also spoke to the LEOs in Marsdale. They figure Nelson was shot early that morning. Rossi would have had plenty of time to do the deed and get back to Uniontown for his event."

Agent Gaskell had questioned Kolchak as well, according to Cavendish, but Rossi's cousin didn't know much about the Ponzi scheme. "I don't think he knows much about anything, to tell you the truth," she said. "Moron is the nicest word I can think of to describe him. And I don't much feel like being kind."

Rossi lawyered-up immediately. But between Kolchak's testimony and evidence Cavendish said they found at his home office, Duncan knew Rossi was well and truly cooked.

Duncan checked the clock. Two thirty. Sally had presented her appeal this morning, but he did not know how it went or when she'd be home. In the meantime, he lazed the day away reading one of her Regency-romance paperbacks.

Rizzo and Pixel snapped to attention and scampered to the back door. A moment later, he heard it open, and Sally greeted the dogs.

"Welcome home," he called. "I'm in the living room."

She came in, stood behind him, and gently put her arms around his shoulders. "What on earth are you reading?"

"It was lying around so I picked it up." He showed her the cover. "It's not usually my thing. On the other hand, I don't want to throw it against the wall because of the ridiculous procedure errors. And I'm getting some great seduction ideas for when my back is better." He kissed her hands.

"You're so bad."

He squeezed her forearm. "How'd it go?"

"Hold on a second. I need wine and to take my shoes off." She left and returned a minute later, holding a glass of her favorite Merlot. She snuggled up next to him on the couch. "First things first. How do you feel?"

"I'm great. Thanks to the meds, I am feeling no pain, as the song lyrics go. Before you lecture me about the fire, it was already laid, so the heavy work was done. The wood is right there. It doesn't take much to put a log on every now and then, but now that you're home, I'll leave that to you." He tossed aside the paperback and draped his arm over her. "Did you win?"

"We did." She proceeded to tell him the whole story, from start to finish, including her advice to Wilson.

"Baronick was there?"

"Yes, and he gave me this little nod after we adjourned. Sort of telling me I'd see him again, I think." She took a drink. "Lucky me."

Duncan chuckled. "I have every faith in you. Will you take Wilson's case?"

She didn't answer immediately. "If he can pay us, sure."

"How do you feel about that?"

She studied her wine, a little too intently. "I'm fine. Why do you ask?"

He hesitated. "Cavendish called earlier. The inmate grapevine at the jail is on fire with the news that Wilson confessed. She heard it this morning when she met with Ned Gaskell about Rossi."

She tensed, then exhaled. "No comment."

The rumors were true.

"What's up with Rossi?" she asked and took a big swallow of wine.

Duncan figured she meant the details about the federal investigation. She already knew about Kolchak's arrest. "Gaskell found a hidden folder on Zander Nelson's laptop. Not only was Rossi involved in the Ponzi scheme, the whole thing was his idea."

She swirled the ruby liquid. "Who gets him first? The commonwealth for murder or the feds for fraud?"

"Luckily, that's not my problem. It's for the lawyers to sort out." He squeezed her shoulder. "Seriously, are you good on the Wilson thing?"

She smiled. "I am. You were right, the other night in my apartment. I'm not freeing anyone. I'm defending the rights of the accused. I did a lot of that in the public defender's office. I can do it again."

"That's you. Saving the guilty." He played with her hair. "Tanelsa is okay with it, too?"

"She is. It's money in the door and nothing we can't handle." Sally stared at the fire as it popped.

"Speaking of your apartment, did you get the keys turned in?"

She sipped her wine. "Right after we adjourned. Mission Move in Five days has been accomplished."

He studied her profile. The lamps were off, and the curtains were half closed. Even though it was mid-afternoon, most of the light came from the fire. It highlighted her hair and reflected in the deep green of her eyes. He told himself again how lucky he was to have her. Then he exhaled as he took in the rest of the room. Rizzo and Pixel resumed their places on the floor, basking in the warmth. A nice house, a roaring fire, and someone to share it with. This was what he'd wanted the first time he got married. He'd become a cop to protect people, not the least of whom included the ones he loved. He knew how fragile it all was, how easily it could be pulled away.

"Sally?" He brushed her cheek.

"Hmmm?"

"Do you want to get married?"

"I guess someday, yes. It's not been top of my mind lately."

"No, I mean to me. Now. Or rather, this coming year. I know these things take time to put together."

Her lips parted. She set the wine glass on the coffee table. Then she gave him her full attention. "What are you asking?"

He swallowed around the lump that had materialized in his throat. "What does it sound like? Do you want to marry me? It's a little out of the blue, I know. You just moved in. This isn't my first choice of setting to ask the question, dogs snoring in the background. I don't even have a ring to give you. I'll get one, I promise. I can't help thinking that now is as good a time as any."

She gazed at him.

"You were shot at. Why wait for the perfect moment to say something? We're adults, we both have good jobs and, well, strike while the iron is hot, right?" He was babbling. "If you don't want to or you need to think about it, I'm okay with that. I thought—"

She laid a finger over his lips. "Yes. I'll marry you."

"You will?" Why did her answer make him feel relieved and a little surprised?

"Of course I will." She leaned over and brushed her lips against his. "I guess I've wanted to for a while. As I said, I've just not thought about it much."

He grabbed her and returned her kiss, feeling the pressure building in his groin as he put all his passion into it. Then his back twinged, and he caught his breath.

She smiled and pushed him back. "Easy, Casanova. Plenty of time for that when you're at full strength." She gave a wicked grin, and her eyes sparkled.

He ran his finger over her neck. "Let's go upstairs, and I'll show you how much strength I have."

"Down, boy." She lifted his hand and kissed it. "I don't think you know what you're getting into, though."

"I've got a pretty good idea."

"I'm not talking about me." She giggled. "When I tell my mother that her baby is finally getting hitched, she'll lose her mind. You think a royal wedding is big? Those people have nothing on Louise Castle."

Duncan sighed. She was right. Louise was sure to plan the wedding of the century. It didn't matter. He could go along with anything. As long as the day ended with Sally by his side, man and wife, until death do they part.

A Note from the Author

If you've read any of the previous Laurel Highlands Mysteries, you know I write real locations. Any of the cities, streets, or landmarks I mention exist, even if I've made up a couple of businesses along the way. However, if you check a map of Southwestern Pennsylvania, there is no Monongahela County or Marsdale. Let me explain.

Jim Duncan appeared in two of Annette Dashofy's popular Zoe Chambers Mysteries books: *Under the Radar* (2020) and *What Comes Around* (2024). This time, I returned the favor by not only using Monongahela County, but featuring both Pete Adams and Wayne Baronick. Annette and I are friends, conference "running buddies," and critique partners, so she was able to advise me and make sure I got both characters right.

I hope you enjoy this little cross-over experience. I sure had fun writing it.

Acknoweldgements

I had a lot of fun writing this book. As always, there are a lot of people who helped me with the process.

I say it every time, but I wouldn't be able to write a book, at least a good one, without my critique group: Annette Dashofy, Jeff Boarts, and Peter WJ Hayes. I'm always amazed when writers say they do it without a group. I know I couldn't, and I'm eternally grateful for all your input.

Susan Helene Gottfried is not only a friend, but a fabulous editor. Thanks to you for finding all the little inconsistencies and illogical ramblings in the finished manuscript. Susan is also a great writer, so be sure to check out her Tales from the Sheep Farm novels.

Thanks to the Dames of Detection, Shawn Reilly Simmons and Verena Rose, for your support over the years. They gave me my break in publishing and have continued to support this series through seven books.

Thank you to Dru Ann Love of Dru's Book Musings for your love for Jim and Sally. It never gets old reading one of your musings and knowing I've satisfied a devoted fan. A crime fiction aficionado, a wonderful person, and now a published author in her own right. My day doesn't start until I've said good morning to you on Facebook.

Special thanks to Leslie Budewitz, who provided consultation on the legal aspects of this story and explained the appeals process. Any errors in the story are completely my own. Leslie is an Agatha-nominated author, penning the Spice Shop and Food Lovers' Village cozy mysteries, as well as "moody suspense" under the pen name Alicia Beckman. Check her out!

I've often been asked what my best advice to new writers is and it's this: Find your people. I am forever indebted to Sisters and Crime and Pennwriters, the blog communities at Jungle Red Writers, Wicked Authors, and Chicks on the Case, and the friends I've made through them.

Readers are the ones who close the circle on the writing journey. Thank you to everyone who follows Jim and Sally's adventures. You are the reason I sit down every day to do this.

To my husband, Paul: Through all the bumps and bruises, we still have each other's backs. Love you.

About the Author

A recovering technical writer, Liz Milliron is the Shamus Award-nominated author of The Laurel Highlands Mysteries, set in the scenic Laurel Highlands and The Homefront Mysteries, set in Buffalo NY during the early years of World War II. She is a member of Pennwriters, Sisters in Crime, International Thriller Writers and The Historical Novel Society. She is the current vice-president of the Pittsburgh chapter of Sisters in Crime and is on the National Board as the Education Liaison. Liz splits her time between Pittsburgh and the Laurel Highlands, where she lives with her husband, son, and a very spoiled retired-racer greyhound.

SOCIAL MEDIA HANDLES:
  Facebook: https://facebook.com/LizMilliron
  Instagram: https://instagram.com/LizMilliron
  Newsletter: https://www.subscribe page.com/newsletteridyllic

AUTHOR WEBSITE:
  https://lizmilliron.com

Also by Liz Milliron

The Laurel Highlands Mysteries

Thicker Than Water

Lie Down with Dogs

Harm Not the Earth

Broken Trust

Heaven Has No Rage

Root of All Evil

The Homefront Mysteries

The Secrets We Keep

The Truth We Hide

The Lessons We Learn

The Stories We Tell

The Enemy We Don't Know